THE CELTIC CONSPIRACY

The characters and events portrayed in this book are fictitious. Any similarity to real persons, living or dead, is coincidental and not intended by the author.

Printed in the United States of America.

The Celtic Conspiracy by Thore D. Hansen was first published in 2011 by Scorpio Verlag in Munich, Germany, as *Die Hand Gottes (The Hand of God)*. Translated from German by Anne Adams. First published in English in 2012 by AmazonCrossing.

Published by AmazonCrossing
P.O. Box 400818
Las Vegas, NV 89140

ISBN-13: 9781612183473
ISBN-10: 1612183476
Library of Congress Control Number: 2012904055

THE CELTIC CONSPIRACY

THORE D. HANSEN

Dedicated to all people who have lost their lives or their freedom through the actions of the Catholic Church. And to those who have realized that historical truth and spiritual self-determination are the right of every human being.

No crime can be hidden forever.
No culture, banished forever.
Every truth shall find the light of day.
If law can become justice,
then a divine culture can return.

PROLOGUE

Since the earliest days of our childhood we have grown used to hearing fabricated histories, and for centuries our soul has been so saturated with prejudices that it watches over these fantastic lies like a treasure until, ultimately, truth appears incredible and the lie, true.

—Sanchuniathon, Four Thousand Years Ago

THE MAGDALENSBERG, NEAR KLAGENFURT IN AUSTRIA – MAY 2, 1945

Major Sean MacClary heard the scream—like something out of a vicious nightmare—moments before the young soldier came running toward the tent where MacClary was awaiting orders from British high command.

"Major, sir, a recruit has fallen into a cave."

In spite of the tension of battle, MacClary felt a momentary sense of relief. "Brilliant, my friends," he said to his nearby troops dryly. "I was afraid I'd lose my men in battle. Instead, they're falling down holes."

The moment for joking passed quickly, though, and MacClary delivered orders for the rescue sharply. The last of the German troops had recently scattered; it was too dangerous to use a light to investigate the area, so this was going to be a more difficult operation than he would have liked.

MacClary took two soldiers and medics with him to find where the soldier had fallen. His left eye began to twitch nervously, a quirk he had developed at a young age when he was under pressure from his teachers. War had only made it worse. In spite of his reluctance to show weakness in front of his troops, he stopped for a moment, took off his helmet, and held his filthy forehead to calm himself down. His dark eyes searched for a point in the countryside where they could focus. As the twitching slowly subsided, he ran one hand through his short, gray hair and with the other put his helmet back on.

When he came to the edge of the cave, MacClary risked using a small flashlight to look into it. About ten feet down, he saw the motionless infantryman.

"Soldier, can you hear me?"

Only a faint groan confirmed that someone was still alive down there.

MacClary turned to the two men nearest him. "Smith and Rudy, rappel to him."

The soldiers quickly did his bidding. As they reached their companion, though, MacClary heard awed whispering that had nothing to do with the wounded man.

"What's going on down there?"

"Major, you have to see this! There's an entrance here to a room filled with all kinds of old stuff."

"What? Wait a minute, I'm coming down."

MacClary rappelled into the cave, following the light that one of the soldiers had turned on once hitting bottom. When MacClary got to the cave's floor, he couldn't believe his eyes. At first he thought they'd found a secret bunker, but he immediately realized that this structure was hundreds, perhaps thousands, of years old. Before the war, MacClary had been a professor at the London Institute of Archaeology. Seeing the artifacts the soldiers had discovered made him weak in the knees and instantly hit him with the desire to go back to the life he'd loved.

"Stay back and rescue the man," he said briskly to the others. "I'm going to take a closer look."

He couldn't make out very much in the dim light, but he could see that this must have been some sort of library or special burial chamber. The condition of the stones, the statues, and the few characters he could make out in the dust-filled air suggested Celtic or Roman origins. That didn't make sense, though, since the Celts were assimilated and converted to Christianity after the Romans conquered them; they would hardly have created this mysterious collection after that. Only the Druids would have had the knowledge and perspective to have hidden these treasures, but that would also have been impossible because the Druids only passed on their knowledge orally.

Was this cave a sanctuary? A place to preserve knowledge and culture? If so, who had built it? Questions shot through MacClary's head like the salvoes of a machine gun, but he wouldn't find any answers now, not under these miserable conditions.

There were few people who knew as well as he that it wasn't the Romans and the Greeks—or the Germanic people—who had first shaped Europe. It was the Celts. True, the fate of Celtic independence was virtually sealed by Julius Caesar, but the culture and its natural religion continued for a long time, until Christianity became the prevailing doctrine in fourth-century Rome. MacClary knew that the loss of Celtic culture had not received nearly enough attention, and its significance reached to the present day. Was this the reason he'd happened upon these artifacts?

Breathing heavily, handicapped by the darkness and the dust that filled the cave, he eyed the pieces as carefully as he could. He saw scrolls that shouldn't have been able to survive a hundred years in this region, but they were clearly ancient. Whoever had made this place had to have looked long and hard for such an unusually dry and warm cave. There could only be one explanation: they wanted to make sure that these testaments to the past would endure, so that one day in the future someone would discover them and show them to the world.

But why?

Among the stone tablets, statues, scrolls, and decorative pieces, a lone chest caught his attention. It was covered with dust and partially disintegrated, but he could make out something through the filth that was written on the top:

DISTURBATIO FONTIS

Was it possible? Was he really standing in front of the records of the persecuted pagans?

MacClary knew that there were German troops in front of them and Tito's troops behind. There was no way he could salvage these artifacts now, and there was very little time to stash them away.

Damn it! he thought. *Why now? What should I do?*

In spite of his confusion and frustration, MacClary felt a familiar and welcome energy. It was as though he were in his lecture hall, surrounded by students hungry for knowledge, devouring his archaeological histories like fairy tales.

"Major?"

MacClary jumped. For the briefest instant, he had been so lost in thought that he had forgotten this horrible war. He ordered Smith and Rudy to bring some new chests from the unit supply over to hold the most important pieces while he tried to think of a way to transport them securely through Austria and then through France to England. The sheer mass of these invaluable cultural treasures created an almost insurmountable obstacle. He felt like one of his medics who had to decide far too often who they could save and who they had to leave to die.

Even if he chose to transport some of the artifacts, it would be impossible to do so under these circumstances without destroying something, especially the parchment scrolls; the fact that they were in such good condition was a miracle. With the oxygen that had rushed in with the cave's collapse, the papyrus wouldn't last long. In ancient times, Egypt was one of the few places on earth where papyrus could be preserved for an extended period without any special conservation method. In damper regions, scrolls were copied for preservation, and it was not uncommon for adulterations to creep in.

He looked at the writing again. It suggested a time only a few centuries after Christ. If this trove were a testament to that period, it would be invaluable to researchers. MacClary almost forgot the circumstances that had brought him here, circumstances that made it hardly seem sensible to think about the future, even for a second. There were only a few hours until he would most likely receive orders to invade Klagenfurt. How could he organize a secure and inconspicuous transport now?

MacClary was well respected and trusted by his soldiers. No major had endured so few losses or made so few bad decisions. Perhaps he could hide the site of the trove and investigate it after the war, when he could be an archaeologist again. As a major and a friend of General Brown, he could have packages and documents declared secret and brought to England without being checked. He would quickly select a few pieces and then have the entrance to the cave closed so no one else would notice it. All he could do beyond this was hope that the dry climate would reset itself and that the damage to the artifacts would be minimal.

MacClary turned to Smith. "Could you seal the cave with a detonation so that no more air can get in, while still leaving the chamber and its treasures intact?"

"Yes, sir, but we need at least sixty feet inside for the blast and the debris."

MacClary shone the light over the room and found more sections of the cave. Maybe his trove would survive the explosion if they moved everything further inside. He ordered his men to bring everything into the back rooms carefully. Then MacClary wrapped up some scrolls, ornamental pieces, and the chest in shirts, pants, and blankets. They would load them up under cover of darkness.

The dawn was slowly emerging. Even if the explosion hid the entrance to the cave, the men were faced with the problem of how to set off the explosion without being noticed.

That was when fortune intervened. They received orders from British headquarters to follow the Seventy-Eighth Infantry Division, which would reach Klagenfurt in the morning. With the onset of combat, a targeted explosion of a cave entrance would hardly be noticed. The detonation went off without a hitch.

Only a few hours later, the British troops marched into Klagenfurt with few losses. News of the German surrender gave MacClary hope that he would soon be able to return to his university work. He had managed to take only a single chest of artifacts with him. Would he ever be able to explore the other treasures of this long-dead culture? If he survived the final throes of war, he would at least be able to bring some of the pieces home safely. That was a start.

Where it would end, though, was beyond anything he could have imagined.

CHAPTER 1

And he who overcomes and keeps my works unto the end, to him I will give power over the heathen, and he shall rule them with a rod of iron, and he shall break them as the vessels of a potter.

—Revelations 2:26–27

LOWER AUSTRIA – MARCH 13, PRESENT DAY

Adam Shane sat on the edge of his bed bathed in sweat. His long blond hair was glued to his face, and his hands grabbed at the edge of the mattress while he took deep gulps of breath, as if he had emerged from the ocean seconds before drowning. A glance at the clock told him that it was six o'clock in the morning. It was time to get up.

Instead, as he tried to rise, he suddenly lost his eyesight.

"My God, what's happening?"

He closed his eyes and fell back. His sense of balance was also gone, and when he opened his eyes again, he could only see his surroundings as different contours of light. Pictures raced through his mind, a collage of human history throughout the centuries blurring past him. Then, as he was about to move from the present into the future, everything suddenly stopped.

His eyes could again fully see his familiar bedroom. His body again controlled his spirit.

Or was it the other way around?

"What the hell was that?"

He should have known better than to ask. This was, after all, hardly the first time this had happened.

It wasn't all that long ago that he had been following in his father's footsteps, working as a blacksmith, a profession that befit his huge physical form. Then his wife was diagnosed with cancer. She refused to put herself through the agonizing treatments her doctors recommended because she knew their chances of success were limited. The path she chose guaranteed her an early death—until the moment when Shane knelt by his wife after the disease had left her as spent and helpless as a child. He willed himself to find a way to help her. And suddenly he was able to do so. Simply by dint of his effort, his wife began to improve palpably before his eyes.

In some ways, his entire life had been leading toward that moment. Since he was a child, while his friends spent their time with sports, motorcycles, music, or plans for losing their virginity, he was thinking about the world and how it could be saved. At fourteen, he was reading books, almost maniacally, that other kids wouldn't pick up unless they were forced to in school. He longed to exchange ideas with others, but this proved impossible in the small, rural, conservative village where he grew up. His upbringing constricted him, and even though he left the town to go to college, the constriction remained.

He shook his head to jostle these thoughts away. They wouldn't do him any good right now. He had to talk with someone. For a second he hesitated, then he reached for the telephone and dialed Victoria's number.

"Adam, why in God's name are you calling so early?"

"I'm sorry, but I'm not doing well. I had one of those incredibly intense dreams and I just had to hear your voice."

Victoria sighed on the other end. "Adam, you have to take care of yourself. I'm afraid you're going to lose it soon if this keeps happening."

She had every right to be afraid. Six months earlier, she had taken their child and gone to live with her mother in London because she couldn't stand Shane's outbursts of anger over his perceptions and despair about what he called the complete collapse of humanity. "This is no way to raise our son," she said to him before she left. He could hardly blame her for going, though he missed her and Jarod horribly.

Victoria paused on the other end. When she spoke again, there was more warmth in her voice. "Tell me about it."

Shane related the details of the dream to her. He was in a forest he didn't recognize. It was cold and the wind was blowing violently. He noticed an old, very large tree whose branches were reaching toward him.

Suddenly, he saw figures in loose, bright robes in a clearing very far away. They were moving as if in a trance or in a ceremony, and they repeatedly turned their gaze to the sky. A sense of peace replaced Shane's fear at this point, a feeling of connection and warmth. He hadn't felt this way since he was a child. The figures seemed so peaceful, so deeply connected to nature, connected by a great love. Shane moved closer and saw that all the figures were old men. They were gesticulating quickly, but they seemed to possess a greater inner peace. It was beautiful to watch.

This clearing had to be incredibly important. The trees were arranged in a circle, all of them the same height, shape, and distance apart. In between them, Shane could make out three rows of seats forming a circle, as if it were a little theater.

Sadly, the sense of peace and community did not last. A horde of men on horseback rode into the clearing, surrounding the old men before anyone could escape. The riders' armor looked Roman. They jumped from their horses, and even though the old men were unarmed, one of the soldiers drove his sword through the stomach of the first man until it came out the other side. Hatred filling his face, the warrior braced his foot against the chest of the old man and slowly pulled his sword out again, clearly taking pleasure in the action. Before he died, the old man shouted something in a language Shane didn't understand.

Shane was stunned, paralyzed, horrified. He watched helplessly as the others were also brought down by swords in a blood frenzy. When the massacre was over, the soldiers got back on their horses and rode toward a small village Shane could see in the distance. He ran after them to witness the horde brutally murdering women and children.

One of the legionnaires had put a severed head on his lance like a trophy. He rode into the middle of the village, which was already ablaze and in chaos. He shouted, and suddenly Shane could understand him.

"Submit! Your gods have left you. Only our god will protect you!"

As if to underscore the point, another legionnaire hurled a spear at a fleeing youth, piercing him through. The carnage continued until everyone in the once peaceful town was dead. Before the pack disappeared, Shane saw a legionnaire with the sign of the fish on his shield ride past him, a scornful smile on his face.

"Victoria, it was like I was really there," Shane said, drained from the experience of sharing his vision. "It was much more than just a nightmare."

"Adam, I see parallels and a message to your own life, here. This eternal frustration with the world that always makes you turn away from any beautiful moment. But the fact that you're sharing this is a first step to overcome your dark world," Victoria said tenderly, and Shane knew that she was genuine. This was as sympathetic as she had sounded since their separation. "I'm here for you if you need me. If you want, Jarod could come stay with you in three weeks' time. I have to go to New York, and he misses you so much. I'll call you on Friday."

"I'd like that. Thanks for listening."

They hung up less than a minute later, but the conversation had done what Shane had hoped it would. It had restored some of his strength. He could think about the vision a little more dispassionately now.

He remembered that in the dream he had visited the village before the attack, feeling very much at home. The village was made up of about forty houses surrounded by a rampart of wood and sand piles. Beyond the heavy wooden gate that formed the entrance was a fountain in a square about a hundred yards away. Arranged in a circle on the square were the house of a blacksmith, a market hall of some sort, and two other houses, one belonging to a chieftain and another to a Druid. Shane had seen many people going about their business on a beautiful, sunny day. The style of the houses and the differences in dress showed there were differences in social class, but no one seemed to be unhappy or suffering. On the contrary, this community, perhaps because of its size, seemed to function well. He would have gladly stayed there.

Until the destruction began.

CHAPTER 2

DUBLIN – MARCH 13, PRESENT DAY

Padre Luca Morati's forehead wrinkled like an accordion. His hands, trembling as they reached for the telephone, were covered with age spots, and every vein was visible through his pale, thin skin. At ninety-four, the old man was well connected in the Vatican and belonged, along with the oldest and most influential clergy, to the Curia.

"Oh, good Lord, I have failed," he sighed sadly as he leaned back in his old leather chair in slow motion, trying to fix his weak eyes on something in the room. Every inch of every wall was filled with books of incalculable age and value. At the window, where he could look out on the entrance to Trinity College, there was a table from the colonial period covered with papers and books, lit by a common library lamp that lent the antique mahogany piece an incomparably warm and typically Irish character.

The line he was calling finally connected. "Si?"

"This is Padre Morati. Put me through—it's urgent."

A moment of silence—during which a fly setting down would have seemed like an earthquake—was followed by the abrupt voice of the person he'd been calling. "How may I help you?"

"Salvoni, I'm afraid the thing we've feared is coming closer. The son is following in his father's footsteps." Morati felt a sudden uneasiness in his stomach, a mixture of uncertainty and a bad conscience. He'd been living with these feelings for decades without ever questioning their source.

"What happened?"

"I think Ronald MacClary has found a clue. He's giving a lecture this weekend at Trinity. Its blasphemous subject matter must have been fueled by new knowledge."

"But Padre, we've known for a long time that he, like so many others, is trying to discredit us with his agnostic lectures and his scientific delusions. Just because he's giving another lecture doesn't mean that he's discovered something."

"The subject matter concerns me, Salvoni. He's drawing conclusions that would require evidence to prove."

"When is the lecture?" interrupted the cardinal, now audibly nervous.

"This Friday, at eight p.m. in the old lecture hall."

"Thank you, Padre. Just to be on the safe side, we'll send someone to listen to his unbearable lies. May the good Lord reward you for your unrelenting vigilance and let you remain with us for a long time to come."

The cardinal hung up without another word.

Morati sank down into his chair, his hands covering his face. Within seconds, his body was shaking with sobs.

For more than forty years Morati had served as vice prefect of the Vatican archives. As such, he was one of the few people allowed to see the priceless cultural objects and the written records and testimonies that the missionaries had stolen during their campaigns against those with different beliefs. He was also allowed into the library outside of Vatican City that contained material that could be dated back to the eighth century. The Vatican's real secret archive was also one of the best-protected places and only known to certain selected members of the Roman Curia. To make sure that the conservationists and researchers who worked there couldn't steal or destroy anything, they had to undergo an extensive procedure at the beginning of every work day. After they had been searched for cameras, recording equipment, radio equipment, knives, matches, or anything else that could be destructive in any way, they were driven from the Sistine Chapel to a place outside of Rome in a car with darkened windows. They were only allowed out of the car in a dark garage and then were taken to work where they were constantly observed in rooms protected from light and germs. At the end of the day, they went through the whole procedure again as they were escorted back to Rome.

Only once had Morati seen the area immediately outside of the library. He was the only one who had ever lived to tell the tale, and he was never allowed to return.

Some of the artifacts Morati had seen in the archive contained unbelievable beauty and wisdom. There were writings here from prophets and spiritual leaders who disseminated very different tenets from those of the Church and whose effect threatened the power of the Church so much that a large portion of affiliated doctrines had already been destroyed. If humankind could see these tenets, the fate of the Church would be sealed. It would be put on trial for the greatest crime in history.

Since Morati had spent half his life reconstructing the evidence of the history of the Celtic Druids and other pagan scholars, he had asked to be transferred back home. He had been retired for twenty years now. Of course, that didn't stop him from acting as protector of knowledge by keeping an eye on the MacClary family, particularly Ronald. The father had attracted enough attention, and, in Rome, people were afraid Ronald might discover something that could cause an uproar in an ever-more-critical Christian world.

Now MacClary's son was creeping closer to a revelation. A revelation the Church could never allow him to experience.

CHAPTER 3

DUBLIN – MARCH 13, PRESENT DAY

Ronald MacClary sat in his office, staring out into the morning light. Dublin in the spring was a mixture of sun, clouds, and rain that teased you with unpredictability. The sun pierced his dark brown eyes, lighting them up like amber and highlighting his three-day growth of beard and his gray-flecked hair.

Ronald MacClary had had a good life. He had been born in Boston just after the outbreak of World War II. His father had met his mother in the early 1930s on a trip to New York, and they were married soon after. After the United States joined the war, they moved to Dublin, where Sean MacClary was soon called to serve as a major in the Eighth British Army Division. His son Ronald, after studying archaeology, had gone to law school in Boston. There, he completed his degree in record time and later served for several years as a judge in the district court of Boston before being named to the Supreme Court, where he had been serving as chief justice for the past three years. But whenever he could, he still came back to his parents' house in Dublin on Arbour Hill, across from the National Museum. There he buried himself in his father's research.

MacClary was rummaging through one of the countless leather portfolios marked with the family crest when his gaze turned to the cabinet where his father's inheritance had been stored for so long. In March 1943, just before he was born, his father had taken over leadership of a large unit of soldiers. Badly wounded, he came back from Austria, and a few years after returning home, he died from a grenade splinter that had lodged in his lung during combat. On his deathbed, he spoke to six-year-old Ronald in a way the boy could barely understand, but would never forget.

They were in a run-down hospital, and his father's body had withered to the point where it seemed as though he'd already been long in his grave. The room reeked of fear, the smell alternating between antiseptic solutions and feces.

"You have to keep investigating my trove, my son," Sean MacClary had said with as much emphasis as he could muster. "You'll find everything in my library. I didn't have time to write everything down, but it's the key to understanding our culture, everything that makes us who we are. It all began with a horrible crime. Look in the..."

The diminished man's breath faded, and only a strained rattle filled the room.

"Where should I look, Father?" Ronald said desperately, knowing that there was more to this and that it was without question the most important conversation of his young life. But the conversation, and his father's life, was over.

As he got older, Ronald looked through every square inch of his father's archives and never discovered anything. Even the scroll in the cabinet hadn't yet revealed its secrets. One thing was clear: his father must have stumbled across something from antiquity, because that was the only thing his archaeological heart burned for. Hardly anyone had known as much detailed information about the Dark Ages, which was to the elder MacClary the blackest period of human civilization. In Sean MacClary's mind, the Inquisition, the two world wars, and all the other conflicts were only byproducts of that earlier period of civilization.

His father's legacy was much more to Ronald than just some historical or archaeological riddle. It was the only possible justification for the man having so little time, or love, left over for him. So many times, Ronald's mother had bitterly cried over how alone and abandoned she felt. Even as a boy Ronald had found it all so unfair, and although in those few moments he'd had with his father he'd gotten excited about the search for the past, it had been the question of justice that led him to break off his studies in archaeology to begin studying law. However, those years of study in his father's library had also made him a critical student of religious history.

Ronald couldn't deny his roots. He had looked after his parents' house and his father's library for decades, watching over it like a treasure. He avoided making any changes for fear of forever losing the opportunity to solve the puzzle his father had laid out before him.

"It's all God's fault," he said with an ironic smile. Then he turned back to his computer to finish his upcoming Trinity College lecture.

CHAPTER 4

AUSTRIA – MARCH 13

Shane had no more time to think about the dream that had catapulted him awake this morning. He needed to get out of bed and on with his day. Within the next half hour, a dozen ailing people would begin filling his office.

He opened the bedroom door and headed to the bathroom. As he did, it occurred to him that all of his things were still in the suitcase in his home office. It had been late last night when he had gotten back from a seminar in Paris on alternative healing and herbalism. Making what was for him an unusually elegant turn, he headed resolutely toward his consulting room in his underwear, opened the door, and reached for his suitcase near the desk.

When he surprisingly discovered that Patricia was already there.

"Good morning, Mr. Shane," she said with an amused smile. "Would you like a coffee?"

He regarded the beautiful twenty-five-year-old woman, not knowing whether to hide his virtual nakedness or pretend as though this were all very natural. Patricia delivered herbs and ointments to his office every Wednesday. Her father, a farmer, gathered them to supplement his income.

Shane reached into his suitcase to get his bathrobe, putting it on quickly. "I didn't expect you here so early, Patricia." He pointed to the large package she was holding. "What's that?"

"That's the ten pounds of horsetail you ordered."

Shane's eyes widened. "Ten pounds? With that I could detox fifty patients at once! And I have enough stock, in any case. I'm sorry, but you must have misunderstood. I hope you can return it."

"Yes, of course," Patricia said, turning her eyes downward. "The rest should be right, though. Should I send you a bill at the end of the month as usual?"

"That would be great, thank you."

"No problem. I'll see you next time."

Without another word, Patricia turned and left. Shane's eyes followed her as she departed, noting the sense of longing that rose up unbidden as he watched her. When was the last time he'd felt anything like that?

Now that he was in his office, he decided to deal with his mail. Among the usual bills, thank-you notes, and advertisements, an envelope made from fine, handmade paper stuck out like a single rose in the middle of a barren field. He picked the letter out of the pile and decided to turn on the television to watch the news instead.

"...the next generation will be particularly affected. After negotiations broke down, Pachauri, head of the UN Intergovernmental Panel on Climate Change and an expert

on the deteriorating state of the earth, warned heads of state about dismissing climate change as a problem for the future. 'The effects will be noticeable during your terms in office,' he said to the assemblage. After his..."

Shane turned off the television. He didn't need a reporter to tell him that humankind had lost virtually all connection with nature. He went back to his mail and this time opened the beautiful envelope. Along with a notice about a meeting of healers and herbalists, he found another invitation in the envelope that caught his attention:

The Systematic Annihilation of Celtic Culture and Indigenous European Peoples and Its Effect on the World in Terms of Culture, Politics, and the Economy: A Lecture by Professor Ronald MacClary

Thomas Ryan had kept his word. A year earlier, he had met the Irishman at a meeting of alternative healers in Vienna. In his opinion, Ryan was a bit of a radical. He lived near Dublin in a commune that had dedicated itself to a return to a life in harmony with nature. Ryan had promised to get in touch with him since Shane wanted to learn more about the project. They'd spent an entire evening together talking about the Celts, the original inhabitants of Europe, and Shane had gotten the distinct impression that Ryan was making fun of the neo-Druids, who, as he put it, had never understood the true message of the scholars, the chieftains, and the Druids. There hadn't been enough time in this first meeting to learn more, but one thing was clear: contemporary excavations suggested a very different image of the Celts than that of a group of barbarians who practiced human sacrifice.

What is happening here? Shane wondered. He'd just dreamt of this exact period and people. *It can't be an accident.*

He sat down at his desk nervously and fished out his calendar, rashly deciding to accept the invitation to the conference. That was when he noted the date. Tomorrow.

Without hesitating, he took pen and paper and wrote a sign that read, "The office will be closed until further notice."

He had very little time before his first patients would be standing at his door. He didn't want to have to turn them away personally, so he needed to leave before they arrived. He added a few clean things to his suitcase, grabbed his passport and his wallet, and got dressed instantly. He performed the high-wire act of pulling his pants on while standing on one foot, while at the same time trying to call the airport on his cell phone. As he did this, something akin to peace suffused him. He put down his cell phone and sat on his office chair, his pants only halfway on.

"Slow down, Shane, slow down. What's going on? You should listen to your logical side and not follow some crazy fantasy."

Could it really be true? Was there really more behind the decline of the Celts than people knew? Ryan hadn't yet succeeded in making a convincing argument for the superiority of the culture, laws, and lifestyle of the Druids, but he also hadn't come anywhere near telling him everything. Shane was thinking about one particular detail from their conversation. Ryan had said that the dubious culture of the Western world, where nature, individuals, and entire peoples were sacrificed to the rule of money, wasn't necessarily the only way. Maybe it was just a small but powerful accident—or an event—that had set Europe on this path. If you could find that point in time and show the alternative, the other path, it should be possible for mankind to go in a new direction.

Ryan was surprisingly confident that mankind would consciously choose to turn away from this path—a path that had cut them off from their true nature, that had made them apathetic and dumb as a herd of sheep—if they only understood the true reasons behind their original choice. There had to be a greater goal than the eternal chorus of growth, competition, and wealth, which was making it impossible for future generations to lead a healthy life, or to survive at all.

"Why do I always come back to this point of frustration when I think about mankind?" groaned Shane. Ryan had promised him that he would learn more about the secret of the Druids and the Celts when they saw each other again. Maybe his dream had been no accident after all and Victoria was right.

There would be time to try to answer that question. For now, though, he needed to pack the rest of his things and make his way to the Vienna airport.

CHAPTER 5

> *But the obligation to chasten and punish is imposed on you as well, holiest of Emperors, and, by the law of the highest God, you must in your austerity track down the crimes of idolatry in every form.*
>
> —Church Father Julius Firmicus Maternus

VATICAN CITY, ROME – MARCH 13, EVENING

Not far from the pope's inner sanctum was the Vatican government building, the true center of power for the little country with exceptionally unusual status in the international community. The building itself was quite unspectacular, with its four floors and modest architecture. Only the oversized crest of the Vatican state made it clear that you weren't in Rome anymore.

Thomas Lambert reached for the telephone, his long day at work wearing on him. As he did, he looked out his window into the courtyard. Even outside of the Vatican,

Lambert always wore black as he dashed from one meeting to the next, running the international affairs of the Church. Almost six feet five, the Briton made quite an impression, especially in Italy. He inspired respect and fear in those around him with his square jaw, steel-blue eyes, and pale skin. There were few who exercised as much influence and control in the "country of God" as Lambert, but after sixteen straight hours, even this Christian giant of the Opus Dei was ready for some rest.

By the time he was working under Monsignor Giovanni Montini, who was later to become Pope Paul VI, Lambert had already risen unimpeded to become the most powerful man in the Vatican. Montini had had an interesting career path; he had worked for the American Secret Service and had also been a member of a Freemason lodge. He had been an easygoing superior who had made it possible for Lambert to bring the second Vatican council to an end, satisfying the modernists inside the Church and the public for quite some time.

In the meantime, Lambert continued his work in peace. He couldn't burn the heretics at the stake anymore, but there were other ways to enforce the pure tenets of the Church. One established method was a network of agents and spies, built up over centuries, for sniffing out the modernists inside the Church and, at the very least, muzzling them. Lambert was so good at his job that not even the current pope—John Paul III—could contest his position.

"Lambert," Thomas barked into the phone.

"This is Salvoni. We need to talk."

"Can't it wait until tomorrow? I've worked long enough today."

"There are some things on God's earth that can't wait. We have some unsettling news from Dublin about a certain Ronald MacClary."

Lambert groaned inwardly. "Please spare me the concerns of Padre Morati. I've already heard them directly from him. God knows we have bigger problems in Dublin than a crazy Irishman who wants to raise the profile of his lost culture at the expense of the Church. If he weren't such a public figure, we would have turned him into a laughingstock a long time ago."

"I'm not sure if Morati has told you everything this time."

"Fine. Come up."

Lambert fell back into his chair, exhausted. Within moments, the door to his office opened and a nervous figure entered the room.

"So, Padre Salvoni, what in God's name can I do for you?"

For a good ten years as head of the oldest secret service in the world, Salvoni had been taking care of matters that should never reach the public ear. He was short, lanky, and athletic, and his small mustache, along with his skin, tanned and pockmarked from acne, gave him the aura of a snake. It was this aura that had ensured his positions over the past years, and even Lambert was never certain of his trustworthiness, as much as he valued his contributions.

"We have to go to Dublin immediately so that we can control the press reaction and the extent of this horrible thing," Salvoni said calmly. "It wouldn't hurt to observe the lecture at the very least."

"What do you expect to gain from that?"

"Certainty. Just certainty."

"You can't go. I need you somewhere else. Send Caloni, but he should only watch MacClary and he should only concentrate on the lecture, nothing else. I don't want an incident with a man who is one of the most important judges in America. To be honest, as much as I value your caution, I don't share your concern here. Do we understand each other?"

With a cold smile, Victor Salvoni nodded and gave Lambert a bow.

"Brother Morati has been watching the MacClary family for a long time now," Salvoni said when he again made eye contact with Lambert. "MacClary is putting the downfall of the pagans in a context that, paired with actual events, could be dangerous."

Lambert's eyes narrowed as he attempted to control his temper. "If you were to make a mistake, it could make the troubled atmosphere around the Church more dangerous than ever. Do you really believe it's worth it?"

"In my opinion, yes."

Lambert suddenly felt more tired. "Fine. I know the Lord has always protected your ambitions. Since I don't think you'll have to do anything about the MacClary situation that our press department can't handle, I expect to have recommendations by Monday about how we can watch out for our lost brothers in Ireland."

"As you wish," Salvoni said before turning to leave.

CHAPTER 6

DUBLIN – MARCH 13, EVENING

Shane was accustomed to the weather in Ireland, where there was seldom a cloudless sky or a summery day, but today in Dublin there was so much rain pouring down that this flight's landing was going to stretch his nerves to the limit. He'd been a horrible flyer for more than twenty years, ever since surviving a near crash. Since then, he boarded every plane expecting the worst. As if to underscore this thought, the plane met the landing strip roughly, just barely coming to a stop before the end of the runway.

"Ladies and gentlemen, thank you for your patience, and I hope that the slight turbulence did not cause you any undue discomfort," spoke the copilot over the intercom.

With a pale face and wobbly legs, Shane stood up.

"Are you all right?"

Shane turned to meet the eyes of an old man who had to be over seventy but swung his carry-on over his shoulder like a kid. Shane had sat next to the man the entire flight, but he had been so preoccupied with his fears and thoughts about the conference of healers that he hadn't engaged his seatmate for a moment.

"I'll be better soon," Shane said, trying to wipe the tension from his voice. "Thanks for asking. I just don't like to fly very much."

"Good man, if God wants you, he'll come and get you, whether it's with a plane crash or a banana peel. Why worry about it?"

"I don't know if I want to leave my fate in the hands of God," Shane responded promptly, his body relaxing, "even though you're probably right. Of course, that leads to the question of which god you're talking about. The old creator who looks benevolently down, guiding the fates of his sheep?"

With an amused smile, the spry man introduced himself. "Eric Fink. I write for the *Standard* in Vienna. It's probably better if we don't start a theological debate, unless it helps you calm down."

Shane chuckled. "What brings you to Dublin?"

The man's eyes twinkled. "I'm writing an article about the blessing that the Catholic diocese has brought to the children of Dublin. That should tell you what I think of your idea of God."

Shane held up a hand in defense. "It's not my idea." He pulled out his conference invitation and pointed to the agenda item that had sent him here. "I'm here for this lecture, which should tell you everything you need to know."

The reporter skeptically examined the invitation, then looked up brightly. "Maybe I'll see you there."

It was time to disembark, and the two said good-bye quickly. The brief exchange with the old man had gotten Shane thinking. What did the Dublin child abuse scandals have to do with the question of God?

* * *

DUBLIN'S INNER CITY

Thomas Ryan was sitting—or rather lying—with his arms spread out on a table in Porterhouse, one of the largest pubs in the heart of Dublin, right near Trinity College.

"Man alive, Thomas," Deborah Walker said, clearly in much better shape, "you have your discussion with Ellison in two hours and you're tight as the last Celt."

Ryan burst out laughing, spraying a mouthful of Guinness a good two yards across the table. "Yep, exactly, as the last Celt. You're completely right, my friend. I realize now what a fool's fest this is every year, and I don't give a shit if Ellison tries to mess around with me. If I'm there or alone, what's the difference? Three hundred years ago, I would have just chopped the head off this wannabe Druid."

He and Deborah made an odd pair. After living through some wild years struggling against the IRA, whom he deemed responsible for the death of his brother Matthew, Thomas had transformed himself from a farmer into an expert in the use of herbs, seeing patients in Dublin pub backrooms. Deborah, with her red curls and old-fashioned glasses that made her still look like a student, was struggling along in Dublin as a lecturer in Irish literature. She was a genius at interpreting old languages, though there was hardly any interest in Welsh or the other original Celtic dialects anymore.

Thomas dragged his heavy body up and pushed his blond hair back. “Wait here, I’m going to get some coffee.” He moved toward the bar, passing the entrance on the way. As he did, a young man nearly barreled into him as he made a swift entrance into the pub.

“Slow down, young man,” Ryan slurred to him. “Or do you want to buy the next round?” Then he paused and took a closer look at Shane. “Well, if it isn’t my curious friend from Austria. Fantastic! It looks like you took me up on my invitation.”

“Yes, I was excited to get it.”

With a loud laugh, Ryan pointed to one of the back tables. “Let’s sit down back there, next to the woman with the round spectacles and the earnest expression. That would be Deborah.”

“Tell me, am I wrong, or is there a meeting of Druids going on here?”

“Of course! And I’m Thomas Ryan, grandmaster of the last order of true Druids.”

Ryan had said this loudly enough that Deborah shook her head slowly and sank down into her sweater.

“Then you’re not too happy to be here?”

Ryan suddenly felt more sober and looked Shane in the eyes.

"No, and this is definitely the last time."

With that, he pivoted toward the bar.

* * *

Shane stood there at a loss, noticing uneasily that some people were looking at him suspiciously after Ryan's performance. Still, he grabbed his bag and went over to Deborah.

"I have to apologize for Thomas's behavior," Deborah said. "He's not having a good day. Sit down. What would you like to drink?"

"A Guinness, of course."

"Are you from Germany?"

"No, Austria. My father came from Dublin, though. He emigrated from Ireland to Austria after the war."

"And what brings you here?"

"Let's say, a strange dream and"—he reached into his pocket—"this invitation."

"Well, you must not have looked at the invitation very carefully. Except for the lecture tomorrow, the conference is over. There's only one discussion left… unless…"

"…unless I can sober up in the next two hours, says my nursemaid," Ryan interjected, sitting down next to Shane with a coffee cup.

Shane looked at the invitation in frustration. It was true; his anxiety had tripped him up again and he had mixed up the dates. He groaned softly to himself.

"Don't worry," Ryan continued, "the most important part is still to come. Tomorrow is the lecture by Ronald MacClary."

"That's the only reason I'm here. I'll gladly do without the pathetic attempts by neo-Celts, Celtic shamans, Wiccans, and other types romanticizing the Druids."

This enraged Ryan. "I'd suggest you talk a little more quietly. There are some here who won't take kindly to your words. And to be honest, I don't either."

Deborah glanced around her as though she were trying to gauge if Shane had already attracted any unwanted attention. "How about a refreshing walk through the damp alleys of our beautiful city?"

Shane took a deep breath to ease the tension that seemed to be shadowing him on this trip. "That sounds like a very good idea."

Ryan stood up, paid for the round of drinks, and didn't speak again until they'd left the pub. "Tell me, Shane, if you're so skeptical about esotericism, what do you make of the fact that you stumbled over me in particular?"

The question surprised Shane. "Let's call it an accident. But I'll confide something to you. I had a dream a couple of days ago. A dream of such intensity, it was like a revelation to me. Then, the same morning, I happened to find this invitation. I'm here because the dream was reflected in the title of the invitation."

"Must have been quite a dream."

"Trust me, it was. That morning, I could smell the earth I had touched in the dream. The dirt under my fingernails could have been centuries old. Just after I woke up, I went blind and lost my balance, and I could only see apparitions of light. Then I saw a trip through history, amazingly fast, steeped in lies and destruction. The whole time I could see legions raging under the banner of Christendom."

Why was he being so candid? What if he was confiding in the wrong people? After all, he was in Ireland.

Ryan stopped walking. "Adam, I don't believe we met each other by accident. There's probably a very simple explanation for what you experienced. You're by no means the only one to have experienced something like this." Ryan, who suddenly seemed much more sober, laid both hands on Shane's shoulders. "You're just remembering yourself," he said, shifting suddenly into German.

"Remembering? How can I remember something without having taken part in it?"

"How do you know that you didn't? Have you ever considered that consciousness could govern time and space? Adam, that was definitely more than a dream. It's an indication that you have a gift that you can train. It's happening to more and more people all over the world these days."

The intensity in Ryan's eyes was more than a little disturbing to Shane.

"There's one thing I'd like to know, Thomas. Why do you despise these new Druids, and what was it about the old Druids of ancient times that was so special?"

"You get right to the point, don't you, Adam? I don't despise the neo-Druids. But a better question would be why the ancient Druids suddenly disappeared. I firmly believe that they had another concept of life for us. But let's slow down a bit. How about this: get some rest and we'll meet tomorrow in front of Trinity College at seven fifteen. Then I'll introduce you to Ronald MacClary. He'll be more than glad to answer any questions that are still bothering you. I think that's enough for today. Patience, my friend."

Shane stood there and looked at him completely confused. "But…"

"I'll just add one more thing, Adam. When I walk through a forest, through a meadow blooming with wildflowers, when I listen to the buzzing of the bees or come upon a spot with mushrooms, shimmering white-gold in the shadows, or hear the call of spring from a chickadee, then I see the gods before me, not a forest to use and exploit. Nature is for me a divine experience. It is the place where I recognize the true mother, the true father. I have no god in heaven, only gods here on earth."

Shane remembered what Ryan had told him in Vienna about his commune and how he had removed himself from modern life to the country to be surrounded by nature.

"Our erstwhile culture will not return if we, like so many here, play the Druid on the weekends, only to drive back to the office on Monday. Only by making decisive changes will we make any kind of difference. But if we are going to talk more about this, first you have to learn more about the fall of the people who once ruled Europe. And there will be time enough for that tomorrow evening."

Shane's first impulse was to contradict him, to continue the conversation, but suddenly he realized that he didn't even have a hotel room for the night. It was really about time for him to take a deep breath and find a place to stay.

"OK, it's a plan."

Ryan clapped Shane on the shoulder. "All right then. Good night, Adam Shane."

* * *

RYAN'S COUNTRY HOUSE, CORK, IRELAND – JULY 18, 1978

It was already dark, and, at eight years old, he knew that he shouldn't be leaving his room again. But he was too curious about who all these people were and what they were talking about. He had to carefully place every footstep so that the creaking of the old wooden floor wouldn't give him away.

From upstairs he couldn't see into the room where almost a dozen men and women were sitting around in heated debate.

"My God, Jane, do you still believe in this myth? I mean…"

"Ron, you have one of the family trees, like everyone else here, and they're so similar to this MacClary's parchment, and it comes from Austria…"

"Yes, and what about it? It doesn't help us if he doesn't have the coordinates."

"Not yet, Ron, not yet, and it can't be an accident that Connor got to know him. We should trust him. He's no friend of Rome, he won't give us away, and he takes us seriously."

"Jane's right. The day will soon come, the time that Dubdrean has given for the return."

"And that leaves open the question of what or who should return. You know the religious aspect of this doesn't interest me in the slightest," Thomas's father, Connor, continued. "But the possibility of giving back to the remaining Celts a portion of their stolen identity—that is too tempting not to follow him."

At that moment there was a loud crash as he fell from his crouching position.

"Thomas Ryan!" came the voice of his mother. "Did I or did I not tell you that it's your bedtime?"

Thomas held tight to his teddy bear. "But I want to be a Celt too!"

Thomas was greeted with hearty laughter from the whole room.

"You already are, my son,"

"Really?"

"I'll bring him back to bed."

"No, let him come down. He won't sleep anyhow until we're done here," O'Brian said.

Thomas skipped down the stairs into the living room. It was warm there, with an open fire, and the light had a yellowish glow. His parents' house was a good two hundred years old, and in winter the cold wind blew through every nook and cranny. The mostly antique teak furniture and the many heirlooms passed down from grandparents made the whole house seem almost like a museum of Irish culture. Ryan cuddled up with his uncle O'Brian, his father's best friend, and mumbled something. He felt so happy to be surrounded by the grown-ups. But then he felt all of their eyes on him.

"What did you say?"

"When are the Druids coming back, Mami?"

"Did you tell him about this nonsense?" his father said in irritation.

"No, absolutely not."

"Who told you about it, Thomas? Be honest," his father asked.

"No one told me anything! I dreamed it a couple of days ago. I saw men in a ship on the ocean, and a couple of them had long robes on, but not all of them. And they came onto land and went off in different directions. But before they did that they took each other's hands and said that they would return. And...no, that was all, but then I heard you talking about the Druids and I thought..."

"It's OK, Thomas, you've heard us talking before. Your mind is playing tricks on you. The Druids we've been talking about, my son, they've been dead for a long, long time."

Suddenly there was a knock at the door, and his mother stood up. Seconds later he heard her scream. "Oh my God, no, God, no, no, no..." Her voice fell to a whimper.

His father ran to the door, and friends of the family carried Thomas's older brother Matthew inside. Matthew was white as a sheet and didn't move. From his chest and leg blood was gushing. A lot of blood.

"My God, will this never end?" Thomas's mother screamed.

He stood there glued to the spot next to Uncle O'Brian, holding his hand tight. "What did they do to Matthew?" he asked.

"They shot him," O'Brian said.

"But why?"

"Because he doesn't have the right religion, Thomas."

"I don't understand."

"No one understands, little one."

"Are the Druids a religion too?"

"No, Thomas, they are old masters who united knowledge and faith, and from this understanding they wanted to create our future. They were spiritual leaders, but not a religion."

"I don't think I understand, Uncle. But I want to know more about it."

"You will, little Thomas Ryan, you will, I promise you."

CHAPTER 7

TRINITY COLLEGE, DUBLIN – MARCH 14

For his entire life, Ronald's father had praised Trinity College in Dublin as one of the oldest and most beautiful oases of knowledge. Beyond its gothic architecture, the university boasted several astonishing things. One of these was the library, built in 1732, that housed more than two hundred thousand ancient texts, among them the famous *Book of Kells*, and the oldest harp in Ireland. Sean MacClary's second home had been the Long Room, a space almost 210 feet in length where the most valuable books were housed. Its corridors, running on both sides and on two floors, had a fascinating clarity and aesthetic. The classical rotunda of the top floor warmed the entire space.

Ronald's lecture tonight was taking place in a no less impressive section of the college—the old Examination Hall, a place that had inspired fear and respect in students simply through its sheer size and beauty, along with its ancient symbols and frescoes. Ronald's father had often told him of his memories, when he was struggling with his own exam jitters, wondering if he would ever make the transition from student to teacher.

Lost in memory, weighed down by his father's legacy, Ronald strode through the venerable halls of the university where generations of MacClarys had, in one way or another, left their mark. He went into the Examination Hall and was surprised to find no one there yet, not even the young assistant, who should have been helping him set up. Confused and a bit unsettled, he looked at the clock over the lectern and then at the invitation he had sent to nearly four hundred people. Then he let out a sigh of relief, his expression relaxing.

"As always, I'm too early."

He'd swung his briefcase onto the lectern and sat down in the first row of chairs when suddenly a voice behind him broke the silence of the hall.

"Ronald MacClary? Is it really you, or just a shadow of your forefathers?"

Ronald turned around, casually crossing his legs. "Jennifer Wilson, what in the world…?"

"I realize you didn't send me an invitation, but do you really believe your avocational ambitions to rid the people of their faith are a secret in Washington?"

Ronald smiled slightly. "Now, Jennifer, we've already agreed that I'm not trying to rid the people of their faith."

"Oh yes, my mistake."

Jennifer walked swiftly to Ronald, and he stood to embrace her. Jennifer Wilson was beautiful, with long, dark hair, a striking and sensual expression, and a charismatic appearance that attracted men while simultaneously inspiring fear in them. Ronald considered her one of the best lawyers he had ever trained, and their relationship went far beyond the typical range of a teacher-student relationship.

"Jennifer, I'm surprised. If I'd had the slightest idea you were interested in this, believe me, then—"

"I know. I've signaled my misgivings about your hobby far too often. Apology accepted." She smiled mischievously. "But you didn't even invite me to the Capitol for the reception for the new judge. *That* I'm going to hold against you."

"You know that I'm trying to avoid any overlaps between our private life and official duties."

Jennifer let her arms fall from Ronald's shoulders and sat down. She looked around the hall and took a deep breath. "OK, if I'm going to be honest, I'm much more interested in a lavish dinner after your lecture. A dinner that has been due you since my exams. I'd like to talk a few things over with you that have been on my mind."

Ronald knew this expression well. Jennifer only wore it when she had something very important on her mind. "How could I say no to that? I can't promise there won't be a few others joining us, though, at least at the beginning."

Ronald reached into his vest pocket and pulled out a note that he offered to Jennifer, grinning. "This is an event the law school is putting on that's taking place at the same time as my lecture. It's about the history of international law and it ends at ten, just before my lecture is over."

"That's, of course, pure coincidence."

"Yes. Even if you don't believe me, it is."

"Fine," she said, turning to leave. "I'll pick you up on time—and don't even think about coming up with an excuse to get out of it."

"Why would I disappoint my best student?"

Jennifer kept walking toward the door as she answered. "You've done it often enough already, Ronald. Women don't like that, you know."

He could just make out the edge of her coat as it whirled like a cloud through the doorway. He enjoyed her presence. Before Ronald had been called to Washington, he had been working in California, responsible for the training of young lawyers, among other things. That's where he had met Jennifer. She was possessed by ambition, but what impressed him even more was the integrity with which she pursued her path. Over the years, a deep friendship had developed.

Ronald heard footsteps and turned around. His assistant and some students were coming into the hall.

"Professor MacClary, you're already here."

"Yes, I slipped up about the hour, but honestly, it was a pleasure to have this room to myself, to experience it after such a long time. Good evening, Ms. Coren. Do you have all the handouts for the audience?"

"Of course. Can I do anything else for you?"

"Could you greet attendees at the door to the building and show them in? It's quite a long way."

"Of course. I'd be glad to. I'll be there about seven thirty. Or should I arrive a little earlier?"

"No, that should be fine. I'm not at all sure people will be that punctual."

Ronald wasn't certain how many people would be accepting his invitation. Many would have simply lacked interest. Others would be staunchly opposed to his ideas, especially when one considered where the lecture was taking place. On the other hand, the opposition to Christian expansion was more evident in Dublin than anywhere else in the world. In Ireland and England, the pagan cultures had not only survived, but had also left a lasting imprint on the traditions of the Catholic Church, though it required a great deal of imagination to recognize the bastardized remains.

A crowd did arrive, though. Ronald recognized several important people in the audience. It made him proud that there was enough of an interest, fueled by recent events, perhaps not surprisingly at the center of the conflict between science and religion. It seemed there was a willingness to talk about philosophical as well as factual controversy. Now he needed to successfully awaken at least a few sparks of enthusiasm for one of the most important questions of their time.

* * *

Thomas and Deborah met Shane in front of the lecture hall, as promised. The Thomas Ryan facing him now was freshly shaven, rested, and alert—in short, completely different from the person Shane had met the previous night.

"Welcome, Adam. I hope I didn't promise you too much yesterday," Thomas said after shaking Shane's hand in greeting. "By the way, there's something I've been wondering about since last night. What's someone like you doing living in the Alps?"

Shane had heard this question before. "About ten years ago, I gave up my job as a blacksmith. Since then I've been working as a healer and promoting organic farming."

"What made you decide to do that?"

"Pure desperation, actually. My wife, or rather, my ex-wife, got cancer just after the birth of our son. The doctors gave her only a few weeks to live. One day I had this feeling I might be able to help her with something very simple."

"And that was…?"

"My physical energy. I gave her unconditional love, and I found a recipe in one of my grandmother's books that contained greater celandine, also known as tetterwort, a powerful remedy against cancer. That's probably what saved her life in the end. Since then, I've just been following my heart."

Thomas grinned and put his arm around Shane, which Shane accepted with a little hesitation. "Now I know why

I trusted you the instant I met you. You see, Adam, I also have the gift of healing, and many of the people who have been here in recent days have it as well. But you're still lacking consciousness—at least, let's say, as seen from a modern perspective. We have so much more to discuss. Come on, you miracle healer, it's time to go in."

* * *

Ronald moved to the lectern, accompanied by scattered applause.

"Ladies and gentlemen, I won't be telling you anything new when I talk to you about a passage from the criminal history of the Catholic Church. And I'll hardly be telling you anything new when I talk to you about the enormous cultural theft perpetrated by this Church, in collaboration with the political elite, since the time of its founding. However, we should open ourselves to new interpretations and look more closely at the impact this has had and continues to have on our culture.

"The first thing I'd like to do tonight is present an incomplete chronicle that proves the fervor with which the knowledge and culture of the indigenous peoples of Europe was crushed out of existence. In the second part of my lecture, I will talk about the impact this has had, and continues to have, on our culture, a culture imprinted by Christianity. This impact is independent from whatever loss in significance this 'belief' is experiencing now, mostly due to recent events.

"Finally, I will ask a question whose answer I already know. That question is: why did the pagans and in particular the Celts disappear from history? The answer is that they couldn't resist this attack, not only because they were militarily inferior, but also because they were mentally, intellectually, and spiritually helpless in the face of such a senseless culture with complete disdain for nature. It simply went against the all-embracing principle of nature and its laws to respond in kind to Rome's actions, which were supported by the Christians. However, the spiritual leaders of the pagans were by no means simply victims, as I will demonstrate. Instead, they reached an exceptional decision.

"Let's start first with the chronicle of events and raise the question of why every last trace of the old masters—not only the Celts, but also the Picts, the Saxons, the Germanic tribes, the Normans, and last but not least, the Vikings—has essentially disappeared.

"In the year 330, Emperor Constantine commanded the closure and destruction of all pagan temples, including the Serapeion in Alexandria and the sun-god temple in Heliopolis. He had the sacrificial altar in Mambre laid to waste and the Aphrodite temple of Golgatha destroyed. In 336, the Trier Christians destroyed the great temple complex in Altbachtal. Fifty chapels devoted to the Nordic gods and Mithraic worship were leveled to the ground. In 346, Emperor Constantine ordered the immediate closure of pagan temples in the cities. In 347, the Church father Julius Firmicus Maternus wrote the antipagan inflammatory pamphlet *On the Error of Pagan Religions* and pressured Emperors Constantine and Constans into the extermination of the mystery cults, the cults of Isis and Osiris, Serapis and Attis, the sun cult and the Mithraic cult..."

* * *

While Ronald continued reading the list to the astonished and somewhat indignant audience, a single man left the hall, unnoticed and unrecognized. As stealthily as possible, Victor Salvoni made his way to the rectorate.

* * *

"We end our history in 1937, when, at the instigation of the Vatican, the prehistoric library of Lussac-les-Châteaux is seized. All of this, ladies and gentlemen, has an origin, a meaning, and a fatal impact.

"The date 314 is more than a year. As most of you know, from this year forward, Christianity rose from insignificance to become the state religion under Emperor Constantine, with the help of the Council of Nicaea, and later under Kaiser Theodosius. With this rise came an unbelievable slaughter in the name of purification, which began with the complete alteration and adulteration of the history of Jesus Christ. During Constantine's rule in Gaul, where Christianity did not yet play a role, the religion and culture of the Celts were unimportant to him, but that would soon change, costing the lives of millions of Celts. It wasn't Julius Caesar who conquered the Celtic culture; Caesar had great respect for the Celts. No, the decisive strike against them was made by Constantine, the man of the hour. The Merovingians, Carolingians, Ottonians, the Holy Roman Empire, and lastly, our entire Western civilization, have all been shaped by Constantine. Seventeen hundred years of history carry his signature; he is the founder of the Western world. However, there is another very different question that's even more crucial…"

* * *

Up on the screen behind MacClary, the audience could still see the list of destruction by the Christian emperor and bishops when suddenly the lights went out. The door opened, and two employees of the college came in with flashlights.

"Ladies and gentlemen, we have a power outage in this entire section of the city. I'm sorry, but I must ask you to follow me and clear the hall."

While the first people started to leave with murmurs of protest, Ronald looked through the magnificent window of the hall to the other side of the street. "Hey," he called to the university employees, "does this section of the city happen to end over there?"

A short, skinny man with thin, graying hair came over to him and shone his flashlight in Ronald's face.

"Put down that light," Ronald snapped at him. "What's the meaning of this?"

"The rector can explain that to you," the man said briskly. "He's waiting for you in his office."

Fuming, Ronald packed up his things and prepared to go find the rector. As he began to leave, Thomas Ryan, standing in the last row with two other men, spoke up.

"Professor, I would be honored if, despite all the excitement, we could accompany you home after this to join you in a glass of wine."

"Thomas! Um, yes, of course, why not. I find myself with some extra time all of a sudden. You'll have to wait a bit, though. I have to settle something with the rector of this honorable institution."

CHAPTER 8

TRINITY COLLEGE – NIGHT

Standing in front of the beautifully embellished fountain at King's Gate, Shane waited for MacClary with Thomas and Deborah. "Can one of you please explain what that was all about?" he said with a combination of amusement and irritation. "Nothing MacClary said today is news to anyone who knows anything about this field. What was the point of the interruption?"

"I think the point of the interruption," said Thomas, "was that the lecture was about to become interesting."

"You Irish confuse me. Who is this MacClary, anyhow?"

"He's a high-ranking judge in the United States."

Shane grinned, the story becoming even murkier for him. "And in his free time he likes to take on the Church?"

Thomas frowned. "It's a little more complicated than that. Ronald MacClary was born in the US, but he belongs to one of Ireland's oldest families and he also has Celtic roots. No one knows more about this field than he does.

More to the point, no one has as much evidence that the Church would love to get their hands on."

"*Almost* no one," Deborah added.

Thomas nodded to his friend. "Yes, *almost* no one."

Just then Shane sensed someone approaching them from behind, and he turned around. In a long loden coat, wearing a hat, MacClary came up to them. Shane's mouth hung open when the judge greeted him first.

"Good evening, Mr. Shane. I'm sorry to have to meet you under these circumstances, but perhaps they are exactly the right circumstances. Come, I think we've all earned a good whiskey."

MacClary hailed a taxi and directed the driver to Arbour Hill. Shane sat in the back seat between Deborah and Thomas and could only see MacClary's eyes occasionally through the crooked rearview mirror. He didn't *seem* crazy. Maybe he was as much of an expert as Thomas and Deborah said he was.

It was a good fifteen minutes before they arrived at MacClary's Georgian-style house. During the drive no one said a word. Even Shane, who had a thousand burning questions, waited until they could speak in private.

* * *

MacClary turned on the light in his office. "Make yourselves comfortable or help yourselves to something from the bar over there."

"What really happened earlier?" Shane asked pointedly.

MacClary smiled, his earlier anger diffused. "Let's just say that the Vatican's contributions to the college have grown very dear to the heart of the director."

"But why did they need to cut you off? You hadn't said anything that people didn't already know."

"People *in the field*, Mr. Shane. You're right, unfortunately. I was planning to take them places they hadn't been before, but I didn't get the chance. Ryan said you had many questions about the role of Christians in the obliteration of Celtic culture. In this illustrious company—and without any outside interference—I can give you some answers. Does the name Porphyry mean anything to you?"

Shane shook his head. "To be honest, no."

"Porphyry was a broadly educated polymath and pagan who was far ahead of his time. He lived before the beginning of the fourth century in Rome as a student of Plotinus, and he wrote a fifteen-book treatise with the title *Against the Christians* that, with impressive logic, decisively denied the divinity of Jesus. Unfortunately, we have only a few excerpts and quotes from it, since the Roman Emperors Theodosius and Valentinian destroyed it less than a century later."

"Porphyry crushed Petrus and Paulus with his intellect," Ryan said. "He's still the bogeyman of the Vatican. No anti-Church treatise before or after him was as detailed, and even modern researchers, if they know nothing else, have to endorse his work."

Shane seemed impressed with this new information, but his face showed confusion. "But what does that have to do with the fall of the Celts? From what I understand, Julius Caesar had already taken care of them two centuries earlier."

MacClary nodded. "Caesar had beaten them from a military perspective, not a cultural one, and he had no intention of doing so. In fact, the Celts in Gaul and Brittany were in the process of regrouping. Remember too that the Celts were not a people, as we understand it today, but rather a culture made up of hundreds of tribes, all bound together by shamans, priests, and the Druids. As Porphyry and the somewhat less knowledgeable Celsus said, Jesus was, compared to Heracles or Asclepius or any other historical religious philosopher, nothing unusual."

"Yes, but—"

"Please don't interrupt, Adam. Like the old philosophers, many lesser-known pagans, including the Celtic shamans and Druids, had recognized that the Christians were in the process of creating a god remote from creation and cut off from the laws of nature. Celsus asked very simple questions, the kind every child asks today. Why would God come to the people on earth? And if he were going to do that, why did he wait so long? How can a body that has been destroyed rise up again renewed? The Christians' ludicrous answer was that for God, anything is possible."

Shane sat forward in his chair. "OK, so everyone but the Christians themselves recognized that a fairy tale was used to—"

Ryan stepped in. "To trap the uneducated masses looking for spiritual sustenance with one of the deities uprooted from the laws of nature. God, or better, the divine, the creation, had always been symbolically or metaphorically worshiped in the pagan religions. This is still true today for indigenous peoples. They worship the elements, the sun and the planets, plants and animals, but as a symbol. For example, the Celts didn't pray to the oak; they worshiped it, because the divine was expressed through its strength and beauty."

Ronald raised a finger in the air. "Correct, but that's exactly the core of the problem. As long as the Christians were themselves an oppressed minority, they were ridiculed and underestimated. Until the point when Emperor Constantine recognized, around 314, that his own power could only be stabilized through the stabilization of faith. He tried out every emerging religion—like we would try out cheese at a supermarket—to see which one would allow him to accomplish this. Unfortunately for the oldest cultures, he settled on the Christians, who had up to that time been underestimated. From that point on, he began what we might call 'Operation One God.' That was the origin of the alliance between the throne and the altar."

MacClary paused to look down at his hands for a moment. "You understand now why the lights go out on occasion when this topic comes up."

It was obvious that Shane was trying to process a great deal very quickly. "Yes, that explains it to some extent, but I'm still missing something from this story. What you describe can't be the only reason for the disappearance of the Celts and the Druids, of all the indigenous European peoples."

"No, you're completely right. Constantine and the bishops shared a common fear. The bishops knew that they were lacking the might needed for their religion to make a breakthrough. So the Church became powerful, but with that power came a loss of freedom, as the Church became part of the Roman Empire. In return they had free hand to destroy everything that stood in their way. The masters of the old world..."

Suddenly Ronald paused, struck by a memory that the evening's events had caused him to forget. "Gentlemen, you'll need to excuse me for a minute. I forgot about a woman, and she'll kill me if I stand her up!"

Ronald grabbed his cell phone and left the room to call Jennifer.

* * *

As the night drew on, there was still a light shining from one window in the government buildings of Vatican City. Thomas Lambert was reading a last appeal for assistance from an Irish bishop who wanted to step down from his position in the face of public pressure. That would be the sixth resignation because of the problems over there. There would be more. Lambert would advise the pope to accept the resignation. He preferred to handle these matters quickly rather than go through tedious debates about the whys and wherefores.

A knock on the door made Lambert jump. He wasn't accustomed to being disturbed at this hour.

"Come in!"

A young priest with a narrow face entered timidly. "Cardinal, I thought this would interest you. I just found it on the Internet." The young man slowly advanced into the room and gave Lambert a computer printout.

After reading it, Lambert only barely managed to keep his composure. "Thank you. Sleep well," he said quietly.

"You're welcome, Cardinal. Good night."

The door had barely closed when Lambert slammed his fist on the desk and grabbed the telephone.

"Salvoni," was the answer on the other end of the line.

"What in God's name possessed you? I ordered you not to do anything that would attract any unnecessary attention."

"I just made sure that, at the right moment, this blasphemer would lose his voice."

"But he *didn't* lose it. Quite the opposite. I just received a headline from the online edition of the *Austrian Standard* that reads, 'Trinity College Cuts Off Lecture Critical of Vatican.'"

"That's still better than allowing MacClary to spread his baseless allegations. We can no longer afford that."

"What we cannot afford, dear Salvoni, is something that I still determine. MacClary's facts come mostly from critics whom we have long since discredited. That's exactly what we are going to do with him now. Do you understand?"

There was a soft sigh on the line. "What do you recommend then?"

"I am going to use my contacts in Washington. The time has come for us to show the judge his limits. Meanwhile, you are going to continue to take care of Ronald MacClary—but with no more incidents."

"Cardinal, everything I do, I do only for the Church, and I pray that God's knowing hand will guide me. We should set aside our little conflicts and place greater trust in our common work, which is so important for our common future."

Those were unusual words, especially coming from Salvoni. "It's not up to me. You're right, the clearer we can be in this confusing time, the better, and—"

"Cardinal, let's not deceive ourselves. We are the ones holding this Church together, and we are the ones who must protect it from further harm. I play only one part in the process whose success has never been more uncertain than it is today."

Apprehension scratched at Lambert. "Salvoni, are you not telling me something?"

"Nothing that has to do with us. Only a feeling, Cardinal, only a feeling. It's better if I work that out between myself and God."

"You have doubts about what you're doing?"

Salvoni was quiet for a moment. "I can't really afford doubts, Cardinal. But questions, yes."

"What kind of questions?"

"You know exactly what I mean. We're both masters of our craft, but are we really aware of our responsibility? Don't worry, I'm probably just a bit overtired from the events of recent weeks."

Lambert believed Salvoni. The massive media attacks about the abuse scandals and the implication of the Vatican Bank in Mafia money laundering had taken a great deal out of him as well. "This Church has survived other crises, and it will withstand this one."

"I know, Cardinal. I'll set everything in motion and will report immediately if MacClary represents any kind of danger."

"Thank you, Salvoni. And thank you for your frankness. It helps all of us. God bless you."

* * *

"Is everything OK, Ronald?" asked Ryan.

"Yes, now it is. In case you don't know this already, you shouldn't aggravate beautiful women. I'll be leaving to meet her for dinner in a short while."

MacClary paused and pulled his thoughts together. "Where were we? Right: the emerging Church and the emperor were both afraid of a return of the powerful Celtic scholars, the Druids. They had supposedly gone into seclusion around 100 AD. In actuality, there are now numerous suggestions that they were building up secret schools, working their way into the court as Romanized scholars, intervening in the affairs of the imperial court to protect the pagans. That couldn't remain completely unnoticed, of course, and it went too far for Constantine when he recognized the threat to his power."

"You mean that the Druids survived Caesar?" said Shane. "We only know about one single Druid by name from Cicero, Diviciacus. Aren't you exaggerating a bit?"

"Not at all. Can you explain to me how the leaders of a culture that spanned Europe can disappear just like that without leaving the slightest trace?"

"Rome had spies all over and at least two hundred years to get it done. The Christians doubtless killed the rest."

Ryan joined the conversation now. "OK, Adam, maybe we should take a step back. Let's assume there was a time when people lived in a state of complete self-determination, responsibility, and freedom. Let's also assume that an educated and power-hungry minority invented a wonderful story intended to keep people from living according to this all-encompassing source of knowledge. The story makes people dependent on a faith, a dependence that results in the slavery that continues today. What would this power-hungry minority have to do to make this happen?"

"They would have to obliterate the source of knowledge," Shane said.

"Correct. And the Druids were, for thousands of years, the Source and the Guide, like the medicine men for Native Americans, the shamans for the Bedouins, and others all over the world. Then, bam! A culture comes along with supposedly biblical instruction, severs our link with the divine, and stamps us practically from birth on as guilty sinners."

Ryan managed to steer the conversation into the middle of the fourth century. He described a day when a small group of scholars had to make crucial decisions. The description was so vivid that Adam felt as if he were actually there—just as he had experienced in his dream.

* * *

ROME – APRIL 28, 330 AD

The columns of the palace of the Emperor Constantine were splattered with blood that morning. Those who had survived the angry mob were herded to the Circus Maximus, where, in front of several thousand whipped-up spectators, they would be sent to meet their maker.

Gasping, Datanos ran through the narrow streets of Rome. He had been lucky. Only a twist of fate had allowed him to escape the sudden attack on Sopatros's school: he had been lying hidden under three dead bodies, and it had been quite a job to free himself.

He didn't dare turn around, and when two men suddenly appeared from an alley barring his way, he thought it was all over for him. But they pulled him to the side, yanked him to the ground, and threw a cloth, some wooden boards, and debris on top of him. Seconds later he heard the sound of horses' hooves and screaming. They had hidden him. Through a small hole he could see the hordes riding by.

"Come along, Datanos, we don't have much time," one of the men said as he pulled him up. They ran past a few houses and disappeared into a cellar. Datanos could feel his whole body trembling. He didn't know which was worse—the impenetrable darkness and the molding stench of the cellar room or his fear of what was happening out in the streets. After a while a door opened, and he could see Aregetorix with several other Druids and a dozen of the philosophers from Sopatros's school.

The room was quite large. In the middle of it was a massive wooden table where a dozen men were seated. The walls were covered with shelves filled with chalices, tools, and storage vessels. Some sun was streaming through the openings in the foundation of the house, allowing him to see his surroundings in the bright bands of light.

"By Jupiter, you're alive!"

"Yes, Mercanus. I can't quite believe it myself. But I have no good news to report. They have killed Sopatros."

A murmur ran through the room, followed by a ghostly silence. Finally one of the Druids started to speak. "Aside from this youth, no one has survived, and more attacks will follow, I tell you. The emperor has answered the intrigues of Ablabius with action."

Datanos looked into the terrified faces of the men. Even the Druids, whose emotions were not normally so easily read, clearly understood the implications of the events of the past hour.

"We have to flee!" one old man said. "They are destroying all the symbols of our gods. The Christians are insisting that every last trace of our presence be wiped out, here and throughout the empire. Twenty years ago, I could already see where things were headed, how much power and influence the Christians were gaining under Emperor Constantine."

"They want to completely annihilate us," one of the young philosophers said in despair. "What kind of god is it that cannot tolerate any other god, that blinds his followers, that incites them to such actions?"

"But it's obvious. They fear our knowledge," Datanos said. "Since Constantine chose to favor the Christians, they have betrayed their own teachings. Everything their apostles have passed down to them has either been destroyed or distorted."

"We have to warn all the scholars," one of the youngest Druids said. "But we can't just leave! Don't you see what's happening here? They are annihilating our world, its entire history of creation and its masters—forever."

"No, my young friend." A soft, deep voice rang through the cellar room. All heads turned to Rodanicas, the astronomer who was said to have a comprehensive understanding of time and space. He was a legend, a man who had had contact with many foreign cultures—no one would dare to contradict him. "No knowledge can remain hidden forever. A lie like this, and a crime like this, against the law of the gods, will be made known.

It is not for us to determine the time for this, but it will come, you may be certain of it." Rodanicas looked around at all the men who listened to him. They were transfixed. "At the end of the fourth sun, our spirit will return. There is nothing more here, nothing worth saving. Everything has been desecrated."

Datanos was wringing his hands in despair. "And will we find a way to protect our knowledge?"

"No. Listen to me. Rodanicas is right," Aregetorix said. Almost seventy years old, he was the oldest and highest-ranking Druid in Rome. Like most of the Druids, he no longer revealed his identity. Instead, he served as a teacher at the imperial court, instructing children in philosophy, mathematics, and Latin. Like his father before him, he was a secret scout, acting as eyes and ears for the few remaining Druids in the rest of the empire. "Our time here has passed. If our bodies should survive, we must assimilate and take on their faith. If our spirit, our culture, and our knowledge are to survive, we must choose exile and leave. Everyone must make this decision for himself. For we Druids, the path is already laid out and determined. We shall return to the promised land. We'll set out tonight. What is the consensus? Who will follow us?"

"Datanos, come with us!" one of the younger philosophers urged. "You have to see that they're not just hunting the Druids anymore, but all scholars who are not prepared to subject themselves to Constantine's insanity."

Datanos nodded. "You're right," he said softly. "They are forcing people into the most abominable kind of spiritual slavery."

* * *

Shane was both intrigued and skeptical, but before he could formulate his misgivings, MacClary picked up the thread again.

"For more than two thousand years, people haven't been able to determine their own lives and their own fate. How was it possible that rulers could, with clockwork certainty, make men go to war? My dear Adam, our Christian-influenced culture has created and maintained regimes that exploit nature and humankind alike. With faith, all things are possible, regardless if it's right or wrong. Still, we have another choice and another chance, but only if we can turn back to the point where we chose the wrong path."

"But more and more people are turning away from the Church anyhow."

"That's hardly the point," Ryan said. "Look inside yourself, Shane. You know what's going on."

Shane held up two hands to concede the point.

"The Christian blessing, the embodied realization of the message of Jesus, originated and continues to originate from individual people," Ronald added. "And these people had to and still must assert the good that they do, often in the face of opposition from the Vatican. These

Christians drew their strength from precisely those Bible passages that are not of Christian but rather of Jewish origin. The commandment to love, for example. And, like Christianity itself, original sin is an invention of Paul. The persecuted pagans probably knew this. The only defense of original sin is based on circular logic. If death is a result of our sins, there must be sins if there is death. Sins, for which God's punishment is death. Therefore, sin is transferred to all of Adam's descendants because they were born mortal.

"But enough of that. Human dignity and human rights exist in Christianity only for believers, because they've been given a kind of amnesty from God. *Nulla salus extra ecclesiam*—outside the Church there is no salvation. And who's inside or outside, who belongs or not, that's again decided by the Church. That's why it's no historic accident that the Christians didn't view the pagans, those who haven't been baptized, as people. As a result, they didn't have to be treated as people. With the Enlightenment came human rights. Meanwhile, the interpretation of humankind standing tall before God had its roots in Judaism."

"And the interpretation that men are themselves godly and possess the godly potential for creation—that has roots in paganism," said Ryan.

MacClary nodded and then continued. "My father was so involved with this during his time as an archaeologist that I can't escape his legacy. As you yourself said, Adam, this question is occupying more people in all corners of our beautiful planet." Ronald looked at his watch. "It's time for me to leave for my dinner engagement. I hope I haven't bored you too much. I would love to invite you to dinner tomorrow evening, so we can continue this discussion."

Adam smiled. "I look forward to it."

CHAPTER 9

RONALD MACCLARY'S HOUSE, DUBLIN – NIGHT

As Ronald MacClary left his residence along with a group of unknown men, George Cassidy waited in a van parked just down the street. A former CIA agent, Cassidy had found employment with the Vatican secret service after his cover had been blown in a botched operation in Argentina. From that day, he'd vowed to never fail on a mission again, and he'd been able to keep that promise.

Now that MacClary and the others were gone, Cassidy and his team entered the house, laden with equipment. He deployed his men quickly, instructing them on preferred locations for the bugs and cameras—the "eyes and ears of God," as Cassidy liked to think of them—they'd been tasked with planting. As he moved to put a microphone in a bookcase, Cassidy's eyes fell on a parchment scroll housed inside a glass cabinet. He knew very little Latin, but he could translate some of the words, enough to feel a frisson of unanticipated tension. He took a quick picture of the scroll and got back to work.

"We have two minutes," Cassidy whispered to the others. No more than ninety seconds later, they left the house as stealthily as they'd entered it. Heading back to the van, Cassidy tried Thomas Lambert on his phone. When there was no answer, he cursed under his breath and opened the door of the van, which was so packed with monitors and other transmission equipment that there was barely room to sit down.

He uploaded the picture he'd taken of the scroll to one of the computers in the van so that he could compare the parchment to other examples and, even more important, get a reliable translation of the few lines he'd been able to photograph.

"Scoot, could you get me a secure connection with the main computer in the archive?" he asked an associate.

"I think so. Give me five minutes."

"OK. Just do what you can."

Cassidy stared out the windshield at the full moon that illuminated the entire street all too brightly for his comfort.

"How far can the signal be transmitted?" Cassidy asked.

"A good twelve miles."

"Then take us as far away as we can get."

The van drove off just as Cassidy was connecting with the computer in Rome. His queries didn't return anything interesting, until the translation of the second line made him break out in a cold sweat.

"The deadly testimony of Constantine..."

Cassidy had long been aware of the potential sources of embarrassment to the Church, so he knew that there were virtually no verifiable artifacts from the period around the year 300. Unless this was an ingenious plagiarism or an elaborate hoax, MacClary was sitting on a discovery whose true importance he couldn't possibly know.

"Damn it, I need Salvoni!"

* * *

"As I said, I might be able to tell you a bit more about the meaning of your dreams," Thomas said as Shane took a sip from his second pint. "I feel that there's a strong bond between us, and I trust you. This is a trust borne out of instinct, and that instinct is the important thing, my friend. Instinct or intuition, or whatever you want to call it, that's what we've lost. Intuition is knowledge, Adam, a knowledge that, if you're truly aware of it, can be an inexhaustible source. It was this source of power and self-determination that the Christians and the Romans fought with every weapon at their disposal, because it threatened their power and would have meant humankind's advancement to a higher level of consciousness. It was this source that they wanted to silence with the greatest manipulation ever constructed. And they've been mighty successful."

Shane's discomfort must have been apparent on his face, because Thomas added, "Hey, don't worry, it's OK. Just find a way to accept what you've been looking for the whole time."

Thomas's words just made things worse. Feeling helpless, Shane broke away. As he did, he noticed the barkeeper turning up the volume on the television. The president of the United States had just begun speaking.

"Few people would have thought that someone like me would one day be making this speech, but it is critical that I do so now. Peace, ladies and gentlemen, has a cause and an effect. War has a cause and a horrible effect. For our own sake, we must put an end to the cause of war. As with every conflict, one side must surrender for peace to truly prevail.

"That is why I have decided, only after intense debate within my own party and in Congress, that the United States shall forgive all debts owed by developing countries. In addition, the United States will ensure that these countries will never again be forced to sell their own raw materials at prices set by the international markets..."

Shane could hardly believe what he was hearing, and he saw that Thomas and Deborah were as astounded as he was. Everyone in the entire pub was listening, transfixed by the words of this woman, announcing a sea change in American economic policy. A change that would send shockwaves through the international financial system.

"My fellow Americans, I know the effect this decision will have on our economic system and on our current doctrine of growth. However, I am also certain that we will be able to limit the negative repercussions if other nations are ready to join us. We need a new world balance. We've known this for some time, long before the last financial crisis. Tomorrow's wealth cannot have its foundation on the senseless materialism of today. Let's

not fool ourselves; our old reliance on growth is a cultural and economic mistake. We need to admit that here and now, and I say this as the leader of a nation that has in the past been one of the worst offenders."

"You see, Adam," Thomas said, the shock at what he was hearing clear in his voice, "that's what I mean. Consciousness is no isolated thing, it's a collective energy, that, in the end, will simply and movingly contribute to survival, factually and spiritually. The universe in which you live is not only a material fact; it's also a very spiritual one."

Shane tore his eyes from the television to look at Thomas. "I know, and the Druids were aware of this. It was a culture based on the interdependence of three factors: God, man, and nature."

"It was man's task to convey the knowledge of the dying from other dimensions, and above all to protect the respect for nature as the mother of all things. With the disappearance of the European shamans, this spell was broken, only then allowing imperial Rome to exploit the earth with a religion that was alienated from nature. You understand, Adam, that if we want to end all of this, we have to show people, to prove to them what happened back then. And that includes those who are beginning to recognize the bigger picture. That's why I trusted you from the beginning. I felt immediately that you have everything in you. You just can't live it yet."

Entirely unbidden, a sob caught in Shane's throat. He took a few seconds to gather himself. "Sorry, but this is all a bit much for me right now. I've been looking on helpless for years, seeing where things were headed, and I always come back to the same point: I just don't see anyone listening."

Thomas shook his head vigorously. "It's not about whether someone's listening to you. If anything, it's about whether they understand you. And that doesn't start in the head, it starts in the heart. What the president just said is testimony to the return of understanding that is fed by the heart, by intuition."

"The difference between Ryan and you," Deborah said, "is that he hasn't pulled himself back into his shell. You need to act the same way."

Thomas became even more animated. "Right. And if you really know what I think you know, and are capable of what I think you are capable of, then you have an even greater responsibility."

"That's an awful lot to swallow, Thomas. Answer me this: what's really the difference between the Christians' beliefs and the Celts' or the Druids'? In the end, isn't everyone just looking for God?"

"The big difference has to do with the form and character of the pagan gods. The old culture's way of life is manifested in their worship of nature and not in a god as the Christians have designed him. In the old culture, devotion, humility, and magic were a normal part of life. They are the mystical metaphors with which the pagans had access to the all-encompassing and permeating universe and its knowledge. They honored and used it for the common good."

"One thing is certain," Deborah added. "If the Christians had shown more tolerance, if they hadn't attacked people of different beliefs with such brutal psychological and physical violence, not only would the Celts and the Druids have survived, but also the culture of the Native Americans and the tribes of Africa and Australia."

Sadly, he's right about that, thought Shane. The scope of this false teaching was enormous, and more people were beginning to be aware of it. The dawning of a new age that he felt within himself was spreading. Maybe Thomas was right. Maybe he could help.

* * *

VATICAN CITY – NIGHT

Victor Salvoni walked through his office and looked out the wide-open balcony doors at the Sistine Chapel. It was a warm evening with a beautiful, starry sky. Salvoni sat down on a small bench in front of the door and let out a soft sigh. In Dublin, his men would have long since finished their work. Thinking about his discussion with Lambert, he realized that it couldn't go on like this forever. One day, mistakes would be made that, in light of the Church's diminishing importance in politics and society, couldn't be covered up with the old methods.

With the number of people leaving the Church climbing at an alarming rate, and many distancing themselves inwardly, the pope had gotten carried away, and in addition to allowing the radical society of St. Pius X, he had also countenanced the statutes of the secret society "Opus Angelorum," also known as "Work of the Angels." The Church was bombed back into the Middle Ages. The Work of the Angels didn't do anything partway: if there was even the slightest doubt about faith, they deemed it the work of the devil. Salvoni had been busier than he liked in the last several months, fending off media attempts to interview the victims of spiritual exercises or to ascribe responsibility to the sects for several suicides.

He'd had to silence the victims of abuse from Catholic schools and seminaries in Germany and Ireland, either with money or by other means. Yet the sheer number of victims made it a hopeless battle. He had set up a broadly based covert action to destroy the traces left behind by the pope himself. But he had long known deep inside of himself that there was only one chance for the survival of Christianity: the return to the true message of Jesus of Nazareth. It had been a long time since the Vatican had anything in common with that.

"One more year, Victor, just one more year, and then you can stop," he swore, the moon shining on his melancholy face.

The ringing of his cell phone interrupted his thoughts.

"Salvoni," he answered.

"It's Cassidy. We've taken care of everything as we discussed, but I found something you should look at. We must have overlooked it more than once, but it proves what Padre Morati feared: MacClary has access to controversial documents."

"What did you find, exactly?"

"I sent you a picture that will explain everything, I think. We also observed three friends of MacClary who had a long discussion with him before we could get inside."

"OK. But for God's sake, be careful, and calm down. It can't be that bad."

"I'll talk to you later."

Salvoni went inside again and opened up his mailbox. What he saw made his blood run cold. The document looked as if it might have come from the cave that Sean MacClary had found so many decades earlier. If this artifact had indeed come from that trove, then they really did need to fear what Padre Morati had always warned about.

Now, everything depended on finding out what else Sean MacClary's son and his friends knew. Salvoni knew he could depend on Cassidy in the coming days. Until then there was only one thing to do: wait, and try not to go crazy in the meantime.

CHAPTER 10

Let the flames of your smelting furnaces roast these gods! Make use of all the gifts of the temple and put them under your control. With the destruction of the temple, you will have taken one step closer to divine virtue.

—Church Father Julius Firmicus Maternus

ARBOUR HILL, DUBLIN – MARCH 15, EVENING

Standing in MacClary's house at his dinner invitation, Shane was feeling much better than he had for the past several days. He felt fantastic, actually. After so many difficult years, here he was finally surrounded by people who shared his interests and his questions, whom he could trust implicitly and with whom he could share his thoughts without reservation. It was only now becoming clear to him how much he had kept bottled up inside. But even that difficult time had, apparently, had a purpose.

Without all the brooding and questioning, without all the battles and despair, he probably wouldn't be here.

MacClary brought his guests into the dining room where the diminutive housekeeper, Ms. Copendale, had just finished setting out their meal. As she left, MacClary told the group how in 1945 after the death of her husband, MacClary's mother, Lisa, had hired Ruth Copendale, then just fifteen years old, to watch her son when she had appointments outside the house or when visitors were there. When Lisa MacClary fell ill, far too young, with a then-unknown immune deficiency, Ruth took on responsibilities that went far above and beyond those of a housekeeper.

The dining room was much too conservative for Shane's taste, but it reflected a feeling of security. You could easily have seated twelve people around the table. The room was filled with tasteful pieces of teak furniture probably dating back to the previous century. The walls were paneled with precious wood, and small, ornamented wall sconces bathed the room in a yellowish light. Pictures decorated the walls, including the signed photograph of Ronald's father in uniform.

"I hope Ryan didn't overwhelm you last night with his theories about early communist Druids," remarked MacClary with a smile in Shane's direction. Thomas glowered at the professor. Shane had had the feeling since the day before that there was a kind of love-hate relationship between Ryan and MacClary. Certainly they didn't always share the same opinion, and their backgrounds couldn't have been more different.

MacClary seemed to notice Thomas's irritation. "Thomas, you have to admit there might have been a far more pragmatic reason for getting rid of the Druids."

"Maybe, but the fact is that Celtic society was based on free accord and a moral order that had developed over more than a millennium. The Celtic people didn't need a centralized government to remain a cohesive society. The Druids always considered property to be collective, for example. Rome, on the other hand, was intensely materialistic..."

"And we shouldn't forget that the Romans considered women solely objects of desire, servants, and breeding machines, while the Celts worshiped them as the source of God," said Deborah.

"Exactly," Thomas continued. "And Rome could control both with their new *divine* business partners. The emperors were no longer dependent on the goodwill of numerous religious leaders. Now they were only dependent on the leaders of the Church, who were as easy to buy off as a prostitute..."

MacClary raised a professorial finger. "But the Druids would have been in a position, along with the few critical thinkers in Rome, to expose the Christians' lies. That's why they had to die."

As excited as he had been only minutes earlier, Shane, who'd had little sleep lately, suddenly found himself overcome with profound tiredness. He couldn't follow the debate anymore.

"Mr. MacClary, is there somewhere I can lie down for a minute?" he said, interrupting the exchange.

MacClary's face showed concern. "Of course, right in the next room. And please, call me Ronald."

Next to the library was a small, comfortable guest room, much more modest than the other rooms Shane had seen in the house. MacClary turned on the light and laid his hand on Shane's shoulder. "I'm sure it was a difficult evening for you yesterday. I know how long Ryan can go on discussing this topic. He's obsessed with the lost knowledge of the Druids. But it *is* lost; we have to reconcile ourselves to that. Lie down for a while. We'll be in the library when you want to join us again."

Shane lay down on the narrow bed. Thoughts raced through his head. He didn't agree with MacClary. The knowledge wasn't lost. He could feel it, even though he couldn't say why he was so sure. It wasn't lost, it was only that the remoteness of centuries had blocked access to it.

As he lay down, he quickly slipped into a trance-like state between waking and sleeping. Before he fell asleep completely, he wondered what role he had to play in this conversation.

A conversation that was still going when he awoke.

"Gentlemen, Rome's motives, even before the rise of the Christians, were always marked by massive economic interests," Thomas was saying. "There was a reason that all the emperors rewarded the priests with incredible gifts after their betrayal of Jesus. Constantine, in particular, inundated the bishops with riches, and from that point on the teachers of the Church, including Ambrosius, Chrysostomos, Hieronymus, and so many others, were subject to him. They wrote praise scriptures for the Christians, adulterated the Bible, and wrote vehement but extraordinarily effective propaganda against the pagans."

Shane quietly made his way back to the library. He saw Ronald reach for his glass of wine as Thomas scornfully added, "Constantine showed which faith he would build on in the future. He betrayed his pagan beliefs, and the Church began to destroy all the pagan places of worship. Then, to add insult to injury, the emperor's money financed the construction of monumental churches on the same sites where pagan shrines had been. That was too much for the Druids."

Ronald nodded. "There you're right. The more the economic power of the priests grew, the more room the Celts had to cede, eventually retreating to our beautiful Ireland."

From the doorway, Shane said, "What Thomas just said is true. Now I understand the deal that completed the betrayal of Jesus's vision. That was his real crucifixion. In comparison, his actual death was practically meaningless."

Ronald turned in his direction. "Ah, Adam, you've joined the living again. Should Ms. Copendale warm up some food for you?"

"No thank you, I'm not hungry."

Niceties dispensed with, Ronald turned right back to the debate. "OK, Ryan, I still think that if we want to understand what happened to the Druids and their knowledge and the source of their power, we have to force the Church to open their archives. But you know as well as I do that's practically impossible."

Unsure that he wanted to enter deeper into this discussion, Shane looked over at a glass case that held a scroll. An almost magical energy seemed to be drawing his attention to it.

* * *

DUBLIN – NIGHT

Jennifer was just finishing packing, though she was still having second thoughts about taking the early flight to Brussels.

"I really think I'm ready for a vacation," she said to herself with a sigh. Dinner with Ronald had gone late into the night before, and she had drunk a bit more than she should have. What had really tired her out, though, was how animated Ronald had been. He was furious with the conrector of the university and was pumped up by his conversations with his Dublin friends, especially this Adam Shane, whom he was convinced Jennifer should meet. Then he simply got carried away on his usual themes. She hadn't been able to get a word in edgewise.

This was unfortunate because she had things she wanted to say. She hadn't wanted to hear him obsess about how to free Christians from the Vatican. She still shared his opinions, but the path he was taking to reach his goals seemed increasingly remote to her.

For the past fifteen years, she had been traveling all over the world, spending only a few days every few months in her little house in Boston, not far from where her parents lived. Otherwise she was in one hotel after another, in New York or London, Brussels or Geneva, The Hague or somewhere else in the world. After fifteen years, she was tired.

She was, of course, proud of the fact that she had had considerable influence on the definition and limits of national self-determination, not least after the disaster in the former Yugoslavia. Ronald's vision, though, was for a redefinition of who would be recognized as a subject of international law. Individual people or the whole of humankind? If the latter, the inevitable result would be to lend credence to the claim of cultural heritage. If this view were accepted, the Vatican could give a papal kiss good-bye to its immunity in the arena of cultural assets. That was what Ronald thought, in any case, and he was desperately searching for a legal foothold to accomplish this. That's why he needed her legal expertise. She just wasn't sure she could continue to offer it.

Just then, her cell signaled an incoming text message:

> We'd love to see you before your flight.
> Love, Ronald.

Jennifer had to laugh out loud, despite herself. She sat down on her bed, fell back, and let herself relax. One day wouldn't make a difference. And anyhow, she would definitely have more fun with Ronald and his "posse" than sitting alone in a hotel room in Brussels.

* * *

Shane was still thinking about the scroll in the case when Ronald offered him a glass of Jameson.

"Oh, thanks. Tell me, what's that parchment in the vitrine over there?"

"That? That's the holy grail of the MacClary family. And it's held up about as well as the holy grail too." Ronald grinned. "My father found this parchment in a cave, sometime near the end of the Second World War, and I've been searching my whole life for some clue he might have left behind that would help me figure out where the trove was."

"Why didn't he tell you?"

"He tried to, on his deathbed, when I was six years old."

Ronald sat down, thoughtfully swirling the whiskey in his glass as he looked around at the group.

Shane stood up and went over to look at the parchment, which had some barely legible Latin writing on it. "I was never good in Latin," he said, attempting to read. "Constantine's false testimony?"

"Not quite. Constantine's *deadly* testimony."

"Oh, I'm beginning to understand why you're all so fixated on this period. What else does the parchment have to offer?"

The assembled group suddenly seemed ludicrous to him. An internationally recognized judge, a bookish linguist, and a healer with Druidic roots. All united in the desire to free Christians from a god whose origin was a lie and in the desire to do justice to the millions of people who understood, felt, and believed in the power of an original connection to the divine.

"This parchment?" Ronald said. "Unfortunately it has nothing else to offer anymore. The rest of the ink was destroyed by erosion. However, just the title gives you an idea of what must still be in the cave, wherever it is."

Shane turned back toward MacClary. "Um, Ronald, your father was an archaeologist, wasn't he?"

"Of course. And not just any archaeologist. He was extremely well known. Why do you ask?"

"Well, if he didn't leave any clues as to the original site of the trove, as you say, couldn't that also mean that the clue is just hidden or not visible?"

"I've of course thought of that, Adam. I've searched through every book in this library. Nothing. No secret note, no code, nothing."

"What's the scroll sitting on?"

"That's just normal handmade paper."

"And how long has it been there?"

"Since the scroll was packed up in the helium vacuum. I never dared release the vacuum. The scroll must have been on top of the paper before that as well."

"And you investigated the paper as well?"

Ronald gave him a penetrating look and stood up slowly. “Well, Adam, you do know how to get my blood pumped up. If I open the vitrine now, the scroll is as good as lost.” The man’s expression made it clear to everyone what he was going to do. “Do you want to spend the rest of your life staring at a few faded letters?” he said, as though no one else was in the room. “Or do you bet everything on the slightest chance of winning the grand prize?”

Ronald breathed deeply, and then a smile lit up his face, making it seem much younger. “OK, then. Ryan, go into my darkroom. I need ammonia and water, cotton, and lemons. I’ll get a hairdryer. It looks like we’ll have to pay Ms. Copendale a late visit in the kitchen.”

* * *

“Dear Ruth, excuse me for bothering you,” Ronald said softly to the elderly woman putting the last plates in the cupboards of the enormous kitchen, “but we want to do a little research. You can retire for the night.”

Ms. Copendale gave the men a sympathetic smile and then clapped her hands in horror when she saw that Ryan was carrying the vitrine.

“Oh my God, Ronnie! I mean, Ronald, you’re not going to…”

“Trust me, Ruth, I know what I’m doing. Or, let’s say our young friend here knows what *he* is doing. At least, I hope so, anyhow.”

MacClary's attempt to calm the old woman down fizzled a bit.

"Oh, absolutely, he knows," said Ryan, smiling benignly and placing the vitrine on the kitchen table. Before anyone started to have doubts about what they were about to do, Ronald let the protective helium gas escape from the container.

"Four people, more than two hundred years old combined, and still acting like children," commented Ms. Copendale dryly, shaking her head as she left the kitchen to go to bed.

Ryan took charge. "Adam, put half of the fluid in a pot and then warm it up over the lowest possible flame. But be careful. It's ammonia. We only need the steam, no explosion."

Carefully he pulled the handmade paper out from under the scroll, which lay, as Ronald had feared, crumbled in pieces. Only the name Constantine held on, like a thousand-year-old ghost left behind.

"Knowing my father, he probably wouldn't have used a normal invisible ink, if he used any at all. But there weren't a lot of options in his day. That's why I'm betting on copper sulfate. If I'm right, we're in luck. If I'm wrong, then we have a long night in front of us."

With gloves and tweezers, Ryan carried the paper to the stove and held it over the pot, from which the biting steam of the ammonia was slowly rising. After Ryan had held the page over the steam for a few seconds, Ronald's jaw dropped.

As if from nothing, the first numbers started to emerge in a brownish color. First a 46, then 43, then 29, and an N, until everything, at last, was visible.

46 43 29 N, 14 25 47 E – 150 m NW from Virunum
down on the slope

With love, Sean

Ronald MacClary stood in the kitchen of his ancestors, his shirtsleeves pushed up, with a smile on his face that hinted at the young boy he had once been. "So, Adam, normally I don't take stock in Ryan's claims about the spiritual visionary power of the Druids, but in this case I can only bow down in awe. You've all just taken the greatest burden from the shoulders of an old man whose life was otherwise full."

Deborah had already opened up her laptop and entered in the coordinates. "There it is, the Magdalensberg in Austria. Parts of the Eighth British Army Division were posted there for the occupation of Austria after the unit had already been dissolved."

MacClary got up and looked at Ryan in relief. He knew that the moment had come, unexpectedly, a moment he had given up hoping for, a moment he had waited for almost his whole life. Yet his exultation was tempered by the knowledge that he couldn't take part in this expedition. His age, for one thing, would make it difficult, and his position, for another, made it impossible. He had known for years that Ryan would have to represent him. Ryan was the only one who commanded the necessary mental abilities, and he trusted him implicitly.

"Now, gentlemen, I think it's time to solve old puzzles and discover the unexpected," Ronald said with a catch in his throat. "In the moment of triumph, for which I have you to thank, Adam, it would be wrong not to mention the sadness I feel. You'll have to go without me. But as you know, Ryan, I've been prepared for this for some time."

With much ceremony and somewhat calculated pathos, MacClary took an envelope out of a small drawer under the vitrine and handed it to Ryan.

"I've spent quite a lot of time with you two over the last several years, preparing you for this unlikely event. You've learned so much, and I know I can trust you without hesitation with my father's legacy. In this envelope you'll find everything you need to rescue some of the artifacts, and I stress, only those that are of interest to us."

The solemn moment seemed to go right over Deborah's head. Like an excited kid, she was rocking back and forth on her chair and typing away on her laptop. "Along with a little memento for each of us, right? Just for private use…"

"Deborah! I've given Ryan explicit instructions to cut off a finger for every attempt!" Ronald half-joked. "You'll take only those pieces that are important to us and make sure that they disappear. Everything else—and I mean everything—we'll hand over to other professionals afterwards."

* * *

George Cassidy shifted nervously back and forth on his small seat in the van. He could hardly believe what he had just recorded. He'd been trying to reach Salvoni for several minutes now, but with no success.

"Damn it, we should've put more in the kitchen," he said to Jean Tamber, who was frantically busy at the computer. This wasn't the first questionable project they'd worked on together over the years. "How long is it going to take to improve the sound quality?"

"At least a couple of hours. I have to let the individual voice recognition programs run on it."

"Keep working. We need this as fast as possible."

The Magdalensberg in Austria. Quick research had shown Cassidy that, since 1948, a settlement from the late Celtic and early Roman period had been under excavation on the south-facing slope. It was here that the Celtic kingdom of Noricum had been conquered and one of the most important Roman trading centers for iron had been created. The Celts had retaken Roman territory repeatedly, and the Druids had returned to places they had lost at risk to their own lives simply because they believed in the power of these places, which the Romans had desecrated and built over. The mountain itself was primarily composed of volcanic rock. The basalt had numerous dislocations that could be remarkably dry for such a damp climate, making it possible to store artifacts. In all, this was a manageable site for an operation. Cassidy would be able to handle this with only a few men.

Finally, Salvoni called.

"Padre, it looks like we have a bit of work ahead of us. Padre Morati has apparently been right all these years."

"What do you mean?"

"They found some coordinates near the parchment scroll. Apparently they correspond to where the trove was found."

"Do you have the coordinates?"

"Wait, that isn't all. They're planning an expedition. The judge has a few friends who are preparing everything as we speak. Someone in Austria is going to help them with the equipment. They just have to catch the next plane. That means we don't have much time. And to answer your question, no, we don't have all the coordinates, but we know that it's somewhere near the Magdalensberg in Kärnten, not far from the Italian border...Padre, are you still there?"

* * *

Salvoni was standing at the window, not even noticing the sunlight on the eternal city. His hand, still holding the telephone, had dropped to his side. His mind was racing. Cassidy needed an answer quickly, but the situation was more complicated than the agent could possibly suspect. If Salvoni followed official channels and charged the judge with excavating an archaeological site on his own, the case would then be made public and Salvoni would be cut off from any information about the site. In addition, it would very quickly come out that his people had been spying on an American judge in his own house, and that would set the Americans against the Vatican. Not good. Official channels were, as usual, a very bad idea.

There was only one real possibility. He had to be at the site with his people before the judge's group got there. To do that, he not only needed the exact coordinates but also the help of the Austrians. Who could he tap in their secret service?

He put the phone back up to his ear. "OK, Cassidy. You stay with MacClary's friends and follow them to Austria. We have everything we need from MacClary. Your job is done there. You can break it off."

"Understood, Padre, but how should we handle things in Austria? I mean—"

"I'll get back in touch with you when I've arranged everything. In the meantime, I expect you to exercise the utmost caution. I cannot tolerate any incidents now, especially when we don't know if the trove will be of any value to us, or if it even poses a threat."

"Of course, Padre, you can depend on me."

CHAPTER 11

DUBLIN – MARCH 15, NIGHT

Ms. Copendale was coming up from the basement with the laundry as MacClary was heading into the library by himself. He stood in front of her, placing his hands on her shoulders. "Thank you, Ruth, but I'll do that," he said gently. "You can turn in now."

"Do you really think I'm going to be able to sleep a wink? I know what this is all about. As if this thing hasn't caused enough trouble already. I can't condone this. I promised your mother…oh, you'll do what you want." Moving at an astonishingly determined pace for someone of her age, Ms. Copendale marched up the stairs to her room, a room that had been her second home since childhood.

MacClary stood on the lowest step, surprised and confused. "Ruth, what did you promise my mother? You've never mentioned that before."

She turned back to him, exasperation on her face. "I promised Lisa I would make sure you didn't fall victim to your father's insanity, which destroyed everything and made her so sick. Do you have any idea how much she suffered because of your father's obsession?"

MacClary lifted up his hands in a helpless gesture. "Yes, I think I do know. I've suffered enough from it myself, but that also means that I need to know if it was worth it."

Ms. Copendale shook her head. "You're just like your father, Ronnie. That's what has always scared me."

Just at that moment, the doorbell rang. It had to be Jennifer.

"We'll talk more about it tomorrow," MacClary said before going to open the front door.

Jennifer was reading some messages on her cell phone when he got there.

"Ronald, are you OK? You look like..."

"I look like someone who has just experienced the most exciting moment of his life."

"Oh no, let me guess: you're going to be the next UN Secretary-General. Or, no, vice president!" A mischievous smile on her face, Jennifer walked down the hall and dropped her coat and purse carelessly on a chair.

"Jennifer, you know how Ruth hates that." Ronald picked up her things and hung them in the closet while Jennifer casually strolled into the library, completely at home.

"OK, so let's hear it," she said when he followed her in. "Did you see a ghost? Have your Druid brothers gone up in smoke? What is it?"

"Nothing like that. Believe it or not, just a few minutes ago we discovered a clue about the trove that my father left behind. There's a cave, and it's on the Magdalensberg in Austria. We have the *exact* coordinates."

Jennifer dropped down into a chair. "That just can't be."

Ryan and Adam came out of the kitchen.

"Jennifer, let me introduce you to Adam Shane. Adam, this is Jennifer Wilson, my most talented student and a colleague for many years at the federal district court in Boston."

Adam stood there, obviously so struck by Jennifer's looks that he couldn't get a word out.

Jennifer stood up and extended her hand. "Good evening, Mr. Shane. Thomas Ryan has already told me about you."

Adam sat down in an empty chair. "Thomas was about to tell me more about the Druids," he said nervously, as though he'd never been in the presence of a beautiful woman before.

With mock despair, Jennifer clapped her hand to her head. "Oooh, and it could have been *such* a nice evening!"

"Now, Adam," Thomas said cheerfully, "the history of the Druids and the philosophers didn't end with their flight from Rome. Not by a long shot. Their first stop was what is now Austria…"

* * *

VIRUNUM (PRESENT-DAY MAGDALENSBERG) – AUGUST 19, 330 AD

The Druids, their students, and the young philosophers had brought several symbols and treasures of their culture with them when they escaped Rome. The journey had been undertaken on foot and with packhorses. It had been an arduous one. The secret system of caves was on one side of the mountain, the Roman administrative seat of Virunum on the other. It was a daring game to get in and out here, but the Druids were insistent that their library be built on this spot, which was for them a holy place.

"Rodanicas, this cave isn't just suitable, it's outstanding!" beamed Datanos.

Now is the time, he thought. *I have to convince the Druids to do something that goes against one of their most holy laws.*

Since the young Druids and Sopatros's three Roman students had been able to steal parchment and tools from the administration in Virunum the night before, the philosophers had begun to write down a chronicle of their experiences in Rome during the Christian grab for power. Where their own memory and experience didn't suffice, they relied on the tales of the scholars who had met a gruesome end after the treachery of Ablabius. The Druids could give them the most information, but the holy men were still reluctant to personally assist in the writing.

"Rodanicas, what will remain if all the Druids die or none of you make it to the Island?" Datanos pressed him.

"Well, you may believe that nothing of us will remain, but that is not the case. At any moment, our spirit can—"

"Rodanicas, please, be logical! You don't know if you can even make it to the Island. You and Aregetorix, you are the keepers of the old knowledge. You could refute the writings of the Christians."

They went into another room, where students had spent the last several days carving the spiral of life into a massive stone. Others had already carved out cavities in the wall, which would provide added protection for the parchment. As soon as everything had been accomplished, these cavities were to be sealed.

"Do you still not understand why we choose not to record our knowledge? We know that no judgment, no reckoning can remain valid forever. Truth must be experienced in the moment. Whatever we would write down now would ossify and become a curse. That's exactly what has happened with the teachings of Jesus of Nazareth. They wrote down his words—set in stone. Do you understand? As if they had shackled him, or locked him up in a dungeon made of stone. Nailed down fast, just as the Romans had nailed him to the cross. And that has brought the greatest harm to the world. The humility that lies in the certainty of uncertainty is the heart of our teachings. I spend aeons with my students trying to get them to understand this. And that, my dear Datanos, is why our knowledge is only passed on to our students in an oral tradition."

"But look at what the emperor and the Christians are doing. At least leave the knowledge of their actions behind for the world."

"Datanos, we believe that everything in Rome will soon change. It is only a brief cultural disorientation, a political game that will end with the death of the emperor. You will see."

"No. You heard for yourself what Aregetorix said!"

"And that is why Aregetorix will remain here."

"What do you mean?" Datanos asked. *Are they finally listening to my pleas?*

"We will set out tomorrow. But Aregetorix is too old for the long journey, and he has decided to remain here."

"Alone?" Datanos looked at Rodanicas in anguish.

"Alone. This was his decision. He will record what your heart is longing for, but we must leave. A messenger will provide Aregetorix with news from the empire, as long as he remains alive. And he alone will decide when these rooms will be closed, and his spirit along with it, and what he will leave behind. None of us—"

"But he's choosing a certain death!"

Rodanicas laughed suddenly. "Do you see Uratorix there, his son? He just chose life, Datanos. We know the passage. Tell the others they should prepare for our departure. And don't worry."

By that evening all except Aregetorix had packed up their things. They would set out in the darkest hour before daybreak, hidden from the Roman scouts. Datanos was standing before the entrance to the chambers, listening to the incantations of the Druids. His heart grew cold. What would become of them? What would become of this world, where only one god was now allowed?

After a while they all came out and made their farewells.

"Here, take this with you," Aregetorix said as he handed Rodanicas a scroll. "This parchment contains our family tree. It will help you to rebuild the schools on the Island. Pass on everything that you know and safeguard this place by only allowing the knowledge to pass from father to son, from mother to daughter. They will know when it is time to free my spirit from this place."

The small group set out on its journey. When Datanos turned around one more time, he saw Aregetorix returning to the cave. He was the last master of ancient times to be seen by the continent. But he firmly believed that one day people would return here. People who recognized the truth.

* * *

Ryan continued. "It's quite simple, Adam. What Ronald and I have in common is this history and our desire to learn everything about it. And Jennifer, be fair, it's at least a serious point of concern for you too, even if it is for other reasons, that the truth finally be accepted. My desire is that we as a culture finally retrieve what was stolen from us."

MacClary considered Thomas's words. The Vatican's secret archive contained many relics of pagan cultures. There, stored in secret, were the artifacts that had not been destroyed over the course of centuries by fanatical myrmidons who often had no idea what they were doing or why they were doing it.

"The message of Jesus Christ was very similar to that of the Druids," Ryan added. "They both had the same basic goals. Jesus, if he really existed, acted out of pure love. He showed humankind the inner and wholly individual path to God."

"I think I know what you mean," Adam said. "You're saying that Jesus declared that the divine spark is in every person. If his message had prevailed, there would have been no need for priests or religious scholars. And because this view was a thorn in the side of the powerful people of his time, he had to die. He wanted to free humankind from every kind of manipulation or requirement about how to find God. That was the Druids' goal as well, although their path respected nature as a symbol of the divine power."

Ryan looked at Adam in approval. "That's right, exactly. And they wanted to slowly dismantle the caste system of that time, which was similar to that of early Indian society, gradually replacing it with a society guided by self-determination and freedom."

"Barbaric propaganda," joked Deborah, coming into the library. "So, ladies and gentlemen, the next flight to Vienna leaves at seven in the morning. How many tickets should I book?"

"Adam, I'm assuming you're coming with us," Ryan said.

"Yes, of course. I can't wait! It sounds like a great adventure right into the center of this insanity we're living in."

"Yes, it should be. Good, then it's agreed. If I've understood correctly, Ronald, tomorrow when we land in Adam's second homeland, we'll pay a visit to someone who'll equip us for the journey."

MacClary nodded. "Right. And if I know him, everything will be ready for you when you get there."

* * *

Shane was standing in the kitchen waiting for the water to boil for coffee. Thomas had just sat down at the table.

"Adam, there's one more thing we should talk about. Your vision, or intuition, whatever you want to call it, that you're so afraid of. The gift of seeing seems so strange to us today because we've forgotten to recognize it as a part of our natural potential. But amazingly, more and more people are returning to this place, practically of their own accord, without even understanding where it came from." He held out a book. "Here, you should read this."

"What is it?"

"Five thousand children with the same story as yours. Scientists have written it off as just a 'phenomenon.'"

He laid the book down on the table, and Shane picked it up and skimmed through the introduction.

"The authors want to explain why children who have just learned to talk can tell about experiences from an earlier life," Thomas continued. "They call the paradigm the 'Akashic Field.' Einstein, Nikola Tesla, and as far as I know Wilhelm Reich called it ether or the morphogenetic field—basically the origin of all things, in which the potential for all phenomena are already present. According to this, the universe contains, beyond time and space, all the experiences of all living things, like a universal quantum savings bank."

Shane had already heard about this. "But that's not a new idea. Clairvoyant people like Edgar Cayce have been referring for a long time to something they call the Akasha Chronicle, which is just the metaphysical name for a kind of world memory of everything that has ever happened."

"Could be. But so few people concern themselves with this. You and I are not the norm. I just wanted to give you some evidence that might take the drama out of your experiences. On the other hand, this is a gift that you shouldn't underestimate."

A glimmer of warmth had crept into Thomas's normally hard demeanor, which surprised Shane. They had only really known each other a couple of days and yet it felt like it could have been an eternity. Shane smiled at him, hoping to exude a similar warmth. "I'm terribly grateful that you're letting me do all of this with you. You know, there's one thing that I keep asking myself: Didn't the Church itself make science what it is today? That is, this pure, rational viewpoint of empirical reasoning with no metaphysical support. I mean, if you ask a physicist if he believes in God, he'll say, 'Of course. I'm a physicist, after all.'"

Thomas burst out laughing. “Yes, and it’s no wonder that the physicists in particular came to this realization. After all, they work day in and day out with God’s materials. But despite their efforts, they only come just so far. As if there was a barrier of some kind, something in the way. The Druids and the other shamans knew about it.”

Shane stared off, dumbfounded. “There’s so much to rediscover.”

Thomas stood and clapped him on the shoulder. “Yes, there is. And we will. Come on, you old Celt, let’s get to bed. I’ll have a few hours of sleep here. We have a very early and very big day tomorrow.”

* * *

Shane stood looking out the window into MacClary’s yard, which was lit up by several small lamps.

“Hello, Mr. Shane,” said a female voice from behind him. “You have a unique gift for setting things in motion.”

“Oh, thanks,” he said, turning toward Jennifer, “but that was just luck, albeit a wonderful kind of luck. I’m still fairly nervous about the whole thing, I have to confess. I mean, I’ve only known the others for a few days, and then all of this…”

“I know,” she said with a hint of wistfulness in her voice. “It can be a bit stressful when you meet Ronald MacClary. How did you end up here, anyhow?”

“Oh, well, you see, for one thing, I’m interested in the art of healing with herbs. And for another, I’ve spent quite a bit of time—for as long as I can remember—trying to fathom our purpose. In other words, asking ridiculous questions that can make one's life a living hell."

Shane looked at Jennifer with a warm smile.

She returned the smile. "Ah, and I always thought that only the Church was concerned with hell."

Shane felt his cheeks flushing. He needed to deflect the focus away from himself. "And what do you do, if I may ask, Ms. Wilson?"

"Please call me Jennifer, Adam." She sat down opposite him and rested her elbows on the small table, supporting her head with her hands as she looked out the window. "I got here, like you, because of my interest in Ronald. When I was just beginning my career as a lawyer, I was hoping for his support to advance my career. But at some point I finally realized that I no longer needed that help. Then, for some strange reason, a real friendship developed."

"Are you as caught up in his quest as the rest of the group?"

Jennifer smiled and leaned back in her chair. Shane couldn't help but look at her. He had never met someone with so much femininity, beauty, self-assuredness, and intelligence all at the same time, and he had to control himself not to give away his feelings. He wasn't accustomed to responding to women this way. In fact, he hadn't felt like this upon meeting a woman since he met Victoria ten years ago.

"Let's say," Jennifer began, shaking Shane from his reverie, "I share Ronald's opinion about the Vatican's questionable history. And I couldn't care less if a crime is a year, a hundred years, or a thousand years old, especially if it concerns murder and torture. Meanwhile, I assume I don't need to explain my opinion about the Catholic Church from my perspective as a woman."

The forcefulness of Jennifer's convictions made her even more fascinating to Shane. "But prosecuting old crimes probably doesn't work that well."

"No, of course not. For that, we would have to have a complete cultural sea change, and such a change is difficult to imagine. Still, historical crimes *ought to be* punishable. And…oh, forget it. I'm just succumbing to the usual sad combination of philosophy and wishful thinking."

With that, Jennifer seemed as though she were ready to leave the room.

Surprising himself, Shane reached out a hand. "Please continue."

Jennifer settled back. "Do you really want to talk about this?

"Absolutely."

And so they did, long into the night.

CHAPTER 12

DUBLIN – MARCH 16, EARLY MORNING

Shane was just finishing his packing after a total of three hours' sleep, wondering why he'd even bothered to pay for the hotel room. Though they never got far from the subject of Ronald's search, Shane still felt as though he'd gotten to see inside Jennifer a bit during their time together. He hoped it wouldn't be the only long conversation they ever shared.

Minutes later, he found Deborah and Thomas waiting in front of the hotel in a taxi that would take them to the airport. As the taxi drove away, Thomas lifted up his hand. "Gentlemen, before we board the airplane, I have something here to fortify our spirits. It should help us to be successful on this trip if we are under the protection of our ancestors."

Thomas took three small cloth bags out of his pocket and handed one to Shane and one to Deborah.

Shane sniffed at his bag. He smelled meadowsweet immediately, then ash leaves, beard lichen, fleabane, ivy, and mistletoe. It was a sweet-tart smell, and he was quietly moved by this present, since it had come from Thomas's Druid heart.

"But that's not all. Deborah also put a bit of Irish wisdom in with it, which, I think, is quite appropriate for you, Adam."

Shane opened the bag carefully, taking out a small piece of paper.

Act, before it happens,
Steer, before it's lost,
The wise man retraces the steps that men have gone,
Working to bring things back to their true nature.
And he fears only one thing: to act against nature
and the unity of all life.

"Thank you, Thomas, and many thanks to you as well, Deborah. Yes, that's it exactly." Shane took Thomas's and Deborah's hands. "I'd like to thank you both from the bottom of my heart."

Thomas and Deborah smiled and squeezed his hands.

"Just one more thing, Adam," Thomas said. "We have no idea what we're about to experience on the continent or what we'll find there, but I'm asking you to trust me, no matter what happens."

"What's the plan, practically speaking?"

"We'll drive to Klagenfurt first. There Ronald's friend will give us all the equipment we need. He has invested quite a bit of money for us three, well, let's call ourselves hobby archaeologists."

"And then? I mean, we can't just walk all over the place and dig."

"Don't worry, Adam," Deborah said. "This isn't the first time Thomas has been involved in something requiring both courage and good planning."

Shane was confused by this for a minute, until he understood what Deborah had meant. Thomas had, after all, spent his early childhood in Northern Ireland.

* * *

Jennifer had postponed her early-morning meetings at Ronald's request. Now she was sitting in his kitchen eating breakfast, a bit the worse for wear after her late-night discussion with Adam Shane. Ruth was puttering around the kitchen, quietly scolding.

"I always knew that this confounded scroll would bring more bad luck," she remarked yet again. "I should have just knocked it over while I was cleaning." She poured Jennifer another cup of coffee.

"Ruth, it's OK," Jennifer said. "First of all, Ryan knows his way around an operation like this. Second, we've made sure that no one can connect Ronald with the whole thing. And third, I honestly don't think they're going to find anything at all."

Ruth looked at Jennifer for a moment, sighed, and got back to her work.

Just then Ronald came into the kitchen. He was holding a stack of papers. "Jennifer, would you come on a walk with me?"

"Sure. Some fresh air would do me good."

In the foyer, Ronald helped Jennifer with her coat. Outside, sunlight was streaming off the puddles left by the morning rain, so much so that Jennifer decided to wear her sunglasses.

"Ronald, tell me what you think this expedition is going to uncover. I mean, you're not going to find Jesus's tomb there."

Ronald seemed unusually serious. "I haven't told you everything up to now. Let me put it this way: my father left details about some crucial items he had seen in the cave but couldn't rescue. This has created a context for me that has always fascinated me as a lawyer and a judge." Ronald handed the papers to her. "Here, please read through this. In these papers, my father describes the results of the Church's activities in culture, economics, and politics over the whole spectrum of our society."

Jennifer was a bit annoyed; she already knew the whole history of Christianity, thank you very much, a history of war and torture, of betrayal and abuse of its own ideals. She also knew all too well MacClary's attempts at taking legal action against the Church. In 1984, he had been head council in the conviction of the Jesuits and the Mafioso Michele Sindona. This man was very well acquainted with Pope Paul VI, friends with the then-head of the Vatican Bank, and responsible for the reorganization of finances in that bank. He had been convicted in what was at the time the largest bank failure ever in the history of the US. But before Ronald could bring additional charges connected to the Vatican Bank's role in Mafia money laundering, Sindona was sent to Italy. Despite being under heavy guard, he was found dead from cyanide poisoning soon thereafter.

"Jennifer, the current abuse scandals, the facts about the Vatican's role in international money laundering, and the sheer mass of internationally active historians who have demonstrated the Church's almost unbroken history of crime—perhaps all of this might offer us an unexpected chance to end the whole nightmare."

"And you think your three Druids will find something in the cave that could help you with this? You're completely crazy, Ronald MacClary."

"I don't think so, Jennifer. My father told me that even the foundation of the Church was a criminal act and that there was still so much to discover, unsuspected even by critical historians." MacClary pointed to his father's papers again. "I also had a meeting last week with Bob Chaney. He's one of the judges on the International Criminal Court. Believe me, with what we now know, the Vatican can no longer be so certain of its immunity."

"Now we just have to hear from the United Nations," Jennifer said, half in jest.

"Spare me the sarcasm. There's really only one country whose legal system might offer us the possibility of attack, and that's the US. Ryan might be able to help us, both with his dual citizenship and his history, but only if you're prepared to represent him. Then we could at least make sure it gets the proper attention and use the media to open the subject for discussion. Can I count on you? Purely theoretically, of course."

Jennifer couldn't believe the course this conversation had taken. "Yes, you can, Ronald, and afterward I'll be your geriatric nurse. You must realize that we'll both be out of a job before a single hearing or even one complaint can be written."

Jennifer stood next to him as if rooted to the spot. The whole story was utter nonsense and had no chance of succeeding. On the other hand, there had been that case in Boston where her good friend Louis Baker, a federal prosecutor, had managed to launch the Blackfoot Indians' action for restitution of old cultural artifacts. Jennifer had handled it so well that the judge admitted the case and Jennifer won it. The museum being sued eventually had to return the artifacts.

Compared to what MacClary had in mind, though, that was a walk in the park.

* * *

Lambert seemed to be walking aimlessly through the Sistine Chapel when Salvoni approached him nervously from behind. "Ah, Salvoni," Lambert said, turning, "I've already heard about the events in Dublin. You have, I think, everything under control for our Austrian expedition?"

Salvoni was surprised by Lambert's calm. "Yes, we'll try to be there by nightfall. Unfortunately we don't have the exact coordinates, but I have some people following MacClary's friends." He had the feeling that the matter could get out of control since his contacts at the Austrian secret service hadn't yet confirmed their assistance.

"Tell me, what is our greatest concern here?"

Salvoni had expected to be berated for the sloppy work in Dublin, not plied with cryptic questions. "There is always the possibility that something could go wrong. Why don't we go the unofficial path and make public what we know? We could declare the discovery the result of our own research."

Lambert answered with unusual indifference. "Oh, Salvoni. In order to hate our history, you'd have to know what it was. And who knows our history? Only the disoriented atheists flailing around in the world of science. The people of faith won't have any understanding of these events."

"But Cardinal, you know that MacClary's father was hot on our heels once. Too close, to be honest. And although we can't really be certain of what the man discovered, we can guess. You must know that the possibility still exists of finding evidence from the period when the Church was founded."

"Even so, I have always argued that you can't apply today's ethical and moral standards to the actions of the bishops of Constantine's time."

Salvoni knew that this was an ambiguous line of reasoning, and he was sure that Lambert knew this as well. “What should we do now, then?”

Lambert’s eyes narrowed. “I’ll say this for the last time: remaining calm is our best option. Go about your work, but don’t take any risks. It’s just not worth it, even if MacClary does find what he’s looking for. Take a couple of men and try to stay two steps ahead of him. But keep your distance at first. Only intervene if it seems prudent. I don’t want MacClary to know that we have any interest in him and his activities.”

Salvoni had his misgivings—the scandals were already beginning to pile up—but he was clever enough not to express these out loud. “Good, Cardinal. You bear the responsibility for this, so we will proceed with caution.”

“Yes, Salvoni, I do bear the responsibility. Thank you, and keep me informed.”

“When will you tell the Holy Father about these events?”

Salvoni saw Lambert’s face redden, and he was certain an explosion was imminent. Instead, the cardinal’s expression softened, and he said, “What events? Please, Salvoni, the Holy Father really has other things to think about at the moment than some treasure hunters and heretical sinners like MacClary. Don’t give it another thought.”

Salvoni knew when he had been rebuked. “Very well, Cardinal.”

* * *

In Dublin, Padre Morati sat at his desk. His mouth and his hands were trembling, partially from age and partially because doubts were beginning to eat away at his conscience again. What had he done with his life? How could he justify belonging to a church that had left such a brutal and bloody trail since the day of its founding? How could someone of his intelligence believe in a god whose death toll was so high?

If Jesus appeared to us tomorrow on St. Peter's Square bringing the same message he brought to us back then, we would kill him again, betray him again, and abuse him, Morati thought as he continued reading his book about land appropriation and the true heritage of his long-loved religion. *Ninety percent of the practices, laws, revelations, and ceremonies were already a part of Judaism. Christianity is nothing more than a bastard child, and it isn't even ashamed of its lack of originality and its thievery. What they didn't steal from the Jews, they robbed from the pagans. In addition, they reviled and abused the people they stole from and even other Christians who tried to live and act according to the true revelations of Jesus. We would be faced with far fewer problems today if we had just followed these laws and not the adulterated Bible.* Morati laid the book down.

He had made an extraordinary decision.

CHAPTER 13

THE MAGDALENSBERG – MARCH 16, AFTERNOON

Shane's fear of flying turned out not to be a factor at all, yet another indication that the fateful events of the last few days were literally changing his life. After a three-hour drive from the airport in Vienna, they arrived in Klagenfurt. Markus Steinberger, an old friend of MacClary's, had joined Ronald in 1970 in a vain attempt to find the site of the trove without any exact coordinates. For decades he had been keeping his silence and, with Ronald's financial support, had continued to purchase the most up-to-date archaeological equipment. Now he drove them in a dark-blue van up the serpentine paths to the peak of the Magdalensberg.

When they got there, an eerie sight greeted them: a church from the Middle Ages built entirely of a yellowish-gray stone, appearing wraithlike in the foggy, raw weather. As they got out of the van, Shane pulled his hood over his head to block out the freezing cold wind blowing in his face, stricken with the undeniable feeling that he'd been here before.

* * *

Yes, it was possible, Ryan thought. Even now, seventeen hundred years later, it was still possible to revive a culture whose divine gifts were so much more authentic and redeeming and whose relevance to Creation went so much deeper than anything the Christian churches had ever been able to accomplish. If it were going to happen, though, it needed to begin now.

They walked silently through a wooded slope for about ten minutes when Shane suddenly pulled up short.

"Thomas, how much further do we have to go?" he asked nervously.

"Actually, we're almost there. It should be within a hundred and fifty, maybe three hundred feet."

Ryan turned around to look at Adam as he balanced on the steep escarpment holding a magnetic field sensor. MacClary had told him he should look for some kind of sinkhole or concavity, a crater that could have been the result of an explosion. As he looked over Adam's shoulder, he noticed a depression that might be it. "Adam, I don't know how you do it, but you seem to have a very strong instinct. There's a pretty big hollow down there, but we'll probably have to go down a good ten to twelve feet. I'll start digging carefully. You two should keep an inconspicuous watch over the area and give me a sign if someone's coming. No matter what, we only go in under cover of night."

Shane and Deborah started off in opposite directions.

* * *

DUBLIN – MARCH 16, AFTERNOON

Jennifer had decided to stay with MacClary to wait for word from Ryan. As she did, she thought about the last thing Adam Shane had said to her during their late-night conversation. He was firmly convinced that a culture was lost when people were robbed of their original spirituality. It would take a long time to revive this, and it would require, above all, evidence, knowledge, and the old, traditional ceremonies.

Jennifer couldn't really argue with him. She knew only too well what had happened to the Native Americans in the US. They had become not much more than lost souls in their own country, ravaged by alcohol, drugs, and crime. In that case it had also been the Christians who, in their delusional belief that they were chosen by God, had taken over the country and treated people of other faiths like cattle. Maybe Ronald was right. Maybe it had to be the US where those responsible could be held accountable.

She was starting to get impatient about finding out what was going on. What would the three scouts find in the cave? She had been staring at the telephone constantly, but there was still no sign of life from the continent.

Ronald, on the other hand, seemed to be almost completely unfazed. Either he really was that calm or he was an even better actor than she had thought. Just now, he was in the library finishing up a telephone call with a colleague in Washington. Ruth had just prepared tea, and Ronald came to sit down with Jennifer. Now that she could observe him more closely, she realized that he wasn't all that relaxed.

"Why don't you call him?" she asked.

"Because we agreed that he would contact me. I don't want to rob him of the satisfaction that that call will give him. I'm almost certain that he's been successful. I know you don't like Ryan, that you think he's too coarse and abrupt, but I know him better than you do. We both have a very, very long family history. And coming from Northern Ireland, he knows all too well where fanatical faith can lead. That's what you're accusing me of, no? Fanaticism."

"I'm not accusing you of anything at all. But you're not laying all your cards out on the table, Ronald. I know you too well not to notice. What if something happens to them? Or if the cave collapses? Or if they're discovered? And what about Adam? He has no idea what you boys are up to."

"Oh, I think he does. He's got at least a basic idea of what this is all about. In any case, they're three grown people. They're old enough to take care of themselves. As far as Adam is concerned, I consider him to be a thoroughly intelligent and cautious man. He and Ryan seem to understand each other very well, which is unusual, as you know."

"You forgot sensitive."

"What was that?"

"Adam is extremely sensitive and intuitive, in addition to being very intelligent."

"All the better," MacClary responded, but she noticed that his thoughts were somewhere else again.

"Oh, you don't understand."

"Of course I do. I could hardly miss the fact that you liked him." MacClary grinned as he stood up. "What I've been able to gather about Adam in the short time I've known him is that he and Ryan have very similar opinions about the spiritual effects of Christian dominance. Just like Ryan, he wants—"

"—to burn the Christians at the stake? No, I don't think that's what Adam wants."

MacClary reacted more angrily than she had ever seen him. "Jennifer, that's not what we're talking about at all! The Vatican is not Christendom. But the Vatican is the origin of an incredible series of crimes against humanity. I thought we had a shared belief about legal ethics. We both know that our field seldom has anything to do with justice, but I want to make a difference here if I can."

"Don't you get it, Ronald? What Adam is looking for is a new balance, one that he's found in the lost tribal culture of the Celts and the other indigenous peoples, before we all got lost in the insanity of this culture of eternal growth. First the tribes lost their inner strength, and then, with the introduction of supercapitalism, the strength of the family. That's where he sees the real drama taking place."

"But he also recognizes that this drama has its origin in a culture that exploited nature and humankind. And Adam is no—"

"I have no idea what he is or isn't. I only know one thing: he is not a vindictive or egoistic patriarch, like you are. You don't understand him at all. The only thing you care about is yourself and your obsession."

Jennifer stood up and strode out of the room. A few seconds later, she slammed the front door.

* * *

Jennifer wandered aimlessly through Arbour Hill in a small park. The quiet was good for her. She sat down to rest on a bench, surrounded by trees. It was colder than she had thought; she should have put on something warmer. Suddenly she thought about her grandfather, who had worked as a healer in County Cork. He was one of the few people there who wasn't Catholic, and he had his own very individual theories about the ways of the world. She must have been about eight or nine when he had tried to explain to her why there were so many poor people in the village. Long ago, he had told her, it was said that there had been great wise people whose spirituality offset the greed of kings and merchants. When these teachers had been pushed out, the quality of compassion was lost, the sense that we are all responsible for each other.

In any case, he had said, these wise men made sure that nature was shown the proper respect. Above all, however, they never separated science and belief, which is why they were at least partially successful in governing matter with their spirit. Was Adam's vision just a part of this gift?

She stood up and continued on. The walk had calmed her down.

* * *

THE MAGDALENSBERG – MARCH 16, EVENING

Cassidy lit a cigarette. How many was that now? He furiously threw the lighter against the windshield of the small van. He had been waiting for hours, not only for reinforcements from the Vatican police and the archaeological specialists in Rome, but also for the reinforcements Salvoni had promised from the Austrian secret service, which, to his surprise, had not shown up yet. Two buses in Rome had been set up with the best equipment to retrieve the artifacts as quickly as possible. All he needed were the Vatican diplomats and he would have no problems managing even without foreign assistance.

Cassidy grabbed his cell phone and called Salvoni, who had insisted on overseeing the operation personally.

"Patience, Cassidy. We need another two hours or so. It wasn't exactly a walk in the park organizing everything here. Were you able to follow MacClary's friends?"

"Yes, of course, and I can tell you now that we're too late. They've found the cave and have probably already broken in. I only have two men here. What should I do?"

"That is unfortunate, very unfortunate, but the cardinal state secretary takes a different view of the situation. Stay hidden and try to get closer as carefully as you can. But don't make a move before I get there."

"Understood. I'll stay hidden and hang back," Cassidy said, like the loyal subordinate he was. He had long ago given up contradicting his superiors.

CHAPTER 14

THE MAGDALENSBERG – NIGHT

Ryan had been shoveling for nearly three hours now. It had gotten dark and the trees in front of the entrance to the cave stood like mystical guards in the soft, thick fog. Adam and Deborah hadn't seen anyone who might unexpectedly interfere with their work, so they came back after a while to join Ryan.

Just as Adam was getting ready to help, there was a crash underneath the earth. The ground gave way. Adam leaned against a tree, grabbing Ryan's hand at the last second; otherwise he would have been pulled down into the cave-in.

After Adam helped Ryan regain his footing, there was absolute silence. Deborah came over, shaking her head in frustration. "That's it, then. We're not going to get through there, at least not tonight anyhow." Resigned, she sat down on the damp ground, cleaning her fogged-up glasses with her handkerchief.

"Nonsense," Ryan said, laughing as he slid down into the hole that had just been created. "Give me the shovel and a flashlight."

Moments later, Ryan's flashlight lit up a hole, about ten feet down and three feet wide. The ground gave way a little more, and Ryan, shoveling like a madman, cleared enough so that he could slip inside.

Ryan had slid down a few steps into the lower chamber, but he couldn't see anything at first since the collapse had caused so much sand to rain down. He looked skeptically up at the cave ceiling, but then the first artifacts grabbed his attention. A moment later he was close to tears. In front of him was a gleaming bronze shield engraved with what were clearly Celtic symbols. Above the shield, the builders had carved the Wheel of Being into the stone. It symbolized the four points of the compass united by a central circle. It also stood for the universe, which consists of four elements—earth, air, water, and fire—and a fifth element that holds everything together.

Ryan knelt down, as if in prayer. MacClary hadn't been exaggerating. The thought that he might be standing in front of the last remnant of his ancestors left him awestruck. His mother had told him that his family, just before they escaped to Ireland, had been very influential at the emperor's court. What would be waiting for him here?

He used the flashlight to look around a little bit more before he discovered another opening about fifteen to twenty feet farther back. Adam, who had been standing behind him, walked forward and went through by himself.

For a few moments it was deathly quiet in the cave, and then Ryan heard Adam breathlessly calling, "Thomas, Deborah, I can't believe this."

Ryan set up a larger light so they could view the entire scope of the cave. They found themselves standing in front of what appeared to be a hundred chests each covered with a layer of wax. Next to them, they could see more shields made of precious metals, swords, countless stone tablets decorated with runes, and even more through another opening. Adam stood there unable to move. In the meantime Ryan had stretched a tarp over the opening, both to keep light from escaping and to keep the outside dampness from penetrating into the cave.

"OK, Deborah," Ryan said when he was finished, "let's open a few chests very carefully. Then we'll know if this was worth all the time and effort."

Adam came up next to him. "You mean these stones, these shields, all the decorations and the weapons, they're not actually worth anything?"

"Of course they are. For the museums in Europe, they would be a priceless treasure. But not for me."

"The stone tablets don't have any information about the purpose of the library," Deborah said nervously. "They're just gravestones of kings or other important figures."

"What we're looking for are the scrolls that MacClary's father discovered back then," Ryan explained.

Then he opened the first chest and sank, frustrated and despairing, to his knees.

Everything was as good as destroyed, although some of the scrolls might offer up a secret or two if they were subjected to computer tomography.

* * *

Shane tore down an old tarp that had the insignia of the British army and went into a second room. Stunned and deeply moved, he stood stock still.

The almost circular room was a good eight hundred and fifty square feet. Man-made chambers had been carved into the volcanic rock, about half the size of a coffin. In these chambers were parchment scrolls, many of which looked, at first glance, to be in good shape, and there were also countless more decorative pieces, bracelets, and smaller stones with engraved symbols. In the middle of the room was a round, polished stone, about ten feet in diameter with an engraved spiral. Shane recognized the symbol: the spiral of life.

He was irresistibly drawn into the center of the stone. At the end of the engraved line, he sat down and looked around in confusion. The impressions that were streaming over him were almost too much for him. He was standing on a spot where the energy of an ancient culture was concentrated. A breath from the past? No, it didn't feel past at all. It was a breath from a culture that he was longing for. Could it really be that the downfall of the Druids and their legacy were manifested here? It seemed pointless to want to turn back the wheel of time, as MacClary was doing. The question of how the development of humankind could have been different was an important one, but Shane felt that this day had more to do with the present and the future than with the past. The opening of this library—there was no other term you could use for the mass of relics left here—would trigger something larger, larger than they could even imagine right now. Of that he was certain.

He looked around again. The room had an almost archaic aesthetic and simplicity that took his breath away. He found himself irresistibly drawn into another passageway. He had to go about fifteen feet through the narrow corridor until it opened up into another, even bigger room, which left him completely dumbstruck.

"Thomas, Deborah, come here, and hurry. I think you're about to find everything you're looking for."

The room was much more chaotic than the other two. Lying all over the place were wooden beams, blank parchment, chests, candles, weapons, pitchers, and more. Then

Shane saw something that made his blood run cold. In another hollow of the cave, there was an enormous table. Underneath it were drawers filled with more parchment. On the table there were countless cups and sticks that looked like writing quills. A chair was next to the table and under the tattered remnants of cloth he saw a skeleton whose skull, decomposed by the passage of time, had fallen onto the table and another parchment.

"Adam?"

"Back here! You have to go through the nearest passageway," Shane called back, his voice choked with tears.

* * *

Ryan's frustration gave way to a wave of euphoria when he saw the parchment in the second room. Deborah found the nearest passageway and continued on into the third room, from where Adam had called them.

"Thomas?"

"Wait, I'm coming, I have to look at this room first," Ryan said, gradually realizing that he didn't know where to start. Without giving it too much thought, he went into one of the chambers and carefully lifted out some of the parchment scrolls. They really were in amazing condition. Would it be too risky to open them and put them straight into his collection box?

As he picked up the first scroll, he realized that this was a sacred moment. Here stood three Irish folk with Celtic roots, and in this moment they had become responsible for helping their ancestral culture regain its place in the world, whether they wanted this responsibility or not.

Just the sight of the writing made him nervous. "Deborah, I need you here," he called in hushed tones.

Deborah squeezed back into the chamber.

"Can you translate this?" Ryan said, showing Deborah the scroll he was holding.

"They're in perfect condition! Are you crazy, opening them up here?"

"Trust me. We don't have much time, and we have to take advantage of this opportunity."

This seemed to convince Deborah, who began to study the scroll. "I can't believe it! It's—there...do you see the numbers? It was written in 315 by a...a Druid, who—"

Deborah hesitated a minute in disbelief. "...who's describing an evening where he, and perhaps another Druid at Constantine's court, was acting as a fortune-teller. He describes a conversation that he overheard, a discussion between Constantine and a bishop. Constantine said that he was ready to help the Christians, since he recognized in their god an important revelation. But their writings were not convincing enough to lead an army. In order to win over people to this faith, it needed more...I can't read the rest. I need something to help me enlarge it. And time, Thomas, I just need more time."

Ryan could see that Deborah was so tense that her right eyelid had started to twitch. But Ryan had heard enough for now. This evidence was worth more than all the gold in the cave. It would prepare the way for a new era if it were to be recognized. At last, they had irrefutable proof of Constantine's true motives.

"That's perfectly fine, Deborah. We'll take this scroll with us. And what about this one?"

In the meantime, Adam had come back to the room with an engraved stone. "Hey, what are you two doing? You need to see what I've found."

Ryan didn't move immediately, but he finally relented when Deborah called him over. He stood at the entrance to the third room and gave a heavy nod, as if he had been expecting this. "This is it, then. I mean...yes, now we've really found it."

"What have we found?" Adam asked in astonishment, looking from one to the other.

Deborah's only answer was to look at Ryan. "Tell him, Thomas." He sighed and sat down at the table where the skeleton lay. "And you should probably sit down on the floor, Adam."

Ryan pulled himself together. "OK, it probably is the right time for this. Adam...I'm a direct descendant of the last Celtic Druid. I have a family tree that stretches back into the fourth century, back to the time when those Druids who could escape Rome's henchmen and who didn't submit themselves to Christendom fled to Ireland and Scotland. According to what is told in my family, in the spring of 331, a group of Druids, including Rodanicas, the Roman Datanos, and six students, arrived in Britain at what is now Dover to make their way to Ireland."

* * *

"The gods were with us," Datanos said.

"I can only guess how many of our tribe they have killed," Rodanicas murmured. They had seen horrible things on their journey. Many of his students and other leaders of the secret schools had lost their lives. He sat down on a stone. The journey had been difficult and dangerous. Just before their arrival, a storm had nearly capsized their ship. Coughing, he looked up at Datanos, who was opening up the sack with the parchment that Aregetorix had entrusted them with. On one of the first pieces of parchment he found instructions for Rodanicas.

"What is that?" Datanos asked in astonishment.

Rodanicas stood up wearily and looked at the parchment.

"These are the records of our ancestors, for every one of us. Aregetorix is the only Druid who was also known and respected by the Island Celts. The honor he is accorded will make it possible for us to get our footing here and start anew," he said. "You, Datanos, you are a Roman. Yet you may come with me. I will offer you the same protection that I am given."

"You know that I will follow you wherever you go."

Datanos took out additional parchment and gave them to Rodanicas. He stood up and turned to the young Druids. "I am giving each one of you your own family tree. Each one of you must seek out a place to live, where you can, in secret, pass on everything that we have taught you.

So will we outlast the time of darkness. Only two of us will pass on the knowledge of the place where Aregetorix is guarding the true testimony. And so it will be—until one day when people go in search of their true heritage."

He ceremoniously handed over the scrolls and then turned to one of the men. "You, Uratorix, you are the other who will guard the place where your father, Aregetorix, has remained." He gave the Druid the last parchment. "We leave at the rift of this time and shall return at the rift of another. And now, leave."

Their faces set, the men embraced each other and went their separate ways, without once turning around to look back.

* * *

"The man you see in front of you is Aregetorix." Ryan suddenly broke off, his breath catching in his throat. How long had he been carrying around this knowledge and all of these questions? "Until now it was nothing more than a legend, but now we're standing in front of the proof. The stories told of one Druid who was left behind to guard everything, as long as he lived. This is the man you see before you now." Ryan sat down, spent, on the ground.

"And you really believe that this is the place?" Adam said, awe evident in his voice.

Deborah had opened another parchment and was studying it carefully. "Frankly, the question has, I think, already been resolved."

Ryan tried to get a better glimpse of what Deborah was holding. "What did you find?"

"Here another Druid, named Cetanorad, is writing a warning to all the Druids and the Celts. It's difficult to translate, dreadfully bad Latin, but I understand at least this much: some of the Druids knew what was going on in Rome. He's writing about falsifications and that knowing this will cost them their lives if they don't escape. And here, oh no…" Deborah fell silent.

"What! Tell us!" Ryan said.

"He attributes a declaration to a bishop, whose name I can't decipher. This declaration was shared with the emperor as a condition for a contract: 'He who would conquer the pagans must destroy the Druids.'"

"And?"

"The bishop demanded that the emperor…wait a minute, the parchment isn't from Constantine's era, though. I don't understand…"

"Oh, that doesn't mean anything. It was mainly Emperor Theodosius I who supported the Church Father Ambrosius in his desire to wipe out anything that smacked of paganism. It was only during his reign that Christianity definitively became a state religion, even though Constantine often gets credit for it. The complete extermination of everyone with different beliefs was, from the very beginning, the declared goal of Theodosius's regency."

Deborah stared around the room. "But then that also means that this library wasn't constructed in just a short period."

"Shouldn't we be calling MacClary sometime soon?" Adam asked.

"Later, Adam," Ryan said. "First we should look around a bit more, so that we can make an intelligent decision about what we should take with us and what we have to leave behind."

He turned in a full circle, gesturing helplessly at the sheer volume of relics.

* * *

THE MAGDALENSBERG – NIGHT

Cassidy was still waiting for Salvoni, contenting himself with the analysis of the conversations one of his coworkers had been able to intercept right before the three Irish interlopers had gone into the cave. Since then, the thickness of the earth had made reception impossible. Just as he was about to dig into the provisions he had brought with him, his cell phone rang. The display read *Salvoni*.

"Yes."

"Cassidy, we'll be there in ten minutes. What's the situation?"

"There's nothing going on here," Cassidy said, almost bored. "They're still in the cave, but what we were able to hear didn't suggest a huge find. Even if the three do discover something in the cave, they won't be able to transport much in the little van they brought."

"Good job, Cassidy, see you soon."

* * *

Salvoni had his men park the bus at the bottom of the Magdalensberg while he drove up to get a better picture of the situation. A good dozen men dressed in black, some of them armed and carrying the most up-to-date equipment for retrieving relics, were getting ready for their assignment. They had received clear instructions from Salvoni. The operation should proceed as quickly and unspectacularly as possible. Under no circumstances should there be any direct confrontation or exchange of fire, since they didn't have backup from the Austrian police.

Salvoni phoned Lambert. "We're too late. They're already inside. They apparently haven't found anything important, if my men are to be believed, but we should still make sure."

"Wait until they come out again, and then you'll know what you have to do."

"But Cardinal, we have to take advantage of the cover of night! What if they don't come out until dawn?"

"Then you have free hand to do what you think appropriate."

Salvoni repressed a sigh of relief with difficulty. *Free hand*. That was what he had been waiting for the whole time. An operation like this was his specialty, and he knew exactly how he needed to run it.

CHAPTER 15

THE MAGDALENSBERG – NIGHT

Shane was working with Deborah to identify more of the scrolls. "My God, when I think about what we've found here! All these records contradict in every conceivable way our current understanding of what was handed down to us by the Druids and the Celts."

"You mustn't forget who was writing the history you read. The true history of the Druids couldn't be written before now because we hardly knew it. One thing is certain, though: everything here suggests that they were the architects of the entire Celtic society." Deborah carefully placed another scroll in the box they had set aside for that purpose. "We know, as far as Ireland is concerned, that there was always a balance between worldly and spiritual power that kings and Druids shared. The idea of an empire was completely foreign to them. There wasn't even a word for it in Gallic or any other Celtic language. It's no wonder that this culture couldn't be maintained in the atmosphere of the *Pax Romana*. The ones Saint Patrick didn't force to convert to Christianity ended up submitting themselves willingly. But here we find the source and…oh, look at this, a complete list of healing herbs and their applications. This must be worth a fortune."

As Shane took another scroll out of the table, Deborah furrowed her brow and hastily scanned the text. "Take that too. That's a description of the ability to communicate telepathically and to have an influence on the weather, animals, and other people. Even if it's only a myth, it's still interesting."

"No, Deborah. I don't think it's just a myth. What if the Druids did have these abilities and this knowledge? That would have been yet another reason to persecute them. I mean, faced with such an accumulated knowledge, the Romans and the Christians must have been terrified. That's why they needed this super god, the one true God. That's the only way they could provide their armies with the necessary force to maintain an empire. I believe that the Druids really did have access to a universal knowledge, to a gift, that exerted an attraction and…"

Thomas had come back into the room. "As soon as we've filled all the boxes and chests that we want to take with us, I want to get out of here," he said in a commanding tone. "In half an hour, I'm going to call MacClary and tell him that there's no way we can retrieve everything here by ourselves."

Thomas turned around and went back into the next chamber.

"And then what?" Shane asked.

"That's it for us," Deborah answered. "That's the deal we made with MacClary. Ryan can take as much as he can and look for evidence that his ancestors left something here. The rest is for the archaeologists. Here, look at this!" Deborah translated another scroll. "*Our time is past. They are torturing us to break our power, to make us come to their source, but they will fail. We know their lies*... Damn, I can't get anything else out of it."

Shane had gotten up and was about to pack a dozen scrolls in one of the boxes they had left at the entrance. Then he saw Thomas, standing with his hand to his forehead. Dust and sand were raining down on him and another parchment, with which he was apparently quite preoccupied. He took a plastic container from one of the chests, which had a spiral inside it, so he could carefully store a parchment in it without having to touch the skin. He was concentrating so intensely on his work that he hadn't noticed Shane at all.

"What are you doing there, Thomas?"

"This is something special. I'll explain later." Shane could tell Thomas was nervous, but he could also sense the relief that had washed over him. "It's the scroll of Rodanicas," Thomas continued, "one of my ancestors. This is what I've spent so much time searching for. It wasn't a legend after all. I can't let go of this parchment scroll again."

Shane sat down next to Thomas. "But that's not everything, is it?"

"No, Adam, that's not it by a long shot. It's not just about me and my family. What we've found here essentially belongs to eight Irish families whose ancestors at the beginning of the fourth century made it as far as Ireland. One of the secret schools we were talking about has survived, more or less, to the present day, so we were convinced that this place really existed and that we had to find it to learn more about our history."

"Then it's really true," they heard from behind them. Deborah was headed to the exit with some scrolls.

"What is MacClary expecting from all of this here?" Shane asked.

"Oh, a lot. As you know, when his father left him with this riddle, it was a heavy burden. He also shares his father's obsession about the early years of the Church. You mustn't forget, the man is a jurist down to his bones, and he sees the genesis of the Church as more like the foundation of a criminal society. He wants to document these facts and arguments so the public will finally accept the truth and the Vatican will lose its influence."

Shane had to laugh to himself. How naïve could these men be? Did Thomas really believe what he was saying? And the judge? Curb the influence of the Vatican! People were simply not ready for that. They had always looked the other way when a crime was committed in the name of faith—any faith. History, even recent history, was rife with this.

"In addition," Thomas added, "a few months ago the British government officially recognized Druidism as a state religion. I'm sure we'll also find proof here that the

Vatican set aside considerable portions of our cultural assets and is hoarding them somewhere. But let's stop talking now and make sure we get out of here."

Shane shook his head in disbelief. "But Thomas, what's going to happen? Who's going to get into the Vatican's secret archive to prove this?"

"Adam, there is no secret archive in the Vatican. That's just one of many conspiracy theories."

"You'll have to explain that to me. There's enough information out there that suggests exactly the opposite."

Deborah jumped into the conversation. "The *Archivio Segreto Vaticano* is, as the adjective *segreto* states, private, and not secret. Only the pope decides which inventory will be declassified, but this archive has nothing to do with the archive of the Congregation for the Doctrine of Faith. And the private archive of the pope is certainly not the place where such things are kept."

"But where then?" Shane asked skeptically.

Deborah shook her head slowly. "The devil only knows, Adam. And I don't use the word lightly."

* * *

DUBLIN – MARCH 17, MIDNIGHT

MacClary couldn't contain his nervousness anymore. *My God, Ryan, just call already!* he thought as he stood in the library. For the first time, he began to fear that Ruth's warning might turn out to be a premonition. Jennifer had made herself comfortable under a blanket in a leather chair in front of the crackling fire in the library fireplace. He turned in her direction.

"So you want to quit. Did I understand you correctly?"

Jennifer looked up at him. "I do. Over the past few years I've started to realize that my career really isn't fulfilling me anymore. The progress we've been able to make is negligible compared to the work that's left to be done. I'm just tired, and I can't take sleeping in hotels or a cold, empty bed at home anymore."

MacClary hesitated a minute and then sat down next to her. For a while the only sound they could hear was the popping of the wood burning in the fireplace. Then he spoke again, softly. "It's not that I'm happy when someone throws away her career, but as your friend, I'm inclined not to make any attempt to stop you."

"You'd just let me go?"

"Do you think I don't see what's going on with you?" MacClary said as he stood up to get himself a whiskey. "Since the collapse of the UN reform, you haven't had any of your old professional enthusiasm."

The telephone rang. Both of them jumped, and Ruth, who happened to be walking by, rushed to the telephone to answer it. MacClary beat her to it, offering her a calming gesture at the same time. His hand on the phone, he paused for just a moment, as if he knew what Ryan was about to tell him.

"Thomas, is everything OK there?"

"More than OK. What we've found here exceeds all of our expectations, and above all, it has fulfilled mine." Ryan's euphoria was palpable. He sounded breathless and spoke so fast that it was almost impossible to understand him.

"Thomas, I'm completely overwhelmed! You really found the parchment scrolls? What else was there?"

"Suffice it to say that your father was right about everything. I can't say anything more right now except that I've found all sorts of evidence here that we've been speculating about."

"So you've finally found evidence of your family. I always knew you would, I—"

"There's a problem, though. There's just too much. It would be impossible to retrieve everything. My suggestion is that I send Adam and Deborah to Dublin with the most important scrolls. The rest has to be preserved immediately, otherwise—"

"I understand, Thomas. I'll use my contacts in the Austrian Foreign Ministry to organize the immediate retrieval of the artifacts. That means that you need to get out of there."

"Absolutely not. I'm staying here to make sure that no trespassers walk in on the site."

Then, without even giving MacClary the chance to try to change his mind, Ryan hung up.

"Damn pigheaded mule," MacClary said, beaming with joy.

* * *

Jennifer sat upright on the edge of her chair looking at MacClary expectantly. "What did they find?"

"What would you say if I offered you the opportunity to end your career with one of the oldest criminal cases in history?" MacClary was grinning as he only did when he was absolutely convinced of something.

Jennifer knew what was coming. How often had they sat together tossing all the legal, historical, and theoretical possibilities back and forth? Could they prove something against the Church? Did they have cultural objects from the Celts or the Druids in their possession? What if the descendants of those Celts or Druids could invoke international law and demand surrender of the objects?

Once, the only recognized subjects of international law were the states, not the people living in them. However, an increasing number of jurists throughout the world tended to view the entirety of humankind as a single subject of international law. If the international community were to get involved in this, the consequences would be incalculable. For example, no more trees could be cut down in the Brazilian rainforest without the agreement of a community of nations. The claim on cultural assets would also be affected—the pyramids, for instance, or the Buddha statues in Afghanistan, for which it was, sadly, too late. Ultimately the claim on historical truth would change as well.

"You're referring to the efforts of Jackson O'Connor?" Jennifer knew the Irish foreign minister from her time in Brussels. O'Connor was an honorable man through and through, with a modern understanding of international law, even if he was as much of a dreamer as MacClary.

"Well, that too. He has always implied that the Irish government is prepared to return all Celtic cultural assets to the descendants in their own countries. And in the same way that Israel is the promised land for the Jews, Ireland is the promised land for the Celts."

"But how in the world are we going to make the Vatican open its archive? Even if we could, they'd have enough time to clear everything out and hide it somewhere else. I mean, what do you want to do, get a search warrant from the United Nations?"

MacClary's expression grew more thoughtful. "I want a signal, Jennifer. A beacon, you could call it. You don't always have to win a trial to achieve justice or even equity."

"In other words, you want to embarrass them. In reality, it's not about justice or equity; you just want to embarrass them."

"Wait until we see what Thomas and the others have uncovered. If Thomas says he's found some piece of crucial evidence, then he has."

* * *

MacClary was trying to calm himself down. As he reached for the phone to call the Austrian authorities and have them unobtrusively secure the site, his father's last words came to mind. Sean MacClary had once said that the reason Rome was so afraid of his work was because he knew how to combine knowledge and rationality with a convincing logic. Had anyone seen Moses receive the Ten Commandments or Zeus help Julius Caesar to victory? He had never enjoyed destroying a person's faith, but the religion that the Catholic Church preached was nothing more or less to him than theater for children, a ridiculous and primitive story, as despicable in its acts as it was dangerous.

He could have no way of knowing the spectacular way that the Curia would soon rush to his aid.

CHAPTER 16

THE MAGDALENSBERG – MARCH17, EARLY MORNING

The other two were at the entrance packing everything in airtight containers for transport when Shane felt himself pulled again into the room with the stone. He knew of no definitive meaning for the spiral, but scholars often believed it to be symbolic of the soul's aspiration to higher spheres. In Ireland, it was often just a symbol for the sun.

Shane had another theory: the spiral stood for time and space. For the Druids, time wasn't linear. It had a beginning and an end, but in between the soul could access everything that had ever happened and anything that would happen. Was that what Ryan had meant when he had explained the theory of the morphogenetic field?

Shane sat down on the stone to gather his thoughts. He had been deeply moved by the evidence left behind by the Druids. How could anyone call the standard-bearers of this culture barbarians? The longer he thought about it, the greater his respect grew for their love of creation and the true divine miracles.

He lay down on his back and suddenly noticed how the stone's spiral was recreated on the ceiling in light, like a living galaxy. Sinking into what was becoming a familiar trance, he could again feel every cell in his body, each one tingling, and he saw the same collage-like pictures from history in his mind's eye. He could recognize people and feel what they had suffered over the past seventeen hundred years from the hegemony of the Christians and the Church's contempt for humankind. He saw Native Americans shot down by British troops, Australian Aborigines driven from their own country like cattle. He saw the enslavement of Arabian and African tribes, women burned in Europe, and so many more horrible things, until he completely dissolved in tears. He took a deep breath. He had begun to understand that he too bore responsibility for ending this insanity. In order for humans—all humans—to be able to heal, understand, and forgive, everyone had to be aware of the beginning of the story. Otherwise there would never be true justice.

He stood up and looked around the cave one last time. It must be so difficult for Thomas to leave this place without being able to see everything. Stored inside this library cave was the legacy of his family. How many more secrets did it hold? He couldn't resist the temptation to pull one more parchment out from one of the lower chambers. The scroll was a bit damp, but it opened quite easily.

"Adam, damn it!" Deborah said, shocking him with her presence. "We agreed that you wouldn't touch anything on your own."

She knelt down by Shane, only then noticing his tears. "Hey, what's wrong?"

"Deborah, the historic truth of this place is immeasurable. I doubt if people will be ready to accept it, because to do so means acknowledging that we've been on the wrong path for so long."

Deborah studied the parchment in his hands for a moment. "You picked out a very appropriate one," she said, pointing at the document.

"What do you mean?"

"This was written by a Druid speaking about the return of the Druids. He says that they will return when people are ready to remember and to end the dark age. He goes on to talk about a legend. I'll try to translate this in Dublin because I can't do it here, but it talks of bringing to the world a new balance and about a few women and men who will make a beginning. The name of the Druid author is Dubdrean."

"Well, we've found more Druids in a couple of hours than archaeologists have managed to find in more than a thousand years." Shane held up the scroll. "Can we take this one with us too?"

"Actually, we have to. Otherwise it will fall apart. I'll see if I can find another box. Then the two of us have to drive back to Dublin as quickly as we can."

Shane was doubly confused. "Drive? I thought we'd be flying. And why just the two of us?"

"Ryan is going to stay here and watch over everything until the archaeologists from Vienna take over. Meanwhile, we could hardly board an airplane with this sensational cargo. We'll drive through France, take the car ferry, then go through England, and then catch the ferry at Holyhead. At that point, everything will go into a prepared room that MacClary is setting up to preserve the scrolls."

Shane just accepted this. What else could he do? He didn't like the thought of leaving Thomas here by himself, but he tried to push aside this uneasy feeling. He was far too preoccupied with what he had just experienced and what was written on the scroll that Deborah had translated for him.

Could all this really be true? The Druids had been, among other things, doctors, jurists, and knowledge-hungry academics with incredible powers of recollection, which they had maintained because of their ban on writing, but they also had a tendency toward exaggerated hero worship. He thought again about the spiral. If time wasn't linear and souls could exist without form and body in this nonlinear time, then it was possible that reincarnation was really the creation of a single large memory. Was it possible that more and more people were remembering?

Thomas's voice tore him away from his thoughts. "Adam, we're ready. Could you help Deborah carry up the boxes and put them in the van? I'll close up the chambers as well as I can."

Shane turned toward Thomas. "So you're really going to stay here?"

"At least long enough to make sure that the real professionals can take over."

I guess you know what you're doing, Shane thought.

* * *

About five minutes later, innkeeper Georg Winter looked out his office window in the nearby inn and saw two figures carrying boxes through the dark. He called his son, who was just finishing up the orders for the next day. Unsure whether they should call the police, they just watched.

* * *

In the bushes on the other side of the parking lot, Cassidy, Salvoni, and a Vatican police officer could see the silhouette of the proprietor in the window of the inn. They didn't want witnesses at this point, so they wouldn't be able to stop MacClary's friends from saving some artifacts.

"Make sure that someone follows them until we can figure out what they've found there," Salvoni ordered. "As soon as they're gone, we're going into the cave."

Cassidy slowly walked down the mountain, where a few men were waiting for the order to go into action.

A short while later, Salvoni called Cassidy.

"Were there originally two or three of them?" Salvoni asked nervously.

"Three. Why?"

"Because only two of them got into the car."

"Then the gentleman is asking for it. We should go in now."

* * *

DUBLIN – EARLY MORNING

MacClary had reported the find to the Austrian Foreign Ministry and was a bit puzzled by their lack of enthusiasm. The authorities told him they would get back to him tomorrow. He couldn't leave Ryan alone for so long in the cave. After pacing around the house a bit, he asked Jennifer to stay by the phone with Ruth and took a taxi to the American embassy.

The building on Elgin Road was impressive, as beautiful as nearly all the US embassies in Europe that were housed in historic buildings. MacClary possessed the rare privilege of being able to use an office in the embassy at any time. He occasionally took advantage of this when he wanted absolutely no interruptions, when he just wanted a change of scenery, or when he had to make confidential telephone calls over a secure line. Immediately after he settled in, he called the American ambassador in Vienna.

* * *

Dave Atkinson was busy at this late hour and the ringing phone surprised him. "American embassy, Atkinson," he said, his voice ringing through the office.

"Hello, Dave. It's Ronald MacClary."

"Ronald! To what do I owe the honor at this ungodly hour?" The two men had worked together on a United

Nations commission devoted to understanding the Yugoslavian war.

"Dave, I need to ask you a favor without your asking me too many questions. I can assure you that it's extremely important to an international case involving an American citizen."

"I wouldn't honor that request from many people, but I will from you, Ronald."

"I appreciate that, Dave. In two or three hours, two people, a young man and a young woman, will come by to see you. The two of them have documents in their possession with which they will not be able to get through airport security. I'd like you to give them diplomatic passports so that they'll have an allowance for diplomatic pouches. Their destination is the American embassy in Dublin."

This intrigued Atkinson, but he'd already agreed not to ask questions. "How quickly do you need the passports?"

"I need you to have them ready when they arrive. Their names are Deborah Walker and Adam Shane. Deborah is Irish, Shane is Austrian with Irish heritage."

"No problem, Ronald. I assume you know what you're doing. I'll arrange everything and wait for them."

"Thank you, Dave. You've been an enormous help."

* * *

Deborah and Adam were headed toward Klagenfurt to get onto the autobahn when Deborah's cell phone rang.

"Professor?"

"Deborah, I don't have enough time to let you drive the van and all of the findings through half of Europe. I've asked my friend in Klagenfurt to take you, with his sons, to the American embassy in Vienna. There you'll receive diplomatic passports that'll let you take everything you have onto an airplane without going through security. I'll wait for you at the airport in Dublin, and then we'll drive directly to the embassy here."

MacClary was speaking so fast that Deborah could hardly follow him. "Good, Ronald, but I think it might take about two or three hours to get to Vienna."

"No problem. The embassy will be open for you at any time. I'll wait here for you. As you can imagine, I'm really looking forward to seeing what you have."

"I think you're going to be amazed. But what about Ryan? How long does he have to wait where we left him?"

"Tell him he should make sure Thomas leaves the cave," Adam said nervously. "I have a strange feeling. Maybe somebody saw us."

MacClary obviously heard Adam because he said, "Don't worry, it shouldn't be too much longer."

* * *

MacClary hung up the phone and walked around the conference table in his embassy office. Just then Jennifer called.

"Professor Reinisch called from the Archaeological Institute in Vienna," she said.

MacClary let out a relieved sigh and sat down on one of the elegant chairs.

"He wanted to let you know that he would be at the site in less than three hours. I think you should tell Ryan so he'll be looking for him at the right time. It'll also help him endure the cold. It gets pretty bad there this time of year."

"I'll try to reach him right now," MacClary said, signing off. He hit Ryan's number, hoping the man's phone could get reception.

CHAPTER 17

THE MAGDALENSBERG – EARLY MORNING

Ryan had lain down on a rock ledge in the second chamber when a sound startled him. At first he thought it was just more earth sliding down. But the sound came again. Something was definitely moving outside the entrance to the cave. As he stood to investigate, everything suddenly went dark around him. The work lights had all gone dead at the same time.

Ryan reached into his jacket pocket to pull out a gun. He didn't get that far. A blow to the head threw him back against the cave wall. The lights went back on and he saw a masked man dressed in black lunging at him. Dazed, but getting back to his feet, Ryan yelled, "Who in the devil are you people?"

Then a second blow hit him. As he fell, Ryan ripped the mask from his attacker's head, taking a clump of hair with him. The enraged man screamed and then delivered a devastating kick to Ryan's ribs. Ryan tried desperately to make out the face of his attacker, but a second later everything went black.

* * *

"Leave him there. He's not going anywhere," Salvoni said coldly, signaling his men to follow him so that they could get to work. He was fuming as he looked around the cave, thinking about how his worries had been trivialized over the past few days and how wrong everyone else had been.

The men hastily began to pack artifacts into the prepared boxes they had brought with them, but Salvoni was sure that the two who had already left had the most important items with them.

* * *

Ryan gradually came around. His head was throbbing, and with every breath he took the pain in his chest was so overwhelming that he wanted to scream. It took superhuman effort for him to keep lying still. If he didn't move, maybe they would just leave him there. He had already tied his scroll onto his back under his jacket, so there was no way he could hide it beneath the debris.

As he lay there, he tried to steal glances at his assailants. One was wearing the ring of the St. Pius X Brotherhood. Apparently one of the shadiest sects inside the Catholic Church had their dirty fingers all over this operation. Ryan tried not to panic as he considered the implications for the world…and for himself.

* * *

Salvoni moved the men on. He knew there wasn't much time left. There were no sightseers at this time of year, and there was not a person to be seen far and wide. But anyone by a window at the inn next door could see activity, and it was quite possible that someone had already called the police. And his men had attacked too quickly and too violently, so they wouldn't be able to learn more from the man in the cave. This was not going at all the way he'd intended.

* * *

Georg Winter had his hand on the telephone when his son, who was standing at the window peering through the foggy night, said, "Just leave it! We shouldn't get mixed up in this. It looks to me like a Cobra special operations unit. We'll make fools of ourselves if we call up the police like some suburban housewife catching someone parking illegally."

Resigned, Winter let his hand drop. He didn't feel right about this, because he was sure he had heard people walking over the lot, maybe coming out of the forest, unusual for this time, but the boy was probably right. It was usually not a good idea to get mixed up in these sorts of things.

* * *

Salvoni gave a last look at the man lying motionless on the floor and crossed himself.

"What should we do with him?" one of his people asked as he made his way to the exit with the last of the boxes.

"Leave him here, set the rest on fire, and close up the cave so no one will notice it." Perhaps it was a good thing that the Austrian special operations unit Salvoni had requested hadn't come after all. Most likely no one would pay any attention to this mountainside ever again. The rain, which had recently started and was getting heavier by the minute, would wipe away all traces that anything had been here.

CHAPTER 18

Having met Markus Steinberger in Klagenfurt, Shane and Deborah were on the empty early-morning autobahn headed toward Vienna, Steinberger and his sons driving a hundred yards behind them.

"Give me your cell phone," Shane said. "I need to find out if Thomas is all right."

Deborah handed him the phone. "You won't reach him. He's still in the cave, and there's no reception there."

"I'm not calling Thomas," Shane said as he dialed MacClary.

"Deborah, is everything all right?" MacClary said, his voice anxious. "I was just about to call."

"It's Adam, Professor. I needed to call you because I don't have a good feeling about Thomas. Why did we leave him back in the cave? If nothing else, we could have stored the artifacts in Klagenfurt and waited for him there."

"We couldn't do that, Adam. Every minute counts. The scrolls need to be preserved immediately. You have to respect Ryan's decision. Believe me, Ryan and I know exactly what we're doing and why we're doing it."

"But—"

"Believe me, everything is fine. The rest of the artifacts will be retrieved by the Viennese archaeologists. We'll try to reach Ryan so he can leave the cave soon, but just in case, I told the head of the Archaeological Institute that he's there."

Shane tried to take solace in MacClary's words, but his tension refused to ease. "All right. Thank you, Ronald. I just want Thomas to come back to Dublin quickly. He should be there when we establish the value of the trove."

"Where are you now?"

"We'll be in Vienna in about two hours, I think."

"Fantastic. Call me when you're at the airport."

Shane hung up and was about to give Deborah her cell phone back when he noticed her looking intently out the right side mirror.

"Deborah, what's wrong?"

"I don't know. Maybe I'm just imagining things, but it's very strange. There's been a car behind Steinberger's following us."

* * *

Cassidy was getting more furious by the minute. There hadn't been a single opportunity to make a move without any witnesses, and he couldn't reach Salvoni to determine a new course of action.

All he could do was drive.

* * *

THE MAGDALENSBERG – EARLY MORNING

Salvoni headed toward the bus. To all outward appearances he seemed completely at ease, but inside, thoughts were rushing through his head. What would be the fallout from this operation? What did it all mean for his own future? He had just learned from Cassidy that the other two, apparently protected by friends, were driving unchallenged toward Vienna. Lambert would go berserk when he found out.

* * *

Ryan had gotten lucky. As the cave burned, he had quickly managed to dig his way through the mud to the surface. Were his attackers already gone? Were they lying in wait for him somewhere?

He tried to stay calm and to clear his head. Finally, he used his last ounce of strength to dig through a narrow hole. His abused body was so weak, though, that every time he tried to pull himself up the last few feet, he slid back onto the steep slope.

He doubled over in pain. It felt as though he had broken several ribs and was bleeding from several wounds in his head. Was this how he was going to die? Knowing he couldn't let that happen, he drilled his hands into the earth and pulled himself, excruciatingly, to the surface.

He slowly tried to get up and go down the slope. As he reached the edge of the forest near the parking lot, pain screaming through his body, a bus turned the curve and blinded him. He dropped down again onto the muddy ground and took cover in the bushes.

* * *

Adriano Paltini was just cleaning his gun when he happened to look out the rear window. Was there something moving in the brush? He was going to dismiss it as a figment of his imagination, but then habit and discipline took over. He went to look for Salvoni to report what he'd seen.

* * *

Ryan lay behind the bush, groaning. The pain was excruciating enough, and now the headlights of the bus had blinded him to the point that he could only see bright spots in front of his eyes. He searched his jacket pocket for his cell phone, but the effort made him double over in pain again.

The first thing he saw when he got his vision back were the lights in the window of the inn. Apparently someone was still awake there, although it had to be after three o'clock in the morning. What if he asked them for help? "You don't have anything to lose, Thomas," he said to himself, trying to get up his courage.

Hopefully nothing had happened to Shane and Deborah. If everything had gone according to plan, they would be close to Vienna by now.

Ryan pulled himself up and began to drag himself toward the inn. As he did, he felt the presence of someone else.

And then everything went black again.

CHAPTER 19

"Father!" the young man yelled at the top of his lungs. "Come down and help me carry this man in the house. He's wounded and he needs help."

"Slow down, now, I'm coming, I'm coming!" The old innkeeper dragged himself out of the house into the pouring rain. "We really should call the police now."

"If we call anyone, it should be an ambulance."

Georg Winter grabbed the injured man under his right arm while his son took the left side. They carried him carefully over the lot and up to the inn. Irena, the young waitress who had been waiting there, opened the door, and the two men dragged the unconscious body into one of the lower guest rooms where they heaved him onto the bed.

"My God," the woman said when she got a good look, "we need to call the hospital immediately."

* * *

Ryan slowly rose again from the darkness. He was lying on a bed and he heard voices. Someone was talking about sending him to the hospital.

"Wait," he said, his voice and the rudiments of his German sounding unusually thick to his ears. "Where am I?"

"We've been watching what's going on," a male voice said. Ryan tried to focus on the figure. "There were quite a few people here and a lot of boxes."

"I can explain," Ryan said slowly, trying to sound normal. The last thing he needed was an ambulance, since it would almost certainly lead to an appearance by the police. "I don't know who those men were, but I know they were looking for the same thing…uh…I was."

"They didn't exactly look friendly," grumbled an older man as a young woman gave Ryan a glass of water.

Ryan took a sip, surprised at how welcome it was. "I need to get going. I promise I won't cause you any problems."

"You should stay here for a while," the younger of the two men insisted. "First, it doesn't look as if you can walk very well yet, and second, I saw some of the men climb out of the bus only about a hundred yards from here."

"That means they saw me," Ryan said, searching for his cell phone. "This is very bad."

"We'll be glad to help you," the older gentleman said, "but you have to tell us a bit more."

"It has to do with something found here during World War II. Apparently the men with the bus didn't want my friends and me to retrieve it."

"Italians," the older man said.

"What?"

"They were Italians. I saw their license plate."

Ryan groaned inwardly, knowing he needed to move faster than his body and his circumstances would allow. If his attackers were actually being controlled by the Vatican, then Shane, Deborah, and even the professor were in serious danger.

* * *

AUTOBAHN TOWARD ROME – 4:00 A.M.

Salvoni sat fuming next to the driver of the bus. He had left some men back at the Magdalensberg to find out if Paltini had just seen a ghost or if Ryan had, against all odds, really managed to escape from the cave.

His cell phone rang.

"Did you find him?"

"The people from the inn did and brought him inside, Padre."

"Unbelievable. How could this happen to us? Did he have anything with him?"

"No, he didn't."

"Let me know if you learn anything else."

Salvoni was simmering with rage. The whole operation was threatening to slip through his fingers. First he had been ordered to wait, then the promised reinforcements never showed up, and now two of the interlopers were serenely making their way to Vienna on the autobahn, and the third, who he had assumed would never again see the light of day, was lying in a warm bed at the inn.

Lambert would waste no time blaming Salvoni for everything. It was always the same story: when a scandal broke, they distanced themselves and pointed to the mistakes of particular underlings. That's how they had managed for centuries to protect the Vatican and the Holy Father from any kind of investigation or harm.

Salvoni's cell phone rang again.

"Yes."

"Padre, what we're recording here is somewhat troubling," one of his men said. "The judge is hoping that the find will allow him to take legal action against the Vatican."

Salvoni's already raw nerves flamed. "Stop your work and get out of there. I'll get back to you with your next orders."

* * *

In Rome, Vincent Contas, the head of the Congregation for the Doctrine of Faith, was getting ready to receive the legendary "library of the pagans." He was rarely at the archive so early, and he felt an eerie silence throughout the rooms where the historical treasures of the earlier Roman Inquisition were stored directly next to the rooms of the Congregation for the Doctrine of Faith. Nowhere else on earth had an institution tried so intensely for centuries to control the most dangerous medium next to the Bible: the book.

Contas was curious why the pagan Druids had been willing to suspend their ban on writing. As he looked around, he could see Padre Econo, who was setting up a room for the examination and conservation of the scrolls. He was one of the best restorers in the world and an acknowledged expert in the field of Celtic cultural history.

"How are you, Padre?" Contas called to him from a good fifty feet away.

"Oh, Cardinal, thank you. I'm doing splendidly. I see the excitement brought you here early today as well?"

"Not so much as you might think," Contas said, playing down the issue. "From antiquity to the present day, lost souls out there who have turned away from the Church are always pouncing on the legends of the Druids. They do this in the vain attempt to prove their pagan ideals, and they'll often use questionable or ostensibly historical sources if need be."

"Now, Cardinal, for every word that has been written about the Druids, there are just as many erroneous ideas. Nevertheless, we know that there's more to the story and…"

"Save your energy, Padre. You know very well I don't share your enthusiasm for this superstition. The time for these soulless denominations has passed, and it won't come again." Contas crossed himself. "The whole uproar isn't because of the actual meaning of these artifacts. It's just that they shouldn't fall into hands that don't mean us well."

* * *

INN AT THE MAGDALENSBERG – EARLY MORNING

Ryan was still lying down in the guest room. He had found the cell phone, covered in mud. His wallet, however, was missing, along with all of his travel documents. He'd managed to convince his rescuers not to call the police, assuring them that he would show his appreciation for their hospitality and help.

"Thank you so much," Ryan said to Irena, the waitress who had bandaged his wounds and laid out some fresh clothes on a chair. He was using a hair dryer in an attempt to dry out the cell phone enough to make it work again. He had to let MacClary know what was going on. He wasn't getting anywhere, though. Frustrated, he turned off the dryer and lay back in bed to rest for a while.

His eyes fell on the box with the parchment. He had been so lucky that the box hadn't hit a stone when he fell back against the wall. Instead, it had slipped into a recess.

Exactly 1,625 years after his druidic ancestor had written this parchment, it lay next to him now. Even with his meager knowledge of Latin, Ryan had been able to translate enough to know what a shattering effect this evidence would have. Most people still believed that the triumph of Christianity had led to a humanization of the wild, uncouth pagans.

Christianity can't imagine faith and love without a death toll, Ryan thought. The image of the crucified God, the passion history, and all the martyr legends apparently served only to prepare and justify their own atrocities toward the heretics and the pagans. Maybe, in the end, his scroll and the things that Deborah and Shane had brought to Dublin would lead Christians to accept their historical truth.

Everything went dark again, but this time it was sleep that finally triumphed over his thoughts.

CHAPTER 20

VIENNA TO DUBLIN – MARCH 18, MORNING

Shane had gotten less than two hours of sleep on the plane before they landed in Dublin. Instead of a commercial airline, MacClary had a chartered jet waiting for them at the airport. Everything else in Vienna had gone incredibly smoothly as well, and Shane was completely overwhelmed with the whole experience. Never in his wildest dreams would he have thought he would get to take part in an adventure like this.

It was gradually becoming clear to him that he had found more than just an explanation for people's rootlessness. Thanks to the discoveries in the cave, he could now see the crossroad in front of him where humanity had made the wrong turn. Who knew what other truths Deborah would be able to glean from the parchment?

Shane gently shook Deborah's shoulder. "We've landed."

The linguist had curled up in the fetal position in her chair and was now looking at him, hollow eyed and pale. "What? Oh…has MacClary called yet?"

Shane pointed out the cockpit window. On the edge of the landing field, they could see MacClary with Jennifer standing next to him.

"Am I glad we're here! I hope the scrolls have held up well," Deborah said, giving one more huge yawn before she got herself out of the seat with some effort.

The plane slowly came to a stop in front of a hangar. There they could already see a delivery van and MacClary's limousine. Deborah grabbed her things and went to the boxes that they had put on the empty seats. The artifacts had to be brought immediately to the place MacClary had prepared for them. "I'll be curious to see what else is coming our way," Deborah said as she opened the door.

"Adam, Deborah," Jennifer said as they deplaned. "I am incredibly happy to see you. Let's start right in packing up the boxes."

MacClary was about to greet them when his cell phone rang. He stepped to the side to take the call. But in the same moment he turned around, his whole face beaming. "Ryan! Where in the devil have you been? There should be an archaeology team from Vienna there by now and—"

The professor's expression dropped. He turned on the phone's speaker so everyone could hear.

"I was within an inch of being killed. Apparently our mission wasn't a secret at all. Who did you discuss it with?"

MacClary shook his head, at a loss. "No one! I don't understand. Do you have any idea where these people came from?"

"I can't tell you for sure who they were, but I can draw my own conclusions. They were very professional, and they didn't think twice about leaving me in a burning cave. It's a miracle I got out alive. The family that's been taking care of me was able to see the license plate of the bus they drove away in. It came from Italy."

"But how could someone in Rome have found out about our plans? Where are you now?"

"I'm still at the inn, waiting until the coast is clear. I'm afraid someone saw me when I escaped the cave. We can't talk anymore right now. Someone might even be listening in on us. I'm going to throw away my cell phone, but I want to tell you one more thing. I've found what I was looking for. The circle is complete, and I won't take any chances. I'm not safe near you right now. The thing that you've been discussing, purely theoretically, with Jennifer, well, let's just say that it might actually be possible."

The color rose on MacClary's face. "What do you mean by that? Please, stay where you are. I'll have you picked up and brought safely to Dublin…"

"No, listen to me. We'll do this differently. Plan B. I think you know the best place for me to go. In any case, I'll need some time to recover. When the dust has settled a bit, I'll contact you again. I have a good friend who can help me. Ronald, trust me, I know what I'm doing."

MacClary seemed resigned to Thomas's will. "One last question, Thomas. What happened to the rest of the artifacts?"

"Everything was destroyed or stolen. Put Deborah on the phone."

"You're on speaker."

Deborah stepped closer so Thomas would be able to hear her clearly. "Thomas, damn it, what happened? You—"

"Ronald will explain it. We don't have much time. Please take care of yourselves. You have to translate the parchments quickly, and they have to be stored in an absolutely secure spot."

"What are you going to do in the meantime?"

"Don't worry about me. I'll join you with the other scroll soon enough. I have to get off now. See you soon."

"Thomas…" Deborah stopped speaking into the phone when she realized Thomas was no longer there. "Why does he always have to be so pigheaded?"

"What happened?" Jennifer asked impatiently.

"He wants to go to Washington," MacClary said. "But I don't understand…"

"Don't you, Ronald?" Jennifer interrupted. "It's pretty obvious what he wants to do in Washington. It was you who put these crazy ideas in his head. Now, apparently, he believes that he really has something there."

"He *does* have something," Deborah said.

Shane had been watching the conversation as though he hadn't been standing in the middle of it. Now he intervened. "Wait a minute; let's go over this again calmly. We have dozens of parchments here. We have Thomas with another apparently explosive scroll, and we seem to have some sort of henchmen from the Vatican who are most likely examining and preserving the remaining scrolls."

"How do you know that?" Deborah said. "Perhaps they destroyed everything. And even if they bring the artifacts to Rome, how does that help us?"

MacClary took a step toward them. "Can we discuss this later? We have to get away from here."

"Where are we going?" Shane asked.

"I was lucky. My many invitations to the bustling embassies in Dublin have given me access to a basement where Deborah can work protected and undisturbed."

Shane made eye contact with MacClary. "And what will you do?"

"First we'll drive home. Not a word to Ms. Copendale, though. She'd wring my neck if she found out about your adventures, and especially about Ryan, and I don't want to burden her old heart any more than necessary. Jennifer and I will fly to Washington as soon as we can. I think it's time to do some investigating."

CHAPTER 21

ROME – MARCH 18, MORNING

Lambert was still waiting for a phone call from Salvoni. He hadn't spoken with the man since yesterday, and he was starting to get a bad feeling. Perhaps he should have taken old Morati's warnings more seriously and paid more attention to Salvoni's advice.

As he turned the corner, he saw to his surprise and relief that the Vatican bus was parked in front of the entrance and that Salvoni's men had already brought most of the artifacts into the archive. Lambert entered and couldn't believe his eyes. He had rarely seen so much activity here. The room was full of boxes, and at least a dozen men were running around, frantically working on the preparations for storing and examining the artifacts. Salvoni was sitting in one of the back rooms making telephone calls. He gave a quick wave to Lambert.

"Good, just keep waiting there," Salvoni said into the phone. "He has to come out sometime. When he does, follow him. You'll be getting more backup. But don't grab him unless he's carrying something suspicious. Do you understand?"

When Salvoni hung up, Lambert confronted him. "Why didn't you report back to me?"

"Excuse me, Cardinal, but your last remarks left me with the impression that you felt Padre Morati and I were wasting our time chasing after an old and irrelevant legend. I have conducted myself accordingly."

"Very well. The good Lord will know what the truth of the matter is. You, on the other hand, still seem to be seeking satisfaction. Weren't you the one who asked for more trust between us? Unless I am sorely mistaken, you are still sworn to God and the Holy See, not to your own wounded vanity."

Salvoni seemed to consider this briefly, then abruptly changed the subject. "Why didn't we get any reinforcements last night? If we had, we would have had no problems completing the expedition."

"Well, unfortunately, recent events have made even our Austrian friends less eager to get mixed up in a sticky situation for us. I managed to arrange plenty of time for you by postponing the arrival of the archaeological team from Vienna. At least I could take care of that much."

"How? I don't understand."

"Your judge just made the find official," Lambert said resentfully. "I only found out about it through a contact in the foreign ministry. That was how I was able to arrange for the necessary delay."

Salvoni looked away and then glanced back up at Lambert. "Well, perhaps you should see what we've brought back, Cardinal."

Salvoni guided him toward the artifacts. Even a cursory glance at the scrolls left a lasting impression. Lambert walked around between the restorers and the boxes until his eyes locked onto one particular parchment. He could only make out a few lines, but the words *Genesis* and *Pharaoh* made him immediately uneasy. As he continued, he found a young worker translating a treatise against the Christians written by a Druid who had lived at the court of Theodosius I. It depicted with startling clarity the practices for which the pagans of Europe had been first denounced and then persecuted, tortured, and killed for having. There was a report in different handwriting about the religious tolerance of the Christians until Constantine seized power. Then suddenly even the original Christians were being persecuted. The report ended with the escape of many Christians into the deserts of the Middle East, or even as far as India.

Lambert sat down and tried to process what he was seeing. He could never have imagined that a find like this would be possible, but he was sure now that what lay before him was as significant as the Qumran scrolls. It didn't matter what else they found. If these writings were made public, they would fan the flames of the atheists, the critics of the Church, and those scientists who were disseminating all sorts of theories about a creation without

God. This criminal nonsense was already fueling speculation among the faithful and the unfaithful throughout the world. Even in the pontifical academy there was an increasing number of people discussing this sacrilege—and with complete impunity.

On another scroll there were drawings of stags, bulls, boars, and hares, the graven images of the Celts. The Druids identified themselves with these animals. They were their familiar spirits, deeply anchored in the Celtic consciousness. Lambert knew from his own research that the ancient religions didn't identify these images with gods; they only used them as representative symbols. The cults related to this so-called idol worship had been used for ages as proof of the animalistic and godless nature of the pagan religions. It didn't matter if Ambrosius or Gregory of Nyssa were called to be the chief witnesses: the extermination of the pagans was from the outset a holy duty of the Church.

The sheer volume of these artifacts was alarming, even more so because a great number—it was impossible to say how great—was in the hands of a powerful critic of the Church. Lambert would have to report all this to the Holy Father. This matter couldn't be swept under the carpet, and as soon as the public got wind of it, it would come back to haunt the Church. This wasn't good. It wasn't good at all.

"Salvoni, I have to beg your forgiveness, and probably even more so that of Padre Morati, but we're concerned here with documents from a time when the young

Church of Jesus Christ had to ward off an unbelievable number of lies and heresies. We cannot allow these things to get into the wrong hands again. What does MacClary actually have?"

"I can't tell you for sure, but before we got there, one of my men saw several boxes being transported away. And then there is this Thomas Ryan, who attacked me in the cave. He got away, but empty-handed, and we have his papers."

"Good. Give them to me. I'll use every channel to make sure we get ahold of him, and you should keep your people there as well. Perhaps we can make MacClary see reason. We'll try to frame him for this. In the meantime, try to figure out what he's planning and what he has."

"Cardinal, I'm afraid that will be difficult," Salvoni stammered. "We had to pull our people out of Dublin. I just can't be sure that we haven't been compromised."

"I don't understand. You weren't recognized in Austria, were you?"

"No, but you yourself said that MacClary officially reported the find. It's possible that he might figure out who got the drop on whom. Then there's this Irishman, as I said, whom we surprised…"

"Salvoni! Do you know what that means?"

"Yes, of course. That's what I've been talking about the whole time! We need a one-hundred-percent airtight denial. Your job, Cardinal. There is absolutely no proof that we were there, and suspicions have never harmed us. In any case, I can think of dozens of secret services who would have an interest in someone of MacClary's stature."

Lambert was astounded by Salvoni's callousness and composure, but it also helped boost his own confidence in the situation.

"Good, then it's about time we make certain arrangements in Washington. We need to show the judge his limits. You go ahead as we've discussed, and I'll take care of the rest."

Salvoni fell back into a chair, his relief apparent. "Yes, Cardinal. The Lord be with you, and thank you for your confidence."

"We'll see, Salvoni."

CHAPTER 22

DUBLIN – MARCH 18, MORNING

Jennifer and Shane had taken a taxi from the US embassy to MacClary's house. Shane found himself, to his surprise, leaning against Jennifer's shoulder when she gently woke him and paid for the taxi.

"I'm sorry, but we hardly had a chance to close our eyes for a minute on the plane," Shane said in excuse, still carrying with him Jennifer's pleasant scent.

"It's fine, Adam," she said, laughing, as she opened the door to the house. "You already know where the guest room is."

Ms. Copendale hurried up to them, bursting with curiosity. "Oh, someone looks like he's in desperate need of fresh clothes and a bath."

"Thank you, Ms. Copendale, but breakfast and forty winks sound even better right now."

"Of course," she said, patting his arm. "Where can I serve you breakfast?"

Jennifer chuckled. "Ruth, we'd love to come into your warm kitchen. You must know that I don't need things as grandiose as the *gentleman of the house*. And you, Adam?"

"What? Uh, yes, of course, gladly," Shane said, nodding eagerly.

Ms. Copendale eyed him with evident curiosity. "So? Have the children found what they were looking for on the playground?"

She'd obviously meant this as a joke, but neither Jennifer nor Shane could manage a laugh. This reaction caused Ms. Copendale's expression to darken. "Where are Ronald, Deborah, and Thomas?"

Since Jennifer didn't seem to know what she should say, Shane took the initiative. "Deborah and Ronald are in the embassy examining the artifacts at a secure location, and Thomas is still in Austria, because he was absolutely set on watching over the rest." He didn't have the heart to sugarcoat it. "Well…and then he was slightly injured when someone attacked him, but he's fine now, I think."

Ms. Copendale looked down at the floor. "I saw this coming all along, but no one listens to me."

"What did you see coming all along?" Jennifer asked.

"Well, it doesn't matter anymore, anyhow." Ms. Copendale took a deep breath before going on. "Ronald's father died shortly after the war, but not as a result of his wounds, as most people think. A doctor found a poison pill in his mouth after his death."

Jennifer buried her face in her hands. Shane shook his head in wonder.

"You mean he was murdered?" Slowly Shane was beginning to realize how explosive this find actually was. And what about the parchment scroll that Thomas had taken with him? He had kept quiet about its true significance—and perhaps about more than that.

"In the short time that Lisa lived after that," Ms. Copendale continued, "she was afraid that the same thing could happen to Ronald. That's why she destroyed any evidence that could lead him in that direction, without burdening him with the truth about the death of his father. But then this Thomas Ryan turns up with his obsession to claim the legacy of the Druids, and since then…"

"Well, and then I come and find the clue straight off. It's so strange, but perhaps it was just the right time for it," Shane said, trying to reassure her.

"Very well. When all's said and done you'll have to bear the responsibility for it yourselves. But never forget how many people will be affected by this. One and a half billion Christian souls live on this earth, and most of them are just good people who need hope. Never forget that every one of these people will be affected by your actions."

With that, she walked away.

"I'll also not forget how many people have already been affected by this," Shane called after her, a bit miffed at her implied accusation.

"Adam, let her be. You have no idea what she's going through. She comes from a time when the power of the Catholic Church had a completely different authority."

"That's not very much compared to nearly two thousand years of terror and banishment, don't you agree?"

"I think you don't completely understand what this is all about, Adam."

"Oh, yes, I do. I can even describe it to you in exact detail." Shane was feeling that pain again, the same that he had felt on the night of his vision. He could see the executed men and the desperate masses. Even trying to talk about it brought tears to his eyes. He steadied his voice with a great effort. "I have seen, and even more, I feel what has happened over the centuries. And it's exactly for this reason that I want to encourage you to keep on this path. It's not just about setting limits for the Church. We have a historic opportunity—perhaps even a duty—to present this historic truth and its immeasurable aftermath. I can no longer stand by knowing that nearly every spiritual legacy of this world has been exterminated. Do you understand? Ten years ago, even the last of the Aborigines said that they were going and leaving the world, leaving it to a changed people, and..."

He broke down in tears, unable to go on.

* * *

Jennifer knew the story. In Australia, members of the last free-living tribe of this oldest culture in the world, the "true people" as they called themselves, had told their story to an American woman. Since their spiritual places and customs had been desecrated and since they were being deprived of the land where they lived, they saw no more reason to live. So they had made a decision to stop reproducing, to leave the earth.

Jennifer had the feeling that time was standing still. She could inhale Adam's sympathy and compassion like the air that she breathed.

She lay her arm around his shoulders. Now *she* was in tears. She was thinking about her work for the Blackfoot Indians. The shattered dignity of this proud people had deeply moved her as well as she watched their last representatives fighting in court for the miserable crumbs of their culture. A court of the country that had destroyed them. Adam's emotional outburst reminded her of a dream that she'd often had as a child. An old Native American in traditional dress squatted on a cliff in the Rocky Mountains, looking down, in tears, into the valley of his homeland and his gods. She had never understood why she had dreamed that, but she had always felt something like a deep weariness with the world, an agonizing memory, which had completely confused her as a child.

"It's time we all started taking responsibility for this," she said softly. "I'll talk with Ronald."

She gave Adam a tender kiss on the cheek, surprising herself with the gesture and unsure how Adam would take it.

"We'll still need a lot of courage, Adam. At some point in court you learn a bitter lesson: if the guilt seems too great and there are too many victims, the criminals have a tendency to portray themselves as victims and look for the most absurd explanations for their acts. Or they develop an unbelievable story to distance themselves from the burden of their responsibility." With that, she began to walk away.

Adam looked up at her, his composure obviously returning. "Hey, where are you going?"

"I have to think, Adam Shane. I just have to think. And for that, I need to get some space. Please, stay here. I won't be long."

* * *

AMERICAN EMBASSY, DUBLIN – MORNING

Deborah was completely transported. Everything she'd been able to translate in the last hour demonstrated the magnitude and wealth of knowledge that had been stored in this secret library. It was like a revelation and an indictment at the same time.

"My God, these sketches are building plans that use the teachings of Pythagoras," she said to herself. "It's true then. The Druids had access to this knowledge." She remembered that only recently on Mont Beuvray, a good thirty miles west of Autun in France, the use of the Pythagorean theorem had been proven in the construction of a water basin more than 2,500 years old.

Proud and awestruck at the same time, Deborah sat in the middle of the embassy basement in a climate-controlled tent and preserved the parchment. First she opened them under high temperatures and high humidity, so that she could photograph them, and then she secured them under glass.

On another scroll there were numerous symbols, including one that reminded her of the Bohr atomic model. "Can that really be?" she wondered aloud.

"So, Deborah, how's it coming?" MacClary said, breaking her from her reverie. He'd unexpectedly come down into the basement room and was walking around like a fascinated little boy among the spread-out scrolls.

"I'm still in a state of shock. Just look here." Deborah pointed to the drawings and sketches she had just discovered.

"Unbelievable. That reminds me of the story of the all-knowing one that my uncle tried to get me to believe," MacClary said as he sat next to Deborah at the table.

"The all-knowing one?"

"Yes, that's what he called the initiates. They were, according to the legend, the preservers of an old advanced civilization that knew the creation story of humankind. They were also supposedly very advanced technologically."

"You're not talking about Atlantis or Mu or something like that?"

"No, no, that would just be more mystic paraphrasing for something that the newly arising centers of power in the East and Rome were afraid of."

"I don't understand a word you're saying."

MacClary took a deep breath and continued. "These so-called initiates, my dear Deborah, were no conspirators.

Quite the contrary, they always represented the forces that tried, with patience and wisdom, to disentangle precisely those conspiracies and that confusion that had been built up to herd the masses into spiritual and material addiction. They tried to explain things in the framework of the perceptible world and to explain the question of 'from where' and 'where to' regarding our genesis and our demise. This was a far cry from using a god to explain this. In contrast to the religious scholars who were always servants to power, the initiates, with very few exceptions, shared all of their knowledge with their inquisitive students so that it could be transferred into the common experience."

"That's incredible! I still don't understand the half of it, but…"

"I'm firmly convinced that truths have been kept from us in a battle that has been waged for centuries, truths that were a key to explaining creation in a way that had little to do with the deities we promoted. It wouldn't be so difficult to explain the history of humankind if it hadn't been hidden in legends or destroyed by interference from the ruling castes."

"And the Druids were…?"

"The last of these initiates. Initiates who could have helped today's metaphysicists, theologists, and philosophers by providing incredible contributions to the clarification of the question of creation—with or without a god."

"That's why they had to die and were persecuted."

"Exactly! The Vatican played a large part in that. What we have lying in front of us here is important, of course, but it's nothing in comparison to what would await us in the Vatican's archives, as long they haven't, in their insanity, destroyed everything there."

"Well, the apple that Adam bit into takes on a whole new meaning, then," Deborah said, grinning, as she turned to open the next scroll.

MacClary roared with laughter. "Very good, my dear friend, very good. You've got a handle on that message from the Old Testament as well."

* * *

MacClary's good humor was soon pushed away by far more serious thoughts. One thing was clear: if humans could really explain their origin, the social and cultural consequences would be incalculable. They might even find God, this god who was perhaps only a word, a thought, a bundle of light waves, or perhaps even completely without form.

Sovereignty, as humankind had known it until now, would no longer be possible. Everything that people had believed in for centuries would collapse and Christian values would have no meaning anymore. In their contemporary debates, modern metaphysicists and religious philosophers were already arguing about whether there actually was a deliberate act of creation.

Jennifer had described it once so beautifully: God is not an object. Perhaps people could find God again inside themselves. Not a tangible god, but rather something to be experienced. Something that was best experienced in love—and in the recognition that everything is connected with everything else. There must have been so much knowledge about this back then, and the destruction of this knowledge was worth everything. If there were a place where they might be able to find more, then it would be the Vatican.

"We have to get in there, no matter the cost," he said to himself as he strode toward the telephone and dialed quickly.

"Mr. Langster, I would like to call a special session of the judges for tomorrow at twelve o'clock noon. This is unofficial. Do I make myself clear?"

* * *

Even just a few seconds ago, Deborah hadn't taken MacClary's words that seriously. Now, though, she began to get uneasy looking at one of the last scraps of parchment she had spread open. There were more riddles here. It wasn't written by a Druid or by a pagan; the Latin was too perfect for that, and it was written in a style that would seem to correspond more to that of a Christian monk from that period. However, according to the author, the leaders of the Celts stood closer to the tradition of the creation story than all the other peoples of Europe.

Just as the Vikings had traveled to America a good four hundred years before Columbus, the Druids had been in Asia before the founding of Rome, specifically in India and the Middle East. If they had had contact with the pharaohs, that would explain a lot. There was no proof of that, though, and the writing further down the scroll was so blurred that she couldn't get anything more from it.

"Ronald?" Deborah called out. "I'm done for now."

"Then drive back with me. There's certainly more to do, and we have to see what we can do for your crazy friend Thomas Ryan. Above all, we have to find out who attacked him."

CHAPTER 23

It is you who should fear the judgment you pass, more than I who am receiving it.

—Giordano Bruno

MACCLARY'S HOUSE – MARCH 18, AFTERNOON

The taxi turned into Arbour Hill and came to an abrupt stop, causing MacClary's head to jerk forward.

"Be careful!"

"Sorry," the driver responded quickly, "but that man wasn't watching where he was going."

A somewhat rickety-looking old man was crossing the street without a care, and MacClary saw that the iron gate to his house was just closing. Ms. Copendale had told him yesterday that she had seen an old man regularly walking up and down the street and seemingly watching the house. She said that he'd once even gone to MacClary's door by mistake. After everything that had happened lately, MacClary had an uneasy feeling. The man didn't look in the slightest bit dangerous, but MacClary wanted to get to the bottom of it.

"Deborah, you go on ahead. I'll be there soon."

"What?" Deborah asked. "What are you planning?"

"I'm just going to take a little walk. Alone."

* * *

While Shane was sleeping in the guest room, Jennifer had made herself comfortable in front of the fire in the library again. This chair had been her favorite place for at least fifteen years, as long as she had known Ronald.

Deborah entered and asked after Adam. Before Jennifer could answer, the front door slammed, and Jennifer heard MacClary mutter a curse as he strode into the library.

"My goodness, Ronald, what's gotten into you?" Jennifer asked. She had rarely seen him so furious.

MacClary didn't answer but went directly to his desk. He wrote something on a pad of paper, big enough that they could all read it when he held it up.

THE HOUSE IS BUGGED. WE'RE DRIVING TO THE EMBASSY.

Jennifer was stunned.

"Where's Adam?" MacClary asked, clearly trying to keep his voice calm.

"He's sleeping, but I'll go wake him."

Jennifer went to the guest room and gently opened the door. Adam lay on his stomach, sound asleep.

"Adam, please, wake up," she said, laying her hand on his head. Her mother had always awakened her like that when she was little because Jennifer would become so frightened when woken suddenly.

Adam turned on his back and opened his eyes slowly. "What? Oh, Jennifer, do I have to?"

Jennifer bent down to whisper in his ear. When she told him why he needed to get up, Adam's eyes shot open wide.

* * *

If what Jennifer said was true, it was the best explanation for everything that had happened in Austria. Who was behind it, though? Shane sat up with some difficulty. Slowly he got dressed and tried to organize his racing thoughts. How far would all of this go? A cold feeling was crawling up his spine. More than anything, he was worried about Thomas. What if his attacker could track him down after all?

Just as Shane was coming out of the room, the doorbell rang. Jennifer and Ronald were already standing in the entryway waiting for him with serious expressions on their faces. Only Jennifer gave him a quick smile.

Ronald opened the door, and three young men, dressed inconspicuously and loaded down with bags, greeted him. "We got here as quickly as we could," one of the men said, somewhat out of breath.

"I appreciate your promptness."

Ronald went on to deliver a set of veiled instructions that Shane understood to be directions for sweeping the house of bugs. He then thanked the men and went out. Jennifer and Shane followed him to his car. As MacClary backed out, he said, "We'll talk when we get to the embassy, all right?" Shane understood that Ronald was worried that the car was bugged as well.

* * *

Jennifer looked out the window for the duration of the trip. How did Ronald know so suddenly that they had been bugged? She was sure he had more to tell them.

The steel gate to the embassy grounds opened slowly after they were cleared. The ambassador, John Baxter, was already waiting in front of the entrance.

"Good evening, Mr. MacClary," the ambassador said. "I hope we could take care of everything to your satisfaction. Have you already spoken with Washington?"

"No, I haven't. I have to clarify a few things, before I get everyone riled up."

"Understood."

The four walked to the office Ronald used at the embassy. As soon as he closed the door, Ronald's face dropped. "Adam, I have no idea how to say this. I need to apologize to you. And to you as well, Jennifer. I neither wanted nor expected that this would go so far. I think it's time we let it go. This insanity must stop immediately."

Jennifer found herself instantly agitated by Ronald's words. "You want to give up? *Now*, when you finally have everything you need?"

"I can't bear the responsibility for this anymore. The news that my home was bugged will spread like wildfire through Washington. The ambassador can't keep it a secret without risking his own head. And then the attack on Thomas... What have I started? I'm going to turn over the artifacts to the appropriate archaeological institute in London immediately. I'm sure someone there will be aware of their significance. But we are out of this."

Ronald sat down, looking older than Jennifer had ever seen him. Adam had been silent until now, but he spoke at last. "Ronald, honestly, I don't understand. You can't really—"

"I can't do anything at all, Adam. I have a responsibility to my position, and I have sworn an oath not to endanger the content and processes of the office with my own private ambitions."

Jennifer couldn't let Ronald continue down this road. "Tell me something, Ronald. Has Ruth ever told you anything about what happened to your father?"

Ronald looked at her curiously. "What could she tell me that I don't already know?"

Jennifer sat to deliver this news. "Your father was ready to risk his life for his work, and he paid for it with his life."

Ronald paled. "What are you saying?"

"So you really have no idea."

"Idea about what?"

"Ruth told us that your father was poisoned. Your mother and Ruth swore that you would never find out about it, and they've spent a lifetime trying to keep you from following in his footsteps. They were afraid that you would suffer his fate."

Jennifer didn't realize immediately that there were tears pouring down her face. Even as she spoke the last words, she knew that this revelation would change everything.

Even her own life.

* * *

MacClary was so agitated that he needed to control himself to avoid sputtering. "Why didn't Ruth ever tell me? I mean…"

"Because things happen when the time is right," Adam interjected. Ronald had practically forgotten that the man was there.

"Please, Adam, with all due respect, how can you possibly know that?"

"Because I have seen things in the cave, in the texts, and over the last few days. Because I've realized why it's sometimes important to follow what might seem to be the wrong path. Ronald, you can't put your tail between your legs and run away just because your reputation as a judge is at stake."

MacClary shook his head sharply. "You have no idea what you're talking about. It's not about me; it's about the possible harm this could cause in Washington toward all the loyal people who took an oath to serve."

Jennifer leaned toward him. "Ronald, you must have known this wouldn't be a walk in the park. And after everything that's happened, you owe it to Ryan to continue."

MacClary stood up and went to the window. There was too much coming at him too quickly. He was deeply hurt that his mother and Ms. Copendale had kept the truth from him for all these years. What Jennifer had told him was entirely consistent with his own memories, though. Just a few days before his death, his father had been completely confident that he would be able to leave the hospital soon. He still had so many plans, and they had even joked a little.

Then he had died, without any apparent reason.

Jennifer was right. He would never forgive himself if he gave up now. He turned away from the window, looked at the two of them, and squared his shoulders.

"So what do you two suggest?"

CHAPTER 24

INN AT THE MAGDALENSBERG – MARCH 18, AFTERNOON

Ryan had slept for a long time. Every breath he took still made his ribs hurt, but the pain in his head was subsiding, and he could think clearly again. He desperately needed to do that. He didn't have many options to get himself out of this situation and safely to Washington. Without papers, it would be almost impossible.

"So, my dear Brian," he muttered to himself, "I think it's time for you to repay your debts."

Brian Langster was an old friend from Ryan's youth. Ryan had saved Langster's life in a shootout in Belfast, and they had been good friends for a long time. Out of concern for his own safety, Langster had left Ireland about ten years ago. The fact that he happened to live in Italy now was an ironic twist of fate for Ryan. On the other hand, though, Italy was the last place people would suspect Ryan to be.

Ryan used his cell phone to find the number, but he made the call from the telephone next to his bed. It took a while before a familiar voice answered. "Brian, damn it, it's good to hear your voice. I need your help, and I'm afraid it's going to be difficult."

"Thomas Ryan," was the deliberate reply from the voice on the other end of the line. "This is indeed a surprise. What can I do for you?"

"I'm sitting in Austria near the Italian border. I'm a bit the worse for wear, and I have to get to Washington in the next few days. I don't have my papers anymore, so the situation is a bit sticky."

"A bit. And someone is looking for you, I presume."

"Yes, but it's not what you might be thinking. I'll explain everything when we see each other."

"Where are you?"

"I think it would be easier if you tell me where I should come. I'm not far away."

"All right. If you take the southern autobahn, there's a country road just across the border, the Via Frulli. Take that for about five minutes to an old cottage above the road. There you'll find an old red camper. I'll be waiting there for you. The best time would be tomorrow, right before sunrise. There will be fewer people out and about then. Let's say tomorrow morning at six. I'll wait one hour, no longer."

There it was again, the old fear. Both of them had spent half their lives on the run. From the police, from IRA terrorists, and sometimes just from themselves. The price for a life of resistance against the Irish insanity was high, and Ryan had walked away with many wounds, of the soul as well as the body. His entire family had suffered in this conflict—they had lost their happiness, their joy in life. He had hoped to escape these wounds with his search to revive his true identity and heritage. Yet now he was right back where he had never wanted to be again, on the run, caught between paranoia and rage.

"All right, Brian. Thank you, and I hope you have a couple of days for me. I'll need someplace to recover," Ryan said, almost choking on his bitterness.

"Don't worry, Thomas. Of course. Do you think I've forgotten what you did for me? See you tomorrow morning."

"Thanks. Yes, see you tomorrow." Ryan hung up, lay back down, and started to think. A few minutes later there was a knock at the door.

It was the younger Winter, the innkeeper's son. "Listen, I looked around a bit. I know everyone around here, and even the tourists are easy to spot. There are some people who definitely don't belong here, and there's too much police activity for my taste. I do believe you, but we don't want any trouble here. You understand, don't you?"

"I understand, of course. You don't want anything to do with problems that don't concern you, and no one can hold that against you. I'm so grateful to you for trusting me and for all your help. Tomorrow I'll be gone. I just have to figure out how to get to the Italian border."

"You need a vehicle, don't you?"

"Well, yes…"

"I have a motorcycle that I don't use anymore. You can have it."

Ryan had a large wad of money in one of his jacket pockets. A habit from the old days. Never leave everything in one place, and always have enough with you to go underground for a while if necessary. He picked up the jacket and pulled out the stack of bills.

"No, really, that's not—"

"Yes, it is. Honestly, it's important to me. You've helped me so much." He pressed some bills into the hand of the young man and clapped him on the arm.

Winter shook his head, then took the money and turned to go. "OK, thank you. I hope you get to wherever you're going safely."

Ryan looked after him until the door closed.

Where exactly was he going?

* * *

AMERICAN EMBASSY, DUBLIN – AFTERNOON

Jennifer and MacClary were with Shane in the basement of the embassy looking at the scrolls and discussing how they should proceed in Washington. The plane would take off in a little more than an hour, but they were nowhere near agreement.

"One thing is clear, Ronald: Rome has always been afraid that documents like these would turn up because they justify every critique of the Church."

"Wait a minute," MacClary said, "let's take another look at where we stand. First, we have several testimonials that provide sufficient evidence. Everyone understands that the Vatican has to have a vital interest in keeping these documents far from the public eye. Second, we have a witness who has gone underground with another scroll and is presumably being followed. We don't have any evidence that the Vatican is directly involved in this, but Ryan might be able to testify to this. With his dual citizenship he fulfills the preconditions for a charge in the US. We have bugs in my home, whose origin is unknown. That's everything, and it's quite a lot."

"How did you suddenly find out that the residence was bugged?" Adam asked.

"I should have been able to figure it out for myself, yet I refused to believe it. Then I received a tip. For the moment, that will have to suffice as an explanation, but this source might be able to help us more in the future."

"If Ryan actually manages to get to Washington without being caught," Jennifer said, "we could definitely file the suit in Boston."

Shane shook his head. "How would that work? The Vatican still has immunity."

"That's relative, Adam," MacClary said. "What we want first of all is attention. You're right; we probably won't be able to obtain a judgment against the Vatican. However, we can win one against the actual perpetrators who might be members of one of the organizations of the Vatican." MacClary looked nervously at the clock. "What we don't know is whether Ryan will manage to get to Washington in time, and how far the people in Rome are willing to go. In every rearguard battle, the Vatican has an infinite number of insider contacts throughout the world. The best protection we can offer Ryan is to file the suit as quickly as possible. And if that doesn't work, then we have to generate publicity."

Jennifer nodded. "One thing is for sure: these intrigues are not compatible with the actions of a religious group. This alone will make judges, as well as the average US citizen, sit up and listen."

"Well, I do have to remind you about the case in Mississippi, Jennifer," MacClary noted skeptically. "The judges rejected it because it couldn't be proven that the Holy See was involved and not just the individual people in the case. But it—"

"Wait a minute, please," Adam said, agitated. "We're forgetting what's in these documents. We have evidence in hand that proves that even the founding of the Church involved mass murder—of the pagans, the original civilizations of Europe. It's at least as horrible as a planned genocide, and it's a direct consequence of the founding of the Church."

MacClary held up a hand. "No, no, Adam. That won't work. That's what our friend Thomas is dreaming about, but we can't let ourselves be that naïve. We won't be able to get a criminal conviction for the crimes of the past, only a moral one. But the reaction of the Church in the present is worth its weight in gold, because it only serves one purpose—to cover up the past. And this evidence is part of humankind's community assets. There are supranational cultural assets, such as, for example, the pyramids. The claim to historical truth and information is an asset that belongs to everyone."

Jennifer was nodding emphatically as she strode across the room with her finger pointing in the air. "If we could establish that as a right, and if there are no international treaties covering it—and there aren't any, that much is clear—then Ryan can lay claim to these documents as a direct descendant of the Druids who were murdered by the Christians by order of the pope. Simple." Suddenly she stopped still and looked soberly at MacClary. "But for that, the retrieval of the artifacts would have had to have been carried out officially from the start. And you didn't do that because you wanted to provoke an incident. Publicity. The whole time, you knew that something would happen, and Ryan was on board from the very beginning."

MacClary looked down at the floor for a moment, abashed. Then he looked her straight in the eye. "An incident, perhaps, but not something like this. Ryan and I had something else in mind."

"I suspected you two were up to some childishness. Well, let's make the best of it."

MacClary was watching Shane, who was looking at Jennifer quizzically. "We don't have time now to explain everything," MacClary said. "We have to get to the airport. I promise both of you that I still have a trump card up my sleeve in case the suit is rejected, but don't ask me any questions about it now." He put on his coat. "Adam, if you've had enough of our adventure, you're more than welcome to hold down the fort here with Deborah."

"I accept that offer gladly. What did you think? I'm not going to miss the rest of this story."

"Great! I think we'll still need to be in touch with both of you when Jennifer and I are in Washington. A driver from the embassy will bring you back to Arbour Hill. Everything should have been taken care of by now, I hope."

* * *

Even before Jennifer and MacClary had packed up their last documents, Shane had left the embassy. As the limousine glided through Dublin, he looked out the window. There were still the same old houses, but things had happened in the last few hours that could change the world. How high would the price be for this change?

And more importantly, who would pay it?

CHAPTER 25

DUBLIN'S INNER CITY – EVENING

Instead of heading back home, Shane had the driver take him to the pub where he had first met Thomas and Deborah. As he got out of the car, he pulled up his collar. He was cold, and he knew it wasn't just the bitter March wind.

Just a few days ago, he had been in Austria, lost in senseless frustration, weary of the world. Now he felt like he had found the answer to all the questions that had been plaguing him. It was a frightening answer, though. It meant that billions of people would have to change their way of thinking, and he couldn't imagine that humankind was ready for this, even though belief in Jesus Christ had nothing to do with the Vatican and the discoveries had done nothing to diminish that belief.

Suddenly he found himself looking into Deborah's face, which caused him to laugh aloud.

"What are you doing here, Adam?" she said. "I'd been waiting for you at Ronald's. He told me you were going to stay in Dublin."

"Yes, that's right, but I felt like I needed a break first, and a nice, big beer."

Shane settled into a chair and gestured for Deborah to join him. As she sat, Shane noticed the excitement on her face.

"I was able to translate another parchment. It's written by a chronicler, not a Druid, talking about the fact that the rising bishops no longer had any interest in people living freely. Meanwhile, they were killing all the priests who were spreading the most important lessons of Jesus's teachings, which was that every person could find God in their own soul."

"That's very impressive, but—"

"Wait, there's more. Women's openness and their sexuality were to be shunned in the future by all officials in the Church. The chronicler depicts this as the greatest of crimes, since originally women had made up the majority of priests."

"That's amazing stuff, but we shouldn't forget that this has been a known and accepted truth for centuries, only behind closed doors. It's just that we're not being burned at the stake for it anymore…though Thomas might manage that too if he keeps on like this."

Deborah laughed—though nervously—and ordered a Guinness.

"Remember that the priests supposedly had an incredibly important task," Shane continued. "They were supposed to be people who knew about the divine potential of every being, who radiated trust and helped people overcome fears. And they were to do this by teaching how everyone could find God inside themselves. By creating an association between the commandment to love and true human encounters, the Church would have had the chance to be a truly divinely inspired movement. But the opposite happened because of the force of the lies the Vatican has piled up since the founding of the Roman Church. Nothing divine can come from that system anymore. In spite of that, I still have my doubts about whether we should get into a battle with them."

"Why a battle? We didn't want a battle. If the Vatican doesn't start to learn from the past, history will wipe out the whole nightmare. No culture will allow itself to be suppressed forever."

"Try telling that to the Native Americans who've virtually been wiped off the planet. I don't know, maybe Ronald and Jennifer are planning an eleventh-hour way of using law to foster justice. I'm just worried about our safety. It's hard to say what the ripple effects of a trial will be."

"I don't think Thomas had a chance to tell you about his vision. He's explained everything to me over the last several years, about the gifts of the Druids and other indigenous peoples. He's convinced that a time will come when people will recognize that the path we've been following has been the wrong one. And we can use what remains of these gifts and the knowledge of older cultures to help us to remember, so that a new consciousness can forge its own way in the world. At least that's what he believes."

"You know, that's what I believe as well. When you translated the scroll of Dubdrean about the return of the Druids, I almost got dizzy. Ryan must have felt an even more powerful affirmation from this text. But with this indictment Ronald and Jennifer are going down a road that could trigger a religious war. It's very possible that we're underestimating the consequences of our actions."

"No, Adam, I don't think so, at least not anymore. There will be resistance from the Vatican, of course, but most Christians have known for a while that the true message isn't to be found behind the Church's power-hungry walls."

"I'm still worried. I think it's very possible that Ronald has something else up his sleeve. What if Jennifer is just a puppet here?" Shane ran his fingers through his hair and rubbed his tired eyes. "I think we've done enough talking and speculating for the day. I propose we drink another round and then go back."

"I'm afraid we don't have time for that. Ronald called me before he left. The scrolls are going to be flown to Washington tomorrow on a special plane so that experts can precisely date their origin. He asked us to come along and stay with the scrolls on the flight."

Another flight, Shane thought with a shudder.

CHAPTER 26

MACCLARY'S APARTMENT, WASHINGTON, DC – AFTERNOON

MacClary had taken Jennifer to the Hotel Monaco and was now sitting in his apartment, not far from the Supreme Court Building, looking thoughtfully out the window. Just as he was about to get out of his chair, the telephone rang. Shaking his head in surprise, he went to his little study. In comparison to the remarkable, almost dramatic antique feeling of his parents' house, this room was much more cold and formal, filled with files and legal books.

"Ronald MacClary."

"Ah, Mr. MacClary. Thank you for answering. This is Bill Axton. The president would like to meet with you tomorrow at five o'clock." Axton was one of the president's closest advisors. The invitation, though friendly, was extended in such a way that it was quite clear it was actually an order.

MacClary grew uneasy. Had the ambassador gone against his wishes and already told the White House about what was going on in Dublin?

"May I ask about the agenda for this meeting?"

"I can't tell you that, but the matter is urgent."

"Very well. I will be there right at five. See you tomorrow, Mr. Axton."

"Thank you and good-bye."

MacClary didn't put down the phone right away. Instead, he dialed the embassy in Dublin and asked for the ambassador.

"Mr. MacClary, what can I do for you? Has something happened?" the ambassador asked when he came to the phone.

"I asked you to keep silent about the bugging," MacClary said sharply.

"What do you mean? What makes you think I haven't kept my word?"

"You haven't told anyone about it?"

"No, and I can speak for all the people who work for me as well. It's absolutely impossible that information about this bugging was leaked out, at least from here."

MacClary could hear the unspoken question behind the ambassador's words. He was deeply embarrassed about his hard tone of voice. "Oh God, I must be seeing pink elephants now," he said contritely. "Please forgive my rush to judge. I've made a mistake."

"Already forgotten. I can understand how these affairs would cause you some concern. Good luck in Washington, and I hope the matter sorts itself out quickly. Good night."

"Thank you, Mr. Ambassador. And a good night to you as well."

Confused, MacClary hung up the telephone. What could the president need to talk with him about? He had never been summoned to the White House before.

There was no likelihood of sleep tonight. MacClary turned on the television and, as if the news had been waiting for him, CNN was reporting about Ireland.

"As was reported today," the well-groomed anchor said, *"the Vatican has for decades been systematically concealing the number of Catholic officials involved in the abuse of minors in Ireland and the US. In addition, reports of a large number of cases involving sexual abuse of children by Catholic clergy have again been reported in Germany and other countries. Pope John Paul III has repeatedly apologized for the abuse. He has requested the presence of the entire College of Cardinals, comprising approximately two hundred members, for a meeting in Rome on the fourth of April to address the abuse cases.*

"Meanwhile, it was reported on Friday that a German bishop was taken into temporary custody related to the cover-up of approximately three hundred abuse cases in the Munich area. It was announced that he had been taken into custody on Wednesday, but has since been released on a bail of fifty thousand euros. The name of the bishop has yet to be disclosed, but Rome has signaled its willingness to do so in the coming days should the charges be confirmed. The bishop has, in the meantime, been suspended from duty."

MacClary sat motionless in his chair. He could feel his customary self-confidence returning as he listened to the news report. There was no going back now, and he was going to make sure that the Vatican stood before the world and their god and took responsibility for their actions.

CHAPTER 27

THE MAGDALENSBERG – MARCH 19, EARLY MORNING

Ryan had said his good-byes to the friendly innkeepers the night before. He had to trust that they wouldn't take any action, at least not before midday, when he'd already have met up with Brian Langster and was miles away over the mountains in safety. Only the son had gotten up with him to set up his motorcycle behind the house.

"I can't thank you enough," Ryan said as he prepared to depart. "When this is all over, I promise you I'll bring my friends back here to celebrate. We'll have a few reasons for a party by then."

As he started up the motorcycle and drove off, though, he could see in the rearview mirror that the young man was crossing himself. *Hmm, well, I might have to rethink that idea about celebrating here.*

It was about thirty miles to the border once he had the mountain road behind him. It was still pitch black, and he hoped that no one had seen him or would recognize him later. When he got to the bottom of the mountain, he was suddenly blinded by lights from a side road. A car started heading directly toward him. Ryan swung the motorcycle around. It started to lurch so much that he almost crashed. Then the cross-country bike started to earn its keep. He cut across a slope and lost his pursuers.

He turned off the light, driving almost blind in the darkness through the brush, until he came back onto the road. He could see his pursuers coming nearer from above, and he pushed the motorcycle as hard as it could go. It took the tight curves squealing. As he desperately tried to get to the autobahn toward Italy, memories flashed across his mind about all the conversations he'd had over the last years about the Celts and Druids with Deborah and MacClary.

He'd soon travelled a solid twenty-five miles on the autobahn. His wounds were still causing him a good deal of pain, but the burning desire to make it to Washington lent him strength. The dawn illuminated the mountains with an orange-yellow light as he approached, and he could already see where he had to get off the autobahn to get to the country road on the other side of the border.

He'd just crossed the open border to Italy when a black helicopter rose up from under the autobahn bridge. Seconds later, he saw a police roadblock about a half mile ahead. That could only be meant for him! He could hear an announcement in Italian coming from the helicopter. Ryan couldn't understand a word of it, but its meaning was unmistakable.

In the next moment, a door opened on the side of the helicopter, and out of the corner of his eye Ryan could see that two sharpshooters were leveling their weapons at him. He began to swerve back and forth, but he realized this wouldn't help for long. How could he get away? To make matters worse, police cars were approaching from behind.

He had to get off the bridge. Underneath him was a wide mountain river with sandy basins on either side, its water glistening turquoise blue in the dawn light. A bit farther downriver he could see a few scattered farms. It was at least sixty feet down, and the water was too shallow to jump from the bridge. He noticed that every bridge pile had a steel ladder on the inside, but before he could do anything with this information, he heard a loud pop, and he felt the motorcycle swerve behind him. The back tire had been hit. He slid to the side and was lucky that his fall was cushioned again by the well-wrapped scroll. He sent up a silent thanks to his ancestors. The fall was still bad enough. His feet slipped toward the crash barrier, which stopped his slide with a jolt.

"Damn it all to hell!"

Ryan gritted his teeth, pulled himself up with a groan, and ran to one of the piles. Carefully he climbed over the fortification, took a wild leap, and landed on a platform where he could get at the ladder. His pursuers were still behind him. The helicopter flew level with the bridge. Shots ricocheted off the cement. He climbed down the pile with as much speed as care, out of range of the shooters. More shots followed. Then he heard the helicopter turn around, obviously unable to fly under the bridge.

Ryan stepped on the last rung of the ladder. As he reached the bottom, he was alone. His pursuers seemed to have disappeared, and there was only one lone policeman who looked down from the bridge as he got to the valley floor and ran away.

"Damn it, what good will it do you to kill me?" Ryan swore in desperation. Then he ran, his face distorted with pain, alongside the river to a nearby farm, as he heard the helicopter return. He reached the other bank and hid himself behind the farm in the undergrowth.

He had to get out. But how? Ryan knew he only had a few minutes until his pursuers picked up his trail again. Not far from where he was hidden, he could see the country road that he had to follow, but he would never be able to make it, not under his own steam and not with a bevy of well-armed people pursuing him.

Desperate, he looked around, his gaze sweeping the river and the fields surrounding the farm. The only living thing he could see was a black horse, contentedly grazing near a shed. Ryan thought for only a few seconds, then he ran in the direction of the shed as another shot crossed his path from some direction or another. There was no time for saddle and halter. As a child, he had been able to win the trust of nearly every horse he met. He hoped now that he hadn't lost this skill.

He ran to the little paddock and laid his hand on the forehead of the gelding.

"I need your strength and your help. Please let me lead you."

Then he climbed on the horse's back and they galloped off. Ryan heard the regular rhythm of the hooves on the stone, felt the horse's mane blow in his face.

They reached the riverbed when Ryan heard the helicopter approaching from behind. Shots narrowly missed him again. "Faster!" Ryan shouted, encouraged by the sight of the looming forest and the rising mountains. There was a ditch that he had to get across. Another shot just under the hooves made the horse jump so high with fear that he crossed over the gap in one enormous leap, making Ryan almost lose his seat. They were almost there. The helicopter turned from its pursuit because of an approaching cliff. Once in the protection of the trees, the path up the mountain traversed boulders and spruce brush.

Ryan gave the horse a friendly pat on his sweaty neck. "You're quite the hotshot, aren't you?" he said, surprised at what an amazing animal he had found just standing on the wayside. They slowed down a bit, and Ryan could see, about a hundred yards away, the inn and the red camper Brian Langster had told him to look for. It was closer than he'd expected.

Relieved, he urged the horse into a gallop and rode down the side road. He could already see his contact standing and waiting for him. Langster took a nervous leap toward his car as the unknown horse came galloping at him like a huge black projectile. Ryan stopped directly in front of the little black Fiat and dismounted with an elegant sweep, landing directly in front of Langster.

He threw his arms around the neck of the horse, who was now breathing heavily, and closed his eyes. "Thank you, my friend, thank you," Ryan said softly and gave the horse a pat on his hindquarters to get him on his way back home. "Well, sometimes one horsepower is all you need." Ryan turned to Langster. "We have to get out of here as quickly as possible."

"I'm going to bring you to a doctor who's a friend of mine," Langster said. "From there you can continue on to the States. But we're maintaining radio silence because we can't take any risks. As soon as you're in the air, you can contact your friends again. Do you understand?"

"Understood."

It would be hard for the others to go days with no word from him, but it was necessary. His bruised body needed the rest.

CHAPTER 28

OFFICE OF THE CHIEF JUSTICE, SUPREME COURT, WASHINGTON, DC – MARCH 19, MORNING

On the first floor of the Supreme Court Building, there is a conference room set aside for the justices. This is where decisions are made, judgments are written, and where trial votes are held on camera to decide whether the court should take a case.

Ronald was nervous. He had no idea how much his fellow justices already knew and how they would react when he brought them into the loop. Until just a few days ago, his activities in the area of Church history had been his own private affair. They weren't looked on too kindly, but as long as he didn't attract too much attention, they were tolerated in silence. But now he would have to explain himself. He had to stop any attempts to attack him and undermine his authority. However, bringing a case forward that hadn't yet been heard, dismissed, or appealed in a district court was a risky business. In the end, all he could do was entrust the matter to his colleagues and wait for their reaction. Most of the justices who had been named by the last four presidents were conservative Christians, but their duty lay with the law, with the Constitution, and not with the Vatican.

As he entered the conference room, there was only one justice there. "Good morning, Ronald," the man said to the astonished MacClary. "I've just heard that Justice Courtney is ill; the session has been cancelled. Didn't anyone tell you?" Justice Bob Johnson was a small, very thin man with gray-flecked hair and a thin mustache. At seventy-five, he was one of the oldest justices on the Supreme Court.

Dumbfounded, MacClary looked at his colleague. "No, but this isn't good at all." For a few seconds he stared at the huge, empty conference table, and then he had a realization. He'd been given the opportunity to talk privately with one of the most liberal justices on the court.

"Here's the thing, Bob. I've been summoned to the White House for a meeting at five this evening. I don't exactly know what's waiting for me there, but it might have to do with certain affairs in Dublin that—"

"I think I have an idea what it's about," Johnson interrupted. "Did you really think that your private feud with the Catholic Church wouldn't have any consequences?"

MacClary sat down, baffled. What had happened?

"Don't look at me as if you don't know what I'm talking about. You're lucky that none of the big newspapers have found out about it yet," Johnson said as he placed an Austrian newspaper in front of MacClary that contained an article about the suspicious interruption of MacClary's lecture.

MacClary breathed a bit easier. "Oh, that! No, Bob, that was irritating, but hardly a reason to reproach me. There was nothing in that lecture that hasn't already been said by others. No, there's another problem. I accidentally discovered that my residence had been bugged."

"What? Who in God's name…"

MacClary took a deep breath. As unpleasant as it was, he had to lie to one of his best friends on the court.

"We don't know, but I can assure you that I haven't had any conversations about our activities over the last several weeks. When I'm there, I am, as you know, in another world. I hardly even answer the telephone. The Guantanamo story came up once, but the bugs hadn't been put in place yet, if the experts are to be believed," MacClary said.

"Good, that's something at least. Still, the whole matter is, at the very least, extremely unsettling. Is there any evidence to suggest who did this?"

"Unfortunately, no, we don't have any ideas aside from the usual suspects. We may never know for sure who's behind it. But there is something else I'd like to discuss with you, off the record. We're apparently about to get a pretty explosive case. I've heard from a lawyer friend of mine that the district attorney's office in Boston intends to bring charges up against the Vatican sometime in the next few days. I don't know the details of the case yet, but she signaled that if it were dismissed she would appeal to the Supreme Court."

"Really, Ronald, I don't understand you. What kind of a parcel of goods are you trying to sell? You're going to get into a lot of trouble if you keep up like this, especially right after this last controversy. You might even be accused of bias because of your private disputes."

"No, I don't think so. We don't even know what this is really about yet. I just want to know where the justices as a whole stand if a Christian institution were to be on trial."

"That's a very good, very prudent question, and you can score some superficial points with that, but in actuality, it doesn't matter in the least. I can assure you that you won't be able to get a majority, even if—"

"Even if it concerns attempted murder, theft of cultural assets, and the destruction of evidence in a case of historical genocide?"

"What? How do you know that? You just said you don't know the details of the case. How am I supposed to trust you if—"

"Wait a minute, Bob. I really don't know exactly, but it might go that way. The question is whether a majority of the justices, when faced with such a magnitude of charges, would speak against the Vatican." MacClary had stood up again. He was starting to get nervous. He was worried he might be completely overwhelming Johnson.

"Well, we swore our oath of office on the Bible, not on the Vatican. In this respect I consider our colleagues to have absolute integrity. But even if I'm right about that, what purpose will be served by the prosecution of a country where almost all the officials have immunity? Honestly, I really don't understand where this nonsense will lead, aside from you ruining your reputation and running the risk of losing your position."

"Bob, we'll have to see. I'm grateful that you haven't lost faith in me. I don't know where this journey will take us, but rest assured: even if I know a lot about the early Church and the crimes of the Vatican, that in no way, shape, or form makes me a biased justice."

"Ronald, you don't have to convince me of anything. I'm no great friend of the Vatican myself, and I consider its claim to omniscience and infallibility more than a little questionable. But there are seven other justices, and I have no idea what the majority will think. If there is enough hard and fast proof, they'll engage in a confrontation like this. But that's the problem, since the prosecution will falter when it comes to the examination and acknowledgment of the evidence. You shouldn't have any illusions about that, and my advice to you is to vote, here in this room, to refuse to hear the case. Otherwise your career might be over soon." Johnson stood up, got his briefcase, and headed toward the door. "Don't let your obsessions control you, Ronald. The Church has less and less sway in the world, even without your judgment. Don't you watch the news anymore?"

"Yes, I do. You're probably right. We'll wait and see, Bob."

Johnson walked out of the conference room without saying another word. MacClary could hear his footsteps fading away on the marble floor. He sat down at the conference table and rested his head heavily on his hands. The conversation had clarified several important points for him. Jennifer and her district attorney would need all the support he could muster for them. Adam and Deborah were valuable witnesses, but their testimony would be useless if Ryan didn't make it to the US. Without him and the proof he possessed, the whole thing would be a ridiculous joke. He had to hold back one chess piece, just in case the action really did blow up in their faces. And this piece had to get to Washington as quickly and unobtrusively as possible.

* * *

WASHINGTON, DC – MARCH 19, AFTERNOON

Shortly after touching down in Washington, Deborah and Shane were brought, along with all the parchment, to a private institute on Walter Street belonging to an archaeologist who was an old friend of MacClary's. It sat well camouflaged in a nice, quiet residential area with tree-lined streets and modest, single-family homes, right near the Capitol. There they waited for MacClary.

In the hall of the laboratory, Shane tried to calm himself down.

"Adam?"

Shane turned around and looked into Jennifer's bewildered, delighted face. She had slipped in behind him and sat down. "What are you doing here?"

"Ronald asked us to come. He seems nervous. Why are you here?"

"I called Ronald earlier, after I found out that there had been an incident at the Italian border." She handed Shane a printout of a report from Reuters.

HIGH-LEVEL IRISH TERRORIST SPOTTED IN ITALY AFTER YEARS UNDERGROUND. UNSUCCESSFUL CHASE BROKEN OFF.

Shocked, Shane looked at Jennifer. "Do you think they mean Thomas? I thought he fought *against* the IRA!"

"I'll give you one guess who's behind this report," Jennifer said with astonishing composure. "Now I understand why he didn't want us to come and get him. If he was able to get away, then he'll be able to make it here as well."

"How can you be so sure of that?"

"Thomas's old friends are used to surviving underground. They know every trick in the book."

"I hope you're right."

Just then Ronald entered. He'd been soaked by the pouring rain, which only added to his agitation.

"Jennifer, Adam, this way," he said, opening an office door and waving them inside. A moment later, Deborah joined them. Ronald slammed the door shut rather loudly.

"Jennifer, have you contacted your district attorney?"

"No, she won't be back from Europe for another two days, but I have an appointment with her."

"All right, we'll need the time anyhow. I've hired three independent experts to work with Deborah to translate the parchments and date them precisely. When Thomas arrives with his parchment, that will be translated and dated as well. With that, and his testimony, we'll at least have a strong motive. And given the cultural and historical dimension of this find, we should have the attention of the world."

"Has Thomas contacted any of you?" Jennifer said as she took some notes.

"No, he hasn't."

Jennifer gave MacClary the Reuters report and fell back into her chair with a sigh.

"Blast!" Ronald roared. "They're doing their absolute best to keep Thomas from getting here. Is what he's carrying worth killing him over?"

"Ronald! He probably recognized who they were. That should be reason enough," Jennifer said and looked at MacClary in surprise that he hadn't realized this himself.

MacClary shook his head in bewilderment. "Yes, I'm afraid you're right. At least he got away. That's the most important thing."

An elderly man in a lab coat suddenly stood in the doorway, several computer printouts in his hand. "Mr. MacClary, I think this might be of some interest to you."

When the man looked at the others and hesitated, Ronald said, "Go ahead. We don't have any secrets amongst this company."

"First of all, we can say with certainty that Ryan's family tree parchment comes from the same period as the scrolls from the cave. Incredibly, we can also find traces of earth and a particular form of pollen on both scraps of parchment, evidence that the documents were made in the same region."

"You're kidding," Shane said incredulously.

"No, no, I'm completely serious," the man who Shane guessed was the laboratory director assured him.

Ryan had told Shane about his family tree, but Shane had dismissed it as wishful thinking and a fairy tale, like all the other legends and myths that swirled around the Celts and Druids.

"That's not all," the man continued. "The other family trees also come from this period, and they were written with the same quill, as if someone wanted to make sure that the background of these families would be definitively documented."

"That makes complete sense," Jennifer responded. "The Druids fled to the islands, but before they left, they had their family trees set down in writing to document their ancestry and their status, to firmly establish their claim to leadership."

"This actually proves that Thomas and the other families are descended from those Druids on the continent who fled the henchmen of the pope," Ronald said. "And that means that we have claim to their legacy, wherever in the world it may be found. Deborah has contact information for all the families. I think we should let them know about this latest development, and I'll also inform the Irish foreign minister. I think we can expect a great deal of support from him, since he was the most vehement in his arguments that Great Britain recognize Druidism as a state religion."

"But Ronald, that doesn't help us," Jennifer said, looking at Ronald in surprise. "We don't have sufficient proof that the Vatican is behind this." Her eyes narrowed. "You know this, of course. That means you have something up your sleeve, something you're not telling us about, otherwise you would—"

"Give me a little time. Wait until I see the president. I still have to clarify a few questions before—"

"Before what? I think it's time that we lay all our cards on the table here," Shane demanded.

"Just give me until tonight," MacClary insisted. "I know what I'm doing."

"All right, Ronald," Jennifer said, taking Shane's hand to signal that everything was fine. "You go to the White House. We'll hold the fort here and keep working on the indictment."

"Good. We'll meet in my apartment tonight."

With that, Ronald turned and hurried out of the office.

* * *

ROME – MARCH 19, AFTERNOON

Thomas Lambert stood in front of the mirror at the entrance to the pope's private rooms and straightened his clothes. He looked pale and bleary-eyed, and the news of the failed attempt to arrest Ryan didn't make his job any easier. He couldn't trust Salvoni, of that he had become certain. He picked up his briefcase, which he'd been holding between his feet, and knocked twice on the door.

As usual, one of the watchmen of the Swiss Guards opened it. "Good morning, Cardinal."

"Good morning. Is the Holy Father already in his office?"

"Of course, Cardinal."

The Swiss Guard welcomed Lambert in. Compared with the enormous frescoes, antique paintings, furniture, sculptures, and other symbols that decorated the holy rooms of the Vatican, Pope John Paul III had furnished his rooms much more modestly. He had even had many things removed that had just been too much for him. Directed through the main room, Lambert opened the door to the office of the pope, who was busy preparing for his upcoming audiences.

"Cardinal Lambert, God bless you. Sit down. Would you like some tea?"

Lambert shook his head slightly. "Holy Father, I am sorry, but I have some unpleasant news," he said, coming directly to the point. He paused for a moment, as if he wanted to give the eighty-year-old man time to prepare himself for what he was about to say. John Paul III's face had very few wrinkles for his advanced age, and his skin had a healthy, rosy glow. He was almost as tall as Lambert, which was somewhat unusual for an Italian, although he had become somewhat bent over with back pain. He had a full head of snow-white hair, and his strong eyebrows lent his dark eyes charismatic radiance.

"You look quite concerned about something," the pope said. "What in God's name is happening to us this time?"

"Do you remember Padre Morati? For nearly forty years, he headed up our ancient archive, with articles from the period of the founding of the Church. Among other duties, he was responsible for working with the parchments from the period of the First Council."

"Yes, of course I remember him. Is he still among us?"

Lambert nodded. "The good Lord has blessed him with biblical longevity. Yes, he's over ninety now. But that's not why I'm telling you this. In 1945, he received an invitation from a fanatical heretic, an archaeologist by the name of Sean MacClary. MacClary asked him if he would like to see a parchment that he had found in Austria. Apparently Morati was shocked by the contents of the parchment, but he always refused to tell us what was in it. Then he must have done something that he regretted for the rest of his life, though he's always stubbornly refused to tell us about that too. In any case, he was convinced that there had to be a place where many more of these scrolls were hidden, and he was just as convinced that these writings would have the power to topple the walls of our Church. At that point, he requested that he be allowed to stay in Dublin to make sure that no more of these scrolls would surface and to be able to interfere if something did happen."

"Wait a minute. What was this man's name again?"

"Padre Morati?"

"No, no, the other. The archaeologist."

"Sean MacClary, Holy Father."

"And Ronald MacClary is his son. I know the man and his work. He has gathered the best critics of the Church around him, and he's practically obsessed with the idea of proving we were involved in a historical crime, a crime that would bring our entire existence into question. An utterly ridiculous idea and a fool's errand. No one denies the failings of the young Church, and these documents—"

Lambert had to make sure that the pope was on his side before he told him about the mistakes he and Salvoni had made over the past several days. At the same time, he wanted to make sure that the old man—as he usually called the pope to himself—didn't learn too much about the dramatic nature of their discovery. This pope was too unpredictable to let him in on everything.

"These documents contain things, Holy Father, which we don't need to have in the public eye just now."

"What sorts of things? I am starting to get irritated with your secrecy, Cardinal. Do not forget with whom you are speaking!"

"With all due respect, Holy Father, the Curia bears responsibility for protecting the Holy See from any harm, and that includes your person as well," Lambert said. He fully realized that he was crossing a line with words like these, but he had to give himself some room to play with so that he could continue to work without interference.

"You're taking liberties!"

"I am, just like you, only a servant of God. I act in the interests of the Lord and in accordance with the Holy Scripture. Like you, I battle every false word, every defamation, and every attack that could harm us. And it's better if you are not directly involved in this conflict." Lambert could only hope that the old man accepted this line of reasoning. It had always worked before. "Several zealous members of the Vatican police followed a tip and found a place in Austria, a place that Morati had always feared existed. We arrived too late and could only retrieve a few of the artifacts. Some men, apparently friends of the judge, were faster than our men, and we couldn't prevent some of the documents from ending up in their possession."

The pope bowed his head and crossed himself. "Cardinal, are you telling me that we were in Austria, acting without the permission of the local authorities?"

"Holy Father, I saw the scrolls with my own eyes. You should see them yourself and form your own opinion. I think you will agree with me that it really was a matter of imminent risk. I'm afraid MacClary wants to make the whole incident public and to oppose us."

"Very well, I will go and view the documents, Cardinal, but I hardly think that we have anything to fear. Particularly the more recent research and hostilities about the period of the founding of the Church are unable to harm us. Pope John Paul II apologized on numerous occasions for the overzealousness and doubtlessly brutal methods of the early Church and the Inquisition, and he led our Church into the present. So what should we be afraid of? Is there something you're not telling me?"

"Holy Father, it's possible that mistakes have been made in the recovery of the objects and in the surveillance of MacClary, but the fact is that we have no idea what he is planning. He has an enormous amount of support, but you could use your influence on the American president to keep him from using his office or his privileges to harm us."

"You question my authority, and yet you want to use it to cover up your mistakes?"

"It is not I who questions your authority, Holy Father, but rather the artifacts themselves that could do that. Our chronicles and records have always said that the testimony of the pagan elites would be dangerous for us." Lambert hoped this was enough. He would only confide his true fears to the old man if there were no other alternative.

"And what do you think I should do now? Call the American president, who isn't exactly in our corner as it is, and complain that one of her most high-ranking justices is speaking ill of us?"

"Yes, precisely, Holy Father." Lambert handed the pope several reports from his briefcase about the goings-on in Dublin. The pope sat down and began to read. His face started to twist in rage.

"This is completely unacceptable. He's trying to exploit our position in the most despicable manner imaginable. Cardinal, I'll draw up a document today. Keep me apprised of the situation. I'll have to think about how to explain this to the president."

"Very well, Holy Father. For my part, I have already registered an official complaint with the US ambassador, but your involvement will give even more weight to the matter. Perhaps they'll start to realize in Washington that they want to win the next election as well."

Lambert stood and kissed the Ring of the Fisherman. Perhaps they could get the whole thing under control after all. He had to find some way to pressure the justice.

"My dear Salvoni, now it's your turn," he muttered as he left the anteroom. "You'll have to perform an unusual service for our flock."

CHAPTER 29

WHITE HOUSE – MARCH 19, AFTERNOON

The black limousine drove up to the back entrance of the White House, where Bill Axton was already waiting for MacClary. MacClary knew that he had to carefully consider every word when dealing with the president, and it made him extraordinarily uncomfortable to have to lie to her, because they had been good friends for many years.

They went through the winding corridor to the Oval Office. When Axton led him in, the president told the man that she only wanted to be disturbed in the case of an emergency. Diana Branks, now forty-eight, had been in office for a little more than a year, having won the election in an upset of her Republican opponent. That the American people chose her didn't surprise MacClary as much as it did many of the pundits. She was eloquent, modern, and had long ago learned how to communicate policy in a way that calmed public fears and gave them the courage to change. She was also up for taking risks. From their conversations, MacClary knew that the president was aware that she probably had only one term to put her plans into effect. Her unconventional manner, coupled with the radical nature with which she greeted the economic and ecological downturn, didn't exactly make everyone her friend and gave ammunition to her opponents. However, one term of office could be a long time if one used it well.

"Ronald, sit down and make yourself comfortable. What we have to discuss will be less comfortable, in any case."

With those words MacClary's hopes of getting off lightly came to an abrupt halt. "Let's get it over with," he responded, trying to keep his voice calm.

Diana Branks looked at the man sitting across from her with a mixture of warmth and great seriousness. "I have here a dispatch from our ambassador in the Vatican," she said, making clear from her tone that she was now speaking as his superior and not as a long-term confidante. "It says that the Holy See is complaining about a not unimportant United States justice who has been in Dublin attacking the Church with baseless accusations, so much so that the director of Trinity College felt it necessary to cut off one of his lectures. Ronald, I know that you are no friend of the Church, but this is going too far. I can't allow someone in your position to attract this kind of publicity."

"Madame President, I'm well aware that the belief in God is one of the most important pillars of our Constitution, but—"

"No buts. I have made my own conclusions. But what am I supposed to do now? The American media hasn't jumped on this yet, but if it does, you could be threatened with impeachment."

"It seems I may have gauged the situation incorrectly. The crazy thing about this is that the lecture was nowhere near as controversial as they are making it out to be. I can only attribute this huge reaction to the position of the Church in Ireland. At the moment, it has its back up to the wall."

MacClary's thoughts were racing as he spoke. He had to borrow time. It didn't make any sense to tell her everything now. After Jennifer had filed her official brief, then he could tell the president more. Otherwise, she could very well ask for his resignation on the spot.

"Fine. So what do you recommend?"

"I will make an official apology to the Vatican and take responsibility for the fact that I didn't examine my sources carefully enough," MacClary said contritely. "I will also express my regret that a private event was made public."

"Good, Ronald. I hope that will smooth some ruffled feathers. I'll convey this to our ambassador in Rome, and I'll expect your note of apology to reach Rome today. I'm sorry to have to rush off, but I have to get to my next meeting. Thank you, and we'll talk again when we get a reaction from the Vatican."

MacClary stood up and headed toward the door. Then he stopped still. He simply couldn't hold back. The matter was too explosive, and too many of the people working with him had already been placed in danger. He had to convince people with the truth, with his heart.

"Is there something else, Ronald?" President Branks asked.

He pulled himself together and squared his shoulders. "Madame President, how pressing is your appointment?"

The president's eyes widened. "My goodness, this isn't like you at all! There is something else behind this, then, isn't there?"

MacClary moved back toward his seat. "You could say that."

* * *

ARCHAEOLOGY LABORATORY, WASHINGTON, DC – MARCH 19, EVENING

Shane, Deborah, and Jennifer had spent the rest of the afternoon looking at Deborah's translations.

"It really is an incredible feeling to be standing here in front of these things so many centuries after they were written," Shane said, sitting at the back end of the laboratory while Deborah and Jennifer were standing in front of the parchment. "It must have been unbelievable for Thomas to see how the circle completed itself. I just wish he'd get in touch with us soon."

"He will," Deborah said. "You can count on it. That boy can't be stopped so easily."

Jennifer took off her glasses and began to clean them carefully. "What irritates me, though, is Thomas's stubbornness. In his paranoid way, he convinced Ronald that the scrolls should never be retrieved by the authorities because the artifacts would disappear in the scientists' laboratories. Of course, he was afraid that he wouldn't have access to them anymore and that the Vatican would seize the most sensational pieces."

"On the other hand," Shane interjected, "I can completely understand his point of view when I look at what's in front of us. We have to move forward now. And judging by Rome's reaction, he was right."

Jennifer nodded, though she seemed weary. "I know. I'm going to see this thing through to the end. Tomorrow I'm meeting with Louise Jackson. She's a woman, African American, and anything but Catholic. She just finished working on the indictment against the Vatican Bank. I'm sure she'll help us. We already have enough evidence here for that, and—" Jennifer broke off as she looked out the window. She slapped her hand on the table. "Hey, there's Ronald. He's outside making a telephone call."

Less than a minute later they heard the door. Ronald came into the laboratory and almost threw his briefcase on the first table, right next to a parchment. He caught himself, realizing how fragile the document was, and instead set his briefcase on the floor. As he looked up, his entire face was beaming. "So, my dear friends, now we have our work cut out for us. It's all gone a bit differently than I had planned, but I think it's the right way—the only way. I just couldn't bring myself to lie to the president. She knows everything and has given me free rein. That means I'm responsible for how this moves forward, and if it becomes too explosive, I'll have to resign from my position. Jennifer, now it's up to you, your district attorney, and Thomas."

Jennifer shook her head. "But Ronald, we don't have enough here! The testimony of Thomas, Deborah, and Adam…that's just not enough."

"Hey, hey, wait a minute," Deborah interrupted. "At the moment there are three places where these scrolls are being stored. We have some, Thomas has one, and we assume that some are in the Vatican, as long as they weren't insane enough to destroy everything. If the archaeologists can confirm that all the parchment comes from the same source, that would be a strong argument in our favor. We just have to find the other scrolls and have them officially seized. Though 'just' is a relative term here, of course. I've also discovered that almost all the scrolls have a very small marking. It's a Celtic protection symbol, a circle intersected by two lines. Here, see? And—"

"Not in the Vatican," MacClary said as the others leaned toward Deborah.

Deborah looked up at him. "What?"

"These scrolls are not in the Vatican. There is an archive outside of Rome, hidden underneath a church. That's where the most sensational documents of the last hundred years have been stored, restored, and prepared for conservation. After being examined by the Congregation for the Doctrine of Faith, they are brought there—most of the time, at least. But we'll never get in there. No judge will give us a search warrant for that."

"We'll take care of it."

Everyone turned to look at Shane, who had spoken so quietly they weren't sure they'd heard him correctly. Jennifer looked from one to the other, bewildered.

"What are you going to take care of?" Ronald asked.

"Ronald, there's much more at stake here than just the formal matter of law. This is a matter of justice, and as you yourself said that night when we first met, it's about historical truth. For that, we have to be willing to take some risks, don't we?" Shane smiled, as if he had suddenly had a fantastic vision. "It's about time that an earthly court puts an end to the heavenly crimes in Rome."

"Where are you heading with this, Adam?" Jennifer asked in concern.

MacClary shook his head decisively. "No, absolutely not. I can't."

"Oh, yes you can, of course you can. I'm not the slightest bit afraid of this. Just tell me where the archive is. I'm sure that Deborah wants to help her friend Thomas in any way she can as well."

Jennifer took two steps in his direction. "So you're just going to march into the Vatican archives and walk out with cases of parchment, which you're then going to get through customs and bring back to Washington? You're completely insane."

Shane tried to remain nonchalant. "Not *cases*; that would definitely be noticed. But one or two scrolls, so that we know where the rest of them are. We'll photograph everything so that we have additional proof that it's not just rogue individuals who are behind this but the

Vatican itself. We would also be able to see which artifacts the Vatican considers to be worth taking these kinds of risks for. We really didn't have enough time to see what the other scrolls might have yielded."

MacClary looked at Jennifer and then nodded to Shane. "All right, but if you're caught, I can't do anything to help you. We all have to be aware that we're increasingly operating on the wrong side of the law to win our case. That has always been a very, very risky way to play the game."

Jennifer still wasn't sold. "My God, Adam, are you really sure you want to do this? And you, Deborah—"

Deborah held up a hand. "I'm with Adam." She grinned. "Thomas has prepared me well for this sort of thing over the last several years."

"What do you mean by that? You haven't—"

"No, no, even Thomas has long given up the old ways. But we've talked a lot about how one would undertake an operation like this."

That surprised even Shane. He hadn't seriously thought that Deborah would be so ready to take such a risk.

"Well, then…" MacClary wrote the address in Italy on a piece of paper, picked it up with the fingertips of both hands, and gave it to Shane. The gesture seemed almost as formal as the Japanese visiting card ritual.

As Shane scanned the information on the paper, MacClary turned to Jennifer. "My dear, I'm flying to The Hague tomorrow and then back to Dublin. Once you've met with Ms. Jackson, we should quickly sit down together and go over everything again."

"I basically have everything ready, Ronald, even the documents for filing an objection in the Supreme Court."

"Good. Thank you."

"Ronald, don't forget that the most important thing here is whether Thomas can lodge a claim as a victim against the elite of the Church or only against individual perpetrators. If the Vatican claims, as they did in the case in Mississippi, that the perpetrators are not affiliated with the Vatican, then we have a serious problem. Even as we speak, the lawyers in Rome are trying to stop the suit in the Kentucky abuse cases using the same strategy. The plaintiffs had to withdraw everything that they couldn't prove."

"Yes, I know, Jennifer. That's why Adam is right. If we can prove that the scrolls are in the Vatican or in an institution that belongs to them, then I can, in any case, assert the claim to surrender stolen cultural assets. That may actually be the only way."

CHAPTER 30

HOTEL MONACO, WASHINGTON, DC – MARCH 20, NIGHT

Deborah had spent the entire evening learning about the area around Orvieto. Right near the gothic dome built by Lorenzo Maitani, there was a hotel named Duomo Orvieto. She couldn't imagine any place in or around the dome where there might be an archive of such significance, but if MacClary were so sure, then it had to be there somewhere. She checked again.

After a half hour of staring at her computer monitor, she let out a little sigh. It wasn't surprising that she had missed it: a small, seemingly unimportant detail in the structural plans of the dome.

In the adjoining room of the large apartment in the Hotel Monaco, where MacClary had gotten them all a room, Adam and Jennifer were talking so loudly that Deborah could hardly concentrate. She tried not to listen to the argument, but certain snippets of conversation kept on bleeding through.

"Adam…"

"…but it's not that hard to understand…"

"…I can't do this anymore…"

"Adam!" Jennifer yelled so loudly that Deborah got up and opened the door.

"It's all right. I understand. I'm just worried that something will happen to you two," Jennifer said, trying to calm down.

"Hey, do you guys need an intervention here?" Deborah joked. "I did a seminar in college on relationship mediation." She ducked as Jennifer threw a ball of paper at her.

"Why are you willing to take such a huge risk, Adam?" Jennifer continued as though Deborah wasn't there. "I mean, you can just go home and be done with the whole thing."

"And why do you follow Ronald?" Adam responded.

"Because…" For a moment there was dead silence, and Jennifer looked into Adam's face. Then she shut her eyes and breathed in and out slowly. "Perhaps because I've always done it. Every time Ronald says, 'Here's what we're going to do now,' I've always trusted him. Believe me, I was just about ready to stop and go my own way, but I can't just leave him in the lurch on this one. You don't have any obligations here, though."

Adam stood up and faced her, clearly agitated "I have a damned obligation to *myself*. I don't want to spend another day like a stupid sheep, just putting up with everything and passively hanging around. I want to begin to act—finally—to put something in motion, and in a very definite direction. I want all the lies to be cleared out at last, and this might be one of the biggest lies of our entire civilization. This is my chance to do something with my life, something I've always dreamed about doing. You and Ronald, you want to bring the Vatican before the law and to see the organization convicted. I can accept that, and it probably is a part of this story. The other part of it, though, is the vision that Thomas, Deborah, and I share, that people will finally be able to learn the truth about a religion that has been foisted upon them by those in power, a religion whose values and doctrine have systematically undermined their own self-determination."

Adam was filled with passion. He'd spoken without pausing, not even stopping to take a breath.

Jennifer remained calm. "I understand that, Adam. And I admire it. Yes, I'll take legal action. That's my job, that's what I've learned. It's just my way of bringing things into balance."

Adam laughed softly. "Yes, I know that, and that's the way it should be. But it's just not everything. The parchments prove what the Druids were aiming for, and it's my goal to show the world what that is. That is my way, and for me it's ultimately more important than the attempt to sentence those who have betrayed our original culture."

Deborah felt the need to interject. "As fascinating as this conversation is, can I remind you that we have to plan a little, insignificant...*break-in* before tomorrow night?"

Jennifer put up a hand. "It's better if I don't hear this. I'm going to bed. When do you take off for Rome?"

"The flight leaves at ten in the morning," Deborah said. "If everything goes as planned, we should be back in Washington early the following day."

"We'll be here on time. That's a promise," Adam said. "Do me a favor, though. Call if you hear anything from Thomas."

"I will. Take care of yourselves, and good luck."

She took a step toward the door, and Adam leaned toward her and kissed her on the cheek, which seemed to surprise both of them. He then watched Jennifer walk away, sighed deeply, and followed Deborah into the next room where she'd laid out the structural plans of the dome and all the necessary maps for planning their escape.

"Not bad," he said. "It looks like you've thought of everything, but where's the archive?"

"Well, it's not directly in the dome, in any case, that much I'm sure of. But you can see on the older plans that there's another chapel with a basement underneath it. I can't find it anymore, but I'm sure that there are at least some ruins there and that we have to go underneath that."

"Do you have any idea what kind of alarm system they have there or how many security guards we'll have to deal with?"

"No, no idea, and we won't know that until we get there." She grinned at him. "I'm bringing my MacGyver suitcase with me."

Adam placed his hands heavily on the table. "Then I guess we'll have everything we need."

* * *

OFFICE OF JUDGE DAVE FOXTER, INTERNATIONAL CRIMINAL COURT, THE HAGUE – MARCH 21, AFTERNOON

MacClary hadn't slept well. Although he was a good friend of Dave Foxter, a British judge on the International Criminal Court, the political realities made what he was going to discuss with Dave difficult. The US had used all the means at its disposal to block the ICC and had categorically denied the extradition of US war criminals to the tribunal. Neither the Vatican nor the United States government had a membership in the ICC, whose decisions were binding under international law.

"Good morning, Ronald," Dave said when MacClary entered his office. "My God, what brings you here? I just found out this morning you were coming."

"I haven't come in an official capacity, if that's what you're wondering. My visit has to do with a case that concerns all of us right now. It doesn't involve our relationship to the ICC, but rather to the Vatican."

Foxter gave a start and looked at MacClary quizzically. "What do you have to do with the Vatican?"

"Well, actually, a great deal and for some time now," MacClary said. "Until now, though, it was always a kind of personal hobby. However, a rather controversial case is emerging in Washington, in which I am not entirely uninvolved."

"Oh, my lord. Does this have anything to do with your father and his thesis about the Church's crimes against humanity? Oh, Ronald, have you been afflicted with the family illness in your old age? I can tell you now that there's nothing we can do, although we might be handling the current abuse cases sometime soon."

"Yes, that is an interesting matter. I've read about your star attorney, a countryman of yours if I'm not mistaken. But it sounded more like a canard to me. Is there really a serious attempt to put the pope on the dock?"

"Ronald, George Caven is one of the most well-known human rights lawyers in the world. If someone like him goes this far out on a limb, then it means something. This could be a watershed moment. Until now, the pope has been protected from any kind of criminal prosecution, just like any other head of state…"

"I understand, and since he's holder of the Holy See and head of the Vatican state, one can't expect that anything will change. In the final analysis, though, everything depends on recognition under international law, and that's what I'm concerned with, Dave. It's a moral and ethical decision of the world community whether we continue to stand idly by or finally draw conclusions from current and historical crimes." MacClary's voice had risen unintentionally.

"Yes, Ronald, the status of Rome…it's a positively grotesque relic from the distant past. Believe me, it's a thorn in my side that a country encompassing St. Peter's, five hundred priests, and little else has such power and influence, and that it's never held responsible for anything."

"Wait a minute, Dave. Caven sees a crime against humanity in the indulgence and facilitation of child abuse, according to the currently applicable international law. And more and more people throughout the world are starting to share this opinion!"

"That may be, Ronald, but the problem is that no one, not the United Nations, not any individual country, *no one*, is ready to act on this realization. Even in the US, it doesn't go any further than lawsuits that are dismissed or withdrawn due to lack of evidence. Where are you headed with this?"

"To another case. It concerns attempted murder, theft of international cultural assets, and the right to historical truth."

Dave's expression dimmed. "My God, Ronald, those are serious accusations, and you know how they've always handled that in Rome. They foist the whole thing off on a single person and say that he no longer has any affiliation with them. Maybe they hand him over, or the Italian police find him under some bridge somewhere."

"Let's assume that we have enough proof, motive, and witnesses. Would there be a way, theoretically, that the case could be tried by you here?"

Dave shook his head slowly. "I'm afraid the whole thing would be over before it began. You've already seen how the lawsuits dealing with even these repugnant cases of child abuse are shot down. The immunity of the pope and other officials no longer applies if they're charged by this court, but the Security Council would have to refer the case to us. What does your president think about this?"

"Oh, she's overjoyed. She had already written off the possibility of reelection and she's behind me one hundred percent," Ronald said, only half joking. "No, in all seriousness, she knows all about the situation."

"If she's really on board, then she could tip the scales in the Security Council. But we're not getting anywhere like this. If we want to keep talking, you have to tell me what this entails."

Ronald looked out of the window for a long couple of seconds, thinking about his next move. Foxter had always been someone he could depend on to keep things quiet. It would be foolish not to take him into his confidence.

"Friends of mine have found scrolls from the fourth century that prove how the church betrayed its own ideals and betrayed millions of people with unmitigated criminality and power hunger. From the very beginning, they violently destroyed almost the entire early culture of Europe and—"

"You don't have to go on, Ronald. I know what you're talking about. I thought that's what this was about, and as you know, I know my way around this topic as well." Foxter gestured to his bookcase, where Ronald recognized works from the most important contemporary critics of the Church.

"Then you agree with me. It's time that we confront the Christians throughout the world with this and show the religion its historical place."

"I completely agree, Ronald, but be careful that you don't throw the baby out with the bathwater. It's of vital importance that you not attack the many, many authentic Christians who are just living their faith and who have nothing to do with the crimes of the Church."

"I realize that, Dave. I know we'll be walking a tightrope with this, but the historical truth seen in light of current events could also be very healing for Christians. If they were to finally turn away from the Vatican, the original ideas of Christianity could be freed from the filth and guilt of centuries. I should also add that my Celtic friends are far more concerned with forgiveness than revenge. I know my role in this, and I'll soon retreat into the background. The future belongs to those who can think into the future. And there are a few of those in my circle. Perhaps you'll get to know them. They want, quite simply, a different world. If you can call that simple."

Foxter pulled a file out of the huge pile on his desk.

"You can still do that?"

"Do what?"

"You're the only person I've ever known who could find the exact file he needed, no matter how many files were lying in front of him," MacClary said with an admiring smile.

"It's like riding a bike." He handed the file to MacClary. "Here, I worked on this not too long ago. It's now common sense in New York, but it hasn't yet been acknowledged. The Vatican has long since gambled away its international legal status, to say nothing of the moral conscience of the world. I will support you where I can, Ronald. The time is simply right for it. If you can call *that* simple."

MacClary let out a sigh. He was gradually realizing that it wouldn't be possible to hold the Vatican as a whole responsible unless his last trump card really delivered what it had promised. "Then a call to the president would be extraordinarily helpful. Right now, she doesn't know if she should send me to the moon or into retirement." He stood up. "Dave, many thanks. When this whole thing is over, we should have a nice long game of chess. I think I'll have a lot more time for that soon."

"I wish you all the luck in the world, Ronald."

"Thanks, Dave. I can use every good wish I get."

MacClary quietly shut the door, took a deep breath, and went back down the corridor to the elevator. He stopped to look at one of the pictures lining the hall. It was a photograph of the Nuremberg trials. Back then, the world had taken a huge step forward in the area of human rights. MacClary buttoned up his coat and muttered, "It's time for the next step. For everyone."

* * *

EIGHTH STREET, WASHINGTON, DC – MARCH 21, AFTERNOON

Shane and Deborah had flown to Italy in the morning. If Ryan had only contacted them before they left, they could have gotten him the papers he needed and transported him to Washington safely. Jennifer could barely contain her anger. How was she supposed to convince the deputy attorney if she didn't have the plaintiffs with her?

She was late. Louise Jackson was probably already waiting in the Belga Café on Eighth Street, where they often met. They had originally gotten to know each other at a law firm in Belgium where they were both doing a practicum. The Belga had an authentic atmosphere, and the amazing Belgian hot chocolate brought them back to earlier days, helping to foster their friendship in its own peculiar way. Louise Jackson was a young, slender, and somewhat feisty woman with South African ancestry. She had made a brilliant career for herself in Boston, where she had been the district attorney at the district court for the last two years.

Jennifer went into the café and smoothed down her hair before spotting Jackson in the back reading a book.

"Louise?"

"Jennifer, it's lovely to see you again. I was worried when I heard your news. Sit down."

"You look radiant! How are you?"

"Thanks for asking. I'm still madly in love—and pregnant to boot. How do you think I am?"

Jennifer suddenly felt a pang in her stomach.

"What was that look?" Louise said. "Did I say something wrong? Oh wait, let me guess, you're—"

"You know, I think you just made me realize something," Jennifer said, smiling sheepishly.

"What's his name?"

"Who?"

"I want to know what his name is!"

"Adam, Adam Shane. He's…but…I'm still not sure, and…"

"Oh God, Jennifer, how long are you going to keep on trying to control everything?"

Jennifer couldn't suppress a loud laugh, followed by a quick sob, which she quickly stifled. "I'll deal with it, Louise, don't worry. I don't have a choice anymore, anyhow. He even has a little to do with the reason I wanted to see you, indirectly at least. Let me get to the point. I've prepared a claim against the Vatican that's pretty explosive."

"No, really?"

"Yes, really. I was afraid you'd react like this. I—"

"No, that's not what I mean. The coincidence is… yesterday I had to make an indictment. A student from a Catholic boarding school in Boston, along with three other victims, came to us and claimed that a bishop currently living in the Vatican had covered up his abuse of these three and—"

"*Another* abuse case? I just get sick thinking about these children. My case is a bit different, though. It's about the historical investigation into the European pagans and the question about which deeds the Church participated in and apparently continues to participate in to cover up the historical truth of their founding."

"Excuse me?"

"Do you think it would be possible for us to go to my place?" Jennifer said with a quick glance around. She didn't want to talk about this in public, especially since the first wave of information had already made it into the White House. Somehow, though, she had to get Louise on her side.

CHAPTER 31

DUBLIN – MARCH 22, AFTERNOON

"Ruth? Are you home?" MacClary was feeling guilty about not saying good-bye to Ruth before he left the last time and about not explaining to her why everything was in such a mess.

"Ronnie? Yes, I'm here. What in heaven's name happened here?" she said, coming into the foyer. "Once a week I go to see my friends, and this time I come back to find the house filled with strange men. At least Deborah was still here to give me some idea of what was going on. Otherwise I would have been scared to death. But I still don't understand why they had to check all the outlets just because the electricity went out. As if it didn't happen all the time! They made a right mess of everything."

"Oh, Ruth, I feel just awful. I had so much to do, and I had to rush off to Washington. I'm terribly sorry!"

Ruth looked at him kindly. "It's all right. Everything is back to normal again. Deborah helped me put things back in place before she left."

MacClary couldn't continue to look at Ruth without thinking of the question that had been plaguing him. "Ruth, why didn't you ever tell me about what happened to my father?"

Ruth looked past him and out the window. "So Jennifer told you. My God, Ronnie, is it really so hard to understand?"

MacClary sat down and looked around. "So many years, Ruth, so many years I've been trying to find a way to bring my father's search to some kind of conclusion. Who knows if I would have done that if I had known that it had cost him his life?"

"Then you should take it as a warning now, Ronald. You really can't understand why I did what I did? I couldn't deny your mother her dying wish. You were all she had after Sean's death. She prayed every night that nothing would happen to you and that you would be able to live your life in peace."

MacClary laughed mirthlessly. "It's too late for that now, and it's just as well."

He headed to the library, rubbing his left eye, which had begun to twitch. MacClary made himself comfortable there. It had become his custom to listen to one of his favorite Mozart symphonies after a trip. Today he put on a CD of the Prague Symphony and sat down in one of the old leather chairs. A few minutes later, he was so lost in the music that he didn't hear the telephone ringing.

"Ronnie…Ronald…" Ruth had to shake him gently to get a reaction. "You have a call."

"Oh, um, all right. Thank you, Ruth."

MacClary stood up and turned the music down before he took the phone from Ms. Copendale.

"Ronald, it's Jennifer. I did it! Louise Jackson filed the suit—expedited, no less—at the district court in Boston."

MacClary's focus returned instantly. "Fantastic, Jennifer, fantastic! That's just what we need. We'll proceed as planned. I'll contact my friend Alan Montgomery today and ask him to arrange a press conference. If we can't get any further in Boston, you can present everything to the experts in the field and make the findings of our consultants public. We can't allow the media to scoop the story and take this out of our hands. Deborah has translated everything, and there are apparently still more surprises waiting for us in the scrolls. We'll coordinate the timing tomorrow. When do you think Rome will receive the written indictment?"

"Judging by the speed that Louise displayed today, I'm sure they'll have it by tomorrow. And if I know Rome, they'll already have a policy in place for a response."

"We just have to hope that Thomas keeps his promise and that our two brave treasure hunters don't fall flat on their faces in Orvieto."

"Yes, we do. We'll see each other tomorrow in Washington?"

"Yes, absolutely."

Jennifer hung up, and MacClary turned up the music again before he sat back down in his chair.

He closed his eyes, gave himself over to the music. Within a few minutes, he was sleeping soundly.

* * *

ORVIETO, ITALY – NIGHT

Deborah had spent the whole day with Adam investigating the dome. They'd been able to find some evidence that there had to be more underneath the structure than just old graves of priests or Etruscans, the original inhabitants of this ancient city.

"I'm wondering how Ronald knew about this archive," Adam said suspiciously. "Even the most esoteric conspiracy theories on the Internet have never mentioned anything about it."

"He knows what he's doing. This dome isn't just some random church, you know. The entire city was constructed by the Etruscans on this rocky plateau. It has a secret labyrinth of cellars, passageways, and cisterns running through it. There's a reason they talk about a 'city upon a city,'" Deborah said.

"You mean, the archive isn't in the dome? It's under the rock?"

"The construction of the dome is based on a legend, the same one from which the Feast of Corpus Christi stems. According to the legend, in 1263 in Bolsena, a little town near here, blood is supposed to have flowed from the Eucharistic bread. But there is another reason I think we're in the right place: in the Middle Ages, several popes were entrenched here, among them Clement VII. All the secret escape routes and cellars would make it an ideal hiding place."

Deborah and Adam looked like a pair of backpackers looking for a hotel late at night. No one took any notice of them as it grew quieter and quieter in the streets around the dome.

"Wait!"

Deborah grabbed Adam by the arm. A car approached the dome. They hid behind a corner of the wall and watched as three priests went up to a side door and disappeared into the building.

"What are they doing here at this hour?"

"Better late than never." Deborah grinned.

Adam pointed to the ventilation shaft they were standing on. "Do you see this exhaust grate? It's not very old. I can see light down there."

They looked at each other in silence, and then a childlike smile spread across Deborah's face. "Bull's-eye, Adam. I think this is it," she whispered. "Now we have to figure out where our late-night supplicants were headed."

A quarter of an hour passed as they stood in the dark watching the parked car. Then the priests came out again and drove away. At the same time, the light from the ventilation shaft went out and they stood in complete darkness.

"This is our only chance, I think," Adam said as he started to use a crowbar to remove the grate from its frame.

"Stop! Are you crazy?"

Deborah took several instruments out of her bag and lit up the shaft. "There's nothing there. We must not be in the right place. And if there's no security here...wait a minute...there is something..."

Deborah shook some fine ash from a small container into the shaft, making it possible to see two moving laser beams. She then lit up the shaft until she could see an electrical circuit behind a casing.

"Is that it?" Adam asked.

"Well, I don't see anything else. It would be far too easy if it were, wouldn't it? But I'll test it anyhow." She took a small netbook out of her bag and placed several firm clamps on the cord. "This is no big deal for Thomas's program."

"*Thomas's* program?"

"Yes, of course. Did you think I wrote it during my free time while I was studying at the university? Still, the security seems flimsy to me. We should be careful."

"No, I can see it. We have to go down here, I'm sure."

Deborah closed her eyes for a moment and then nodded. The scene reminded her of that moment at MacClary's when they were all standing in front of the vitrine. Without Adam's uncanny intuition leading them to the coordinates of the cave, none of the events of the last few days would have been possible. They pushed an iron stake into the ground and tied a rope to it.

"I'll go first," she said, already letting herself down carefully. When she got to the bottom, she called, "Adam,

I think…I think we've really found it, but…oh, come down, and see for yourself."

Adam wrapped the second rope around his chest, tying it with a climber's knot. When he landed, he shone his flashlight through the bars of the grate. They could see bookshelves filled with old files and another entrance next to the door opposite them, just visible through a glass pane. There was a sign that said something about conservation and restoration, and it had the seal of the Vatican.

Deborah had already begun to loosen the bars with a chisel and a rubber hammer, finding it surprisingly easy to do so. "They must be awfully sure that no one will find this place," she said. "Somehow I can't imagine we're really going to find what we're looking for here. They should have all sorts of security devices here."

"I'd be just as happy to do without any more hurdles."

The last bar slipped out of her fingers and fell with a loud clang onto the floor. "Damn it," she whispered into her turtleneck, and they both ducked down. However, after the clanging subsided, it was replaced with absolute quiet.

"Do I have to pray now, or what?" Adam joked.

"Did you hear something?"

"No, not a thing."

"Good. Still, we don't have much time. Someone must have heard that. I'll go first."

Deborah noticed that her hands were trembling. Adam must have noticed as well.

"Hey, wait a minute," he said. "Give me your hands."

"What?"

"Give me your hands!"

She gave him a skeptical look but stretched her hands out obediently. Adam took them firmly into his own. Two little hands in his own enormous ones.

"Trust me, OK?"

To her surprise, Deborah could feel herself calming down in Adam's warm grasp. "That helped. Thank you."

"Now go."

Deborah pushed her upper body through the opening and let herself down silently. The room was enormous. The walls were lined with shelves full of old documents. "I don't believe it. This is a collection of the forbidden books of the Inquisition. Here, look…"

"We don't have time for that," Adam said sharply. He carefully opened the swinging door to the corridor. It was pitch black and deathly quiet. Was it really possible that no one had heard the bar fall? Could they really be that lucky?

Just as Adam started into the hall, the door slammed against him, hitting his forehead. He threw himself back against the door so hard that his assailant slammed against the opposite wall and slid to the floor.

Deborah ran into the hall, scanning up and down the corridor with her flashlight. She saw a dark figure running away, but he was too far gone to stop him. If he went to get help, they had at most a few seconds before they had to get back up the shaft if they were going to avoid being seen.

"Adam, we need to get out of here!"

"Not a chance! Let's take your pictures."

As if she were operating on remote control, Deborah got her camera out of her pocket and took all the pictures she could. She cursed softly as she realized that the flash was throwing light everywhere, even on the street in front of the ventilation shafts.

Adam gesticulated wildly with both hands. "Come in here!" Using a crowbar, he broke open the locked door to the conservation room and turned on the light.

"Are you insane? Turn out the light!"

"It doesn't matter anymore." He pointed to the back table, where several scrolls were spread open. "Quick, give me a box."

With lightning speed Deborah took one of the boxes from her shoulder, just like the ones she had used in Austria for transporting parchment. Seemingly uncaring of the danger they were in, Adam rolled the scroll into the box. Deborah got a fleeting glance of the writing on it.

"Wait a minute, that's…a scroll about Sopatros…he was…"

"We can get to all of that later," Adam said, closing the box and running toward the ventilation shaft.

Both of them pulled themselves up the shaft as quickly as they could. They sprinted toward the narrow streets right next to the dome. Deborah saw an armed man coming out of the dome and running toward them. They hadn't seen him before.

Suddenly there was a shot that just missed Deborah and hit a wall. As stone shards sprayed, she ran into a side street just in time to avoid the next shot. One street to the left, then again to the right. Both of them were running as fast as they could. They were lucky: the streets were too narrow for a car to follow. Somewhat relieved, but still frantically looking over their shoulders, they kept on until they reached the dark safety of one of the many labyrinthine back courtyards.

Deborah and Shane waited there until almost dawn before they slowly inched their way back to the rental car. There was no one around. The police and their pursuers from the dome must have given up at some point. Relieved, they fell into the car and drove to the airport.

CHAPTER 32

VATICAN CITY, ROME – MARCH 23, MORNING

The knock on the door was so loud that Salvoni jumped at the sound.

"Salvoni, where did you store the parchments?" Lambert barked as he entered.

"We had them brought to Orvieto after the Holy Father examined them. He was quite shocked."

"Who arranged it?"

"Who arranged what, Cardinal?"

"The transport of the parchments to Orvieto. What else have we been talking about here?"

"Excuse me, I'm confused. Contas arranged it, Cardinal."

"Damn it, I do not understand. Is everyone here doing exactly as they please now? Is there even the slightest trace of coordination left in this organization? I clearly said that the material should on no account leave the Vatican before the matter is concluded."

Salvoni was trying to get his wits about him, but he was having trouble. "What happened? Orvieto is the most secure location we could—"

"Your *secure* Orvieto was broken into! Without the brave intervention of the priests and guards, it could have been much worse. Apparently nothing is missing, to which I can only say thanks be to God." Lambert crossed himself three times and then pulled out a handkerchief with trembling hands, wiping the sweat from his forehead.

"I have a good idea who's behind it," Salvoni muttered ruefully.

"So do I. It's not exactly difficult to figure out, is it?" He regarded Salvoni darkly. "Salvoni, it's time that we face the music. I may not be able to keep you on anymore, and I have to ask you to perform one last service for us."

Salvoni had known this moment would come one day. His fate had been hanging over him like a shadow for years. He had grown tired to his core, so horribly tired, that he was ready to agree to anything. All that mattered to him now was that he would soon be done with this miserable torment. "Yes, Cardinal."

"First, make sure that everything in Orvieto is destroyed. The old archive will be dissolved and brought here. And every last one of the parchments from Austria will be destroyed, no exceptions."

Salvoni couldn't even comprehend what Lambert was ordering. He was talking about ancient artifacts, documents of incalculable value and huge importance for the study of antiquity. There were articles about the Druids' medical science and trade agreements with Rome that proved how advanced the metalworking of the Celts had been. And of course there were countless writings of the old philosophers, which the Druids, in their thirst for knowledge, had collected and assimilated.

"But Cardinal, only a small portion of our collection is concerned with the foundation of the Church. Couldn't we just secure the rest of the documents in the Vatican? I mean…no matter what happens, if we destroy these invaluable documents now, people will just demonize us all the more. It won't be easy to hide the library of the Druids from the public eye, but to destroy it…" Salvoni didn't have anything to lose, and he could feel, to his own astonishment, how calm that made him. "We both know that the really sensational documents aren't in Orvieto anyhow."

Lambert nodded. "You're right, Salvoni, we both know that. Ronald MacClary's friends must have found precisely those scrolls which would be most effective to use against us."

The two men remained silent for a minute, and then Lambert calmly continued. "You know, Salvoni, I just read a book by one of our harshest critics. The title is *The Vatican Walks in the Devil's Shoes*. Sensationalistic, but from the author's viewpoint, very apt. For centuries we've managed to keep these critics in the tiny, manageable confines of their scientific community and to protect the faithful from their venom, but how much longer can we continue to do this? How much longer, Salvoni?" Lambert sat down. "The abuse cases have heated up criticism of the Church. We've always argued on the basis that humans have their foibles and make mistakes, even within the Church. But this library of the Druids, as you call it, this could bring an end to this line of reasoning. And what then?" Lambert folded his hands behind his head. He looked almost relaxed, but Salvoni knew that appearances were deceiving.

"What then? I don't know, Cardinal, but I know that it's a mistake to destroy this new discovery. It may be that, in the end, it could help us to make amends."

Lambert slowly nodded. "All right, Salvoni, perhaps you're right. Just destroy the most controversial parchments and bring the rest to the archive of the Holy Father. But it has to happen today, do you hear me? And one more thing: If my sources are to be trusted, a lawyer in the United States is attempting to call the Vatican to account for the operation in Austria. The woman must belong to MacClary's circle, but I don't know anything more than that. If this case is really taken up, then you know what must be done." Lambert looked at him sharply.

Salvoni would not wither under Lambert's gaze. "You will remember, Cardinal, that this was my suggestion. We need an airtight official denial, and I am ready to be the one to take responsibility for it. And the Holy Father?"

"He knows everything that he needs to know. I think he will know how to conduct himself and how to use his influence in Washington."

"What does that mean?"

"Our lawyers are doing everything necessary for our and your protection, as much as is possible. If it is enough, then you...then we all will have been lucky. You see, Salvoni, the Holy Father is acting for all of us."

Salvoni shrugged his shoulders. This was the first time he had seen Lambert worrying about the fate of an individual. Until now he had always talked about the greater good, inspired by the belief that he had to protect God's work. Something had changed.

"I expect you to return from Orvieto immediately after everything is taken care of," Lambert said.

"And then?"

"Then we will use every resource available to us to make sure that Thomas Ryan doesn't slip through our fingers again."

Salvoni tensed. Inside, the little spark of hope that he had just felt flickered out again. Nothing would change as long as people like Lambert were steering the fate of the Church. "I understand, Cardinal."

"And Salvoni, if you should fail, this is the number of a Swiss account and an address in Rome. I'll arrange for your discharge papers, which are backdated to December." Lambert pressed a credit card, a key, and an address near the Colosseum into Salvoni's hand. "I hope you won't need it."

* * *

WASHINGTON, DC – MARCH 23, AFTERNOON

As they approached Washington, they looked for their Irish diplomatic passes, which had come in handy on this trip. "I still can't believe we got out of there in one piece," Deborah said, laughing erratically. Shane thought she might be a bit hysterical from exhaustion and being shot at in Orvieto.

"I have to admit, I've always thought those huge security systems were just something you see in movies, but we were incredibly lucky to find a weak spot," Shane said, taking a deep breath as the plane started to land. "To think, I used to be afraid of flying."

They drove from the airport directly to the laboratory and handed over the only scroll Shane had grabbed for radiocarbon analysis. MacClary had flown back to Washington the night before. Jennifer hadn't been able to sit in her hotel room anymore and had been in the laboratory for hours brooding over Deborah's translations.

"You little devils actually did it!" Jennifer exclaimed as Deborah and Shane came into the laboratory break room.

"Yes, we did. We managed to photograph everything, as promised, *and* we brought a pretty exciting document," Shane said. Just then he remembered how Deborah had been preoccupied with the parchment. "So who was this Sopatros, anyhow?"

Deborah jumped right into academic mode. "He was the most important head of the neo-Platonic school in Rome, and he most likely took on several students who had been educated by Druids. He was a very well-regarded advisor to Constantine until he was executed in 330 by imperial order because of his pagan beliefs and because he refused to desist with his anti-Christian writings."

Shane shook his head. "Yet another victim I didn't know about. I should start a tally sheet. You know, the more familiar I become with how the Vatican thinks, the smaller they seem to me in their massive, lordly robes. The more I learn, the less I can comprehend why they don't simply admit what they've done. On the contrary, they still see themselves as the great leaders of religion." He played with a pencil, lost in thought.

"They still think they have an exclusive hold on salvation," Jennifer said. "It makes me sick. But with this library, we can break their absolute claim to truth. And I swear to you, I'm going to pull out all the stops to accomplish it."

Shane was surprised that Jennifer's anger failed to motivate him. "I think we need to shoot higher. This library gives the entire Western world a chance to ask ourselves what we are doing, what kind of society we want to create."

"I know what you mean," Jennifer said. "Maybe it really would be enough to make everything we have public and then wait and see what happens. But I want more, Adam. I want the few remaining descendants of the Druids and the entire world to have claim to the historical truth." Jennifer turned and looked through a window, watching the scientists working with a scroll. Shane was wondering if she ever doubted herself.

"Where is Ronald, anyhow?" he asked. He was a bit surprised, and not a little disappointed, that MacClary hadn't been there to give a warm welcome to his two heroes. After all, they now had nearly all the proof they needed.

"He's meeting with the justices all day today," Jennifer said matter-of-factly, "sorting out our options."

CHAPTER 33

ROME – MARCH 24, AFTERNOON

Pope John Paul III was standing in front of the window in his private rooms and looking out onto St. Peter's Square. He was resting his hands heavily on the windowsill.

"Holy Father? Cardinal Lambert is requesting a brief audience."

The pope turned around slowly. "Very well. Tell him to come in."

With slow steps, Lambert entered and bowed down. "Holy Father, I have—"

"Cardinal," the pope interrupted him, his voice serious as he showed him the papers the Vatican lawyers had given him that morning. "I expect to have an honest answer. Now. Who is responsible for this?"

"Holy Father, please! It's better if you know as little as possible about this. It's—"

"As God is my witness, tell me the truth, now!" the pope ordered. "You never told me it had escalated to violence. I have to—"

"I have already dismissed the person responsible, Victor Salvoni, a member of our police force. He was the one who acted without consulting anyone. Even I can't tell you exactly what happened in Austria."

The pope relaxed slightly. "Good. That means Padre… he is a padre, isn't he?"

"Yes, Holy Father."

"Then Padre Salvoni will take official responsibility in case our defense fails?"

"Yes, he will. I have already discussed everything with him."

The pope nodded slowly. "Do we know the contents of the scrolls that are presumably in Ireland or the United States?"

"No, unfortunately not, Holy Father."

"Well, Cardinal, from what little I have seen, this is extremely dangerous, especially given the overall situation we find ourselves in."

The pope had spent half his life studying ancient history, but like so many of his predecessors, he hadn't felt the need to face the consequences of this bloody history. Now he shuddered to think about the consequences of these wars, wars fought against cultures under the command of the Church. He couldn't let Lambert see the slightest doubt or weakness.

"I don't need to tell you what kind of impression it would make if we were to be officially accused of using violence to obstruct the discovery of this library of the

Druids. I will try to use my influence in Washington. Pray that I am successful."

Silence and cover-ups. There are so many reasons to hate us, the pope thought, *and everything motivated by the fear of taking responsibility*. One of these days this mindset of the Church would break more than just its back.

"Yes, Holy Father, I will take care of things going forward."

"Keep me informed on a regular basis. Good day, Cardinal."

* * *

In front of the door to the president's office, Bill Axton had spent the last few minutes reorganizing the president's speech, which he had dropped to the floor. He sat down and waited, but, finally, he couldn't wait any longer, otherwise the president would miss her next appointment. As he opened the door, she waved him inside and Axton could see that she was boiling mad.

"There is one thing I cannot do, Holy Father," President Branks said sharply, her face crimson. "I cannot and will not interfere with our judiciary. If your lawyers are unable to get the case dismissed, my hands are tied. I can make sure that news of the case is not leaked to the public, for now, but that is all I can do."

Axton groaned inwardly. The last thing this president needed now was a dispute with the Vatican. If it should get out, it would turn a huge number of voters against the Democrats, and that would give the Republicans that much more fuel for the fire they wanted to set for her.

"Yes, Holy Father, I promise you that I will take care of the matter personally," the president said. There was a pause as the pope spoke. "Thank you, Holy Father."

After that, she hung up the phone. Her advisors, who had been unable to avoid listening in, looked at her questioningly. She looked around the room. "Everyone out. Bill, you stay here. Ask the justice to come here immediately, and find out in which court the charges are being brought. I want it on my desk by five this afternoon."

"Yes, Madam President, I'll take care of it. What about your appointment in the Cabinet Room?"

"Cancel it, and tell MacClary that he has until six tonight to show up here. Oh, and another thing. I need tomorrow's speech by eight tonight. I'm going to need to make some changes."

* * *

MACCLARY'S APARTMENT, WASHINGTON, DC – MARCH 24, AFTERNOON

MacClary hung up the phone and looked resignedly out his window at the dome of the Capitol. As they had hoped, Boston had dismissed the case due to lack of evidence. The call he had just received from the White House hinted that the judge in Boston had acted so quickly because someone in Washington had lent a helping hand.

The first summons to the White House had been extended in a relatively friendly fashion. This one sounded much more like a command. What in the devil had gotten into the president? He had taken her completely into his confidence. Would she crumble after all out of fear of public opinion?

He was interrupted by the ringing of his doorbell. He stood up slowly and walked to the door.

"Adam, Deborah, Jennifer. Come in."

"Guess what, Ronald?" Adam said. "The head of the institute confirmed in his report that the parchment comes from the same period as the trove we found in Austria. The pollen and radiocarbon analysis can't lie. Exactly as we had hoped! It's proof that it came from the cave."

MacClary looked at him, confused. Then he shook his head to clear it and come back to the present. "Excuse me, I was somewhere else. First off, my hearty congratulations to you both. I have to say, you both showed a great deal of courage doing this."

"And we needed it when they were shooting at us," Deborah added.

MacClary gasped. "Why didn't you tell me this yesterday? That means they know you were there! Damn it!" MacClary slammed his fist against the wall.

"That's unlikely," Deborah said, "since we were only there a few seconds. We had just enough time to take some photos, grab one of the scrolls, and get out of there. If we're lucky, they won't notice anything missing."

"Well, there's nothing to be done. We can't waste any time."

Jennifer walked over to his desk, where she saw the fax from the district court in Boston. "When did you get this?"

"A few minutes ago. I should have called you right away."

"But this is what you wanted," Jennifer said in astonishment. "I'll pass on everything to the Supreme Court tonight and then—"

"Wait, Jennifer. I just got an unpleasant call from the White House, and I can assure you it wasn't a casual invitation to tea. Something isn't right there. I'll need your help now to move forward. So I'd like to ask you all to come with me to the White House."

* * *

"I hope the president is aware that you aren't coming alone," Axton said politely.

"No, but she'll soon find out," MacClary answered with a slightly arrogant grin.

"As you wish."

When they found themselves standing in front of the president a bit later, Shane could feel his hands starting to sweat.

"Ronald, what is the meaning of this?" the president asked sharply.

"Madam President, may I introduce you to Adam Shane and Deborah Walker, two of the three people who were involved in retrieving the artifacts in Austria," MacClary said confidently. "And Jennifer Wilson, a lawyer friend of mine who has joined with the district attorney in Boston as a prosecutor of the case in Thomas Ryan's name. He has been missing since the retrieval of the documents we've discussed in Austria and is supposedly being hunted down in Italy as a terrorist, an apparent use of targeted misinformation from the Vatican."

"Stop, Ronald! This can't all be true! I personally spoke with the pope today on the telephone and—"

"And he will have knowingly or unknowingly avoided telling you the whole truth," MacClary said, trying to preempt an accusation.

"The Vatican wants to ensure that they are not connected with the events in Austria. The responsibility for the so-called attack belongs with a one-time member of the Vatican police, who was relieved of duty last year and—"

"Excuse me, Madam President, but that is impossible." Shane heard his own voice sounding unnaturally loud in the room before he was even conscious of the fact that he had spoken. "We were able to obtain proof that certain artifacts from the Magdalensberg cave, which would cause quite a stir when viewed in the light of Church history, are being kept in a Vatican archive."

"Is this true, Ronald?"

MacClary hesitated for a moment. "Yes, Madam President, and that means that the Vatican is quite definitely behind this. They didn't have all the facts in Boston and were apparently not all that concerned with motive."

"How do you know they have all the facts in Rome? Do you think I always know what my ministers, my party, or the CIA are fighting out behind my back? Do you know how often I have to back a decision that I know nothing about and that I still have to accede to? So much for the power of my office, Ronald."

Ronald was well aware of the exposed position Diana was in, and it almost made him sorry that this had all come up during her tenure. On the other hand, she had the fighting spirit the situation needed.

"Diana, that's not the whole story. I'd like to ask for your trust. Let us explain everything to you now."

The president balled up her fists. Then she went to her desk and pressed the speaker button of her telephone. "Bill? I'm not to be disturbed for the next half hour," she said before turning back to her visitors with a sigh.

CHAPTER 34

NIZZANI COUNTRY HOUSE, ITALY – MARCH 24, AFTERNOON

Ryan sat on the terrace, a glass of red wine in his hand, as he looked at the gorgeous Italian Alps. In the midday light, enveloped in fog, they looked like giant watchmen, millions of years old. How small and insignificant these couple of thousand years had been when humankind, in its egocentric way, believed it could rule the planet, instead of living in natural harmony with the earth. He needed to keep reminding himself that an increasing number of people were becoming aware of this. Langster had brought him to a friend, a very wealthy doctor, who had treated his wounds and given him a place to stay where he could recover for at least a bit. The whole time he was plagued by thoughts about what had happened. How was he going to explain to the others why he had been labeled a terrorist? Langster had forbidden him to pick up the phone, but he couldn't wait anymore.

"Well, how does it feel to be a member of one of the oldest families in the world?" Langster joked as he sat across from him.

"Oh, better, much better. But it doesn't seem to be sitting all that well with other people."

"I'm sorry, but I need a couple more days to get you back to Washington safely. You're still on the Italian police's wanted list. The doctor has said he's willing to take you to Washington in his private jet as soon as it's possible, and then—"

The thought of more time out of contact made Ryan's heart lurch. "Brian, I can't wait that long. There's too much at stake. I have to at least let them know that I'm alive."

Langster said nothing for a second and then locked eyes with Ryan. "Of course. Here, here's my cell phone. Try to keep it under a minute." In Ireland, he had always had a reputation for being exceedingly cautious. His successes spoke for themselves; no one had yet been able to track him down.

"Thank you, Brian, I'll be brief."

* * *

WHITE HOUSE, WASHINGTON, DC – MARCH 24, EVENING

After a good hour, Shane, Deborah, Jennifer, and Ronald left the president's office. All of them were beaming. Even MacClary's relief was written all over his face.

"Ronald, you can depend on my people," the president had said. "We'll find Thomas Ryan and bring him safely home as soon as he gets to the airport."

"Why didn't you tell us about this before?" Jennifer asked when they got into the corridor. She was still completely bewildered by the information that Ronald had kept to himself until now.

"Quite simply, I promised. And please, Jennifer, not a word to Ms. Copendale. She knows him and has no idea about his past. That goes for you two as well."

Deborah nodded obediently. Shane didn't say anything. In the last hour, the president had honestly and bluntly admitted how limited their options really were and how powerful Rome's influence still was. Even in the United States, elections were still won based on religious faith.

But what had impressed Shane the most was the president's idea of a shift in economic policy. She'd had several books open on her desk written by the most renowned scientific philosophers and alternative economic theorists. It all boiled down to a complete renunciation of an economy based on growth. The president's ideas about a new worldwide ethic were a revelation to Shane, a revelation that he had given up believing could be possible.

Ronald and Shane had been able to convince her to play along, but the game was a long way from being won. Ryan was still missing, maybe even dead. They had no idea what Rome had up its sleeve to make it look like its hands were clean. That left only Ronald's secret source—and even that was unpredictable.

"If she gives this speech in front of the United Nations, she'll be out of the game," Ronald commented, a bit too coldly for Shane's taste.

"You will be too, Ronald," Shane replied.

"What? Yes, that's possible, but I'm assuming that the president will be giving one justice after the other a good talking to and that she will insist on them following their juristic obligations and not their beliefs. What was that text you gave her that helped changed her mind?"

"In the last few days I have felt so completely overwhelmed by everything that's happened, and after I was shot at for the first time in my life, I could suddenly sense Ryan. Now don't look at me like that. I really did sense him, as if he were right there next to me. It was eerie, but I was stomping around in his past…" Shane trailed off for a moment before continuing. "I was thinking about the symbol in the chamber again, the spiral of life, and about what Ryan had told me about the field of memories, in which everything that has ever happened is stored in what amounts to an enormous databank. If I correctly understand the parchment of the Druids that deals with space and time, each one of us can travel in this spiral of time. We can use our experiences if we seize the information and if we are open to the possibility of understanding history not in a linear path, but as the sum of all experiences. The more people who do this, the more this experience will escalate, until it has reached a critical mass that is prepared to develop a new consciousness from the sum of these experiences."

"Not necessarily a new consciousness, Adam," Deborah added, "but in any case one that is bound with a life characterized by balance and harmony with the land and the earth. The end of all the bedlam."

Shane nodded vigorously. "Exactly. There would come a moment when a high official, an ideal ruler, in an historic or mystical instant would grab the world's attention by initiating a noble and benevolent government. This government would escape the confines of time and space because of its experience and love for creation. It will find itself at a point of intersection where it will have to act with integrity and authenticity."

Ronald looked at him, astonished. "That's what Thomas has been talking about for years."

"But what does that have to do with the president?" Deborah asked.

"She is standing at the point of intersection. Her willingness to act, without thinking about her own ego, for the benefit of all life, is what the Druids called the King of Worlds."

"And the Christians called him the Messiah," Deborah added.

"Yes. It's just that the Church has completely distorted this, and in so doing, has actually prevented the coming of the Messiah. We're not talking about a person or even a form, but about the coming of a new consciousness that can realize its potential in each one of us. It doesn't matter which religion you look at: the Messiah, the Savior, or the good ruler, they're all really just synonyms for humankind's longing for a higher consciousness. That means that the president herself is no shining light; she is just the point of intersection where everything connects. Just like in set theory."

Shane felt as though he could suddenly understand everything. That's what the return of the Druids meant: a state of consciousness that made it impossible to go against the laws of nature and balance. People had to take responsibility for their own salvation.

"She will give the speech," Ronald said, "I'm sure of it. Now I understand why she finds the impending conflict with Rome so useful."

"But Adam, why do you think the president is this person?" Jennifer asked.

Shane shrugged. "I just know. I can't give you any other reason. That's the vision I had. And to get back to your earlier question, that's why I greeted her with the short, inspirational greeting of our ancestors."

* * *

Just then Ronald's cell phone rang.

"MacClary."

"Ronald, it's Thomas."

"My God, Thomas! Where in the devil are you? Do you have any idea how worried we've been? The latest news reports were a shock for all of us, and—"

"Ronald, I'm so sorry. I hadn't counted on anything like that either and—"

"How can they simply label you an IRA terrorist when you were fighting *against* them? The Italian police can't be manipulated that easily!"

"I'll explain everything when I'm back in Washington. It'll be another couple of days, though, because I'm still on the wanted list. I'm getting some papers and I'll be flown to Washington on a private jet."

"Take care of yourself, Thomas! And remember, you have to come see me first. We've already gotten quite a few things rolling here. Right now I'm standing in front of the White House. They'll help you in any way they can when you've landed, and hopefully you'll soon be standing in front of the Supreme Court." Normally no witnesses were heard in a case tried before the Supreme Court, but in this case, the justices would hardly be able to object. They had made too many mistakes in Boston.

"Understood. I'll contact you again when I have more specific info. How are Adam and Deborah? Did they get everything back safely?"

"Not only that, Thomas, but Adam has blossomed into a real Irishman. If you knew what the two of them have been up to…"

"That's good, but I didn't really expect anything less. I rarely make mistakes with people, Ronald. I have to get off now. I'll call again tomorrow. Thanks for everything."

"I'll take care of—" Ryan had already hung up.

Relieved, the justice looked around at the present company. "Now let the old men in Rome play their games. We'll do what we discussed with the president. Jennifer, have you finished the documents?"

"Of course. They're already at the court. You just have to set a hearing."

CHAPTER 35

SUPREME COURT, WASHINGTON, DC – MARCH 26, MORNING

MacClary had spent the whole morning thinking about how he could create some confusion in Rome. What did they already know? What were they afraid of, and what was their next move?

Suddenly he jumped up and scrambled through his notebook for the telephone number for Edonardo Vasaci, a journalist in a Roman news agency. He'd been combing his memory for the name.

The phone rang for quite a while before Vasaci finally picked up.

"Hello, Signore Vasaci, I hope you still remember me."

"Honorable Justice! I'd recognize your voice anywhere! Tell me you have another story for me. I still owe you for the last one."

"No, no," MacClary said, smiling. "This time you can pay me back for the last time." Several years ago, MacClary had passed on some sensational information to Vasaci about the government of Andreotti.

MacClary could hear a vacuum cleaner outside the door of his apartment. The cleaning service was making its weekly rounds. This was one of those moments when he longed for Dublin. He was sick of the noises in this town; it never rested. "I would be incredibly grateful if you could float a story for me. It won't be long. I'll call you back when you can retract it as a hoax."

"Understood, Justice. I'll do anything for the story, even thumb my nose at my job."

"Thank you. Thank you very much."

MacClary knew he could depend on Vasaci. When they'd finished talking, it was time to meet with the other justices. The president should have had the chance by now to exert her influence on them. He picked up the phone again.

"Mr. Carrington, I'll need a ride in twenty minutes."

"Very well, sir." Ronald's driver was one of the few people who somehow managed to arrive on time, no matter what the traffic in Washington was like.

Some of the justices would continue to resist Jennifer's appeal, but he knew he had two or three securely on his side. Plus the court in Boston had dismissed the case far too quickly; just the formal irregularities were serious enough. Ronald knew that everything was coming down to the wire now. His—and the president's—political survival was hanging from the thread of Jennifer's seamless marshaling of evidence and his clever maneuvering to provide for any contingency.

The telephone rang.

"MacClary."

"Ronald, it's Jennifer. I just heard from Democratic Senator Jeff Bukake that one of the justices in the court is trying to mobilize against you. There are rumors that a Republican in the House of Representatives wants to mount an impeachment process against you if you vote to take on my appeal."

MacClary wondered on what basis someone could launch an impeachment process. His lectures couldn't possibly be enough to discredit him to that extent. Had Rome come up with something insidious?

"Well then, I have to get enough of the justices on my side to make my vote unnecessary, Jennifer," he said, surprising himself by how calm and composed his voice sounded.

"Ronald, if what I've heard is correct, it will be enough that you're still a member of the court, let alone the chief justice. If the case is adopted, there won't be any way of stopping it anymore."

"Jennifer, there are three months until the congressional elections. The president has a respectable majority right now, and by the time any impeachment procedure comes to a vote, this whole thing will be long over."

"Not necessarily. You know as well as I do that a hearing can be postponed until the process against you has been resolved one way or another."

"Jennifer, please! Are we really still so backward that we're going to let attempted murder, theft, and cover-ups simply go unchallenged?"

He could hear Jennifer sigh. "Ronald, be honest. How many justices do you have on your side?"

"Well, I have Bob Johnson, Ian Copter, and Barbara Andrews for sure. I confirmed that this morning. I don't think a single one of the justices would take the risk of going behind my back like that. If it should come out, they'd be in hot water themselves. But who knows. I'll be at the court in an hour and I'll speak with Alex Winster. I hope I can make him see the light. I might have to play my trump card earlier than I had planned. I'll discuss it with Ryan, and then we'll see. Oh, and another thing. Yesterday I spoke with some delegates from the Irish Parliament and told them about our find. The Irish Foreign Ministry has clearly committed itself to our cause and wants to make this clear under international law. They stand ready to do more."

"That's good news, Ronald. Good luck in court."

"Thank you. I'm afraid I'm going to need it."

* * *

VATICAN CITY, ROME – MARCH 26

Salvoni had finished his siesta when he heard the news broadcast on the radio. One item made his afternoon coffee superfluous. Could he really be so lucky?

He quickly got up, pulled on his pants and shirt, and ran out of the room as if his life depended on it, straight into a priest who was coming toward him in the corridor and who was now getting up again, cursing the whole time. When he arrived at the press department, Salvoni attacked the most recent Italian wire copy.

"I can't believe it! Thank you, Lord, thank you." Salvoni pulled his cell phone from his pocket and tried to reach Lambert, to no avail. He ran through the gardens of Vatican City to the Government Palace, ran up the steps, and stormed into Lambert's office.

Lambert sat in an adjoining room making a telephone call in English. He threw a grim look toward Salvoni, but Salvoni's beaming face made him take the telephone away from his ear.

"What is it?" Lambert whispered.

Salvoni hurried over to Lambert and gave him the wire copy as Lambert asked the person on the telephone to wait a moment. As he read the news he almost dropped the telephone. "Mr. Carrington, I'm afraid I have to interrupt our conversation for a bit. I believe our situation has taken a dramatic turn. I'll call you right back."

Lambert hung up and looked at Salvoni. "Has this been confirmed, Victor?"

That was the first time in nearly thirty years that Lambert had addressed him by his first name. "Yes, I think so. He was found in Austria."

Lambert smiled darkly. "Are you aware that this changes everything? Be ready for a trip to Washington. We shouldn't miss this opportunity to snatch the justice's triumph against the Holy Church from his hands. Have you had everything taken care of in Orvieto? Are the rest of the scrolls here?"

"Yes, they are in the archive of the Holy Father." Salvoni was suddenly plagued by doubt about the reliability of the news, about the possibility of opposition. "As much as I would enjoy it, isn't it a bit too risky, just flying off to Washington?"

"No, don't worry about it. Not only do we have diplomatic immunity, we also have the full support of the Holy Father."

Salvoni knew that Lambert was a sly fox. He was always amazed at Lambert's ability to protect the Vatican from any kind of criticism or even criminal prosecution. That's what assured him his almost untouchable position, and Salvoni, not for the first time, was convinced that he was standing in front of the next pope.

"I will inform the Holy Father," Lambert said. "You are welcome to come with me. I think you have earned the right."

CHAPTER 36

SUPREME COURT, WASHINGTON, DC – MARCH 26, AFTERNOON

Even though he felt as though his talk with Jennifer had brought him to a new level of understanding, Ronald could hardly contain his rage. For more than a quarter of an hour he'd been sitting in the conference room waiting for the justices. And something else Jennifer had told him was bothering him even more. Not only had Ruth Copendale lived all those years with the horrible knowledge about the death of his father, but she had apparently also prayed for Ryan, Shane, and Deborah on the evening before their departure for Austria. He had never known her to pray outside of church.

"Ronald!"

"Elora, I'm glad you got here first, I—"

"You don't have to explain anything to me, Ronald," Justice Elora Spencer said. "It might surprise you, but I will be voting to approve this petition if I'm convinced by the lawyers and the facts. The president called me yesterday. I didn't vote for her and she's not a member of my party, but in this case she was able to convince me that

I shouldn't let myself be guided by my respect for the Vatican, and I won't. You, however, are still a problem."

"What do you mean by that?"

"How could you get involved in this matter in Dublin, Ronald? There are two possibilities as I see it. Either you tender your resignation now or you take the risk of being forced out of office. No matter what you decide, we won't block the hearing. I've spoken with the other justices, and if we count your vote, we'll have a majority—"

"Well, that should make you happy!" John Faster said, plowing into the room. "This Church founded our civilization, with all its strengths and foibles, and you go and stomp on it." Faster, as always, was ready for a fight. Enraged, he slammed his briefcase on the polished conference table.

Elora Spencer leaned forward a bit and laid both of her hands on the table. "John, could you calm down a bit, please? None of us has any intention of indiscriminately harming the Church. But we've already discussed all of this. You'll have sufficient opportunity to pick apart the lawyers."

Faster reluctantly calmed down and sat, his face crimson red, at the other end of the conference table. The remaining justices methodically entered the teak-walled conference room. An enormous Persian rug gave the room an air of warmth.

Ronald opened the session as usual. "Dear colleagues, we're speaking today about the urgent application from the district attorney in Boston and the attorney representing

Thomas Ryan, a US citizen. In light of recent events, I would like to make one thing absolutely clear: my private research and lectures have no influence on my professional integrity, even if one of the justices present today has tried to discredit me for it."

A murmur went around the room.

"It's a good thing there aren't thirteen of us and that you, Faster, are not Judas, otherwise people might think we were at the Last Supper here. Of course, it's possible that Senator Bukake was simply mistaken yesterday."

Faster stood up and slammed a copy of the Constitution on the table. "Mr. Chief Justice, this is our Constitution. Perhaps you'd like to sue the United States as well, since we haven't always followed our own rules."

"I'd be happy to discuss that after our session. However, the United States is not claiming to be the representative of God on earth." Several of the justices couldn't refrain from laughing at Faster's tantrum. "Now please sit down."

Faster, frustrated, complied.

Barbara Andrews, one of the justices whom MacClary had always respected and admired, entered into the conversation. "My dear colleagues, our problem lies not only with the public reaction to the proceedings. There is also the matter of the Vatican's status under international law. We should perhaps follow the opinion of the ICC and the majority of states, which—"

"What do you mean by that?" Ian Copter interrupted.

"Let me explain. Based on recent developments, it is quite possible that the next General Assembly of the United Nations will adopt a resolution to withdraw recognition of the Vatican as a subject of international law."

"That's completely ridiculous!"

Feelings were starting to run high, but Justice Andrews didn't let this sway her.

"As I said, Justice Copter, that is the new opinion of the community of states. According to the classic rules of international law, what is missing from this construct is the essential feature of a state, namely citizens. The unusual thing about small nations is that membership is only given for a limited amount of time and—"

"That is irrelevant here. Until otherwise decided, the Holy See is a person governed by international law, and its members therefore enjoy the privileges appertaining to it," Adrienne Morburg said. "But what are we talking about here anyhow?" Justice Morburg was usually somewhat shy, but she was also a very clever jurist who didn't let herself be dragged into politics so easily.

"Let me finish. There is a gradual recognition that the diplomats of the Holy See are just a pale reflection of their former glory. They are relics from a time when the pope was intimately bound to the emperors and kings of Europe."

Faster snorted. "And what does that have to do with this case?"

"A great deal. Above all, my esteemed colleagues, it should show us quite plainly that we cannot allow ourselves to have any hesitation in handling this case like any other. If it should be determined that the case in Boston was dismissed with undue haste—"

MacClary put up his hands. "My dear colleagues, please, calm down. Justice Andrews is completely right. I was just in The Hague a few days ago. Even there, international law is experiencing a certain structural change. Still, I suggest that we concentrate here and now on the concrete case before us and look at what went wrong in Boston." Andrews had done him a huge favor with her stance on international law and international significance, but he was trying not to be too obvious in his show of appreciation.

"An excellent idea," Elora Spencer remarked dryly. "I have spent quite a bit of time with this case already, and I am voting for adoption of the petition." She magnanimously looked around at the astounded faces of her colleagues. "Let's hear what the lawyers have to say. And Faster, I'd like to take the liberty of saying one thing to you as a justice, but also as a wife and mother. For years I've been observing the victims of sexual violence in psychiatric clinics, and a not insignificant number of them involved church dignitaries. These people are with us in spirit at this table as we decide if it's possible to bring the Vatican or even members of the Vatican to trial. As a Christian you should be the first one to lay aside your double standards and feel sympathy for these victims and for the millions of victims who have died over the past centuries because of the Vatican's aggressive claim to power."

She said this with such piercing clarity that even Faster sank down into his chair and didn't say another word.

CHAPTER 37

HOTEL MONACO, WASHINGTON, DC – MARCH 28, MORNING

Two days had passed. Despite Jennifer's fears, nothing had been heard from the House of Representatives. Justice Spencer's lecture had apparently made Faster come around. She was sure that he was behind the attempt to remove MacClary from office.

That morning Jennifer had invited everyone to the Hotel Monaco for breakfast to go over the final plan. While Deborah and Ronald were arguing over the best time for a press conference for the scientists and Jennifer was making last-minute notes, Shane was wearily staring at the television in the hotel bar, dozing off.

When the bartender changed the channel, Shane was jolted awake. CNN was reporting from Europe.

"Hey, could you turn that up, please?" Deborah asked the bartender.

"As announced today, a lawsuit has been filed in Boston against the Vatican. According to as yet unsubstantiated reports, it is not related to the current abuse cases. Instead, it concerns an internationally relevant cultural theft in which an American

citizen was reported to have been seriously injured. According to the charges, members of the Vatican police stole extremely provocative documents from the time of the founding of the Catholic Church from a private archaeological team from Ireland. The Vatican is said to be in illegal possession of a substantial number of the parchments. A team of experts and scientists in Washington has already substantiated the dating of other documents from the find and is attempting to sort through the first translations.

"According to the experts, the parchments are from the fourth century, the time of the founding of the Church, and are reported to reveal controversial details about the circumstances surrounding the Church's beginnings. According to reports by the director of a private institute for archaeology in Washington, Joseph Pascal, this information will be made available to the scientific community in the coming days.

"The charges are being vehemently denied by the Vatican's American legal team. Since the case has already been dismissed in Boston, the appeal will be heard starting tomorrow in the Supreme Court in Washington because of its international significance. Since news of the trial was announced, several hundred people have already gathered in front of the White House to demonstrate against any premature condemnation of the Vatican. It is rumored that Cardinal State Secretary Thomas Lambert has flown to Washington and will make a statement about the charges tomorrow.

"We turn now to Rome, where our correspondent Tom Leaver is in St. Peter's Square to report on initial impressions there."

MacClary stared speechless at the television.

Jennifer put a hand on his shoulder. "Ronald, we knew it wouldn't remain a secret for long."

"Yes, of course, that's not what's bothering me. We can't let the demonstrations escalate. We have to be very careful to rein in the media tomorrow." He turned to look at her. "Jennifer, you know that we can't talk with each other in the courtroom. Please, no matter what happens, don't reveal any more than necessary in the first hearing. In the second hearing, you're free to do what you will. I can't tell you more than that right now. They really think that they're going to get out of this unscathed." Shaking his head, he turned back to the television.

"Tom, what can you tell us?"

"Well, here in Rome, the reaction to the charges is relatively calm, and it's rumored that the Vatican is trying to play down the whole thing as a mistake, that the case actually revolves around the actions of individuals rather than the Church. Many priests here are sure the facts of the case will be cleared up as quickly as possible."

"Thank you, Tom. We'll be bringing you continuing coverage of this in the coming days. As our reporter in the White House has learned, demonstrations have been reported in front of several US embassies, including those in Germany, Italy, and France.

"And now, a summary of the news from Europe."

* * *

Jennifer looked at Shane's face and could tell he wasn't happy.

"Adam, what's wrong?"

"The same thing that's bothering Ronald," Adam said, still staring, transfixed, at the screen. "We knew people would revolt. There have been too many horrible things for too many years to avoid that."

Jennifer understood what he was saying. The first reactions from the churches demonstrated how much aggression this whole thing was unleashing, but then there were also voices like that of the American Bishop Ellington, who was calling for reforms in the Vatican and more courage in the face of historical truth.

"Jennifer, don't you see what the danger is here?" Adam continued. "If people are reacting this way now, before a single detail about the actual content is made public..."

"I know, Adam. We'll take care of that."

"I hope so. I don't want to be party to something that leads to widespread violence."

"I know," she said quietly, taking his hand. "I don't either."

"Then hang on to that feeling you have right now when you're making your arguments in the Supreme Court tomorrow. We have to learn to stop the dogma, Jennifer. Let's just lay the historical facts on the table and let the world show us what the legacy of the original inhabitants of Europe looks like."

Jennifer thought about a conversation she'd had with Ryan a little while ago about his experiences with religion and revenge in Northern Ireland. Christianity determines who would be the next victim. How long was this insanity going to go on? How long would people be allowed to use faith as a justification for murder, rape, and slavery?

Adam had started to stand up, but Jennifer grabbed his sweater and pulled him back down so that he landed right next to her on the bench.

"I have to tell you one more thing, Adam," she said with a tenderness she rarely heard in her own voice. Then she took his face between her hands and pulled him gently toward her. She gave him a long, passionate kiss, trying to believe that no one was watching, even as she knew that couldn't possibly be the case.

She pulled back. "What I wanted to tell you," she said with a softness that belied the beating of her heart, "is that I love you, Adam Shane. Thank you for coming into my life."

She wasn't going to allow herself to wonder what had made her choose this moment to make that declaration. Instead, she stood up, took her coat, and went toward the exit at her usual quick pace.

When she got there, she turned around one more time. "I'll see you all tomorrow. Be on time."

CHAPTER 38

SUPREME COURT, WASHINGTON, DC – MARCH 29, NOON: FIRST HEARING

Salvoni and Lambert had landed in Washington early that morning and were meeting with the archbishop of Washington, Cardinal John Jasper, who had been trying without success to exert some influence on the Supreme Court. They were headed toward the Supreme Court along with a dozen bishops from all over the country.

"Keep calm, Salvoni," Lambert said sternly. "With God's help, we'll be done with this soon enough."

Salvoni tried to take heed, but he didn't have a good feeling about things.

* * *

It took them almost half an hour to get there. There were hundreds of demonstrators in front of the Supreme Court Building that morning. Jennifer rode with Louise Jackson through the crowd while Deborah and Shane followed in another taxi. She looked at the countless banners that were calling for an end to the hearings. Others read

"Peace for the Pope," "Shame on you—God won't forget this," and other similar slogans. When Jennifer arrived, she saw reporters waiting for her at the entrance to the Great Hall. Until now, she had been an unknown face in Washington. Both of them managed to make their way through the crowd without having to make any comment, though they'd been barraged by camera flashes.

Jennifer sat down in the first row, her gaze fixed on the nine chairs of the justices. So much history had been made in this room. Even though the building had only stood since 1935, it looked as if it had been built during the time of the founding fathers. The white marble columns in front of the flowing red velvet curtains gave the entire hall a curious combination of warmth and power.

The hall was packed with people, among them numerous bishops in their red and white robes. Way up in front she could see the cardinal state secretary, Thomas Lambert. How sure of themselves these men were! And how uneasy she felt herself.

That morning, she had received a call from Ms. Copendale, who reported worriedly that someone had thrown a red paint bomb at the façade of Ronald's house. Just to be on the safe side, Jennifer had called the police in Dublin, who immediately promised to patrol the area on a regular basis and, if necessary, to put a police presence in place to protect the house.

Ronald had told everyone that morning that the European media had run a brief report stating that Ryan was dead, which had caused a powerful reaction in the

Vatican. This kind of misdirection was right up Ronald's alley.

As these and other thoughts flashed through her mind, the justices started to take their seats. Ronald was the last one to enter the hall. As he had warned her, he didn't even glance in her direction. With two hammers of the gavel, the marshal opened the session.

"The honorable chief justice and the associate justices of the Supreme Court of the United States. Oyez! Oyez! Oyez! All persons having business before the honorable Supreme Court of the United States are admonished to draw near and give their attention, for the court is now sitting. God save the United States and this honorable court."

Jennifer stepped up to the lectern. She could feel her heart beating in her throat, making it nearly impossible for her to speak. *God save the United States, yes*, she thought, *but please not the Vatican.*

Ronald began to speak. "We are hearing today the urgent petition of the Boston district attorney and the attorney Jennifer Wilson in the case of United States citizen Thomas Ryan vs. the Vatican. I am giving the floor to attorney Jennifer Wilson."

Jennifer took one more deep breath. She would need it. A hearing in the Supreme Court was more like a cross examination, and in this case she had to be ready for anything that might throw her for a loop. "Mr. Chief Justice, if it pleases the court, we are making a motion for a new trial in the case before the district court in Boston, since we are able to prove that members of the Vatican have not only stolen internationally relevant cultural artifacts—"

Justice Copter interrupted her. "Hasn't the petitioner himself attempted to seize these artifacts without consent and as a foreigner?"

"Two other participants in the retrieval had made the site known to the Austrian Foreign Ministry on the same evening before the attack took place," Jennifer responded. "The communication has been documented. The two witnesses confirm that they found the cave with Thomas Ryan and were the first to open it."

Jennifer presented the confirmation from Austria to the justices, made an elegant turn back to the lectern, and continued more confidently. "In addition, the commando attempted the deliberate murder of petitioner Thomas Ryan. After he had been struck down—"

Justice Faster tried to intervene. "How do you intend—"

"—the cave was set on fire," Jennifer said, pushing through. "The petitioner was left in the burning cave and was only able to save himself through a combination of luck and the help of witnesses who happened to be present."

"I asked how do you intend to prove this, especially in the absence of the petitioner?"

"The petitioner is currently in a private clinic and will be brought to the United States within the next three days. Immediately after his rescue, he made contact with the present witnesses and members of the expedition, who were on their way to Vienna with some of the artifacts."

"Is the petitioner able to identify his attacker or attackers?" Justice Faster asked.

"We only know that he saw one of the attackers wore a ring of the St. Pius X Brotherhood. Most of the men were hooded. He was able to tear the hood off one of them before he was struck down."

* * *

Salvoni slumped down. She couldn't have invented that. He had just been too slow with Ryan. He looked at Lambert's shocked expression. Salvoni had left out this detail for obvious reasons, and he could see that it was making Lambert nervous as well.

* * *

Ronald spoke next. "How do you come by the assertion that the Vatican could have been behind this? And if that were the case, why would they take such a drastic course of action?"

"Well, that is the nature of the beast, Mr. Chief Justice. As you have been able to hear from various media sources lately, this find is not only the greatest sensation since the discovery of the Qumran scrolls, it also relates to the direct charges by contemporary witnesses, the Celtic Druids, which prove that the history of the founding of the Church has been falsified and covered up to the present day."

"That is not the subject of the proceedings," Justice Morburg said.

"Your Honor, I am only attempting to answer the question of the chief justice. The contents of the parchments almost exactly correspond with the charges of the most renowned Church critics of our time. In addition, it has been internationally recognized that humanity itself, as a subject of international law, has claim to historical truth. The Vatican, or at least members of the Vatican in this case, attempted to impede the disclosure of historical truth using violence and—"

Justice Faster interrupted again. "How can you substantiate that claim?"

"With the statements of the witnesses present here today and with evidence for which we need a bit more time, which they apparently did not have in Boston."

"To the best of my knowledge, the Druids are nothing more than a myth," Faster said sharply. "Please!"

Jennifer could feel herself rapidly coming into her own. She had the upper hand. Most of the justices were clearly impressed, otherwise she would have been bombarded with far more interposed questions. As she turned to the side, she looked straight into Lambert's pale and cold face. Apparently he hadn't counted on her tenaciousness.

"Did the Boston court have these expert opinions and the other facts at their disposal?" Justice Johnson asked.

"Yes, Your Honor. In addition, it has been established that one of the scrolls comes from a direct ancestor of the petitioner. This was proven by way of a forensic examination of a family tree that has been in the possession of the Ryan family for centuries."

Johnson scowled. "That's completely impossible."

"No, Your Honor, it has been scientifically proven by this independent expert." Jennifer again handed a certificate to the justices. "Thomas Ryan, along with the members of eight other Irish families, are descendants of the Druids who built this library, which…" Jennifer pulled up, thinking about MacClary telling her not to give everything away. She would say only as much as she had to today to clear the hurdle of the first hearing. "…which substantiates the petitioner's claim to these cultural artifacts. Thomas Ryan, Your Honor, by his own admission, has this scroll with him."

"That means that we need to wait until the petitioner gets to Washington," Ronald said.

Jennifer could see how MacClary's plan was falling into place. The Vatican would feel as though they were safe until the point at which Ryan and MacClary's trump card arrived for the showdown in Washington.

"Yes, Mr. Chief Justice."

"Thank you, Ms. Wilson. I will turn over the floor to attorney Roy Watson."

"Mr. Chief Justice," Watson said, "I have been charged with the defense of the Vatican, but to be honest, I am not sure what I should be defending. The charges are not only completely unfounded, but they are also, in light of the damage they have already caused, reprehensible."

"Leave the assessment to the court, Mr. Watson, and continue," Justice Courtney said.

"I am in any case astonished that no one is aware of the following facts. Not only is, or rather *was*, the petitioner wanted in Europe as a terrorist, but he was also found dead two days ago in Austria."

Justice Winster leaned forward. "Excuse me?"

"This is according to this news report, Your Honor. In addition, the St. Pius X Brotherhood performs no function within the Vatican. They operate as an autonomous entity. That means that even if the attack were to be substantiated as being carried out by the St. Pius X Brotherhood, neither the Vatican nor the Holy See can be held responsible for it. We move to halt the proceedings."

Ronald turned to Jennifer. "Ms. Wilson, do have any explanation for this?"

"Mr. Chief Justice, that is not possible. I just spoke with Thomas Ryan this morning. We are sure that the matter can be cleared up quickly, as well as the suspicion that Thomas Ryan is a terrorist," Jennifer said. That was the point she had been waiting for. Now the hearing would need to be interrupted, and they would have gained valuable time to await Ryan's arrival.

MacClary looked at the other justices, who seemed at a bit of a loss. He spoke quietly with them, out of the earshot of others. Then he turned back to the public in the hall.

"This hearing is adjourned. The next hearing will take place the day after tomorrow at twelve o'clock noon."

The marshal's gavel ended the theater for the day, leaving everyone staring at each other in surprise. No one had expected such an abrupt end to the day's proceedings.

Jennifer took a deep breath. She had survived the first round, but the ice she was walking on was very, very thin.

* * *

"Why didn't you tell me?" Lambert barked at Salvoni as the two rode back to their hotel.

"What are you talking about?"

"Why didn't you tell me whose face Thomas Ryan saw? And how could anyone be so unbelievably stupid as to wear a ring like that in an operation like this?"

Salvoni was crumbling inside. He was a man who had always taken responsibility for his actions. He could no longer find any justification for his chain of embarrassing mistakes. "Cardinal, I will take personal responsibility. We have to make sure that the Holy See—"

"I know, Salvoni, I never doubted that you would. But I'm afraid it will be difficult to contain the damage. They won't let go. The Church critics, the atheists, the nihilists—they'll all—"

Lambert's cell phone interrupted them. "Yes?"

Lambert rolled his eyes as Salvoni watched him for some reaction. "Very well. Have it handed over to the US ambassador. We'll bring everything here to a close. I'm staying until the end of the hearing in Washington. Yes, I'll let him know."

Lambert hung up and took a deep breath.

"The Holy Father thanks you for your willingness to take full responsibility for the events. I'll make sure that you are tried in front of an Italian court. We will do everything we can to make sure that you are treated as well as possible."

Salvoni had been awaiting this fate. "Thank you, Cardinal. I hope that this takes care of everything."

"Your Thomas Ryan really is alive. The justice seems to have used the same tricks we have, Salvoni."

"I suspected as much, but I let myself be swayed by my hope that God would protect me from this burden. Now I see that it's too late."

Lambert nodded, an expression approximating compassion on his face. "Later today, the Holy See will be lodging a complaint with the United Nations about the hearing, stating that international treaties were violated."

The driver turned the radio on.

"...was interrupted after the attorney for the petitioner was able to make a credible argument that the case in Boston should not have been suspended prematurely on formal grounds. As was recently announced, the first violent altercation between demonstrators and the police took place in front of the United States Embassy in Switzerland. One member of the embassy staff suffered a severe blow from a stone thrown by the demonstrators and has since succumbed to his injuries. Switzerland and eight other nations have summoned their ambassadors to the United

States today to return home and demanded an end to the hearing. They have stated that the attempt of one nation to condemn another impinges on international law. The White House issued a statement confirming that they will not intervene in the work of the judiciary and that the hearing is only intended to clarify whether the Vatican itself or only individuals were involved in the events in Austria. If the charges are not substantiated, the proceedings will be immediately suspended, according to White House spokesman Steve Thomson."

"Turn that off," Lambert ordered the driver.

CHAPTER 39

HOTEL MONACO, WASHINGTON, DC – MARCH 29, NIGHT

Shane and Deborah had driven back to the hotel after lunch. Jennifer had gone to lie down for a bit. She was exhausted, but she knew there was no chance of getting any sleep.

She felt too dependent on MacClary's strategizing. What if his dubious source didn't even exist? Had he just invented this so-called trump card to keep them all on board, in the hope that there would be enough evidence when Ryan finally got here? Restless, she got up again and went into the spacious living room of the hotel suite.

"…never experienced anything like it," Adam was saying to Deborah. "When the justices ended the session, I looked at MacClary's face, at Lambert's, at everyone's. Everything seemed like it was suddenly going in slow motion, and I could feel everyone's presence. It was as if I were observing everything from far, far away, and everything I saw was horrible."

"What was horrible?" Jennifer asked.

"The roles, Jennifer, the roles we're playing here. If I've learned anything in the last several days, it's that, even though the Druids and the other indigenous peoples were aware of this contrast of good and evil, they meant something different by it. I don't know how to explain it. They knew that everything that we do or think creates the reality that we live in."

"And what does that have to do with this hearing?" Jennifer asked, half asleep.

"At some point I started not being able to tell the difference between the intrigues of this ice-cold cardinal and Ronald's actions. They are children of their time. They know no other way besides going up against each other. And what's happening out there on the street? Exactly the same thing. Irreconcilable extremes come into conflict with each other and play Cowboys and Indians. Damn it all, when are we finally going to grow up? When will we realize that all of these divisions exist only in our own deluded minds? Here, the latest news. Look at it."

"But Adam—"

"Look at it!"

Jennifer looked at the European newspapers. Several people had been severely injured in demonstrations in St. Peter's Square.

"When we were in the gardens at the White House, I told you what I had found in the scrolls and what the Druids had meant by a change of consciousness. And you and MacClary can't come up with anything better than—"

"Stop it, Adam! You knew from the beginning what Thomas and Ronald were planning. And yes, not everything has gone as we had expected, but what do you think we should do now? Just throw it all away?"

"Well, in any case I won't be going with you on this path anymore. Even the president understood that."

"But Adam, we don't have any other choice but to show the world how the Vatican betrayed its own values! Yes, damn it, I gauge people by their acts, what else? For me, history is the history of humanity. Step by step, we're approaching a better world."

"Who says that your justice system is the right one? I recall that one of your presidents almost set fire to the whole world with it. With a single sentence."

"Adam, I don't need any lessons in penal law."

"He said: 'We're waging a crusade against evil.' And what exactly are we doing?"

"But that's—"

Deborah walked between them. "Really, Adam, don't you see the differences anymore? On one side you have the path of the Church fathers, using a written tradition to open the doors to rigidity, dogma, and quiet manipulation. And they did this so efficiently that the Vatican is scared shitless to admit even a hint of it. On the other side you have the Druids, who tried to prevent precisely this manipulation by using an oral tradition. All we're trying to do is bring things back into balance again!"

"Yes, but it's precisely because of this inflexibility that the Vatican's time was over a long time ago. It's just that no one noticed. My God, Jennifer, the facts of our find are enough. They can't escape it anymore. We don't need this huge showdown!"

"That may be, but stop accusing me of thirsting for revenge. I have nothing but sympathy for the victims of this church. I want to get rid of their control. That's the only way we can even begin to turn this almost two-thousand-year-old curse into a blessing."

"That may be, I have to admit, but it would be more healing for all of us if the pope made this step himself without our having to force him into it with this verdict. And what about Ronald? Are you going to tell me he doesn't have any desire for revenge? Who murdered his father and why? Do you know the true motive? Was the culprit only a victim of his own mistaken beliefs? This world will never change if we don't learn to forgive! Criminals, victims...how else do you want to divide it up?"

"Adam, that's enough already. If you mean what you're saying, then it's better for everyone if you fly back to Austria now. There's nothing else for you to do here," Jennifer said, despairing and hopeless. Then she turned around and left the room.

"Whew." Deborah clasped her hands behind her head and looked at Shane critically. "You expect a lot, my friend. Every revolution has its victims, of one kind or another."

"But I don't want a revolution. And it isn't even about what I want as an individual. It's about change. We don't have any more time for this petty reckoning."

"But maybe we do need a transition, Adam," Deborah said, the argument clearly upsetting her. "You know, the teachings of the Druids also talk about truthfulness. And that's what's going on here in this court. It comes down to clever discourse and truthfulness." Both of them could hear the sobs coming from Jennifer's room. "And this isn't the solution either, if one of us is suffering," Deborah said, looking at him reproachfully. Then she sat down and buried her head in her laptop, not deigning to look at him again.

Shane walked over to Jennifer's door, where he knocked cautiously.

"Come in already," Jennifer said with a last sob as she blew her nose.

"I'm sorry."

"It's fine, Adam. I overreacted. It's strange, but I'd just been thinking about this myself, what we're doing and where it's headed. I—"

"Well, how do I know what role my identity is playing here?" Shane smiled. "Again, I'm sorry."

"If you're looking for an answer to the question about your identity, I can tell you where you'll find it, my wise Druid."

"Hmm?"

"Within yourself," Jennifer said gently.

Deborah knocked and stuck her head in the room without waiting for an answer. "Hey, the president just announced that she'll be giving a speech about the

Supreme Court hearing tomorrow morning at eleven," she said in excitement.

"I think we're not all that interested in that right now, Deborah."

Deborah stared at the two of them and then went red in the face. "Oh, um, sorry." She left the room as quickly as she had entered it.

Shane felt helpless. The tension between them was almost palpable. He stood in the room a bit lost and looked at Jennifer questioningly.

"Get over here already." Jennifer scooted over to make room. When he got over to the bed, she took his hand and pulled him to her side. "I'd like to find out what it feels like."

Bowled over by Jennifer's directness, he lay down next to her and pulled her to him. He could feel her warmth, her firm thighs, and the softness of her curves, and he felt like he was holding something infinitely precious.

He laid his large hand protectively on her head and could feel for the first time the tenderness of this woman who was so tough in her job. Ms. Iron Heart, Thomas Ryan had called her once. How many light-years ago was that?

"Forgive me," Shane said.

Something seemed to fall away from Jennifer. The pressure to always be strong had become almost unbearable in the last few days and hours. She nestled closely against him. Right now his chest offered her a feeling of being at home, and she felt safe. It was something new for her, that a man wasn't just trying to have sex with her. It was a deeper intimacy. Two people in love, two hearts almost terrifyingly open to each other. Her senses opened up, her energy sank into his body, and she was one with him, even before their bodies joined.

Adam could sense an almost unbearable tension. This woman had fascinated him from the first moment he met her and had drawn him to her like a magnet. It was only the excitement of the last several days that had made him hold himself back. Now, when he let himself go, a passion broke out of him that extinguished everything else.

* * *

WHITE HOUSE, WASHINGTON, DC – NIGHT

> ***Christianity is the most perverted system that ever shone on man.***
>
> **—Thomas Jefferson**

The entire day the president had refrained from saying a single word in public concerning the worldwide protests about the hearing. That afternoon, she found out that the Irish Parliament had decided to call a special session of the United Nations. In light of the dramatic turn of events and the accumulation of internationally relevant crimes committed by the Vatican and the members of the Catholic Church, eighty-six nations had come out in favor of the special General Assembly within hours of its announcement. Even the Security Council was going to meet to discuss the worldwide clashes between those opposing and those supporting the imminent trial after radical Christians had thrown incendiary devices at many of the US embassies and numerous deaths had been reported throughout the world as a result of the unrest.

The president looked out onto the street from her bedroom window in the Executive Residence of the White House. The last demonstrators were still in front of the White House fence and had lit candles. She knew that her political fate hung on the speech she would be giving the next morning. She lifted the receiver of the telephone on the small, antique table next to her.

"Bill, could you please bring me the draft for the 'Butterfly' project. I want to work on it again."

"But Madam President—"

"Bill, please, no discussions now."

A few minutes later, there was a knock at the door.

"Come in, Bill."

"Madam President, I must inform you that neither the Cabinet nor the Senate wants an open debate on this project at this time."

"Thank you, Bill, that's all."

"Very well. Good night, Madam President."

Project Butterfly was one of the many possible strategic plans economists had been working on after the last financial crisis. It was radical—too radical.

When will people be ready for this? she thought, suddenly too tired to read through the material. With a sigh she put the document on the table, stood up, and went over to her bed. She lay down on the bedspread and pulled out a pillow. She just wanted a couple of minutes to think.

Instead, she slipped into a state where she was hovering between sleep and consciousness, like a space between realities.

She could see herself standing in front of all the cameras the next day in the White House Press Office looking into perplexed faces. Suddenly Lisa, her five-year-old daughter, came in holding a parchment from the library of the Druids in one hand and the Declaration of Independence in the other. Lisa gave her both of the documents and asked if it was true that the earth was a living creature and that it was sick and would soon die.

Behind her came Adam Shane carrying a stack of papers on which an enormous, beautiful butterfly was sitting. She looked into the eyes of the butterfly, and then it flew away from the stack of papers and through the room. Little Lisa cheered it on, crying, "Fly, fly, butterfly. You'll make the earth well again!"

Slowly the president awoke. To her surprise it was five in the morning. At some point, she must have fallen asleep.

She let herself sink back down into the pillow. She remembered that her daughter had asked her this question a couple of weeks earlier. As far as the parchment of the Druids was concerned, it had developed the notion of mankind's freedom and self-determination to a much deeper level than even the Constitution of the United States. Though a landmark document, the Constitution came at a point after people had long since oppressed those cultures that were able to live in harmony with nature.

The decline of the aboriginal people had certainly not been a natural phenomenon. For centuries it had been politically motivated with the support and justification of a faith that had been nothing but a lie from the very beginning.

The president heard Adam Shane's words: *What does it mean to develop a spiritual consciousness for the original culture of the Celts if you also just stood by and watched as the last tribes of the world perished?*

"That is the truth, uncomfortable as it may be," the president said to herself decisively. "And I always thought you would be the first one to retire, Ronald MacClary."

CHAPTER 40

WASHINGTON, DC – MARCH 30, MORNING

Jennifer turned up the volume on the television as Adam and Deborah took their seats in front of the screen. The president's speech was about to begin.

"Good morning, ladies and gentleman of the press, my fellow Americans. I would like to use the opportunity of the current events in Washington to discuss several questions of faith. My daughter asked me a couple of days ago if the earth was so sick that it was going to die. Lisa is, as most of you know, five years old.

"How should I answer her? Should I lie to her?

"Because we really have arrived at an historic turning point. We are headed down a descending path of social, ecological, political, and economic crises in a period of global power struggles that threaten our survival. We have to reorganize our lives into lives that are peaceful and that will allow our children a world with a future. The choice is still ours to make, but it all depends on our values, our convictions, our visions, and our communal planetary ethics.

"You will perhaps be surprised when I maintain that these communal ethics have existed before. They were known to the

original inhabitants of this country as they were to all other indigenous peoples. 'Take nothing more than you need' was the guiding principle of these cultures. The reverence for the actual wonder of creation, of our earth, was a given for the indigenous peoples. This is also the message we can glean from the recently unearthed trove from the Celts and Druids, the original inhabitants of Europe, which is now being argued about in the Supreme Court. The resulting unrest in Rome points to fears that I will not touch on today. There is only one thing I know for certain: our current consciousness will be determined by the assessment of this trove and by the assessment of Church history, the consequences of which I can only briefly outline. It will determine whether the unity of humankind can now become concretely known to us or if we will degenerate further.

"Ladies and gentlemen, none of us in this world can do anything without it affecting everyone else. Many things that we have assumed to be reversible are no longer so. The hierarchies of our societal order have disenfranchised people. We need people with self-determination and a sense of personal responsibility. Our highly lauded efficiency and material growth is misguided. Technology is no longer the answer to our problems, and the next new thing is not always better than the tried and true. We cannot continue to live as if the future is irrelevant to our present.

"Out of respect for our judiciary, I will make no statement on the current hearing against the Vatican other than to say that we all have claim to historical truth, and we are duty bound to take note of this. We have built a culture on convictions, whose effects we are now beginning to feel and which could lead to our destruction. If we are not ready to create something that will

produce an uncompromising balance between nature, technology, and faith, it will no longer be a question of faith on how long we will continue to survive. It is most likely no accident that the testimony of this ancient culture in particular is coming to us now.

"It is sometimes easier to return to a place where we have made a wrong turn than it is to hope that we will find another path to our goal. The laws that nature has provided us require every one of us to take responsibility for our own actions here and now. The older cultures can be a great help to us in this. Let us learn from everything they have left us and beg forgiveness for the results of our arrogance and ignorance. That applies to every person, regardless of his or her faith or nationality.

"I would like to introduce you to Project Butterfly. It was created through the vision of one of the best scientists in the world. The measures, which I will explain to you now, will become a great challenge for the United States in the coming years. But we can only implement them within a global context. I will devote myself to this in the time remaining to me in office. It is time for us to again have faith in ourselves and in our potential. Then I will be able to tell my daughter that together we will heal this earth.

"Now to the specific measures..."

Jennifer turned to Adam with a contented smile. "Well, you big Druid, are you happy?"

"I'm overwhelmed. Butterfly, what a beautiful name. And it promises so much." Shane laid his cheek against Jennifer's face. That he felt close enough to her to offer such casual affection gave her heart a thrill.

A second later, her cell phone broke the spell.

"Jennifer, it's Thomas Ryan."

"Oh, Thomas, it's damned nice to hear from you."

"Can you tell me why I was declared dead?"

Deborah stood up and took the cell phone from Jennifer, putting it on speaker at the same time.

"OK, so now you've been resurrected. Could you please get your legendary ass here sometime soon? I mean, you do actually understand what's going on here, don't you?"

Ryan laughed. "I'll be in Washington soon, and I can't wait either, so calm down. Give the phone back to Jennifer again."

"Lazarus only wants to talk with you today," Deborah said, turning off the speakerphone and handing it back with mock indignation. Jennifer could tell, though, that Deborah was hugely relieved.

"Thomas..."

"Make it fast. I can't talk long."

"OK. The FBI will pick you up at Reagan Airport and bring you to a hotel. When are you coming, exactly?"

"Not until the day after tomorrow. The plane lands at six in the evening."

"Can't you get here any sooner? The next hearing is tomorrow and I need you here *now*."

"That's not a possibility."

"All right. I'll see if we can manage to postpone it again. Take care of yourself, Ryan."

She hung up and looked around the room.

"What now?" Adam asked.

"Nothing. We'll have to stall the court. But I've already thought of something."

Hopefully Ronald would keep his promise.

* * *

VATICAN CITY, ROME – MARCH 30, EVENING

The announcement of a special morning session of the United Nations Security Council unleashed a firestorm in Rome. The security situations stemming from the increasing violence at the worldwide protests would be discussed. The pope could no longer accept the view of numerous diplomats that the Vatican had abused its status in the past to avoid criminal prosecution.

He called a member of the Swiss Guard.

"Yes, Holy Father?"

"Have Cardinal Catamo come here," the pope said gently.

"Of course, Holy Father."

Eduard Catamo was the head of the Vatican's press office. Among his other responsibilities, the older gentleman had for some time made sure that a person looking for literature on the pope in a bookstore would have a far easier time finding a tribute to him than criticism of the sort that was now spread out on the pope's desk.

After the draft of the European Constitution was written without any reference to God, John Paul III had intensified the offensive to turn Europe once again into a Christian continent. But then all of their efforts were nullified with a single blow. The involvement of the Vatican Bank in Mafia business and, above all, the worldwide explosion on discussions about abuse cases abruptly disarmed his new crusade against modernity.

"Holy Father?"

"Come in, Eduard. What do you know about Cardinal Lambert's involvement in this insufferable story?"

"I cannot imagine that Padre Salvoni acted on his own, Holy Father."

"Listen, I know that the cardinal is doing everything he can to succeed me on St. Peter's chair, and I also know that he is your superior, but I am still this Church. If the cardinal bears more responsibility for this matter than I know, I want you to tell me about it now. You can see for yourself what damage he has already caused."

"But Holy Father, when I see what is coming at us from the historians who analyzed the first scrolls, then—"

"Then what? Do you see these books? Everything, and I mean everything, is already known to the world if one wants to know it. This Church has seen emperors and kings, dictators and revolutionaries. They come and they go. We have survived the Middle Ages, the Reformation, and the Revolution of the Moderns, and we will also survive the writings of a couple of Druids or pagan philosophers that have been completely misinterpreted."

"But Holy Father! I think we have to look ahead and defend ourselves. They've been meeting in New York for the past hour."

"Cardinal, the ancient religions were not destroyed by us. They collapsed under the weakness of their many gods and a lack of piety and unified moral teachings. If we are not careful, the same fate will soon await this Church. We have to show the world now what the appeal of our faith is."

Catamo bowed his head. "Holy Father, I will ensure that Italy's Catholics use the Sunday Angelus of the pope to make an avowal of faith to the Vatican. We will show the world the power of a clear faith."

"How many waves of conflict have there been? How many ideological movements, how many modes of thought have rocked the little boat of the Church? And yet, we've never been so threatened as we are today, Eduard."

"The documents, well, they prove..."

"A genocide. Just say it. Yes, they probably do prove that and more. But that is history, Eduard, a history that shows that the world and the acting bishops and the emperor needed a transition period to become true Christians. Will this nonsensical discussion never stop? I need to ask you for a favor now, in God's name. We have to protect this Church, whatever else happens." The pope held a document out to Catamo. "Here, take this and follow the instructions to the letter. It is important that it arrive in Washington in time."

Catamo looked at the papers and gasped.

"But Holy Father, are you—"

"Eduard, I must be able to rely on you."

"Yes, Holy Father. I will take care of it."

"Good, thank you. And another thing: I would like you to contact this attorney. I think it makes sense if I have a conversation with one of the people behind this case. We have to make it clear to them that the distant past is not the present of this Church."

Without another word, Catamo left. The pope watched him go, and then his glance fell on the books he'd been reading. Yes, the truth had been off limits for far too long. For as long as he could remember, he'd believed that if society said God was dead, then people would say that they are God. Then the world would lose all of its standards and all of its morality.

Now, for the first time, though, he wasn't so sure.

* * *

RONALD REAGAN AIRPORT, WASHINGTON, DC – EVENING

MacClary was getting very nervous. He'd seen footage from Rome right after the president's speech. Around two hundred thousand people had streamed into St. Peter's Square that morning, among them representatives of every political party, including the leaders of a small party with notorious links to the Mafia. They estimated that more than a million people would be demonstrating their loyalty to the pope that Sunday.

If everything went well, the hearing would be long over by then and the man that MacClary was so eagerly awaiting would play an important role in ending it.

The limousine, followed by a half dozen White House automobiles, drove up to an outlying hangar usually reserved for diplomats and government officials.

As he was waiting for the airplane to land, his cell phone rang.

"MacClary."

"Ronald, it's Adam. I know that we're not supposed to—"

"It's fine. What's this about?"

"The pope wants to speak with us."

"The pope wants to *what*?"

"The pope wants to speak with us. In person. In Rome. Jennifer got a call from an ambassador in New York. The pope wants to speak with someone who was present when the scrolls were retrieved, unofficially. Ronald, I have a feeling that the pope doesn't know what happened in Austria."

"It may be, Adam, but don't start thinking he doesn't bear any responsibility because—"

"No, definitely not that. I'm going to accept this invitation, though. I want to know what's behind it, and one thing is certain: if he relents and distances himself from the operation, we should—"

"Adam, that's completely ridiculous. This pope has taken more conservative steps to reverse progress than his predecessor did, and no matter what he comes to you with, everything that he has written is an attack on free and open society."

"Don't worry, Ronald, I've read his writings. I know who I'm facing, but something just isn't right here."

"Very well. You have to decide this for yourself, but don't forget: you're essentially acting as a representative of this case. The Vatican has been expert at this game of intrigue for centuries. I don't have time for debates right now. Take care of yourself and keep me informed. I'll see you the day after tomorrow in court."

"Thanks. See you soon."

As MacClary hung up, he saw that the jet had landed. After the plane had taxied in front of the hangar, the door opened and a man dressed in dark clothing came slowly down the steps to get into one of the limousines. *Well, that's taken care of*, MacClary thought. At the same time, though, a shiver ran up his spine. What secrets surrounded this man? Would he, Ronald MacClary, be able to handle what he would learn in the coming days?

CHAPTER 41

It is my firm opinion that Europe today represents not the spirit of God or Christianity, but the spirit of Satan. And Satan's successes are the greatest when he appears with the name of God on his lips...I believe that European Christianity is a corruption of the Christianity of Jesus.

—Mahatma Gandhi, September 8, 1920

WASHINGTON, DC, AND ROME – MARCH 31

Flying to Rome and back in a day was not something Shane welcomed, but it was going to have to be that way. He wanted to be back in Washington that evening so as not to miss the next hearing. Some of the Irish families had arrived in DC. Their presence should help to reinforce Ryan's claims, since he hadn't reached the States yet. When they were shown the scrolls and translations in the laboratory, many tears were shed over the losses and the crimes that had taken place so long ago.

Deborah had insisted on accompanying Shane on his trip, claiming that she wanted to stand face-to-face with the man who was still teaching that she was a second-class citizen. When they landed, Vatican diplomats met them at the airport. They drove for more than a half hour through the horrible Roman traffic. After they had gotten through the swarms of people that had been gathering in St. Peter's Square for days now, they found themselves standing in front of the power center of the infallible.

When they arrived at the pope's private rooms, one of the diplomats approached Deborah. "I am sorry, but the Holy Father wishes to speak with only one person."

"Now why doesn't that surprise me?"

The man turned to Shane. "Are you familiar with the customs regarding how you are to speak and greet the Holy Father?"

The implication irritated Shane. "I will not ignore the normal rules of politeness. I pay every person the same respect. If you require something beyond that, I will have to disappoint you."

The man gave a brief shrug, and then he opened the door. What Shane saw when he entered was an average man, an old man in his white robes with a surprisingly peaceful expression.

"Leave us alone," the pope said, waving the guard away.

The door closed, and the two of them stood across from each other.

The pope pointed to the latest news of the day, which reported an ever-increasing escalation in the worldwide demonstrations. "You are playing a dangerous game, Mr. Shane."

"That is probably the price for change."

Shane noticed a slight darkening of the pope's expression. "Do you believe in God, my son?"

"I am only the son of my father. No, I do not believe in your constructed god, one who only knows guilt and sins, who supposedly sacrificed his son for humankind. I hope you didn't call me here to have a discussion about your god."

The pope sat down and looked at him contemplatively. "Very well, then. Please tell me what actually happened in Austria."

Shane began to tell his story. It wasn't long before the conversation became heated, with the pope trying repeatedly to justify the actions of the Church. Shane attempted to keep his temper in check, but it finally got the best of him.

"Tell me one time when the Church was truly Christian under the leadership of a pope. The time of the Merovingians? The Frankish raids? The Crusades? The burning of heretics and witches? With the Cathari, the Waldensians? The Hussites? The extermination of the peoples of North and South America, the persecution of the Jews, the Thirty Years' War, the First and Second World Wars, the Vietnam War...there must have been one time that you followed the gentle example of this Jesus, who wanted to guide people to their hearts and to love and—"

"You forget who you're talking to!"

"I do not have time for a theological debate with you, but I can tell you one thing: the Inquisition wasn't the first time you hunted down my people, the pagans. The more freedom and power Constantine and the emperor conceded to you, the more ruthlessly you went after the original inhabitants of Europe."

"That is your interpretation of history."

"It is the truth of this period, and it had nothing to do with the laws of Jesus and everything to do with a secular lust for power."

"We took the people out of the swamp of ignorance and barbarity and gave them a direction."

"Yet you can't give me one example of when the leadership of the Church, your popes, bishops, and cardinals, truly embodied Christian values. By denying your historical truth you yourself are bringing your Church to the edge."

"If you measure the Church only by its critics, then you will cause exactly what you are trying to avoid. The frailties of mankind reveal nothing about the power of God and his message. People like you will lead the world back into barbarian darkness. Explain to me how this volatile situation around the world will help?"

"I'd rather have you explain to me what justified a murder in Austria a few days ago."

The pope winced, which was not the reaction Shane anticipated. "If it really was one of us, then there is no justification for it."

"Really? Wasn't the justification fear that proof would be found, proof that the Church committed mass murder of the pagans in order to obtain and maintain its power? A pure, cold-blooded, planned, and executed genocide."

"Be quiet! That is blasphemy!

"It is the truth, and you should finally start coming to grips with the consequences of it. The consequences of the extermination—"

"Stop!" The pope grabbed at his chest and sat down. "Do you understand what kind of responsibility I have for a billion and a half Christians? Believe me, young man, the fall of this Church would bring down the world with it. Then you could look on as the decline of values and customs finally lead humankind into darkness and confusion."

"No, your attempt to stand in the way of modernity, democracy, the freedom of women, and people's sexual self-determination—that is the old attempt to imprison a free society with a monopoly of faith. For me, that contradicts in every way imaginable the gift of humankind, to be able to develop by means of their own reason. Morals and ethics are not the achievements of the Church, not even the Bible."

"You think that the pagans would have created a different, better world?"

"Everything that I've seen and experienced in the last several days tells me that the Druids have one thing in common with all the other indigenous peoples. Their goal was a balance between God, humankind, and nature.

They would never even have thought of developing a morality where humankind was the pinnacle of creation, lording it over nature and the animals. Is it that you won't or that you can't understand that this teaching has led us to the point where nature will soon no longer be able to sustain us?"

"Don't you see that to the modern man everything is relative? That he no longer sees anything as absolute and that everything comes down to the individual and his needs? The Church is not responsible for that."

Shane shook his head vigorously. "That is *your* world-view. Only when we accept that there is more than one worldview will humankind realize that it has to take responsibility for its own. I see more and more people who have a clear understanding of what is acceptable and ethical, and I had hoped we could have a conversation about that with each other." He looked down at the floor, feeling spent. "I think it's better if I leave now."

The pope let the moment hang for a second and then said, "May God be with you on your false path, Mr. Shane."

Shane shook his head hopelessly. "You must see that the Church is not in front of this tribunal only because of the parchment we found. People can sense that a new age is upon us."

When he got no answer, he turned to leave in silence. He had his hand on the doorknob when he heard the voice of the pope one last time.

"Mr. Shane, no verdict will free us from the need to forgive one another."

Shane turned around. "That's the first time I've been able to agree with you, but I cannot trust you. Give us what belongs to us."

CHAPTER 42

WASHINGTON, DC – APRIL 1, MORNING

On the morning of the second hearing, Jennifer had driven calmly to the courthouse. If MacClary's plan worked, the justices would have enough to keep them busy with the proof from the Italian police about their tragic mistake and with the retraction by the Italian news agency regarding Ryan's supposed death. In addition, she still had Orvieto to play out. Even if Rome had completely emptied out the archive, the hearing would have to be postponed until a review could be accomplished.

The hall was again filled. Only the press was, as usual, not allowed inside. To her surprise, neither the cardinal state secretary nor any other high-ranking representative of the Church was present.

* * *

In the Cathedral of St. Peter on Capitol Hill in Washington, Victor Salvoni was sitting in one of the back pews. In his hand he held a small golden cross that he was playing with nervously.

Salvoni gave a photograph to the man sitting in front of him. "You're sure you can take care of this?"

"Signore, I've taken care of things just like this under far worse circumstances. But I have to be able to recognize him in the crowd in front of the court before he can get into the building."

"That shouldn't be too difficult. The authorities have assured us that the area will be closed off because of the demonstrations, even for journalists."

"Then you can count on me. With God's help, this will be the end of the matter for you and the Church."

Salvoni bent forward and kissed the man on both cheeks. "Thank you."

"You're welcome. You saved my life once. Now it's my turn."

Salvoni's cell phone rang. He searched nervously through his pockets until it finally fell onto the floor. He had to search under the pews to pick it up.

"Salvoni...Cardinal! I can't hear you very clearly, where are you?...What do we have?...You certainly have nerve, I'll say that much. That changes everything..."

While still on the phone, Salvoni tried to run after his friend, but the man had already left the cathedral.

"Yes, of course, Cardinal. I will be at the hearing on time...Thank you, Cardinal, thank you for everything."

Salvoni pulled his rosary out of his jacket.

* * *

WASHINGTON, DC – EVENING

> ***Deep is the wellspring of the past. Should we not call it unfathomable?...For the deeper we dig, the further down we penetrate and grope in the underworld of the past, then the rudiments of humanity, its history, its civilization, prove to be utterly beyond our grasp...***
>
> **—Thomas Mann, *The Story of Jacob***

"I have a strange feeling," Adam said as soon as he saw Jennifer. "I think you should be ready for anything that would divert attention from the Vatican's guilt."

"We're still negotiating, Adam," Jennifer said calmly. "The Italian police looked at everything in Orvieto, and you won't believe this, but—"

"There was nothing left to find there, right? Somehow I knew that. It was naïve to think that we could get away with that."

"Wait a minute," Deborah said. "The experts from the CIA and another institute have confirmed that the photos weren't fakes. And Ryan's testimony should be enough, shouldn't it?"

Jennifer tipped her head toward Deborah. "The experts are arguing about that as we speak. What concerns me more is that the Vatican's lawyer wants to present a witness tomorrow who is supposed to disclose the perpetrators. And they aren't members of the Vatican. If they succeed in doing that, the matter is over and done with."

"Damn it all!" Adam exclaimed. "What about the bugs in Ronald's house? That's where everything began! Who else could it have been?"

"Adam, if it gets out that Ronald is the cause of this whole mess, not only would he have to resign, but then there would be no proof that the Vatican or even the pope—"

"Jennifer, it's for you!"

"What?"

Deborah handed her the cell phone. "It's Louise."

Jennifer quickly grabbed the phone. "Yes?"

"I couldn't reach you on your own cell phone. We have a problem."

"What's happened?"

"The Vatican just presented the court with an authorization for the retrieval of the artifacts from Austria. It's dated February third, long before Thomas Ryan got there."

"Damn it. Louise, that's a fake."

"That may be, but that's not all. They're maintaining that they engaged a private archaeological team to perform the excavation. And they were—get this—under the direction of a one-time senior member of the Vatican police. The authorization for excavation was issued by the Austrian Foreign Ministry."

Jennifer's head was spinning. "How can that be? The only way they could have learned about the exact location of the cave was by listening in on Ronald's home. We have to find out who bribed these officials."

"I don't think we'll be able to do that quickly enough, and even if we did, then there's still—"

"Wait, Louise; it's still one person's word against another's. Ryan wasn't the only person there, after all. What about the people from the inn? Would they be willing to make a statement?"

"When they found out what this was about, they made it quite clear that they don't know anything. They never saw Ryan, let alone helped him. That's their story, anyhow."

"Great. Well, we have to keep our heads and just continue as we've planned. I can't imagine that Ronald wasn't expecting this kind of move. Louise, I'm sorry for this."

"It's OK, honey, I'll survive this somehow. But what about you?"

"I don't have any other choice now but to trust Ronald. Thank you for everything, Louise. I'll see you tomorrow."

CHAPTER 43

ITALY AND WASHINGTON, DC – APRIL 2

Ryan had said good-bye to Brian Langster that morning. The doctor had done a fantastic job: Ryan felt much better, and he could hardly wait to land in Washington. He had a brief cell phone call with MacClary, who explained the background of the story about his pseudodeath. The entire thing seemed at once creepy and funny. What he did not find so funny, however, was MacClary's plan to leave the others in the dark about his further plans. He knew that it was sometimes necessary to lie, even to your best friends, to make sure that something remained secret. In this case, though, MacClary was demanding an awful lot of his friends without laying all of his cards on the table.

Despite a huge storm, the plane landed with only a little bobble on the runway. In the distance, he could see cars with blue lights, his escort presumably, which didn't make him at all happy.

"Thank you, Mr. Ellis," Ryan said when the plane came to a stop. "I'll never forget what you've done for me."

"It's OK, Mr. Ryan," the elderly physician said as he opened the door to the cabin. "Brian's friends are my friends. I hope that you are successful. It's about time."

The first thing that Ryan saw as he deplaned was a cloud of red hair, and then Deborah was hugging him so tightly he could barely breathe.

"Thank you for bringing this crazy man back to me," she said to Ellis before kissing Ryan's cheek.

Ryan warmed at her greeting. "I was really afraid that I wouldn't see you all again."

They locked eyes for a moment and said nothing. Then Ryan noticed Adam and Jennifer and sent them an elaborate wave.

"You're going to have to tell us how it feels to be resurrected," Adam called up to him with a grin.

"Well, it's not as uncommon as you might think. The people in the time of the pharaohs already knew the resurrection story, and now I'm just one of the many mystical figures who were used to keep people from worshipping the sun."

Deborah laughed, but Ryan could tell that Jennifer was having a tough time showing any humor. "What's going on?" he said when he came up to her.

Jennifer handed him a piece of paper. "The wire copy came a couple of hours ago. The Irish government has recognized your claims and those of the other families..."

"...despite massive protests by the Catholic Church," Ryan said, reading from the text. "Hey, but that's good news!"

"There is enough of the bad kind to go around. We'll explain everything during the drive."

They got into a car, and the convoy started to make its way to the hotel. Ryan was still feeling weak and just wanted to sleep. Before they'd even left the airstrip, he was asleep on Deborah's shoulder.

CHAPTER 44

HOTEL MONACO, WASHINGTON, DC – APRIL 3, MORNING

"What time is it?" Ryan asked when he awoke the next morning. "What about the court session? Have I missed something?"

"Don't worry. You're staying here today," Jennifer said, surprisingly brightly after she was so somber the day before. "Ronald decided that you shouldn't come to court before noon tomorrow, so you can take it easy today. But I have something for you here. Actually for everyone."

Ryan walked deeper into the main room.

Jennifer chuckled. "A number of church dignitaries have announced that they'll be there tomorrow, and I started to wonder how the Druids might have dressed."

She went into the next room for a minute and came back pulling Adam behind her. He was dressed—apparently not completely willingly—in a flowing robe. It looked like the robes that the Druids supposedly wore to protect them from the elements, but it was made out of an elegant fabric and cut in a more contemporary style.

Under the light gray cowl and robe, Adam was wearing black, loose clothing.

Ryan didn't know if he should laugh or be irritated by the whole thing. And how could Jennifer be in such a good mood when they had tomorrow's session hanging over their heads, when people were going to try to destroy their case using falsified documents and cover-ups?

"Jennifer, please, you can't be serious!" he said. "Do you want us to look like Jedi knights?"

Jennifer seemed surprised by his protest. "Isn't this robe a suitable expression of your culture and position? It will set you off very well against these priests with their red robes and funny hats. Besides, where do you think George Lucas got the idea of the Jedi knights anyhow?"

"Um, I think we need to give this a little more thought, Jennifer," Adam said. Then he suddenly burst out laughing. For a moment, all the tension in the room seemed to fall away.

Deborah had been watching all of this. Now she went to the door of the suite and said to Ryan, "I have something to show you that I think you'll like quite a bit more."

As she opened the door, Ryan yelled out, "No! I don't believe it! My God, it's great to see you here. O'Brian, Jane, Uncle Patrick, and little Paggy. Sarah, Ian, and John Lord…my God, are there more of you out there?"

He threw himself into the embrace of the assemblage.

"The others are in town," O'Brian said. "You'll see them all at court. Let me look at you. They really did a number on you, from what I've heard."

"Yes, you could say that. And it was quite an odyssey getting here too. But I'm here, and I'm sure there are those who won't be very happy about it."

O'Brian shook his head in admiration. "I can still remember you as a child, how anxious you were to learn everything about our culture and about the secret of the Druids. Back then, we had nothing more than a couple of dubious legends to offer you, but now you're the one who's revealing more and more. I just want to thank you. I wish your father had been able to be here to experience this."

"Maybe he's known for a long time. You know, Uncle O'Brian, everything is relative with time and space, and death is only a transition. I can sense Father every day. He's always with me."

"That's enough now," Jennifer said brightly. "There'll be time for your metaphysical ramblings later. Right now Sarah wants to show you something."

Sarah was the youngest in the O'Brian clan and had been studying the myths and legends of the Christianized Druids in Dublin for years. "Ryan, as you know, the caste system of the Brahmans was a model for the Druids, but with a subtle distinction: anyone could become a Druid, regardless of family background, if he was suited for it."

"Yes, my clever little cousin, I know. A person is a Druid by calling as well as through a very particular education. But where are you headed with this?"

"We would like both you and Deborah to head up the study of the scrolls in the future. Here."

Sarah held up the model of a public space with trees that had just been set up near the Irish city of Cork. A building was being designed just behind it, in which all the artifacts of the Celts and Druids were to find a new home.

"Sarah, did you remember to bring the swords with you?" Ryan joked.

"Excuse me?"

"Well, you see, the head Druid was actually voted in by the other Druids. But when there was no clear decision, they sometimes fought it out at the point of sword." As he said this, Ryan pretended to lunge at Deborah.

But Deborah just stared at the model in excitement and ran both of her hands through her mane of red hair. "I'm…I'm speechless. This is incredible! Where is the money coming from?"

"There are a few rich Irish people who have always hoped that the relics of our culture would be brought together in a central location," Sarah responded. "They are financing this project with some help from the Irish government."

"People, I can understand your excitement," Shane interjected. "This is fantastic and everything, but I keep thinking about the others. I wish that the other indigenous peoples of the world would have a similar opportunity."

"Adam, I've got something for you here that I've been wanting to show you for a long time," Jennifer said with a serene look.

She reached for her bag and pulled out an old newspaper clipping. It was an article about Bolivia, specifically about the inauguration of the first Native American president of a South American nation since its colonization by Spanish conquerors. Shane read the president's speech and was deeply moved.

"Today a new age begins for the original inhabitants here, a new life, where we can strive for equality and justice, a new era, a new millennium for all peoples..."

"So what about a Druid as president of Ireland?" Shane asked, half joking, as he passed the article on to the others.

"Why not?" O'Brian responded. "One day that too will be possible."

Shane sat down and looked around at everyone again. They were right. When he thought about what had happened in the past couple of weeks, anything was possible. And then there were all of those small groups throughout the world that had broken off from the Church, not wanting to live any longer with the old dogma and working toward a monumental change in their own consciousness. All of it was important in the grand scheme of things and on a smaller level as well.

He looked at Ryan's laughing face as he held Paggy in his arms, flourishing in the company of his family.

* * *

WASHINGTON, DC – APRIL 3, EVENING

Lighthouses are more useful than churches.

—Benjamin Franklin

Cardinal Lambert had made himself comfortable in his hotel room. He had just finished discussing everything with the lawyers for what he presumed would be the last hearing. Salvoni had already lain down and was tossing and turning in his bed.

In spite of his coup with the authorization for the excavation, Lambert was still plagued with doubts. Too much had already come into play. After Catamo had told him about the pope's unexpected audience with one of these godless pagans, he had to ask himself what was going through the Holy Father's head. Who knew what the pontiff was planning next?

He slowly and deliberately dialed a number on his cell phone.

"This is Cardinal Lambert, Camerlengo. What do you know about the conversation that the Holy Father had with Adam Shane?"

"Only a little. But it was very loud. In any case, it was over faster than expected, and both of them left feeling rather disappointed, at least as far as an outside observer could tell. But to be honest, Cardinal, I'm more concerned about the automatic resignation with which the Holy Father entrusted Catamo."

The Argentinean cardinal Rodrigez Perona had been elevated to the trusted position of camerlengo at the age of sixty-eight, directly after the election of John Paul III, a fact that Lambert had never been able to get over. It was the first time that a Latin American cardinal had moved up into the innermost power center of the Church. Lambert would never have let anyone know, especially since he didn't want to lose his most important source of information, but this competition irritated him enormously. In his position as camerlengo, Perona would take over the leadership of the Vatican for a short period upon the death of the Holy Father. He would take care of the pope's funeral and organize the election of a new pontiff. It was no wonder that a man with these powers would also be an important personal advisor during his life as well.

"Excuse me?"

"The Holy Father gave Catamo a document with his automatic resignation," Perona said. "It's only precautionary, in case the United Nations should revoke the status of the Holy See."

"I don't understand. We've done everything to ensure that no one can hold him personally responsible," Lambert said, trying to reassure Perona.

"That may be, but in the investigations about the—"

"Yes, of course! I forgot about that," Lambert said in consternation. After the loss of immunity, the pope, as head of state, would have to subject himself to investigation about the cover-ups of the abuse cases. For months, several influential lawyers had been trying to obtain an arrest warrant for him, either to charge him in a national court or in front of the ICC in The Hague. At the very least, he would be questioned as a witness in one of the many lawsuits where damages were being sought.

"But that's not all, Cardinal. He also gave Catamo something else, and Catamo is remaining insistently tightlipped about it," Perona said, only adding to Lambert's uneasiness.

"Very well, Camerlengo. You know that I have always considered you a possible successor to the chair of St. Peter. We have to be ready, if necessary, to call a new conclave within hours. Make it clear to Catamo what his position is and find out what he knows. And I would ask you to keep a close eye on the Holy Father. Above all, be his ears. Do you understand me?"

"Yes, Cardinal, I know what I need to do."

"Make sure to contact Cardinal Contasiera and Cardinal Huber privately. Both of them will help you if there is an emergency."

"Very good. May the Lord be with us and the hand of God protect us."

"Yes, may the hand of God protect us. And another thing, Camerlengo, give me hourly updates about what is going on in New York at the United Nations. I'll be returning tomorrow immediately after the hearing."

Lambert's suspicions had proven correct. This pope had become unpredictable. From this point on, anything could happen in the eternal city, and he would be hard-pressed to stop it.

* * *

WASHINGTON, DC – NIGHT

The history of the early European peoples and the history of the Church would have to be rewritten. That was the subject of many newspaper headlines the day before the next hearing. The first press conference by American historians had awakened international interest in the trove. However, the headlines told only part of the story. Other scientists felt that the scrolls only confirmed what anticlerical historians had been writing about for a long time, although the general public was only now taking them seriously.

MacClary had his driver take him to the institute so he could make up his own mind about the historians' independent evaluations. Now he was sitting in the room with the scrolls, thinking over the past several days. Emotions were running high on both sides. Essentially, he couldn't plan more than a day in advance. What would the court do next? This whole thing had to come to a close tomorrow, and it would, one way or another.

"Good evening, Ronald," Joseph Pascal said in greeting. Pascal had been picking apart the Old and New Testaments for a good thirty years, and he had been following MacClary's efforts for a long time. Pascal was one of the scientists who, just before the press conference, had analyzed parchment that the archaeologists had rescued from the charred remains of the cave in the Magdalensberg. Not only could the parchment and the writing be conclusively dated, but a small emblem, a druidic protection symbol, was on every one of the scrolls, including this one.

Every attempt by an opposing assessment to prove that the parchment originated from a much later period or that they came from outside the cave had been disproved, much to MacClary's relief.

"Good evening, Joseph. What do you have to tell me?"

"Not much, except that despite the less-than-optimal circumstances, this is really a breathtaking find. It's almost as if we had found the first pharaoh. We've always known that he had to exist, but now it's as if we're standing in front of him. At least that's what it feels like."

"Go on."

"The assumption of God's existence and its significance and the resurrection of his son Jesus are of central importance to the Christian faith. Both assumptions were, until the time of the Enlightenment, the explanation for everything that happened. Since the Enlightenment, however, they only play a role in religious debates.

That's why we regularly hear from the Vatican that the decline began with the Enlightenment. This isn't so far off, really. The only question is, *the decline of what*."

"Yes, but what does that have to do with what we discovered? It's not exactly revolutionary thinking."

"That's what you think, and I think so too, but the Vatican finds itself in the position of finally allowing people to open up a critical investigation of faith with the aid of scientific methods and their results. They can't simply continue to be immune to every criticism, do you see? The Enlightenment was the first logical evolutionary leap. Now here come the testimonials from these old masters, and it's quite astonishing. I don't think that we have all the historical facts here about the history of the Church's founding, but they are nevertheless some very important facts. And the impact of the scrolls alone should ensure that people make a return to knowledge and reason."

"I understand what you mean, but Rome will never allow critical thinking that could potentially lead to atheism."

"Of course they won't, Ronald, but the negative image of the aging Vatican has already made it clear to most Christians that salvation is not to be found in the Church."

"So my father was right all along."

"About what?"

"If the philosophers, and I include the Druids among them, had managed to secure the favor of the emperor in this small window of time in the fourth century, the

Enlightenment would most likely have come much earlier. The Christians, with their systematic persecution of educated people, pressed the cultural stop button."

"'What if,' Ronald, is one question that historians never ask," Pascal remarked with a twinkle in his eyes as he started to get ready to leave. "At least not if there's the slightest chance of anyone overhearing them. Anyhow, what holds for Christian texts would also have to hold for these scrolls. They were written for the people of their time."

MacClary nodded his head. "They make statements about the events of their time, Joseph, but that doesn't tell us the slightest thing about their intended audience. I'm not sure who they were written for. Perhaps the writers knew far more about the concept of time and space than we can imagine. Perhaps they were expecting us."

With that, MacClary took his coat, cast a last thoughtful look at the documents, and headed back to his apartment.

CHAPTER 45

UNITED NATIONS BUILDING, NEW YORK – APRIL 3, MORNING

It was cold in New York. It had even snowed the night before. In front of the United Nations Building, dozens of journalists were gathered to present live coverage of the first major speech by the relatively new president in front of the United Nations.

This day would either change the world or Diana Branks would no longer be in office that evening, or both, she had told her advisors, who left the room shaking their heads after they found out what she was planning.

A special General Assembly of all member states was an exceedingly rare event. The fact that the United Nations Security Council would be meeting two days later heightened the drama even more, as did the fact that the diplomats of the Vatican were no longer being admitted into the assembly.

Diana Branks felt like a racehorse at the starting gate. She gave a last look at her wristwatch. "Bill, do you have everything?"

"Yes, of course. And this just came from Rome."

"From Rome? Give it here."

"The pope requests that we await the results of the hearing before taking further steps that would harm the Church and the state of world peace and—"

"Oh good, nothing new, then. If you've run fresh out of ideas, just lump the well-being of the Church with world peace. I think I can read this later, Bill. Thanks anyhow."

"Understood. Good luck, Madam President."

Although Bill had experienced quite a lot in his time at the White House, he seemed exceedingly nervous, wiping his sweaty hands on his pants.

"What's wrong, Bill? Still worried about losing your job?" The president gave an ironic smile. "Then we have something in common. But that's the risk you take, if you're going to put an end to lies and illusions."

* * *

More than ten thousand demonstrators had gathered in front of the United Nations building. There were fierce confrontations between outraged Christians and opponents of the Vatican. At the same time, throughout the world, more and more influential members of the Church were joining with atheists and Muslims in calling for profound reforms and the avoidance of all violence. The World Council of Churches in Geneva called on Rome to open up a historical debate.

* * *

The president entered the hall where three hundred heads of state and diplomats from all over the world were gathered and went to the lectern.

"Ladies and gentlemen, nations of the world, as I was thinking once again about recent events and the position we will be taking with respect to the claim of the Republic of Ireland, I remembered a statement made by one of our senators during the Cuban Missile Crisis. He said then that it was God's decision when we die and not that of the president. He was trying to question the ability of the president to make such a monumental and assuredly fateful decision to engage in nuclear war.

"I would not like to live in a world where I was no longer able or allowed to make profound decisions on my own in my capacity as the president of the United States or in my capacity as a citizen of this planet. I would like to live in a world in which every human being possesses the maturity to take responsibility for their own decisions. I would like a world in which we understand that it is an act of our will, and not divine providence, when we wipe each other off the face of the earth in a war or in reckless acts.

"If we miss this opportunity to make central decisions about which common values and visions we want to use to construct our future, then we, and our children, no longer have a peaceful future worth living, and that is more certain than a church's amen. I cannot and will not leave our destiny to a fatalistic belief in God. If we remain on this low level of consciousness, one that only serves our egocentric interests, our questionable needs, then…"

* * *

People around the world watched their televisions and computer screens in astonishment over what was unfolding in New York. There were few who didn't have strong feelings about what was happening here. The president of the United States was dropping the Vatican and calling, in all seriousness, for a new world order.

In Israel, Jewish and Christian children were sitting and praying together. In Jordan, Muslims were staring at the television and discussing their own faith. And in Austria, the son of an innkeeper started to feel uneasy as he began to understand that, without knowing it, he had been a participant in dramatic events. Yes, they had helped this man who had come from the cave badly injured. They may even have saved his life. Who knew? But when they realized that the Church was mixed up in the case, they had denied everything to the police.

"We should have told them everything," he said now to his father, who was raising his hands defensively. "We should never have lied to protect the Church."

* * *

"I have here in front of me, as do you all, the draft of a reform of international law, about which we will have to make a decision in the coming days. In this draft, the experts come to the conclusion that the Vatican is no longer entitled to its old status, independent of the many international lawsuits currently pending against it. But I also see all the important contributions performed by many organizations that are supported by the Vatican and other Christian churches, for peacekeeping missions and humanitarian relief for example.

"Therefore, I am charging the United States to rescind the Vatican's recognition as a state under international law and to give every individual organization the status already accorded to other relief organizations within the structures of the United Nations. This will create more parity moving forward. The period in which the Vatican was able to exert direct political influence here and in nations throughout the world is, in our viewpoint, a relic of the past. But it is important that Christian relief organizations and bodies such as the World Council of Churches in Geneva be allowed to continue their work, unimpeded, as nongovernmental organizations.

"Any and all clerical influence that goes beyond this is to be rejected. The world community should unambiguously unite in rejecting any further religiously motivated politics, and the United States of America will support such a unification."

* * *

After the president had concluded her speech, the Secretary-General was hard-pressed to keep the heated emotions of the pro-Vatican representatives under control before he could turn the floor over to the next speaker.

Diana Branks sat down in her chair, her knees weak and trembling. She had pushed her luck. Whatever might happen in the days to come, though, she had said what had to be said.

* * *

Outside an apartment building near the United Nations building, two passersby were arguing about the position of the Vatican. A poor soul sat on the stairs begging.

One of the men interrupted the argument and stopped on the stairs.

"What are you doing?" the other asked.

The first man pulled a ten-dollar bill out of his wallet, went over to the man on the stairs, and placed it in his hat.

"God provides, God provides," the beggar said. "Thank you, sir."

The man who had given the money turned back to the man he'd been talking with. "What was I doing?"

"A good deed? Well, yes, that's brotherly love and sympathy, but—"

"Do you need a pope for that? A podium for dogma? St. Peter's Basilica? Do you need thick books, the Bible, showy bishops' palaces? In short, do you need the Vatican for that?"

The other man looked at the homeless man who was still enjoying his good fortune as he headed off to get something to eat, and most likely to drink.

"No."

"Now you've understood the most important of Jesus's teachings."

* * *

VIENNA – APRIL 3, MORNING

In the Austrian Foreign Ministry, State Secretary Anton Schick was looking out of his office window at the Minoritenkirche, one of the oldest churches in Vienna and the center of the Italian-speaking community. For hours his telephone hadn't stopped ringing since the American embassy had asked for administrative assistance with a rather explosive matter.

"Who called you?" Schick asked Josef Angerer, who had headed up the group of Austrian archaeologists at the Magdalensberg that discovered nothing but charred remains in a sooty cave.

"A Mr. Rudolf, Mr. Secretary."

"What time was it?"

"It was one in the morning, and the sun hadn't yet risen when we got there," Angerer replied. Ministry staff had been questioning him for hours, trying to figure out why he and his people had gotten to the Magdalensberg so late. All signs pointed to the fact that an official had intentionally waited to pass on the necessary information.

"And what did you find there?"

"We could only rescue a couple of artifacts. Shields, swords, some decorative pieces. And one scroll."

Schick was quickly checking who had been on duty that night.

"Good. Wait here, please."

The state secretary motioned to two police officers to follow him.

* * *

In his office, Alfred Steiber was feverishly busy erasing information from his computer when suddenly, without notice, the door opened and a furious state secretary came into the room. The police officers stood outside the door.

"Why did you wait four hours before passing on the information to the Archeological Institute?" Schick questioned him threateningly. "Do you have any idea what you've done?"

"I don't understand..."

"Steiber, don't make things worse than they already are! I know you have connections with the Vatican. I need you to tell me who instructed you to sit on this information."

"Mr. Secretary, I have no idea what instructions you're referring to. I could see no urgency in the matter. Only after I got a second call from your office did I understand the seriousness of the situation."

"I am going to ask you one more time. Who gave you instructions to hold off? I'm warning you, either you tell me immediately who in the Vatican convinced you to do this or I'll have you arrested on the spot."

As if on cue, the two police officers entered the room. When he saw them, Steiber again started frantically pressing the delete button on his computer, but one of the police officers intervened, yanking his hands away from the keyboard.

"Let go of me, you bastards, I have—aaah!"

After the police officers had secured the flailing man with handcuffs, Schick sat down in Steiber's chair. "Now I think we'll take a closer look at that recycle bin."

Minutes passed, during which Schick sat there furiously muttering, occasionally letting an "I can't believe this!" escape his lips. Then he nodded to the officers. "You can take him away."

Hearing all the commotion, the head of the press department came into the room.

"What's going on here?"

"Ah, just in time. We have something to do."

Completely confused, the department head followed the clearly enraged state secretary to his office.

CHAPTER 46

ROME – APRIL 3, EARLY MORNING

The pope had just had a long conversation with the president of the Italian Republic to find out how the Italian authorities would react if the Vatican's status under international law were to be revoked. All over the Vatican, you could sense how nervous everyone was. Even Lambert's sly attempt to block the case in Boston wasn't improving the mood. Meanwhile, thousands of people had gathered in St. Peter's Square to voice their sympathy.

John Paul III gave a quick look out the window and sighed. The support of the masses was indeed comforting, but in the last few days he had become painfully aware that the situation was far worse within the holy walls. There were only a few people he could really trust. Lambert had managed over the course of the past several years to portray him to the whole Curia as an unreliable zealot and to enflame fears that this pope would take up the reforms that his predecessors had done away with: the commitment to ecumenism, peace, and conciliation. Many of the alpha dogs who had spent decades protecting their territory were afraid, plain and simple, of losing their positions of power.

"Holy Father, you sent for me?"

"Yes, Perona, come in. I hope you've set everything in motion."

Perona entered the room slowly. "Yes, Holy Father. I just got off the phone with our spokesperson at the UN. It doesn't seem that they are close to having a majority yet for Ireland's proposal."

"Have you spoken with Cardinal Lambert?"

"Yes, Holy Father. In spite of everything, he is optimistic that this will all be over tomorrow when Victor Salvoni testifies."

"Still, if I read the situation correctly, are we not in illegal possession of scrolls which, either way, are thought to belong to the world's cultural heritage?"

"Yes, Holy Father, but, officially, we only subsidized the excavation. In addition, the scrolls aren't even here."

The pope nodded slowly. "Good. Let everything be brought to a central location and make sure that Lambert knows we will be turning all the parchment over to an international delegation."

"But how will we explain that?"

"Quite simply. We exerted influence on the team we hired to make these scientifically important parchments accessible to the general public." The pope knew, and he assumed Perona did as well, that this wasn't a huge loss compared to everything else that had been made public.

Perona seemed to be considering this, and the pope wondered what was really going on in his mind. When it became clear that Perona wasn't going to respond, he continued. "Just one more request, Perona. I would like you to supply me with a list of all the bishops who are younger than sixty years old and who have distinguished themselves especially through their commitment to social responsibility."

"Holy Father, what—"

"Please, Perona. Even you must realize that we cannot continue as we always have. Even if the situation in New York and Washington ends up resolving to our advantage, without visible and tangible reforms, we will lose more and more."

"But Holy Father, our office is inundated with letters expressing the people's deep affection, hope, and admiration for you."

"Yes, of course, Perona! You've completely misunderstood me. This isn't about my successor, it's about the next cardinals to be named. We need to have less emphasis on politics and concentrate on giving the faithful recognizable signals that this Church doesn't only consist of internal strife and scandal. That doesn't remotely suggest that our world doesn't still need to be spiritually cleansed by the Christian faith. But we need to have people at the forefront who will bring God back to the center of religious, philosophical-scientific, and political thought. You yourself must see how your work for the Pontifical Academy has brought a renewed public awareness of the mortal sin of abortion and has created a mood of affirmation."

"Thank you, Holy Father."

"Don't worry, Perona." The pope smiled in a fatherly way. "I have one more thing: when Cardinal Lambert returns, tell him that you are no longer his informer."

"Excuse me?"

"Do you really think I don't know how Lambert has been carrying out his own agenda behind the scenes?"

"But Holy Father, I would never dream of doing that!"

"Do you think I don't know how many popes—both within and outside of these walls—have died a very unnatural death? I do not intend to be the next one."

"Understood, Holy Father."

* * *

SUPREME COURT, WASHINGTON, DC – APRIL 3, MORNING

The white van parked near East Capitol Street. From here there was a good view of the side entrance of the Supreme Court. Here, far from the main entrance, was the one used by the witnesses and justices of the court. The telescopic sight had jammed a bit, but now the weapon was ready, and from a distance of at least three hundred yards there would be enough time to slip away from the scene.

* * *

That morning Shane had been in the hotel café with Jennifer and Ronald discussing what lay ahead. Only now was Ronald letting them in on the significance of his secret source. It would put the Vatican lawyers in an untenable position, but MacClary would have to resign if it became necessary to use this source. He had prepared all the documents for that day's hearing and had put them in an envelope for Jennifer to unveil if there were no other alternative. Now everything depended on whether the justices believed Thomas's testimony and the photographic evidence from Orvieto.

"Where's Deborah?" Shane asked as they entered the courtroom.

"She's coming with Ryan," Jennifer said, looking nervously at her watch. "It's starting."

Shane felt weighted down and feverishly uneasy at the same time. An ice-cold fear was making his heart beat rapidly. He could hardly stand the tension. In front of the main entrance of the Supreme Court, the authorities had drawn a buffer zone. The first bishops were coming in. Outside the barrier, ten thousand demonstrators surrounded the courthouse, with some engaging in occasional street fights with the police.

The mood in the hall was tense. Jennifer had told Shane that the other side would have the floor first. They were presumably quite confident at the moment.

* * *

The justices had taken their time and were finally coming to their places.

"I give the floor to the attorney for the Vatican," MacClary said while he looked into Salvoni's nervous eyes.

The Vatican attorney began. "Mr. Chief Justice, if it pleases the court, we repeat our request that this hearing be concluded immediately. I have here an authorization for the aforementioned excavation. Although it was contracted by the Pontifical Academy, it was carried out by a private security firm headed by the previous head of the Vatican police who is here today, Victor Salvoni."

"What does 'previous' mean in this context?" Justice Andrews asked.

"Victor Salvoni left the service of the Vatican more than one year ago and now works for a private security firm in Rome. This firm was charged with guarding the excavation in Austria."

"This sounds like an attempt by the Vatican to protect itself with the use of fallacious claims," Justice Andrews said. "The old methods are not as effective as they once were. The Vatican can no longer escape its responsibility by simply stating that cardinals, bishops, or employees do or do not count as one of their citizens. The recent considerations of the United Nations have not escaped notice by this court, esteemed colleague."

Justice Faster stepped in. "In addition, how do you explain the unanimous confirmation by all the experts that the photographs here in front of us from the Orvieto archive are not, after all, fakes, contrary to your claims?"

"The head of the expedition used the rooms temporarily for the initial sorting of the documents," the lawyer answered. "I would point out that the dome in Orvieto does not belong to the Vatican. It is, however, understandable that the contractor placed the rooms at the disposal of..."

MacClary placed both hands on the desk, leaned over, and looked sharply at the man. He simply could not understand the audacity with which the Vatican was trying to shirk its responsibility, nor the coolness with which this lawyer was collaborating in the game.

Regardless, the Vatican representative continued speaking undeterred. "Apparently it is simply a case of two competing groups crossing paths. I stress again that no member of the Vatican was involved in this. Victor Salvoni is taking full responsibility for the unfortunate incident."

"Are you maintaining that all the events and the escalation at the site were not known to the Vatican before they received this charge?" Justice Copter asked. "And why are we only seeing this excavation authorization now?"

The lawyer held up his hands. "Indeed, all of these events were unknown to the Vatican. The head of the Pontifical Academy, who had commissioned the excavation, was unable to provide a timely clarification due to a hospital stay. In addition, the members of the expedition are unanimous in their statements that they did not interfere with anyone, but rather that they themselves were attacked by three unknown men."

MacClary nearly laughed out loud. "Can you prove that the, as you say, *previous* head of the Vatican police is no longer a member of the Vatican police?"

"Of course, Mr. Chief Justice. His termination papers from last year are in front of you. In addition, we have received confirmation today that the rest of the artifacts are already outside of the Vatican in the Castel Sant'Angelo, where they are being examined by government archaeologists. Any discussion of secrecy or concealment is, therefore, completely inappropriate."

MacClary leafed uneasily through his documents, taken by this ingenious move.

Ingenious, at least, to the public eye.

* * *

SIDE ENTRANCE TO THE SUPREME COURT BUILDING, WASHINGTON, DC – MORNING

Despite the countless demonstrators, Ryan and Deborah had clear access to the driveway to the side entrance. They could see the demonstrators from a distance and their continued tussles with the police.

Ryan held the box with the parchment of Rodanicas tightly in his hands. They'd had this parchment examined the previous evening, and it had been certified as authentic. Together with the family trees of the Irish families, this completed the lineage from the fourth century to the present day. He felt as if he had been redeemed. The motorcade arrived at the side entrance. A dozen FBI agents climbed out to secure the area. The door of the armored car opened and Deborah got out. Ryan put the strap of the box over his shoulder and exited. He looked around briefly before he went up the steps, surrounded by agents.

The pain came quickly. It burned like fire. Ryan suddenly had trouble breathing. Next to him, an agent fell to the ground. Blood flowed from the man's head onto the bright concrete of the steps. Several agents threw themselves on top of Ryan and Deborah to protect them from the bullets.

More shots came and another agent fell to the ground, badly injured. Shots ripped through concrete.

"Back there!" yelled one of the FBI agents, pointing at a van. Three agents were kneeling down in the open field of fire. Another one was hit and fell backward. The agents launched a fusillade of bullets at the van. Finally the driver's door seemed to open on its own, and a man fell out. He was definitely dead. But was he the only shooter?

Two other agents ran to the van to secure the location. Ryan slumped down and tried to use everything he had to shut out the pain of the burning wound in his chest.

One of the agents was already tending to Ryan. He quickly examined the gunshot wound and pulled out his radio.

"Agent Rupert Cook. I need an ambulance at the side entrance of the Supreme Court immediately! And send a helicopter! Yes, numerous injuries, one life-threatening, at least two men dead. No, I can't tell you anything further right now."

Deborah knelt next to Ryan. "Thomas, Thomas, no, please don't! Please, please don't! Damn it all, get some help! Please, please help us!" Her jacket was soaked with Ryan's blood.

Ryan could barely muster the energy to speak. "Give me your scarf, Deborah."

"What? Why?"

"You have to help me. I can't do it alone. Bind the scarf around my chest and pull as hard as you can."

"What are you talking about? We have to get you to the hospital. Oh God, Thomas!"

"Deborah…I need to. I want to go in there. You have to help me. Otherwise I'll lose too much blood before I get to the courtroom."

CHAPTER 47

SUPREME COURT, WASHINGTON, DC – NOON

In the courtroom, Jennifer was nervously looking at her watch. *Where is Ryan? He should have been here a long time ago.*

The lawyer for the Vatican had pulled out all the stops to make everything look like an unlucky combination of circumstances, and the mood of the justices seemed as if it were being swayed. Suddenly MacClary started to speak.

"In light of what must now happen, I must recuse myself from this case. In expectation of this possibility, the president has entrusted Barbara Andrews as my successor."

Jennifer opened the envelope containing the documents MacClary had given her the night before. A murmur swept through the court. Even Salvoni didn't understand what was about to happen. They hadn't overheard the justice talking about any other evidence, had they? So what was all this about? Was the justice going to testify? Lambert picked up his coat, as if he were planning to go.

"Order!" Chief Justice Andrews said. "This court will come to order. I turn the floor over to attorney Jennifer Wilson."

Jennifer stood. "Madam Chief Justice, we have here confirmation from the Austrian Foreign Ministry that the authorization for archaeological excavation is illegal and was issued after the fact. The official concerned has already been taken into custody in Vienna."

Lambert sat there stunned. Nervously he whispered something to his lawyer.

"Second, I am able to inform the court that Victor Salvoni's termination papers have been falsified as well. This morning we received by special courier the actual termination papers for Victor Salvoni from the Vatican's special envoy to the United Nations. They were dated yesterday and personally issued by the pope. It is therefore an impossibility that Salvoni left the service of the Vatican more than a year ago."

Another murmur swept through the crowd. Heated discussions were breaking out in the audience, and from the bench of bishops and cardinals loud cries of protest could be heard.

Chief Justice Andrews again called the court to order and requested that Jennifer continue.

"Madam Chief Justice, aside from the testimony of the petitioner, who should be here any minute, we have a witness who can prove that the Vatican acted as the contractor in connection with the excavation at the Magdalensberg, and in a manner that can only be construed as exclusively secular, not religious. In addition, we can prove that this man, the witness himself, has been spying on the MacClary family for decades, since the Church was afraid—"

"Is this witness at least here, if the petitioner has not yet arrived?" Andrews said.

"Absolutely, Madam Chief Justice."

The door opened, and a man entered the courtroom, his body completely hidden by a monk's habit. From his bent figure and gait it was clear that he was quite old.

An expectant silence fell upon the room. Seeing the man, Salvoni was shocked to the core. He had already started to have his suspicions about who the witness might be, but hoped he was wrong. Now every cell of his body was flooded with fear as he saw those gaunt hands covered with age spots. When the witness finally pulled back his hood, Salvoni crossed himself, lay his hands behind his head, and took a deep breath. Now everything was going to come out.

When Lambert recognized the old man—Padre Morati—he clenched his hands on the edge of his seat. "You'll burn in hell for this, you bastard," he said as Morati passed by.

The old man paused a moment in front of him. "I've been burning in hell my whole life," he responded quietly, composed.

Jennifer began to speak again. "Approximately three weeks ago, the witness Padre Luca Morati informed Victor Salvoni, who is sitting here today, about a possible threat. He suspected that Ronald MacClary might have access to the parchments that are before the court, the scrolls of the Druids and several Roman philosophers."

"How do you intend to prove this?" Justice Winster asked.

"I will come to that presently. The Vatican police only learned the actual information about the location of the cave where the parchments were stored by wiretapping Ronald MacClary's residence in Ireland. Both the wiretapping operation and the party responsible were confirmed by experts from the American embassy in Dublin."

"How do you know that the bugs were placed by employees of the Vatican?"

Shane could feel the fear emanating from the cardinals and bishops. He saw Salvoni seething with rage. Others were cursing old Morati as well, who had sat down between himself and O'Brian in the first row. None of this seemed to affect the old man.

"I have here a report from the FBI that documents the origin and whereabouts of the bugs. They were purchased by the Vatican police approximately four years ago in the United States."

The cries of protest from the bench of cardinals and bishops became more agitated, forcing the chief justice to hammer her gavel forcefully on the desk.

"Either this court will come to order or I will have the courtroom cleared. Continue, Ms. Wilson."

Jennifer continued. "In addition, the padre has gone on record as saying that he spoke with the cardinal state secretary about the circumstances of his discovery."

"Where are you going with this?" Justice Copter interjected.

"As you know, Cardinal State Secretary Lambert is one of the most important senior figures in the Vatican City State. If he was involved in all of these matters, that further justifies our complaint against the Vatican City State."

Lambert conferred with the Vatican's lawyer again. Morati looked at him for a few seconds, contemplating the cardinal's horrified, furious, inhuman face, then he pulled himself together and seemed to have come to a decision. With difficulty he stood up and signaled that he wanted to say something. Although it was not customary to hear witnesses in this court, Justice Andrews gestured that he had permission to speak.

O'Brian stood up and gave the old man his arm for support. Between the pressure of the situation and the burden of his confession, Morati could hardly stand up on his own.

"I am too weak to tell the entire story, but I can assure you of one thing: in the upper levels of the Vatican, the fear has always been present that one day it would become clear with what inhumanity we stood opposed to the Enlightenment and reason, and how much we wanted, from our earliest days into the present, to make our teachings irrevocable law. I myself…" Morati swayed, looking as though he were about to collapse. "I have regretted it my entire life, but I…" Tears were running down his face. With his last ounce of strength, he finished. "I myself have killed a man for it. When Sean MacClary, the father of the honorable Justice Ronald MacClary, refused to tell us the location of his discoveries, I was also responsible, shortly before his release from the clinic…for poisoning him."

His voice shook with every word he spoke. He was slowly collapsing. O'Brian wanted to help Morati sit down on the chair, but one last thing came from the padre's lips.

"I can only ask for that which we as a Church have failed to give in the face of our critics, although we still hold it as one of our core values. I ask for forgiveness."

There was a shocked silence in the courtroom. Even MacClary sat as though he was paralyzed. Morati had so far only told him that he knew the murderer—not that he himself was the murderer.

Shane turned around expectantly, but when he saw Deborah's tear-streaked face and her blood-soaked clothes, his blood froze in his veins. A moment later he saw the FBI agents helping Ryan into the courtroom.

Everyone in the room could see that something horrible must have happened to Ryan. He seemed weak, but still his pride radiated from within as he looked into their shocked faces. "Leave me, I can manage the rest alone," he said to the two people who had been helping him. He went up to the justices' desk. His face was contorted with pain, his clenched hands betrayed the incredible pain he was trying to suppress.

Salvoni didn't know what do anymore. Was this really the man he had knocked down in the cave? It had all happened so fast.

Paying not the slightest attention to court protocol, Deborah ran over to Jennifer in a panic. "Someone shot him. He's losing a lot of blood. Jennifer, please, hurry and finish this up," she begged through her tears.

"What? Oh no."

Shane felt sick. Yesterday they had all been so full of hope. Every last one of them had felt that for all of them, but especially for Ryan, a long journey was finally coming to a happy end. And now this.

He had the feeling that the pain of an entire age was reflected in the suffering, the horror of this moment. Issues of faith, power...when would it end? He wanted to get up to help Ryan, but Jennifer motioned him to stay seated and wait. When she continued speaking, it was clear that she was struggling to remain calm.

"I am unfortunately forced to interrupt the response to the testimony you have just heard. This man is the petitioner, Thomas Ryan, and I believe it is of the utmost urgency that we hear his testimony now, since he has just been shot in front of the courthouse."

"Please go ahead," Justice Faster responded.

"I am Thomas Ryan, rightful heir to the library of the Druids, descendant of the Druid and scholar Rodanicas, which this parchment substantiates." With his last ounce of strength he opened the box, took out the parchment, and rolled it out on the lawyer's desk in front of the justice's podium.

"And this man"—Ryan pointed his finger at Salvoni, who was watching his fate unfold as if in a trance—"this man tried to kill me at the Magdalensberg."

Ryan pulled out a hood from underneath his coat, a hood that belonged to Salvoni and which still contained a clump of hair that he had ripped out during the struggle. The courtroom was filled with a dead silence. Even the church officials sat in their seats in shock.

"I condemn you, and I am asking that one day all of this..."

With a groan Ryan slumped to the floor. The door to the courtroom opened and paramedics rushed in. Deborah knelt down and took Ryan's head in her arm.

The pent-up emotions in the courtroom suddenly exploded into a tumultuous scene. While several of the bishops continued to hurl curses at Morati, Justice Faster gave a signal to two court officers to take Salvoni into custody. Salvoni had been staring at Ryan as if paralyzed and didn't put up any resistance when they placed the handcuffs on him. In the commotion, Lambert tried to sneak quietly around the side and out of the courtroom.

When he got to the door, he found two police officers standing in front of him, accompanied by Luciano Verosa, the Holy See's envoy to the United Nations.

"Let me through this instant! I have to get back to Rome on urgent business," Lambert said in his usual authoritarian manner. However, the handcuffs that one of the police officers had pulled out were impossible to ignore.

"Cardinal, I have been ordered to have you taken into custody with regard to your participation in a theft and attempted murder in Austria," Verosa said coolly and calmly.

"Are you crazy?" Lambert said as he tried to force his way past the officers. "And in any case, you know that I have diplomatic immunity."

"I am afraid that you are mistaken, Cardinal. As of yesterday you have been removed from office and are no longer a member of the Vatican City State. Here are your termination papers."

"But that's absolute insanity. Who...?"

Suddenly Lambert was struck as if by lightning. Morati's testimony had severely incriminated him, and apparently Rome had already been aware of this testimony before the old man had appeared here. The Vatican's strategy of getting rid of suspicious employees was backfiring on him.

"The Holy Father personally arranged for your termination, and I don't believe that you really need an explanation for the rest. Take him away."

Lambert could feel the cold metal of the handcuffs, along with an unambiguous shove from one of the officers.

In front of the justices' desk, the paramedics were still fighting to save Ryan's life. Deborah was kneeling down next to him, looking into the indifferent faces of the bishops. Disgusted by the horrible events unfolding here, a few—but only a few—had discarded their robes.

"Is this how you interpret the message of your prophet? Murder? Lies and betrayal?" she yelled at the group. "You tried to kill this man because he wanted to find his own identity, our identity, because he wanted to bring our culture back to life. I hate you, I hate you..."

Shane came over to her and took her in her arms, her sobs muffled in his jacket.

Ryan could feel the blood coming up his throat and running out of his mouth. "Hey, you heroes..." He grabbed the paramedic's hand. "Please, just leave me alone with my friends."

Shane, Deborah, Jennifer, Uncle O'Brian, and MacClary knelt down next to Ryan on the floor.

"Stop talking about hate, Deb. All of you. You have to forgive them. What was it their prophet supposedly said? They know not what they do. You'll always be able to find me. In here."

Ryan lay his hand on his heart.

"You're not alone, do you hear me? You have these people here and you can be sure that they will help you. We're one big family. You'll never be alone...I...I love you all. Now bring me home."

Ryan's eyes looked up to the ceiling and went still. A trickle of blood spilled out of his mouth.

With a gentle motion, Shane closed Ryan's eyes. Then he sat back down, wrapped his arms around his knees, and cried like a child. Jennifer was holding Deborah, who had completely broken down in sobs.

Hidden beneath the raw surface of a healthy friendship, a great love had grown between Thomas Ryan and Deborah Walker, unseen: in the crazy years with MacClary, with the lectures and all the conspiracy theories that they had concocted together; in the countless hours in Dublin's pubs, where they had dauntlessly argued with everyone about the true legacy of the Celts; on the fields of the short summer in Cork; at the sacrificial stones of their ancestors, always with the feeling that there must be another way to life, one where the respect for nature was closer to that which the indigenous peoples had always had.

High above them, the justices of the Supreme Court were shocked and paralyzed with horror. Suddenly there was absolute quiet in the courtroom. Only Deborah's sobs could still be heard. She seemed to be miles away as she gently brushed Ryan's hair out of his face. She took her handkerchief and wiped the blood out of the corners of his mouth. The others were all kneeling down next to her.

As Shane was watching this, he was suddenly overcome with a strange feeling, almost a premonition of things to come. He stood up and waved Jennifer to the side. "Jennifer, the dismissal of Salvoni and this cardinal isn't just a strategic move. It's an act of desperation. I think there's a bitter power struggle raging in the Vatican right now. A pope is elected for a life term. That means he dies in office, one way or another, do you understand?

When the president showed us the limitations of her own power, I realized that this all-too-human situation applies to the pope as well. I have to get there, fast."

"But Adam...I...I mean...we need you here."

Shane looked around. In the middle of the courtroom, several people were gathering around Ryan's body while the guards led Salvoni and Lambert out.

"I know. I hate to go, but I have to do it."

"But Deborah needs you! I need you! Or maybe I'm just afraid that something will happen to you."

"Don't worry. I know that nothing will happen to me. It's not about me now. Trust me. Perhaps this whole insanity will be over soon."

"Hold me," Jennifer said softly.

Shane nodded and held her tight. He could feel her fear. "We'll see each other in Dublin. I promise."

After the paramedics had laid Ryan's body on the gurney and brought him out of the courtroom, the chief justice adjourned the hearing until the next day.

Tomorrow the decision would be made.

CHAPTER 48

VATICAN CITY, ROME – APRIL 3, EVENING

International reactions to the dramatic events in Washington were not long in coming. Within the walls of Vatican City, the cardinals and priests, as well as the pope, watched in shock as the events unfolded on their screens. Three Latin American cardinals had announced their resignations and were calling for reforms.

Pope John Paul III was sitting at his enormous desk, putting the finishing touches on a letter to the secretary-general of the United Nations. It was an urgent plea for forgiveness for the actions of his subordinates, who were, after all, only human and therefore fallible. The letter hadn't been easy for the pope to write; he had lived far too long with the idea of inviolability and infallibility. However, as news of the escalation in Washington reached the Vatican, the mood in St. Peter's Square changed as well. People were chanting for him to make a statement, their unanimous support apparently a thing of the past, and he was devastated by reports of people around the world leaving the Church.

The pope had not yet named a successor to Cardinal State Secretary Lambert. This power vacuum was causing utter confusion in the College of Cardinals regarding the pontiff's next step. How much would Lambert's actions spill over from his own office and affect the fate of the Vatican?

"Holy Father?" Cardinal Catamo said from the doorway.

"Come in, Catamo, come in and sit down. But please, no more bad news."

"I have at least a pale ray of hope to offer you, Holy Father, that in the end only Lambert, Salvoni, and of course Morati will be held accountable for this matter. But we have to be clearer in distancing ourselves from these events. We have to speak in plain words and characterize the events as what they were: a conspiracy within the Vatican that we deeply regret. Your efficiency concerning the parchments and the dismissals—"

"Don't be naïve, Catamo. You have your finger on the pulse of public opinion. The enemies of our church are whetting their knives now, but that's nothing new or surprising. We've been suppressing their voices or waiting them out for centuries now. But if we don't tend to our own people now, the ones that live in the dioceses and parishes, then we really will lose ground. I have an open letter here that was published yesterday in newspapers all around Europe. Since then, the letter has received hundreds of thousands of supporters on the Internet. It's like a tsunami."

The pope gave Catamo the page from the newspaper. The open letter asked when the church would abandon its own teachings about violence, referencing St. Augustine, who hailed torture as a cure for the soul, or St. Thomas of Aquinas, who thought that unbelievers should be sent to the state executioner. It spoke at length about Emperor Constantine, who adulterated the bible and the history of Jesus Christ. Its main question, however, was this: how many people would have to die before the Church put out the fire at its stake?

The cardinal only gave a cursory glance to the opening, then handed it back. "But Holy Father, that's not what our Church is anymore."

"Isn't it? As long as all Christians indirectly feel that they share responsibility for the crimes of the cardinals and even the popes, we are this old Church. People think that we only stopped burning at the stake under pressure from human rights movements, Catamo."

Catamo shot a concerned look at the door. He guessed that the camerlengo was standing outside and listening. Every snippet of conversation that he managed to hear could be dangerous. "We are not alone, Holy Father."

"So be it. In the catechism of my predecessors, it is said that for the harm that our sins cause to another we must do everything possible to make reparations. Catamo, I think it's time that we mustered a bit more courage."

"What do you mean by that?"

"We have to overcome the fear of change and concentrate on the spirit of our faith and its core values.

We can no longer overlook reality, Catamo. I would like to call a meeting of the cardinals in the Basilica the day after tomorrow. This is the time to call for a Third Vatican Council. If we want to have a future, we must take responsibility for the past, and we must speak about it."

The pope handed Catamo a draft for a press release. Catamo looked at the release and sat down heavily.

"Don't look like that, Catamo, as if a council were the end."

"When...when should I release this, Holy Father?"

"For now, just hold on to it. And have the security in front of my rooms increased." The pope's earlier tiredness had given way to a renewed energy, even as it was tinged with worry and sympathy for the man sitting across from him. Would Catamo stand up to the pressure and remain loyal? "Give that to the press while I am speaking with the cardinals. Not a minute before then."

"But they haven't even reached a decision in Washington yet."

"Yes they have, Catamo. I am sure of it."

Catamo took a moment to absorb this statement. "Holy Father, I have another message for you. Adam Shane would like to speak with you again."

This caught the pope by surprise. "Adam Shane? Did he say what it was about?"

"He called me an hour ago. He said he was just following an instinct, that only in the last several days had he begun to understand many things, and he wanted to warn you about something. I found this somewhat cryptic, but that's all I could get from him."

"Now, Catamo, I think that could be a conciliatory gesture that would benefit us all. Tell him he should come any time. Now, if that's all, let Perona in before his ears slip through the keyhole. Thank you, Catamo. May the Lord protect you."

With his right hand, the pope blessed Catamo, who was already opening the door to the anteroom.

Outside the door there were only the usual guardsmen. No sign of Perona.

"Holy Father, the camerlengo is no longer here."

"Very well. Please remember the security request."

* * *

WASHINGTON, DC – AFTERNOON

Shane was in his hotel room packing up a few things for his trip. Deborah, Jennifer, and Ronald had driven to the forensic analysis department at the FBI. They still hadn't clearly established the identity of the shooter, but initial evidence pointed to a former CIA agent who had moved in the circles of the so-called Legionaries of Christ and had been in contact with Victor Salvoni.

Shane sat down on the bed. His flight was in a couple of hours. He still had a little time, and he tried to reach Jennifer one last time. After the second ring, she picked up, and a mixture of relief and tenderness flowed over him.

"Jennifer, it's me. I just wanted to hear your voice for a minute," he said, trying to sound calm. "How is Deborah doing?"

"About as well as can be expected, which means not well at all. Have you seen the news?"

"No, why?"

"It's unbelievable. I had thought that the violent protests would increase when it came out, but they haven't."

"When *what* came out?"

"It's virtually certain that the majority in the United Nations will vote to rescind the recognition of the Vatican as a state. Most of them are demanding above all the surrender of the cultural artifacts that do not belong to the Vatican. Adam, this doesn't just affect the parchments. They're demanding that the Vatican archives be made open to exploration by a UN commission, and—"

"That's fantastic! When?"

"It won't happen that fast. Don't forget that Italy still stands in the way. It will probably be weeks before all of this is formalized, and that's being optimistic."

"Yes, I understand, but still, it's a devastating sign. And I can't imagine, especially after Morati's testimony, that anyone will cause any more trouble."

"Yes, devastating is a good word for it. In any case, it will put more pressure on the justices not to view this as just the acts of Salvoni and Lambert. Still, don't forget that Morati was shielding the pope. So please, Adam, if you really think you have to go there, take care of yourself. I have a very bad feeling."

"Where will you be after the court makes its decision?"

"We'll be flying straight to Dublin. Ronald wants to talk with Ms. Copendale. She's probably completely beside herself."

"I still don't understand what she has to do with this."

"I don't either. Will you come to meet us when you leave Rome?"

"I'll be there. You couldn't keep me away."

Shane hung up and leaned back. Suddenly, he could feel Thomas's presence. He caught sight of the parchment that Deborah had secretly snuck out of the laboratory. It had the same symbol on it as the stone where Shane had had his last vision.

That feeling of clarity and pain overwhelmed him again as he thought of how many generations had been betrayed, murdered, and banished. Incredibly, the older scholars and Druids had apparently accepted their fate with stoic calm. He could feel them as they wandered through Europe, harassed and hunted down, never able to settle anywhere. They simply kept moving westward, finally finding safety on the island where all paths ended. But how was it possible that these family trees had been passed down for so long? Why were they only now being discovered? It couldn't be a coincidence. Something was missing from the puzzle. Maybe he would learn more, or understand more, when he was in Rome.

CHAPTER 49

WASHINGTON, DC – APRIL 4, MORNING

Waking up was horrible the next morning. MacClary had hardly been able to shut his eyes, still feeling intensely guilty about Ryan, even though Deborah had tried to assure him the night before that Ryan was solely responsible for his decisions and that she didn't blame anyone for his death. MacClary managed to struggle out of bed and hoped that he would get back to Dublin in time to help Ruth Copendale understand what had happened. She rarely watched television, but she must have read the newspapers by now.

The streets were full and he was so late that he nearly missed the last meeting. In front of the Supreme Court there was dead silence. After the assassination the day before, the buffer zone had been enlarged. Security had been increased and armed security officers could be seen everywhere. When the first busses with the cardinals and bishops arrived, the atmosphere seemed even more haunting. In their red-and-black robes, they went up the steps to the main hall.

* * *

Jennifer and Deborah had ridden in a bus with most of the Irish families. A depressive mood lay over them. O'Brian and Sarah had been talking with Jennifer about why the court might still dismiss the case. The pressure on the justices was too intense. No one knew for sure if they would rule according to the facts of the case or if they would still take the political situation into account. Since the pope himself had gotten involved by dismissing Salvoni and Lambert and handing over the parchments, the uncertainty had only increased.

Sarah was the first to get out of the bus, waiting for Deborah at the bottom of the stairs. She gave her a concerned look. "Do you think you'll make it?"

"I have to, Sarah. I owe it to Thomas. I owe it to myself. I just hope this is over fast. Then I just want to go home with all of you."

As Jennifer was getting out of the bus, she was suddenly afraid. Shane was going to meet with the pope shortly after the pronouncement. She looked up into the clear, cloudless sky.

Deborah was standing next to her, looking searchingly into her worried face, and folded her arms around her for a brief instant.

* * *

When MacClary arrived at the court through a back entrance, Chief Justice Barbara Andrews was already in front of the conference room, waiting for him.

"Good morning, Ronald."

"Good morning, Barbara. I hope you got some sleep, at least."

"Not really. But we did arrive at a decision. We have decided to approve the motion. Only Faster was against it at the beginning, but he finally changed his mind after we made it clear to him the importance of a unanimous decision. Not counting your abstention, of course."

MacClary looked at the ruling. They had all followed his lead. This exceeded even his wildest expectations, but at that moment he could only feel profound exhaustion. There was simply no room for joy.

"Good. Then let's get this over with," he said, heading toward the conference room to put on his robe, most likely for the last time in his life.

"Ronald." The chief justice looked at him reflectively. "We would like you to be the one to read the decision aloud. We think you've more than earned it," she said.

* * *

The marshal announced the justices for the last time in this hearing. The chief justice announced that the decision would be read by Ronald MacClary.

The tension in the courtroom was palpable.

"I will now read the decision," MacClary said. Suddenly he could feel his emotions. The grief at the horrible loss of a friend. The relief that this tension would soon be behind him. The joy of victory. The appreciation for everything that had happened in the last several days and weeks. And the deep bond with his father. Today the history of the world would be changed, and an era of lies and crimes in the name of faith would finally end.

MacClary looked at the back wall of the courtroom and took a deep breath before beginning to speak. "Ladies and gentlemen, as you know, I abstained from voting on the motion made by the district attorney's office in Boston because of my personal involvement in the case."

The courtroom grew restless again. One of the cardinals couldn't control himself and called MacClary a heretic. The chief justice gestured to two guards to escort the cardinal out of the courtroom, which just increased the volume of the man's tirade.

MacClary watched the cardinal leave and then continued. "The Supreme Court is more than cognizant of the unusual circumstances of this case. Still, we must consider it like any other, soberly and unemotionally. Accordingly, the motion from the Boston district court against the Vatican regarding the international theft of cultural articles has been deemed acceptable and is referred back to that court for a new trial."

Ronald had hardly finished that sentence when the Irish group broke out in deafening cries of jubilation. Deborah hugged Jennifer, laughing and crying at the same time, and was pulled into the embrace of the Irish families. This decision was no more than a start, but they knew their cultural heritage would come home from the Vatican archives sooner or later.

The chief justice attempted to calm the uproar. "This court will come to order," she cried into the crowd.

Ronald continued. "The present evidence and testimonies lead us to conclude that the people involved in these illegal actions were not only individuals, but highly placed individuals within the Vatican. In addition, the court finds that this is not the first time that the Vatican has taken possession of a people's cultural heritage. They did this to suppress historical facts, and in doing so were responsible for committing criminal acts. These incidents, however, are not the subject of this hearing, which is hereby concluded."

Indignant cries again came from the bench where the cardinals and bishops were sitting. The lawyer for the Vatican just looked at the ceiling in resignation.

"For the last time, order in the court!" the chief justice roared, as more guards entered through the two side entrances to enforce order if necessary.

MacClary continued. "On the orders of the UN Security Council, Victor Salvoni and Thomas Lambert will be turned over to the International Criminal Court in The Hague this week for attempted murder and suspicion of murder. The appropriate files will be immediately delivered to the ICC for further investigation and hearing of the evidence."

* * *

Jennifer leaned back for a moment in relief. *That's it*, she thought. *That will open the way. The Vatican will no longer be able to shirk its responsibilities*. The only one who had been acquitted today was the imaginary Christian God, in whose name murder and terror had been spread over the entire globe for nearly two thousand years. How would this Church—which had, with no real sign of remorse, placed itself morally and ethically above the law—react to the decision?

Jennifer couldn't shake the nagging feeling that the next days would bring even more dramatic events.

CHAPTER 50

> ***It is the essential human, who, bound and blinded by his body, captive to his drives, only dimly aware of himself, is longing for deliverance and redemption, and can find them in this world...***
>
> —Karl Jaspers

ROME – APRIL 5, MORNING

Shane was sorry that he hadn't been at the Supreme Court for the ruling. On top of this, he'd forgotten his cell phone in Washington. He tried reaching Jennifer on the hotel telephone but to no avail. Apparently the lines were as overwhelmed as they'd ever been. He tried other numbers but couldn't reach anyone. He hated that he couldn't touch base before heading to the Vatican.

In St. Peter's Square, an increasing number of people were gathering, but the aggression and the loud protests had been replaced by a strange calm. People were talking with each other. Many of them simply praying. Everyone was waiting for whatever would come next.

It took Shane nearly a half hour to cross the square even with the help of the police, who'd blocked it off and were only admitting people after searching them and checking their papers. Every access point was completely jammed. In their black uniforms, with helmets, black protective padding, and weapons, lined up in three rows, the police reminded Shane of the Roman legionnaires he had seen in his dream. This filled him with an odd feeling of danger, as if he had slipped through time. What had truly changed since the Roman legionnaires had fallen on unarmed Druids? This question reminded him of when he was only about twenty years old and stood in the Colosseum at the site where the Roman leaders had made decisions of life or death with a simple motion of the thumb. What *had* changed since then?

* * *

After he had received the written report about the decision in Washington, Pope John Paul III was plagued again with despair. Seated at his desk, he read the ruling another time. "My Lord, what have we done? It can't go on like this. Lord, please, help me in these dark hours."

As he turned around, he knocked over a large gilded cross that was hanging on a bar. He felt like everything was going in slow motion. He wanted to stop it. For a moment, he had to hold his breath, and his legs threatened to buckle under him. He looked on helplessly as the cross broke into thousands of pieces with a deafening crash. Now thunderous silence filled the room. He stared at the shards on the floor.

He couldn't see any way out of this. The strain on his conscience was only getting worse. How could he lead the Church into a new era? He could see very few ways to defend the Christianity—and the world—in which he had believed for his entire life. With a last helpless look at the shards, he fell back into a chair. He looked at the desk near the window and the buttons underneath it that operated the loudspeakers for St. Peter's Square. He wasn't surprised by what had happened in Washington. He had expected this decision, even if there had still been a glimmer of hope until the end that Morati's exculpatory testimony about him might allow the Vatican to be spared one more time.

In any case, the news from the US confirmed his decision. Calls for a Third Vatican Council had been made for years now. Even Vatican II, a desperate attempt to align Church dogma with the realities of the time, had ultimately failed. The conservative factions would do their best to make this one amount to nothing as well. The cardinals of the Curia, Lambert in particular, had always fought against another council, feeling that it might threaten their power and influence. Now that Lambert was no longer around, the pope believed he might be able to move things in a positive direction.

He was just about to get up again when there was a knock at the door.

"Holy Father, Mr. Adam Shane is here."

The pope welcomed Shane into his offices and appraised him. "Mr. Shane, I have to say, it took a lot of nerve to come here."

"I felt compelled to do so. I do not believe that the arrest of your state secretary was just a tactical decision, but rather a—"

"You're *concerned* about us?" the pope replied in surprise.

Shane hesitated for a moment. "Why does that surprise you so much? Is it beyond your imagination that a person can respect another person who has a very different conception of life and God?"

The pope sat down and contemplated Shane for a while. "I can assure you that I am deeply shocked by what took place in the courtroom in Washington. And I am just as shocked at what has apparently been going on for decades in a small circle of this church, out of fear—"

"Out of fear of the truth. And with complete disregard for your own teachings. You know as well as I that your Bible was written for the people of ancient times and only made sense in that context."

"Even if that were true, do you really understand what you've started? What the social and cultural consequences of your actions will be?"

"I think so," Shane said, sitting next to the pope on a velvet-covered chair. "I even think I can bear the responsibility for these consequences."

"Well, in regards to your concern for our Church, I can tell you that you're only accelerating something that has been simmering within these walls for a long time. In a few hours I will be announcing to the cardinals that we will be holding a council. You will be glad to hear that in this council we will be rethinking several doctrines of the Church and, where necessary, adapting them to present times."

* * *

A couple of doors down the camerlengo was sitting at a desk with nothing on it except a simple speaker with raspy voices coming out of it. For centuries, double walls, hidden doors, and secret passageways had sufficed for what today could be accomplished with a couple of simple, electronic components. He looked into the grim faces of the two cardinals sitting across from him and shook his head.

"I'm telling you, we have to take action," he said.

* * *

"I don't think that that's enough," Shane said sharply. "Inside of these walls, and in your Church throughout the world, nothing will be sacred until you acknowledge the changes wrought by time and the crimes of the past. And the changes within seem to be the hardest for you. This doesn't really surprise me, since this change would mean the loss of power." Shane could sense that the pope was trying to cover up how nervous he actually was. The man was hiding something, that was clear.

"What makes you so sure that you will succeed in dissuading the people from their belief in God?"

"Where did you get the idea that I want to convince people to give up their faith? I wouldn't be able to, and that was never my goal. Why do you believe that the writings you're referring to haven't been adulterated?"

"Believe me, we are well aware that traditional Christianity is experiencing a crisis of its absolute claim to truth, especially in Europe, but you cannot seriously expect to sell me on the writings of these Druids and the other so-called scholars as an alternative!" Pope John Paul III said scornfully. "The parchments found in Austria are really not a threat to us, even if you choose to see them otherwise. Only the foolish actions of Cardinal Lambert and Victor Salvoni have attracted so much attention to them, and it won't be long before your Druids have disappeared back into a drawer in some university."

"You are mistaken, I'm afraid. Only the power of faith supports Christian scripture, but it cannot withstand any rational scrutiny. The philosophers during the time of the founding of the Church knew this. I have come to understand one thing in the last few weeks and in my study of the parchments: The original scriptures of Christianity, Islam, or Hinduism are no more believable than those of Druidism. No one can rightfully claim to be in possession of the sole truth. I don't have to be an agnostic to understand this."

"The Celtic texts originated after Christianization, Mr. Shane."

"That may be, but how does that differ from the original texts of your religion? The original Aramaic texts were written long after the death of Jesus, translated into Greek, and then into Latin, a huge operation that brought errors into the texts. The first Christian text was actually the Apocalypse of John! Then the letters of Paul the Apostle. The Gospels were written even later, at least in the form that we know them today. The parchments of the contemporary witnesses, Sopatros or Porphyrios, for example, are authentic. You would be ill advised not to view the Irish texts as equal in value to your own."

The pope smiled with little humor. "Do you want to establish the Druids as the better religion?"

"No! What the Druids taught was not a religion, and even if it were, they've been dead for as long as you've been keeping up your lies. That's the point! Still, these teachings deserve the same respect as the texts of Christianity."

Shane didn't want to engage in this debate any further. He could tell that the certainty the pope had radiated at their first meeting was long gone. This was nothing more than the last gasp of the battle. Still, he pressed on.

"Do you still not realize what happened in the courtroom in Washington? Your zeal has cost millions of people their lives and caused massive confusion in people's minds. For centuries. Yesterday many of us lost a very good friend, and for what? Can you tell me that?"

The pope shook his head slowly. "Christianity is not simply based on mythical images and ideas whose justification—"

"I'm really not here to discuss your faith with you. I'm concerned with something completely different. I have seen and felt how torn you are. I can sense the unbelievable amount of resistance you are up against here. I have just one request: give back to us, give back to humanity, an important legacy. Do it of your own free will. It belongs to us all."

"I don't understand you, that's already...I've already turned over all the documents to the institute for—"

"You understand me quite well. I mean the items that are still hidden in your archives."

The pope massaged his forehead with his fingertips, sighed deeply, and looked at Shane with an expression of profound sadness. "My dear young friend, I thought you were brighter than that. Have you been taken in by this old tale? Mr. Shane, there is no secret archive. I know there are all sorts of wild conspiracy theories floating around out there, but it's just another myth. Our archive has been open for years, though initially only to researchers sympathetic to the church."

"I...I just don't believe that. You're saying that there is nothing about the Druids in the archives of the Inquisition, that you know nothing of their scientific genius? It must have scared the Church at least as much as Copernicus once did, or Giordano Bruno, or the critical writings of a Porphyrios or Sopatros. If that is true, there can only be one reason—these documents were systematically destroyed."

The thought was fascinatingly simple, horribly simple. If it were true, than Druidism was dead and gone for all time.

"Yes, I'm afraid that is one of the shadows that hangs over this Church," the pope said, looking out the window in resignation.

"Then I can better understand why we were followed and almost killed in Austria. You don't want to reform this Church. You don't want to accept a humble role for the Church that puts it on a level with all other religions with no claim to the ultimate truth. But that will ultimately destroy you. Just look around you!"

The pope, to Shane's surprise, remained silent.

"You heard the American president's speech," Shane continued. "The planet is joining together. A planetary code of ethics is the logical next step to ensure our survival. These ethics are not the accomplishment of the Church, but perhaps it is at least the legacy of the original Christian teachings of compassion and brotherly love. But this is also about the necessary respect for the true miracle, for nature, and for that which can still nourish us. Only humankind can stop the internal and external exploitation of resources by taking responsibility for everything. For that to happen, we need self-determination. We are the creators. Each of us carries the divine spark within us."

The pope remained quiet, staring at a desk strewn with books criticizing the Church.

Shane pressed on. "You are holding the faithful and all humankind in spiritual slavery. Religion has great power. I don't have to tell you that. You can drive people to war, as any child knows by now. But it's more than that. The longing for redemption and the thought that the end of the world is near kills every impulse to shape our future. We don't have any more time to leave the leadership of this world to people who think like this. Here, read this!"

Adam handed the pope the translation of a parchment by the Druid Aregetorix, which he had brought with him in one of the boxes. John Paul III read only the first lines before he crumpled down in his chair. When he looked at Shane again, tears were in his eyes. Shane knew what he'd read.

"A great continuum is now ending, and the world will be all the poorer for it. You have looked on silently as the legacy of our ancestors was destroyed. You have attacked our roots, abused our mother, and rejected our belief in divine inspiration. You have rejected the faith in every individual human that nothing is impossible for him. If humans forget that they themselves are divine, they will become victims to the dark powers, slaves for eternity..."

The silence hung heavily over the room until the pope finally stood. "Mr. Shane, I can assure you that I realize more than you might believe at this moment. What do you think I should do now? Go out and say, 'I'm sorry, we've been wrong for two thousand years?' I understand now that you are no enemy to the Church, that you are not my enemy, that you may be no one's enemy at all. You would have waged this crusade against any other institution, I believe, and I will act in a way that I think will appease you."

CHAPTER 51

DUBLIN – APRIL 5, NOON

The flush of accomplishment at winning the first round in Washington having faded, MacClary, Jennifer, and Deborah arrived the next morning in Dublin. MacClary had a hard road ahead of him.

"Ronald, what is tormenting you?" Jennifer asked.

"I'd like to finally have some clarity about the past. And I want to take the burden of responsibility from Ruth," MacClary said softly.

The taxi turned into Arbour Hill. As MacClary opened the door, the workers were busy removing the last bit of paint left behind by the paint bombs thrown at the house. A guard was still posted at the door. He gave them all a friendly greeting.

"Thank you," MacClary said to the guard. "You've been protecting a jewel."

Everyone went inside. Ronald treaded heavily toward the kitchen to find Ruth. Deborah and Jennifer were going to retreat to the library when he quietly called after them. "She wants you to be here with her."

And so they sat together and heard firsthand the story of Sean MacClary's death.

* * *

In August 1945, Sean MacClary had been strapped to his bed after receiving a local anesthetic. No one thought anything of it, since he had been having seizures after a bullet was removed from his spinal column. No one was surprised that the patient was alone in a room meant for four patients. He had received several visitors, among them two priests. The nuns working in the clinic had been surprised at that, since Sean MacClary had until that time expressed no desire for spiritual assistance. In reality, the visit had nothing to do with spiritual assistance, as one of the nuns later unofficially reported. The conversation had gotten quite loud in the room and it had had something to do with a trip to Austria, where the two men wanted to accompany the patient. Sean had categorically refused. A bit later young Ronald and his mother came to visit, and the men hastily left the clinic. Not a half hour later, Sean was dead. The murderer had apparently been so surprised by the family's visit that he had forgotten the most important evidence—the capsule in Sean's mouth.

* * *

Ruth Copendale sat at the kitchen table, completely spent after finishing her story. The *Herald-Tribune*, which lay in front of her, was wet with her tears.

"So now you all know everything. I am responsible for Sean's death. I confided everything to this Morati, everything. I brought the devil into the house. Oh, Ronnie, I'm so sorry. I never wanted this. I only wanted to help. I had the idea that Sean could trust Morati because he seemed to be a more critical priest and at least he knew a lot about the antiquity..."

"Ruth, please, *shh*. You didn't have any idea, and I know my father agreed to meet with this man. And my God, I saw how much Morati has suffered having allowed himself to do such a thing."

Deborah laid her hand on Ms. Copendale's arm.

"But Ryan...my God, I can't forgive myself for that."

"Yes, Ruth, you can and you must," Jennifer said. "You are not guilty if someone else breaks every ethical rule there is."

"Ruth, what Jennifer is saying is damned important," MacClary said, tears running down his face. "Ruth, you know that I've always loved you like a mother. Please, listen to us. They will all be punished as they deserve, and we can find peace. And perhaps we've gone a long way toward helping many more people find peace as well."

"But what will come next?"

MacClary had gradually pulled himself together. "Well, we'll be spending a lot more time with each other, I think, since I don't really have any work in the United States anymore. But above all, I'm sending you into retirement, as well as offering you a home in this honorable house for the rest of your life."

"What? Excuse me?" The sight of her confused face made everyone laugh, even if it was through their tears.

"Well, I don't think I owe this world anything else. And you're making all the early retirees look bad," Ronald joked.

Ruth took a moment to comprehend this. "Where is Adam?"

"Well, that's a bit difficult to explain. He's..."

"He's in the lion's den," Jennifer said with a wink. "But don't worry, Ruth. I believe our Druid in training will be here soon, hale and hearty."

CHAPTER 52

ROME – AFTERNOON

"I cannot promise you that you will find the remnants of your culture inside of our walls, but I can promise you that this church and this faith will prove their worth," the pope said, to Shane's surprise.

"What do you mean by that? How can you still prove yourself? Each individual has the right to his own reality. That is the root of awareness. Tolerance results in the possibility of diversity, which we could have looked forward to. Don't you see that even the claim to the possession of the sole truth perverts faith?"

The pope got several documents out of his desk and put them in a leather briefcase.

At this moment, the door flew open and a man stormed into the room. Shane saw the weapon in the intruder's hand, and panic flooded over him. The pope had been standing with his back to the door. Now he turned around, more surprised than shocked. Without giving it another moment's thought, Shane threw himself on the unknown man.

"No!"

He desperately grabbed the man's arm holding the weapon and pulled it up and back with all his strength. The shot narrowly missed the pope and shattered one of the vases on the desk. Shane jabbed his elbow as hard as he could against the assassin's temples, and the man fell to the floor unconscious. A completely bewildered guard ran into the room and took the weapon out of his hands. "We wouldn't have let him in, Holy Father, if we had had the slightest idea. But the camerlengo, of all people…"

Another guard helped Shane up. "Thank you, thank you. You have saved the life of the Holy Father."

The pope was looking at the camerlengo lying on the floor in complete shock. Things had come this far then. They were ready to kill him for fear of losing their power. Shane breathed heavily. He looked at the pope in despair. "Do you see what I mean now? Everything here revolves around power and greed. Do you want to experience a miracle? Then be one yourself and act, Holy Father."

"You don't believe in God and you despise the Church that I head. Why in the world do you call me 'Holy Father'?"

"Because you still have the chance to do something truly holy, something healing," Shane said, his whole body still trembling. He had never experienced as much violence as he had in the past few weeks. "Tell the world the true message of all religions. Free us, and recognize the Celts and Druids as that which they were. I am asking you for this after all the suffering that has befallen us and all of humanity over the course of a hundred generations."

That was the first time that Shane had labeled himself a Celt and really felt like one. He felt pride and dignity at the accomplishments this culture had left behind for the world.

"You have to understand that I do not face history without a conscience." The pope sat down again, spent, and watched as the guard carried the camerlengo out of the room. "I'm only afraid that this world would come apart at the seams if the Church opened the door to doubt."

He really believes this, Shane thought. "The message of love knows many forms. Let the people free. Look at the world with the eyes of all religious traditions. They all refer to the beginnings of the world, the gods, and to the moment when a chosen being began to announce a joyful message, and to the hope that this being would one day return."

The pope closed his eyes.

"Perhaps it was always just a single message, that a new consciousness would be created. In each of us, alive and not dogmatic. Don't you see how absurd the fight about the true revelation is? Most of the Druids and the ancient philosophers recognized that they themselves were the Messiah and that the liberation from suffering would be fueled by a new consciousness. In the end, we are responsible for our own fate."

"So what do you think I should do now? My fate lies in the hand of God, my son, even if you are unwilling or unable to believe it."

"You still have the opportunity for independent action."

The pope paused for several seconds before speaking again. "I have learned from these dramatic days as well, Mr. Shane, and I will act. But you must go now, as you can help me with one last service."

The pope gestured to a guard to come in.

"Please accompany Mr. Shane safely out of the Vatican and to the US embassy. Mr. Shane, our ambassador to the United Nations will be waiting there for you. The camerlengo, whom I trusted, can no longer assume this duty. Bring this briefcase to the ambassador. He should make its contents public immediately, and then you will see what I am prepared to do."

Shane nodded and reached out his hand. He didn't understand what this man had up his sleeve, but he decided at that moment to trust him.

"Mr. Shane, I respect you more than you think. You have a good heart, and I hope I will be able to see you again under other circumstances."

What was this man planning? Shane had to work hard to control his nerves, and before he left the room, he did something that surprised everyone in the room, most of all the pope. He embraced him.

"Thank you, Holy Father."

"Go now. You don't have much time."

Two men from the Vatican police came up and signaled that everything was ready.

"Lock my rooms," ordered the pope, "and let no one else in under any circumstances! Mr. Shane, take this."

The pope stood in front of Shane so that no one could see what he was placing in his hand.

"But—"

"Take this, and take care of it."

As Shane looked at the item in his hand, he had to keep himself from crying out. He looked at the pope in disbelief, turned around quickly, and went out with the armed policemen.

* * *

The two guards walked on either side of Shane, escorting him through the rooms and down the stairs. He saw several cardinals and priests who recognized him, giving him a look that was a cross between hatred and despair. They cursed the Swiss guards as traitors and threatened them with eternal damnation.

When they came out on St. Peter's Square, Shane could sense that there was no turning back now. It was only with great effort that he restrained himself from looking inside the briefcase to see what was in there. What had the pope given him?

"Come, Mr. Shane, we need to hurry. You must leave the Vatican territory as quickly as possible. Didn't you notice the men behind us? And please be so good as to turn the briefcase around. That papal seal makes you an easy target."

A few men in priest's robes were following them. At least one of them was obviously armed.

"How are we going to get through the city safely?" Shane asked the guard as he started to move as quickly as he could through the throngs of people. "Why didn't we go out a back entrance?"

"We will get into a car at the Via della Conciliazione. It's only another few yards. Any other route would have been too dangerous."

"To be honest, I find this quite dangerous enough," Shane said as he looked over his shoulder to see that the men following them had fallen back a bit. It was difficult for anyone to make their way through the crowd. There was a ghostly atmosphere hanging over the entire square, a mixture of fear and anticipation that felt as if it could explode at any moment. Or did it just seem that way to him?

The Via della Conciliazione was packed with more than ten thousand people.

"A car, you said? Well, that could take a while," Shane joked out of nervousness and helplessness. Their black-clad pursuers were catching up with them.

"It looks like we don't have any choice but to go to the Castel Sant'Angelo where the next car is waiting," one of the men said. "Go on ahead, I'll catch up."

"What? What are you going to do?"

The man had already disappeared into the crowd. Shane turned around, but the second guard pulled him along. Shane ripped his arm away and stood still.

"Mr. Shane, please, come, we have to get out of here."

Just then one of the pursuers fell silently to the ground.

Shane clapped his hands to his mouth. "My God, why?" he asked the guard in despair, but the man just kept pulling him on.

"Don't ask. Just come with me now. We have to keep moving."

"What is in this briefcase that someone would be willing to murder for it?"

In response, the policeman pulled out a weapon.

"If the Holy Father wants this message to reach the world, then I will make sure that it does. If you don't cooperate, it will happen without you. I am not joking, Mr. Shane. This is neither the time nor the place for that. They've found what they were looking for. I can't tell you any more than that."

"Very well, I'm coming," Shane said. His decision was made easier by the fact that he could see other people pursuing them now. Without this man's protection, he would have been completely helpless against them. "How far is it to the embassy?"

"At least a mile and a half. Come, follow me."

"Do you have another weapon?"

"What?"

"I'm starting to get a bit tired of being unable to defend myself."

One of the men pursuing them was shoving people out of the way. By that point, the second guard had made his way back to them, and he'd heard Shane's request.

"Here, take this one."

Shane almost had to laugh out loud. The man had a weapon secured under his pant leg, like in a bad spy movie.

* * *

While the cardinals were waiting for the pope in the Basilica, the pope opened the windows of his rooms and turned on the loudspeaker.

"My brothers and sisters, the Church has suffered much harm in recent days. The original Christians proclaimed the unadulterated peaceful and charitable message of our Lord Jesus Christ almost three hundred years after his death. They knew that Christianity is based on the commandment to love our brothers, to love our enemies, on the commandment not to steal and not to kill, and yet we must now realize with horror that the people who work within the Church have often disgracefully betrayed these commandments. Yes, they have even taken up arms."

The crowd on St. Peter's Square was deathly silent. In the Basilica, there was at first a wave of murmuring, and then agitated calls to listen. Some of the irate cardinals were headed toward the pope's rooms, taking those armed guards along who remained loyal to them. However, the anteroom had already been barricaded by the other guards. They stood at the ready, their weapons drawn, determined to follow the pope to their death if necessary.

Two warning shots were fired, and then a tense silence could be felt among the intruders.

The pope had stopped for a minute as the tumult in front of his door had gotten louder. Now he continued. "I must recognize that the belief in our dear Lord Jesus Christ's Sermon on the Mount and his true message are no longer emanating from this Church, if they ever did. I beg the people of this earth for forgiveness for that which has been so despicably perpetrated by this Church in the name of God."

In the anteroom, the intruders were desperately trying to overwhelm the guards again and to silence the pope. One of the cardinals screamed hysterically: "He's been possessed by the devil! He's destroying God's work on earth. This is the coming of the Antichrist! The revelation of Johannes is coming true! The end is near!"

* * *

Shane and the two guards had fought their way through the crowds to the Castel Sant'Angelo on foot.

Finally they saw a police car in front of them. One of the guards gesticulated wildly toward it and already had the key in his hand as Shane felt a burning pain in his right hand. Stunned, he looked at the back of his hand, where a bullet had been shot clean through. Pain and shock brought him to his knees. The guard closest to him had targeted the shooter and shot him directly in the middle of his forehead. Passersby were screaming and dispersing in panic in every direction.

"You have to get up, Mr. Shane!"

"Damn it! It hurts like crazy!"

"Show me."

Somewhat roughly, the guard turned Shane's hand over, making him yell again. Then the man pulled his white shirt out of his pants and ripped a strip of cloth off for a makeshift bandage.

Shane could see more men in the distance. Their pursuers were no longer making any attempt to conceal their weapons.

"Come on, get in!"

His face drawn with pain, Shane sat down in the passenger seat while the guard backed up at full speed, bearing down on their pursuers, who had to dive headlong in the street to avoid being hit. They still managed to fire several shots at the car, spraying shards from the windows everywhere.

"Damn it, who are these people?" Shane shouted.

"The guards of the honorable Cardinal State Secretary Lambert, Mr. Shane. Who did you think?"

The guard raced like a madman first over the Via Tomacelli and then through the narrow streets to the Via Veneto. They stopped directly in front of the US embassy, where they were received by armed CIA officers and brought rapidly into the building.

"Are you Mr. Shane?" asked a slim, fifty-year-old Italian man with a resonant voice. He was remarkably calm, considering the circumstances.

"Yes. Why?"

"Come with me."

They went to an office. Shane's attention immediately went to the television broadcasting a live event. "What's happening on St. Peter's Square?"

"Do you need a doctor, Mr. Shane?"

"No, no, it'll be fine."

"Could you please give me the briefcase now?"

"Yes…yes, of course."

As they stood in front of the television, the ambassador opened the briefcase, leafed briefly through the documents, and crossed himself.

Shane was stunned by what the pope was saying on the television.

"It is my wish that you all have the freedom and self-determination to follow that faith that will bring you, personally, closer to God. As I had to learn in a most painful way, since that path is different for every person, any claim to an absolute truth can no longer be substantiated. I therefore resign from my position."

The pope symbolically threw his zucchetto, his circular head covering, out of the window, and the murmur of ten thousand people could be heard.

"It is time that we join together to follow the true message of Jesus, the message of the Sermon on the Mount, and also the message of the many other revelations, which all speak of the one spirit of divine creation that resides in each of us. This includes the traditions of the Druids that have been discussed so much recently. We owe it to their few descendants to pay the same

respect to the historical accomplishments of these scholars that we pay to other spiritual beliefs.

"Before my resignation, I set a radical reform of the Roman Catholic Church in motion. All the archives will be opened as part of humanity's legacy. I admit that this Church's claim to absolute truth and to the representation of the one God was a mistake. My resignation is only a symbol. It is done out of love, respect, and a deeply felt sense of responsibility. It does not, however, mean the dissolution of the Church. We must come together even more to help solve the problems of this world. We will not abandon the people who need our practical and spiritual assistance, but we will set aside the misguided claim that we are the sole representation of God on earth. I ask from my heart that you pray for our weaknesses in brotherly love and tolerance, in whichever form you are able and desire to do. In all humility, I beg you for forgiveness and pray for healing for us all."

The guard standing next to Shane said, "Now they'll say he's insane and shoot him through the head. Then they'll vote in a new pope."

"That will no longer be possible," the ambassador said, still deeply shaken, as he laid the documents on the table. "Mr. Shane, did the pope give you anything else?"

Shane grew nervous. Should he tell him? "Yes." With his uninjured left hand, Shane took the Ring of the Fisherman, the symbol of papal power, out of his pocket and held it out to the ambassador on his outspread palm. "May I now find out what kind of documents I was carrying through the city?"

The ambassador ignored Shane and quickly took his cell phone out of his jacket. "I need to call the master of ceremonies. He must bring the news to the cardinals before any other needless damage is done."

"What are these documents?" Shane asked again. "What kind of news?"

"These are the termination papers for every cardinal throughout the world. Together with the missing Ring of the Fisherman…" Suddenly the ambassador, who had showed no emotion until now, began to tremble and broke into tears.

The guard caught on quickly. He looked at Shane half in awe, half amused. "You see, if there are no cardinals in office, there can be no new election for a pope, and at the same time, the cardinals can only be named by the pope. Add to that the fact that you are carrying the unbroken Ring of the Fisherman, and you theoretically hold the highest office in this Church." He shrugged his shoulders. "Theoretically."

Shane was growing uneasy. He wanted to go back to the Vatican. He wanted to protect the man who had just become a hero.

In the meantime the ambassador had reached Cardinal Pertrose, the master of ceremonies. But as he explained to him what he had in his hand, he heard only a strange sigh and a loud thud.

"Cardinal? Cardinal? Are you still there, Cardinal?"

Just as Shane was about to leave the room to return to the Vatican, the door opened and Catamo entered.

"Oh, thank the Lord, Catamo," the ambassador said. "I have to talk with you. You need to make this public as quickly as possible. But brace yourself, this will be your last official duty."

"I know. The pope took me into his confidence several days ago."

"What?"

Shane looked at Catamo's face and gave him his uninjured hand before hurrying out of the room and the embassy.

The guard followed him and hurried to meet him. "I think it would be better if I go with you, Mr. Shane."

CHAPTER 53

All over the world, television stations had interrupted their normal programming. The pope was standing in silence at his window and praying. Most of the people had knelt down or were just standing there quietly and praying with him.

For many, however, this moment wasn't the end, but a new beginning, and it was such a liberating moment that they fell into each other's arms in tears. People of all faiths were sitting in front of their television sets, Copts in Egypt, Jews in Jerusalem, Muslims in Tunisia, Buddhists, and many more. They all watched, awestruck by what this man had realized and accomplished. It was the strongest imaginable sign for peace throughout the world, a peace that now seemed possible.

In her first comment on the events, President Branks hailed this step as a historic moment, the dawn of a new era in which fundamentalism and claims of omnipotence would be replaced by tolerance and freedom. She maintained that it would apply to politics as well, which in the future would be focused on the potential and the value of every living being and not on the greed and excess of a few.

"The West has knelt long enough before the idol of commercial growth."

* * *

Shane and the guard had the driver get them as close as possible to St. Peter's Square. When Shane felt the weapon in his back pants pocket, he took it out and gave it back to the guard. "Thanks, though it didn't really help me much."

The car came to a stop.

"Are you ever going to tell me your name?"

"Peter."

"I'm Adam. I'd love to talk, but I don't want this man to be killed, like so many before him who wanted to change the world. Least of all him, since what he's accomplished is really a miracle."

Shane opened the car door and got out.

The Vatican had been taken over by pure panic. As the cardinals found out about their dismissal and the death of the master of ceremonies, some of them sat in the Basilica, stunned. Others were standing together, dumbfounded, in front of the pope's rooms. All attempts to break through the door had suddenly stopped. At some point, the first of the church dignitaries took off his hat and left with his head bowed. Some of the others followed, while others continued to stand there, unable to move.

In the rooms of the pope, the guards could breathe a bit easier as the noise abated. The pope had taken a normal priest's robe out of the cupboard and put it on. Then he had two of the guards open the door, and those standing outside saw something that no one in the world could have imagined possible two hours earlier: the pope was going to leave the Vatican as he was—a simple man, a simple priest.

When Shane and Peter had fought their way through the crowds to the entrance to St. Peter's Basilica, the heavy doors suddenly opened. First came two Swiss Guards in traditional dress with their lances outstretched, then several cardinals who had remained true to the pope. As a sign of their solidarity, several of them had also put on simple robes. Then came the man himself, Giuseppe Mardi, who, until a few hours earlier, had been known as John Paul III.

The last pope went slowly down the steps. When he saw Shane, he waved him over to his side.

* * *

In Dublin, everyone was sitting in front of the television set in MacClary's library.

MacClary ran his hands over his face. "I'm overwhelmed. Just overwhelmed. God, look at that."

"I don't believe it," said Jennifer. She saw Adam Shane—*her* Adam Shane—walking next to the pope through the crowd. The people were making way for them out of respect.

“He’s wounded,” Jennifer said with a concerned look at Adam’s bandaged hand. What on earth had happened in Rome over the last several hours?

“What’s going to happen next?” asked Ms. Copendale, who had been watching everything from her chair.

“He’ll come to Ireland,” Deborah said, never taking her eyes from the screen. “The pope, I mean. The Irish government has agreed to take him. But this picture here…isn’t it incredible? Aregetorix was right after all. The return of the Druids isn’t a literal return. It’s simply the return of consciousness, that the divine expresses itself in an unending variety of ways. Do you realize that we’re watching this happen right now?”

* * *

The last pope turned to Shane and whispered, “Have I kept my promise?”

Tears were streaming down Shane’s face. Suddenly a feeling he had never experienced flooded over him, a mixture of grief and joy, deference and dignity, all at the same time. For a brief moment, the two men stood and looked into each other’s eyes. The crowd around them grew still, as if it could sense that something was happening here, something so intensely overwhelming, the like of which had not been felt here for a long time, if ever.

“You are a hero, Holy Father.”

“From now on, please call me Giuseppe, Adam.”

Slowly they continued on to the waiting limousine, where the driver was already holding the door open.

"If you want to go to Dublin, my dear Adam, then come with me," said the former head of the formerly most powerful church in the world.

* * *

"I'm slowly starting to believe that this is finally over," MacClary said to those assembled around him. "This day will never be forgotten, and you have played a huge, painful part in it. I'd love to embrace you all."

On the television screen, the limousine was leaving the square.

CHAPTER 54

> ***And suddenly you know: it's time to begin something new and have faith in the magic of a new beginning.***
>
> **—Meister Eckhart, Christian Mystic**

GLENDALOUGH, IRELAND – APRIL 8

The United Nations had recognized the claims of the few direct descendants of the Druids, and after international experts had been allowed to look around the archives, they actually found a few more valuable items: philosophical tracts about the healing arts and architecture, works of art, and many other ideas that finally put to rest the image of the supposedly barbaric Druid tribes. MacClary had the three-ton stone with the spiral of life brought from the Magdalensberg to Glendalough as soon as he could. The transportation had cost a year's salary, but he didn't regret a single cent.

Glendalough, in the middle of the Wicklow nature sanctuary, was one of the most beautiful treasures of Ireland and an important site in Ireland's church history. From the surrounding hills, there was a breathtakingly beautiful view of two lakes. There were streams, forests, and little waterfalls, a mystical spot for dreaming. In the neighboring forest, the stone now rested in the middle of a circular clearing and gave the spot an almost solemn atmosphere, even if it was only a symbol of a culture long past. Who knew what the new culture would produce connected to remnants of the old?

Shane had sat down a bit apart from the others. His cell phone had rung, and when he saw the number on the display, he felt hot and cold at the same time.

"Victoria? I'm…I'm sorry that I haven't called, but I'm guessing that you've got some idea of what's been going on…"

"You don't need to apologize, Adam. But I have someone here who wants to see his father," Victoria said without the least hint of reproach in her voice. "I hope you've finally found what you were searching for."

"Yes, Victoria, I think I have. Where is Jarod?"

"A better question might be, where we both are," she said with a soft laugh.

"Why? What do you mean?"

"We're in Dublin. I thought it was high time Jarod saw where his grandfather came from."

"Victoria, you should come—"

"I know where you are, and we'll be on our way within the hour."

"There's something else you should know," Shane began, but she had already hung up. Shaking his head, he put his cell phone back in his pocket and went deeper into the woods. Jennifer and Deborah should be there somewhere.

Ryan's journey here ended at midday. His body had been brought in the cargo hold of an airplane from Washington to Dublin, and then he had been driven here. O'Brian and Sarah had carefully prepared everything that morning and his body had been laid on a pile of kindling at least six feet high.

On the other side, many Irish people had laid another fire that would offer warmth to the guests in the evening. It would be a long night.

Jennifer and Deborah watched the setting sun at the edge of the woods.

"He would have liked this," Jennifer said, giving Deborah a hug.

Deborah was slowly recovering by being with her friends and had mustered some courage again. "Yes, he would have. I still can't quite believe that he's not here anymore. I keep thinking he's going to come around the next corner any minute. It's hard, Jennifer, even though I can sense his spirit here. But somehow things go on, and I am eternally thankful to you all that I can be here with you today. When I'm finally able to start cataloging the parchments, it will be better, though." She smiled at Jennifer, took off her glasses, and began to clean them carefully.

Shane came up from behind and sat down with them.

"So is everything ready?" Jennifer asked.

"Yes, we're ready."

The paths leading to the clearing followed the four compass points, and several wooden buildings had been constructed in the forest. Here the remains of Celtic culture would finally find a home, in a central spot of the promised land of the Druids.

"It's an amazing place," Shane said, his face beaming.

"Tell me, how did you convince the pope to take this step?"

"Me? I didn't do it at all. He had already made up his mind, but he was waiting for the right moment. The man knew quite well that he was in mortal danger. If the Curia had even the slightest inkling how much he understood..."

"But you told him something, didn't you?"

"Yes, an Irish legend that Thomas told me once."

"Do I have to twist your arm or are you going to tell me of your own free will?"

Shane leaned back and crossed his arms behind his head. "In the tale of the sea journey of Arth, son of Comn, a young hero loses a game of chess and is forced to make a dangerous journey in search of a certain maiden. He has no idea where and how he can find this young woman, but he can't get out of searching for her, so he travels off, from one dangerous situation to the next. He takes many wrong paths and endures much suffering, but when he finally finds her and returns home years later, the people greet him with jubilation and joy because his success also helps his people. The happiness of one is the happiness of all."

"That's beautiful," Deborah said, deeply moved.

"Giuseppe must have understood the message behind it, since the unknown maiden was a metaphor for his search for God and for himself. This alone, apart from any control that could be found through a doctrine of salvation, means happiness for everyone in the end. In this story, the visionary Druids only wanted to express that each individual can achieve a large measure of insight if they develop their potential and remain free of indoctrination."

"How did all this get into your head?"

"I can actually answer that. I learned it in my body, on the stone that is now in the clearing. Thomas had the theory that there is a universal knowledge that is saved for eternity like a memory. That is exactly what I experienced when I was lying on the stone in the cave. My memory. This kind of experience is possible for everyone."

Jennifer considered this. "Yes, the last few weeks have probably prepared every one of us for something that will awaken memory and this longing." She stood up and stretched. "OK, enough philosophy for today. Come, it's almost dark and nearly everyone is here already."

As Jennifer, Shane, and Deborah entered the clearing, they were stunned. People from every direction were streaming into the circle. Many of them were already standing in the middle. Ruth Copendale, Ronald MacClary, and the other Irish families were positioned in the first row around the stone.

Then Shane saw several figures making their way through the crowd with torches, including a man in simple white clothing.

"I don't believe it."

"What is it, Adam?" Jennifer tried to get a better view.

"Don't you see him?"

Jennifer's eyes grew wide as she recognized the approaching figure of the one-time pope. As the old man arrived at the inner circle, the people welcomed him into their midst. Shane went up to the pope and with a smile took the Ring of the Fisherman out of his pants pocket. "A lovely thing, Giuseppe, and it's a great temptation to keep. But I think it would be better in your possession," he said as he laid the ring in his hand.

Deborah stood next to Giuseppe Mardi as everyone in the circle held hands. Now Adam Shane spoke for the first time in front of the last descendants of the Druids. His voice was as fragile as autumn leaves as he looked at the pile of wood with Ryan's body on it.

"I am here today because I followed my heart and a vision that brought me to my roots. Our world often seems to be on the edge of a precipice because we are cut off from each other and feel helpless. But we are all bound one with another, even in death. I, you all, everyone here has an unending divine potential. The key to our freedom lies in self-determination and in the rejection of false feelings of guilt. The true miracle is that we are all in control of how we create our lives."

Shane gave the pope a penetrating look and then continued.

"Even the last seventeen centuries were necessary to come to this point of forgiveness. Today is a good day to invite all cultures to create this planet anew with our perception and our strength. We can do this. In humility and grief, I bow down before you, Thomas Ryan, descendant of Rodanicas, and release you into the *autre monde*, the other world, where you may find peace and serenity."

Together with Deborah, he walked up to the pile of wood and lit it with a torch. All of them stared into the flames that flickered around Ryan and everyone bid farewell to him in their own way.

Then the long night began. From all four directions, more and more people streamed into the forest. Their faces reflected a mixture of redemption and excitement about what this turning point would bring. Everyone at that place knew that she or he would have a part in it.

From the United States came a particular request from President Branks. She hadn't forgotten what Adam Shane had entrusted to her the night before the announcement of her ambitious economic plan, and she invited him to work as an advisor for her.

Jennifer and Deborah pulled Shane aside. "What do you think? Are you going to accept her invitation?"

"Well, after this little cultural confusion, I don't really know where I'm headed, but why not?" Shane said, half in jest.

"Little?"

"What are a couple of thousand years, Jennifer? In the last few weeks, I've realized that our spirit creates our reality."

Together they stared into the flames that were slowly engulfing Ryan's body, the last Druid. Shane remembered his time with Thomas Ryan and his ability to recognize the whole universe in a leaf.

EPILOGUE

I must create a system, or be enslaved by another man's. I will not reason and compare, my business is to create.

—William Blake, Irish Poet

Shane stood on the spiral of life and looked up at the stars. Tears of grief and joy had sprung into his eyes. Jennifer joined him on the stone and took his hand. They both looked up at the sky. Near them, children were dancing around the fire, his son Jarod among them. He was happy to see Jennifer and Victoria talking with each other. A little bit later they came up and sat down with him on the stone.

Shane let the memory of the last few weeks wash over him. Someone had spoken of success, even of victory. He couldn't even begin to think of using terms like that. He hadn't been the one to make the Church collapse, nor had it been the group of people with whom he'd spent the last few weeks. And so many of the Druids' secrets remained hidden to them and would probably never see the light of day.

But humanity had a chance. *Perhaps we can finally accept the possibility that there is no divine plan and that we are alone with that which we have*, he thought. *And perhaps we can finally value what we have.*

No, he didn't feel any sense of triumph. The Druids, like the Roman and Greek philosophers, had been concerned with rational knowledge. In the interest of power, other influential thinkers had allied themselves with the political leaders of their time and given people what they longed for, in their fear and helplessness: the concept of a single God. Just as the Christian tracts and the practice of the Catholic Church had very little in common with Jesus Christ, the countless brotherhoods and lodges who were bidding farewell to Thomas Ryan this evening had no clear idea of the original Druidism.

It just wasn't enough to make a Druid robe and to insist on the legitimacy of any kind of ritual. Still, there was the possibility of searching for the spiritual and ethical principles that lay behind these legends and songs and hero's tales. There was the possibility of remembering, as the Christians had just remembered the true message of Jesus Christ in St. Peter's Square and throughout the world. Shane was sure that the respect for different faiths, for different perceptions of reality, was as much a part of this as the respect for the earth.

For a moment he felt an enormous responsibility resting on his shoulders. But then his gaze passed over the clearing, the people, the happy children, and finally rested on Jennifer's face, and the love that radiated from her eyes.

ACKNOWLEDGMENTS

I would like to thank my publisher, Christian Strasser, who not only had his heart in the right place, but also recognized the signs of the times, a time in which a new consciousness is searching for historical truths. In particular, I am grateful to my editor, Ulrike Strerath-Bolz, for all the inspiration and a fantastic working relationship. And my thanks as well to Wolfgang Ziegert, who has been a true teacher, friend, and discussion partner for a long time.

Thanks as well to Naomi L. Kucharsky, who so successfully championed this novel. I am especially grateful to my partner, Verena Strobl, an uncompromising reader and visionary who coached and inspired me, and I must also thank my parents, who have supported me in everything I do.

Further thanks are due to the numerous experts in ancient history and jurisprudence for their generous advice, and to the numerous critics of the Church, from whose experience and writings I was able to learn so much.

ABOUT THE AUTHOR

Photograph © Mathias Lenz, Wien

THORE D. HANSEN was born in Northern Germany in 1969. Since completing his studies in political science and sociology, he has worked as a journalist and communications consultant in Germany and Austria. In 1994, he did research at MIT in Boston on US-foreign affairs. A relative of Nobel Peace Prize winner and North Pole explorer Fridtjof Nansen, Mr. Hansen has become an avid student of his Scandinavian heritage. His passion for the cultural historical backdrop and consequences of monotheistic religions as well as the pagans of antiquity brought him to his first novel, *The Celtic Conspiracy*.